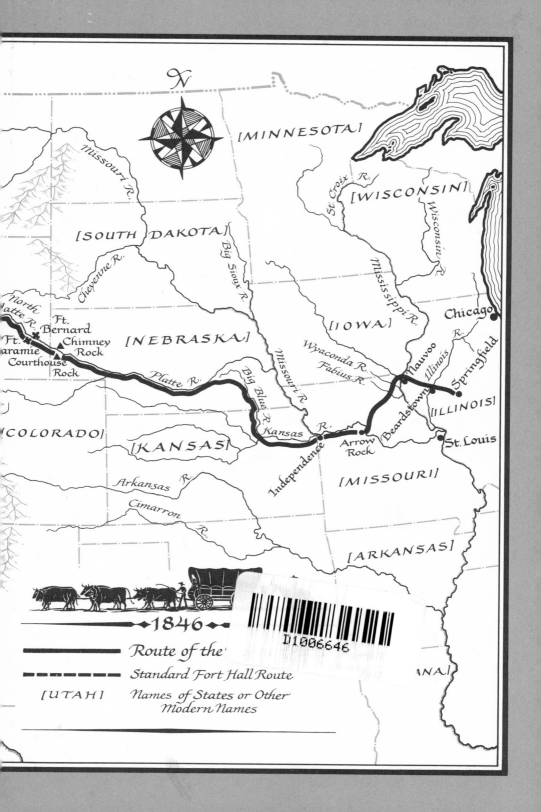

N

[MINNESOTA]

[WISCONSIN]

St. Croix R.

Wisconsin R.

Missouri R.

[SOUTH DAKOTA]

Big Sioux R.

Cheyenne R.

Mississippi R.

Chicago

[IOWA]

North Platte R.

Ft. Bernard

Chimney Rock

[NEBRASKA]

Missouri R.

Wyaconda R.

Fabius R.

Nauvoo

Illinois R.

Springfield

Ft. Laramie

Courthouse Rock

Platte R.

Big Blue R.

Beardstown

[ILLINOIS]

[COLORADO]

[KANSAS]

Kansas R.

Independence

Arrow Rock

St. Louis

[MISSOURI]

Arkansas R.

Cimarron R.

[ARKANSAS]

◆ 1846 ◆

ID1006646

──────── Route of the

- - - - - - - - Standard Fort Hall Route

[UTAH] Names of States or Other Modern Names

[ANA]

TAMSEN

OTHER WORKS BY DAVID GALLOWAY

Criticism
The Absurd Hero in American Fiction
Henry James: The Portrait of a Lady
Edward Lewis Wallant

Editions
Pioneering in Art Collecting
The Selected Writings of Edgar Allan Poe
Ten Modern American Short Stories (with John Whitley)
Calamus (with Christian Sabisch)
The Other Poe: Comedies and Satires

Fiction
Melody Jones
A Family Album
Lamaar Ransom: Private Eye

TAMSEN

DAVID GALLOWAY

HARCOURT BRACE JOVANOVICH, PUBLISHERS

San Diego • • • • • • • • • • New York • • • • • • • • • • London

Requests for permission to make copies of any
part of the work should be mailed to: Permissions,
Harcourt Brace Jovanovich, Publishers, 757 Third Avenue,
New York, N.Y. 10017

Library of Congress Cataloging in Publication Data
Galloway, David D.
Tamsen.
1. Donner Party—Fiction. I. Title.
PS3557.A4155T3   1983   813'.54   82-23232
ISBN 0-15-187992-3

Designed by Joy Chu
Printed in the United States of America
First edition
A B C D E

FOR CHRISTIAN

In October of 1846 a party of seventy-nine men, women and children under the leadership of George Donner attempted to cross the Sierra Nevada Mountains to California. Trapped by early snows, thirty-five of them perished. Those who survived sustained life by consuming the flesh of their dead comrades. This account of their ordeal makes liberal use of the mechanisms of fiction, but at no point does it intentionally depart from the evidence preserved by history.

I
DEPARTURE

1

HE MOVED BAREFOOT ACROSS THE BRIGHT GEOMETRIES OF THE turkey carpet as though they concealed thorns. The flannel night-shirt clutched at his knees, and Tamsen felt the same tightness in her throat that she had known when her children risked stiff-legged first steps into her beckoning arms. In seven years his approach to their bed had never lost the shy, stumbling gait of the young bride-groom, though he was thrice married. When George Donner courted her away from her schoolroom and her brother's farm, he was already a grandfather, and affectionately known to all of Sanga-mon County as Uncle George. He had carved homesteads from the forest as casually as idle men whittled a stick, and with the same easy assurance he had dismantled the cage of her grief, liberating her from chaste and somber widowhood. But even after she had borne him three children, he came to her each night as though fearful she might turn him away or bruise him with careless laughter.

The man stood beside the high bed and stared down at her with eyes like faded scraps of blue gingham. When something gave him pleasure, the color shaded toward violet, as though his whole being quickened and concentrated then, and in those bright moments Tamsen could imagine the gaze of the young man who was once so impatient of horizons. The eyes were drained of color now, as the knuckles of his hands had been blanched throughout supper, rigidly clutching knife and fork and carving his food with exaggerated precision, while she had spoken her mind.

Tamsen's lungs stiffened as she waited for him to reach out and drown the wick of the lamp. She listened for the brief splutter of the dying flame as though only its gift of darkness would ease the mounting pressure in her chest, but a draft swelled the light, and she heard only the sound of the coarse fibers being raked by the blaze. In its uncompromising glare she watched as the man slowly raised the nightshirt to his shoulders, fought free of its folds like a swimmer urgently surfacing for air, and dropped it at his feet.

The sight struck her like a dull blow. His nakedness was a stranger who had invaded the house, groped in her neat cupboards, spilled books to the floor, pawed in her embroidery basket and tangled fine skeins of silk into angry knots. The lock had been wrenched from the prized larder whose key she carried proudly on a jeweled fob pinned to her waist. Within the silvery, hickory-lined interior, bags of flour and salt were gashed open and jars flung to the floor, trampled into a reeking mass whose stains would never be scrubbed away. The stranger's blunt fingers had shattered the fragile silhouettes of pressed flowers, and he had thrown a smothering shadow over the beds of her three sleeping daughters. Now the clumsy intruder had thrust his way into her bedroom, hovered like a clenched fist in the noisy light of the lamp.

For she had never before seen this massive display of his nakedness. She had removed splinters from his broad hands, pressed mustard plasters against his chest, lifted his swollen feet into steaming buckets of salty water, rubbed his strained shoulders with camphor. But something in his own almost maidenly reserve made her turn away when he stepped into the copper bath angled before the kitchen fire. And when George Donner joined his body to hers he was a dark mass that seemed to obliterate even the reluctant moon-glow that sometimes filtered through the single window of the room. Her husband's body was as familiar to her and as remote as the distant range of hills she had known in daily walks with her father —a snug and solid counterpoise to the fickle margins of the sea.

The relentless lamplight accented the stain that dyed George's face and neck, forearms and hands, in the ancient walnut hood-and-sleeves of the farmer. The rest of his skin was the translucent white of skimmed milk, scarcely interrupted by the wiry silver hair that matted his chest. His flesh had thickened in recent years, and the bulk hovered over her as though compelling her to read each syllable of the history of toil and yearning and belated contentment recorded there. The man assaulted her with his nakedness, perhaps even sought to punish her, but every fold and crease and scar he bared was also a plea. His very decay beseeched her, like the faded hue of his eyes, to brace him for a while longer against the irreversible drag of gravity.

He sat heavily on the bed, and Tamsen felt her own unresisting body slope toward the hollow gouged in the feather mattress. She awaited a reprimand for her opposition during supper but he made none, and the pardon she might have asked stayed mute. The children should not have been made witness to her disobedience, even if she had so fiercely resisted his plan on their behalf, and she had then wronged their father even more, seeing him as a clumsy intruder who vandalized the darkened house so carefully secured with bolts and bars of his own devising against the coming of the night. For her to speak first might reveal that greater offense, while silence could seem mere stubbornness, and tears would signal womanish submission to his wishes. The charge of stubbornness she had known since childhood, and so Tamsen waited in silence, though she trembled slightly when the man's hand dragged at the hem of her chemise, scraped along her thighs, and flattened against her stomach.

His palm seemed rough as pine bark, though at first it rested lightly on her skin. Then the fingers began to knead and probe her, as her own might have worked a resisting mass of dough. Firmly, yet without giving real pain, they squeezed and pressed and rolled skin that had three times been stretched taut as the rind of a melon with the daughters he had planted there. The motions stopped briefly, then became those of an animal burrowing frantically for shelter, and she winced as its groping became more urgent, insistent, as though it would not rest until it clutched her thundering heart.

"Mr. Donner," she breathed. It was less a protest than an acknowledgment, uttered in the same brisk rush of syllables with which she might have greeted an acquaintance passed rapidly on the streets of Springfield. "Mr. Donner," she repeated, but the sound was now a plea—not merely that he excuse her defection, but that his newly awakened hunger should not end by consuming them all, like a serpent slowly engorging its own tail.

The hand stilled, but its pressure held her to the mattress as firmly as a moth impaled by a pin. Her eyes were clamped shut but could not seal out the presence of the pulsing light that filled the room with its restless and unaccustomed brightness. She felt her legs being eased apart, the surge of the mattress as George slowly raised himself and knelt between them. He stroked her thighs, his thumbs curving against stiffened muscles, but shame and confusion had dried the streams of her body, and even his persistent caresses would not end the drought. When he arched forward and rapidly entered her, a wedge seemed to be cleaving her apart, and she groped instinctively for the bedstead, gripped it and braced herself against the pounding rhythm. Irrelevantly, she heard the branch of a tree scratch the window, then the ropes supporting the bed creak and chatter in response, and she thought of sails fattened by the wind.

As suddenly as he had begun, the man paused and drew away from her, leaving an emptiness as severe as the pain he had inflicted. Tamsen looked up to see him propped on tensely muscled arms, hanging over her like a rack of clouds, but his eyes were bright glimpses of a deepening blue sky beyond. "We'll be goin' to California," he announced, and entered her again, but more gently now, and her body opened to receive him, while her fingers released their grip on the bedstead to seek the familiar contours of his shoulders. As he labored above her, lustrous with sweat, she sensed that it was neither her flesh nor her spirit that he sought to master, but the land itself, and that she was only a necessary instrument in that struggle. He had conquered tangled acres in Kentucky and sprawling farmlands in Indiana and Illinois, but the merciless plains of Texas had defeated him. There must be no more defeat. There was no time now for defeat. As he plunged and shuddered to a peak, his breath sang a pleading melody into the hollow of her neck. In that instant she knew, and with a sureness that his words could never have achieved, that the treacherous journey of which he dreamed was a crusade against death itself.

"Child," he whispered hoarsely, and carefully stroked away a pinfeather that had caught in the moist corner of her mouth.

"Daughter . . . ," he began, but his voice lifted into a question as he said, "we'll go to California?"

The hair on his chest had the sweetly musty fragrance of rain-damp straw, and Tamsen buried her face there. "Yes," she replied, and the word signaled neither submission to his will nor compromise of her own. It was a solemn and irreversible pledge that they would confront the adversary together.

2

February 2nd, 1846

Dear Sister,

I had it before me to write you at Christmas, but we have all been down with fever this winter. Not the ague or the bilious fever, thank mercy, but the California fever! As you know, I was reading Mr. Emerson's essays to our weekly literary society, but then our neighbor Mr. Reed acquired from Cincinnati a copy of *The Emigrants' Guide to Oregon and California,* and Mr. Emerson could not compete. The papers are all full of talk about Lansford Hastings, the author of this guide, who claims to have discovered a new and shorter passage through the mountains to California. We have had an uncommon hard winter, with much sickness, and everyone made saucer eyes over Mr. Hastings' descriptions of hollyhocks and sweet-william blooming everywhere in California at Christmastime. Wild clover, he says, stands five-feet-high, and cattle never require to be artificially fed or housed.

We have not only read all of Mr. Hastings, but Captain Frémont's journals and the complete works of Mr. Farnham and the latest speeches of Senator Benton. Numerous of our friends and neighbors seem bent to join up with the Great Overland Caravan scheduled to leave Independence, Missouri, in early May. Most are partial to Oregon, though Mr. Reed argues strongly for

California, as does Mr. Donner. It is claimed that but one man in all California ever had a chill there, and it was a matter of such wonderment to the people of Monterey that they went 18 miles into the country to see him shake. A favorite joke is about the man who lived to be 120, got bored with life, and went back east so he could die. The body was shipped by sea to California, where the health-breathing zephyrs instantly resurrected him!

Outfitting for the trail and laying in goods to trade for land with the Mexicans is nothing for poor folks, and most who talk of emigrating will have to settle for the talking, which can be bought by the bale for a pair of coppers. It is certain, though, that the Reeds will go. Mr. Reed is a handsome, gabby Irishman with elegant manners, much favored by all the Springfield ladies. He lets it be known that his grandfather was a Polish count, and the way he shows his aquiline profile when he talks keeps reminding you not to mix him up with the shanty Irish. He has a town named after him and owns a cabinet factory, rides the fastest thorough-bred in the county and has a weakness for flowered waistcoats. His wife is a poor, sickly thing, but full of spirit, and she will accompany him. Her mother will go, too, if she lives through the winter, and her daughter Virginia from another marriage. They have three little children of their own, and two of them just the age of our Georgia and Eliza.

Have you guessed by now that your poor sister will number among their traveling companions? Yes, Mr. Donner has the California fever, too, and so does his brother Jacob. Mr. Donner's son William, who accompanied him to Texas some years ago, will remain here for a time, but is determined to join us later. Each family is to have three great wagons, all to be special made for the journey, and every night we make new lists and then lists of lists that remind us of what we require for encamping along the trail and for our settlement in California. Few of the necessaries are to be had on the Pacific shores, and those at criminal prices, due to the long passage by sea.

It grieves me that Mr. Hastings will prevent your seeing your little namesake, Eliza Poor. She has adopted all my chickens and given them names, and is convinced they will only eat from her hand. I fear we shall not have roasted chicken on the table again unless it is imported from the market in Springfield, and even then Eliza P. is likely to accuse us of eating some distant cousin of her little brood. Georgia makes good progress and can at last walk quite normally, though her knees seem to tangle when she tries to run. Frances is quite grown up, and would not dream of appearing in town without a hat! When not scowling about as lady of the manor, she is pretty as any fairytale princess, and her daintily regular features remind me of our own mother. Her younger sisters are, of course, a great burden, but she suffers them bravely and occasionally invites them to take tea with her dolls. With these three and his two elder daughters and his wife, Mr. Donner is a little like some Ottoman sultan with his harem, but the company of females, he says, helps keep him young!

Our property in Chicago is to be sold to make a nest egg for sunny California, but we will retain the farm on which we are presently residing. It consists of nearly 250 acres of land (about 80 under improvement) and an orchard with bearing trees. There is also an 80-acre lot of good timber included. Part of this is to be deeded to Mr. Donner's married children, with 110 acres reserved for the five younger girls, lest they should determine someday to return to their birthplace. Though I shall be glad to put the continent between my dear family and the hideous fevers of the eastern States, I go with heavy heart from good neighbors and from these orchards and barns. And our big white house is a sturdy ship even in the cruelest winter gales. After all my wanderings this seemed a safe anchorage, but perhaps I was destined after all for the life of a gypsy.

I shall not be idle along the way. Mr. Francis, publisher of the *Sangamo Journal* in Springfield, desires that I send him despatches whenever possible—scribbles about our adventures among the Indians and the buffalo herds! Palmer and Fray of Chicago have consented to publish a botanical treatise describing the wildflowers and herbs of the West, with my hand-drawn illustrations rendered by them as engravings, and I am sketching a little every day to instruct my fingers. I have also ordered several presses for preserving botanical specimens. As there seem to be only a few popish schools attached to the California missions, and these intended largely for the conversion and civilizing of the Mexicans, I shall be obliged to return to the schoolroom and intend to establish California's first academy for young girls. You may easily guess the names of my first pupils! We must thus transport abundant writing materials, water colors and oil paints, materials for handiwork, and other necessary school supplies. With all the sorting and packing and mending and making, we are in a frenzy from sunup to sundown. The older girls are a great assistance, and even Frances has learned to plait the trimmings left over from our endless sewing and quilting. We will stitch them into rag rugs as remembrances for the friends we leave behind.

Since you have never seen your pretty nieces (and may not get to California before they are married!), I am sending you a daguerreotype of myself with the children. It is the handiwork of Mr. N. H. Shepherd, who established a temporary photographic parlor over Mr. Brookie's drugstore a few weeks ago. He has developed a new process guaranteed not to fade, but takes some liberty in the coloring, as you will guess. My hair is not quite such a geranium red, and Georgia's eyes are more like periwinkles than gentians, but otherwise we are just as plump and sassy a quartet of gypsies as we appear.

Please send me news of yourself and Mr. Poor and the children. We expect to begin our journey in early April, so as to allow ourselves ample time to join up with the caravan that is to leave Independence in early May.

Your loving sister,
T. E. Donner

3

THE PHOTOGRAPH IS AN ELONGATED OCTAGON MEASURING 3¼ inches high and 2¾ inches wide. The fashionable octagonal shape has been formed by cutting away the four corners of the oblong glass plate on which the image is exposed, and though this gives the whole the classic appearance of a medallion, it seems to crowd the four figures who pose here and give, at first glance, the feeling of an abstract density of rounded female curves, of lace and shirred taffeta and embroidered grosgrain. With this abundance of pleating and drapery, they might be mannequins thrust hastily together in the tiny octagonal window of a millinery shop. In the center of the picture a woman sits rather stiffly on a simple, straight-backed chair which lifts one fluted finial over her right shoulder. The finial is, however, only partially visible, for it is cupped in the plump hands of a small girl approximately six years old, whose bonneted head is nonetheless on a level with that of the seated woman. Either the child stands on a box or the woman is of strikingly diminutive stature. To the right (but on the woman's left) stands a younger girl, symmetrically posed, and with her arms raised. Presumably her hands clutch a matching finial on the chairback, but they are obscured by the broad ribbon that trails from the side of the woman's bonnet. The seated figure is angled slightly to the left, and on her lap she holds a third child, who would appear to be two or three years of age. The woman's left arm curves about the child's body and her left hand grasps the tiny forearm. Her right hand is flattened across the child's knees. The posture is graceful, and it has a protective, motherly air, but something in the positioning of the woman suggests the exertion of force, as though she clamps the restless sitter in place, immobilizing her for the two minutes it takes the gaping mouth of the camera to drink in their image. But she cannot control the child's eyes, which dart about the improvised studio, flicking across crates of chemicals, a collapsing settee, the photographer's brightly polished gaiters, the broad gold bands on her mother's fingers. In the photograph this continuous motion makes the child's eyes seem vacant, blurred, like those of an antique doll.

Faded, too, are the crimson and ochre and azure tints with which N. H. Shepherd originally colored the plate; aging chemistries have also blurred certain details, and carelessness has pitted and flecked the surface. Nonetheless, this portrait of a mother and her three daughters remains a valuable historical document—both as one of the earliest surviving daguerreotypes made in what was then designated as the American West, and as a remarkably vital, artistic example of the work of N. H. Shepherd. Soon after he had twisted and prodded these four sitters into a perfect cameo of female shadow and curve, he produced portraits of the attorney Abraham Lincoln and his wife, which would eventually hang on the wall of their bedroom in the White House. Shepherd was amazed by the success of his stay in Springfield. His announcement in the *Sangamo Journal* had indicated that he would be present over the drugstore of J. Brookie from January 10th until February 1st, but in fact business was so brisk that he was still in residence on April 15th, and thus joined the festive crowd that milled about the nine heavily loaded wagons of the Donner and Reed families bound for California.

At first glance one might take this for a photograph of four sisters. Certainly the figures are linked by blood and not merely by occasion. The family relationship is immediately apparent in their eyes—strikingly large, widely spaced, and deeply set beneath the straight, heavy line of their brows. This, together with the severe center parting in their hair, threatens to give them all the stern, scowling air of the offspring of a fanatical country parson, but is immediately contradicted by the teasing smile they share. The upper lip is narrow, scarcely more than a fine pencil line, but the corners dimple in a suggestion of suppressed laughter, and the bottom lip is plumply full. This plumpness complements the generous oval shape of the faces, the rounding of the cheeks, thus contributing to the total effect of sleek and somewhat pampered femininity. There is a surprising beauty here, and one that cannot be entirely accounted for by individual features, though there is something striking in the sculptural symmetry of the four faces, in the way the thick hair descends from the severe center parting and coils softly against the cheeks. The hair is obviously drawn together at the back of the neck, but its ampleness resists all efforts to flatten it into a glossy cap. Like the smile that hovers in the corners of their mouths, it defies control. The beauty comes in part from this quality of playful eagerness that threatens to break free of convention, of stays and bindings and sashes, of the contrived geometry of their pose.

That these are not four sisters becomes apparent only when the photograph is studied in more detail. It reveals faint crescents beneath the eyes of the seated figure; these are obscured at first both by the heavy shadow of her brows and by the distracting brightness of the eyes themselves. There is nothing haggard or worn about these dark crescents, but they are nonetheless an unmistakable notation of the flesh, a record of the agonies and toil and separation and loss the woman has survived. Oddly, the lines lend her face both dignity and vulnerability, as though the mischievous glow of confidence and health she radiates is a fragile veil that could easily be torn apart. It has been torn before, and the curves beneath her eyes are evidence of the hasty mending. Thus, despite the diminutive stature, the girlish merriment of her suppressed laughter, the seated figure is clearly a mature woman. Her fashionable clothing, the confident angle of her head, the casual self-assurance with which she poses for her first photograph—all these suggest a woman of intelligence and of comfortable circumstances. The children surrounding her (unlike her first two) have survived infancy, and this tight cluster of their bodies, this dense gathering of female flesh, is testimony to their victory. The girls who stand to the left and right in the photograph press against their mother's body; the child on her lap is firmly circled in her embrace. Her arms are arranged to hold the youngest daughter steady for the camera, but they also act as a shield to ward off invisible dangers.

The name she enters in the photographer's register is Tamsen Eustis Donner, and the middle name is written with particular flourish, with a graceful scroll descending from the "E," and another twining from the "s" to cross the "t," giving the name the effect of an elaborate monogram, set protectively between the sturdy but humble supports of "Tamsen" and "Donner." She thus pays tribute to Captain William Eustis, who earned his honorary title in the Revolutionary War. A widow's only son, he was not yet sixteen when he enlisted for duty, but quickly caught his superiors' attention as the most alert and eager sentinel at Boston's Old South Church when the British launched their spring offensive. In the concluding months of the war he had languished as a prisoner aboard the *Count d'Estang.* Colonel Eustis cultivated a stoically unsentimental public image as the Roman soldier-scholar, but he doted shamelessly on his miraculous daughter Tamesin, lavishing on her the praise and wonder and discipline and instruction and luxury which fathers classically bestow on the eldest and on the youngest of their daughters, and she was, in fact, both. Tamesin was the first and the last of his six children, and her very existence was an elaborate negation of death.

The first Tamesin was born in 1786, and her quick, inquisitive spirit seemed perfectly matched by a vigorous, robust body. Molly, born three years later, was a sickly infant subject to fevers and fits that left her face twisted and blue, her tongue distended like some monstrous larva that sucked her breath. John and Elizabeth both nearly died from the measles. Meanwhile, Tamesin thrived, resisting the onslaughts of whooping cough that recurrently flowered in the nursery, the ague that swelled the joints of her younger sister Elizabeth. Thus, no one was prepared for the brutal swiftness of her death. Three months after her tenth birthday cholera clutched her roughly, squeezed and pressed the juices from her body, shriveled her cheeks and bloated her stomach, filling the house with the stink of her brief, agonized dying. Captain William was still unconsoled when his second son was born in 1799. The baby's protuberant maleness seemed to be another of nature's cruel mockeries, and though the boy was named for him, no mere William could replace the cherished Tamesin. On the 1st of November, 1801, his wife bore him a sixth child, and this second Tamesin ascended the vacant, grieving throne of his affections. As though she had been spirited away by evil fairies, he welcomed her triumphant and miraculous return, treating her not as a child, but as a reincarnation of the first

Tamesin, who would have been fifteen when her successor was born. Before her hand could properly hold the quill, he guided it in forming the alphabet, and he passed over nursery rhymes to read to her from massive, gold-edged volumes of botany. He taught her Latin and mathematics, the little Greek he knew, and the names of all the first-magnitude stars. After the death of Mrs. Eustis in 1808, the passionate communion of father and daughter became even more intense.

There is some obscurity in the spelling of the child's name, apparently originating with the mother who bore her, and who designated herself at various times "Thomazin" and "Tamazin" and "Tamesin," though she seems to have favored the last spelling for her daughters. George Donner's third wife chose yet another variation for their wedding announcement, identifying herself there as "Tamozine," but usage seems to have simplified it to Tamsen, the spelling she herself eventually came to prefer. The origin of the name is puzzling. It may have been coined originally as a simple female equivalent for Thomas, or even as a variant on the mythic Tammuz, the ancient Syrian god of vegetation viciously slaughtered by a wild boar, and whose blood is said to reappear as anemones to redden the slopes of Mount Lebanon after the winter rains. In one variation of the myth, the exquisite body of Tammuz is devoured by Sheol, the goddess of hell.

When Colonel William Eustis died of a stroke in 1821, his daughter Tamsen quickly found application for the tuition he had begun in her infancy. For a time she taught French and botany at the Conservatory for Young Ladies in Newburyport, Massachusetts, but the promise of a milder, healthier climate to the south encouraged her to move to Elizabeth City, North Carolina, in 1825, and there she taught school for a further three years, rejecting a series of prosperous landed suitors who sought a sturdy young wife to tend their hearths and nurture their motherless children. Her choice fell instead on a dashing and somewhat irresponsible haberdasher, a strikingly handsome man rather younger than herself. Tully Dozier had a countywide reputation for his devotion to poetry and to pretty young women. Tamsen seemed to suffice the latter need, and she enthusiastically shared the former. Tamsen bore Tully a daughter and then a son, and between Christmas and New Year of 1831 she nursed husband and children as they died of cholera. The urgent pumping of their lungs, as the three dragged in ragged scraps of air, seemed to vibrate the walls of the small frame house, and their uncontrollable fever suffused the bedroom with tropic heat. The disease mysteriously spared her—perhaps, she later thought, because it had already claimed one Tamsen as its due. In the months that followed, her own clumsy animal survival seemed an act of unspeakable cruelty, and she ached to follow her husband and children into death. Her mind struggled against the body's extraordinary will to survive, which seemed to her then a faceless enemy that had forced its way inside her, laying pitiless siege to the sorrow in which she yearned to dissolve. Eventually, she took her small inheritance and returned to Massachusetts, but Newburyport, too, reminded her of the loss of her gallant heroes, of the sheltering Captain William and of the gentle, silken-skinned Tully, and there followed vacant, wasted months, horrors from which memory instinctively recoiled. Thus, when her brother William wrote to complain of the difficulty of tending to his own brood of motherless children, she instantly agreed to join him on his farm in Illinois.

Tamsen muffled grief with physical labor, a city girl tuning herself to the rhythms of the land and the variety of unaccustomed demands the simple farm made on her, asking no more than mind-dulling weariness from the tasks she performed. She milked cows and dipped candles, mended clothing, baked bread, learned to handle a team of oxen, recruited the children to help turn the earth for an herb garden. Gouging a precarious balance with the heels of her crude brogans, she grappled between plunging, water-slick legs, and dragged whimpering calves into the saving air. A cough from one of the children was sufficient to startle her into icy wakefulness, and she dosed them heavily with mixtures of bark and quinine, with Wallace and Diller's Western Tonic, and with Dr. Braggs' Indian Queen Vegetable Sugar Coated Pills. But finally her own nightmare fears were banished by the robustness of their growing bodies, and then she could allow herself the luxury of being distressed by the shameful neglect of their education. Instructing her nephews and nieces, wandering with them through meadows and fields to clarify lessons in surveying and botany, stirred the old joy she had known as a teacher. It forced its way now, insistent and green, through the brittle husk of her grief. Awakened, too, was the conviction, inherited from Colonel William, that the gift of knowledge incurred certain responsibilities. Thus, she returned to the schoolroom, first in Auburn and then at Sugar Creek, where the pupils were older and more advanced. Scarcely five feet tall and weighing less than a hundred pounds, she was smaller than most of her pupils, but her clear, firm voice and vigilant eye (perhaps a further inheritance from her soldierly father) more than compensated for the discrepancy of size. The only significant opposition she encountered was from the Auburn Board of School Trustees, which was unhappy to learn that the new teacher regularly knitted during recitations, and ordered her to give up either the school or the handiwork. Instead, she invited the trustees to her classroom and knitted resolutely while lessons were heard, criticized, explained. The following day she learned the Board's decision: "Mrs. Dozier shall keep her school and her knitting too." The episode only confirmed the local judgment that she was "a right peppery little thing."

Tamsen Dozier first saw George Donner in the summer of 1839, at a horse race just beyond the Springfield town limits. He was astride a sleek black stallion named Arabian Leopard. At fifty-five he was the eldest of the competitors, but clearly the most popular, for the crowd urged him on to victory with surging choruses of "Uncle George!" He had recently returned from Texas, where he and his brother Jacob had farmed for a year. George's eldest son William had accompanied them, and William's wife bore him a son there. Kids, said the grandfather, were about all you could harvest in that parched hell, and though Jacob was the elder, it was George Donner who led the little tribe back to Illinois. They had always been wanderers. The brothers, born in Rowan County, North Carolina, were still children when their father pushed through the Cumberland Gap into the wilds of Kentucky, scarcely more than boys when they made their own pioneering way into Indiana. They cleared land, hauled boulders and stumps from the fields, put in a crop, harvested it, and dreamed of moving on. The wilderness might have been a personal affront to them, a cosmic oversight they were deter-

17

mined to correct. They stripped away its tangled undergrowth, fenced it, sliced their mark into the earth with the brightly honed point of a plow, scattered seed in the furrows and commanded it to grow. Even as they watched it sprout, they seemed to grow restless. Before the first crops were laid by, they were talking about clearing new acreage, putting in orchards, sinking a second well, adding more pasturage to the south, damming the creek. Their thick, eager, work-roughened fingers prodded the land, shaped it to some instinctive formula, and then groped after new earth on which they could impose their irresistible will. Their conquests invigorated the two brothers, gave their step a springy assertiveness as they measured off their ripening domains, but the wives were slowly worn away, exhausted by unvarying cycles of clearing and planting and harvesting, of childbirth and nursing and weaning, of tending the sick and cooking for famished husbands and hired hands and growing children. George Donner married for the first time in Decatur City, Indiana, to the youngest daughter of the owner of the General Merchandise Emporium. She presented him with five children before her death, and when the Donner brothers wandered into Illinois in the autumn of 1828, the widower lost little time in taking Mary Blue as her successor. They settled with George's five children on 240 acres of land east of Springfield, on the road to Mechanicsburgh, a few miles from the acreage bought by Jacob Donner, now also a widower. Jacob soon found a wife in Mary's widowed sister, adopting her two small children and subsequently giving her five more. George and Mary Donner produced seven children in nine years, and Mary died giving birth to the last of them; only two daughters —Elitha and Leanna—survived infancy.

Perhaps George hoped to find a new wife, as well as a new empire, when he departed for Texas with his brother and his eldest son, but age had made him more cautious, and he retained the Sangamon County farm. The hard Texas soil resisted his will, the sun scorched him, the sudden fierceness of winter stabbed mockingly at his bones, and after harvesting a single scraggly crop he returned to Illinois. In the summer of 1839, when Tamsen saw him astride Arabian Leopard, he seemed on the verge of accepting the comfortable role of patriarch, and was widely consulted for his seasoned judgment on crops and deeds and horseflesh. His prosperity not only guaranteed a carefree old age, with others to labor for him, but had provided farms for his adult children, a kind of extended kingdom where he could warm his aging body with the affection of his increasing progeny. The man's curling beard and pale blue eyes, which softened his broad face, reminded Tamsen of the hand-tinted engraving of a prophet in the family Bible. As the horses thundered around the improvised track, spraying the air with dense yellow clouds of dust, she sensed the fierce determination with which he sought victory over his younger comrades, and somehow this knowledge startled her. Without the aid of whip or spurs, he nonetheless pushed the stallion to its limits, until she feared its great heart would burst with the effort, but he also leaned forward, stroking the tensely muscled neck, and he might have been chanting an ancient incantation to the rhythm of its pounding hooves. The following day, when she closed the door of the Sugar Creek schoolhouse, he was waiting for her, with Arabian Leopard tethered in the shadow of a tree. He had not announced his visit, and the sole explanation he offered was in the long, appraising look he gave her as she fumbled with the massive iron key, puzzled and annoyed by the sudden incompetence, the helpless female surrender, of her hands. She shared her father's suspicion of religion, yet she had more than once thought of herself as the widowed and exiled Ruth, and as she walked with George between fields of corn that fluttered golden tassels in the summer breeze, she knew that he would be her Boaz, her lord and her protector. George and Tamsen Donner were married at the German Prairie Christian Church in September, 1839, and the first of their three daughters, Frances Eustis Donner, was born on July 8th, 1840.

It is Frances who stands to the left in the photograph, clutching the back of the chair on which her mother sits. The bonnet she wears is a miniature version of Tamsen's and seems far too old for a child who has not yet celebrated her sixth birthday. Made of fine straw and worn far to the back of the head, it has a two-inch brim that rises abruptly in the front to form a kind of tiara, almost entirely covered with clusters of miniature silk flowers. Broad bands of embroidered silk ribbon, drawn into plump bows over each ear, trail down onto the shoulders, and a ribbon of the same stuff is tied just under the chin, holding the bonnet snugly in place. The faces of both mother and child are thus framed in coronas of silk, and the result is touchingly picturesque. On the other hand, the ribbons so firmly knotted under their chins compel them to hold their heads rather stiffly, as if any sudden movement would court strangulation. The child's self-consciously adult air has been cultivated by her pivotal place among the five Donner daughters. Her half-sisters Leanna and Elitha are now twelve and fourteen, and she wishes to be accepted as their companion; simultaneously, she claims seniority over her own two younger sisters. There is something possessive, even domineering, in the way she grasps the back of the chair on which her mother sits, as though Tamsen is there by her sufferance, as another of the children it is her matronly duty to tolerate and, from time to time, encourage. Or perhaps it is only the weight of the bonnet that forces her to hold her head at such a rigid, imperious angle. Her parents were old enough to be her grandparents, and at her birth she became aunt to a dozen nephews and nieces; this too may contribute to her precocious womanly air.

It was, at any rate, more than calendar years that gave her such canny understanding of the awesome events that occurred a year later on Prosser Creek. "We shall have to begin on those who have died," her mother said, without pity or desperation or apology, but as calmly and casually as she might have noted that the supply of firewood was growing low.

With some deep female prescience Frances had grasped the words, and she had freely collaborated in carrying them out, but for more than thirty years she was unable to utter the name of the woman who had squatted beside her, turning the sizzling meat on an improvised spit. The youngest of Frances's own children was then eight years old, and she had no doubt that it would be her last; the first had already married and begun a family of her own. Thus, when her courses stopped, she judged it to be the early beginnings of the turn of life, denied her pregnancy until the child within her stirred, thrust against her heart in a demand for recognition, and she responded with the banished name—not in a whisper but in a cry that slashed the air: "Tamsen!" Frances was then thirty-eight, as her mother had been at the time of her own birth.

None of this subsequent history is immediately visible in the little daguerreotype, though it is perhaps implied in the intensity with which the mother and her eldest daughter stare out from the massed flourishes of their ribboned bonnets. Certainly it is impossible to read a similar text in the blurred, restless eyes of the small child cradled on Tamsen's lap, or even in the bright, mischievous stare of Georgia Ann Donner, who stands at the right in the photograph. The latter is four years old, and the baby will soon celebrate her third birthday. They have amply shared the childhood denied to Frances —linked not only by the closeness of their age, but by the fact that Georgia was painfully slow in learning to walk and to talk. She was only a few months old when she tumbled from her parents' high bed, despite the firm bulwark of feather pillows that wedged her in place. For the next year she was fretful, colicky, and when she finally began to walk, her knees were held so stiffly that the slightest hesitation sent her toppling like a felled tree. She and Eliza Poor (named for Tamsen's favorite sister) would cling together like frail old women, clutching wildly for balance, then tumble to the floor in fits of laughter that led Tamsen to dub the pair "my chubby giggles." Inseparable playmates, they developed a secret language, resembling the urgent cooing of pigeons, with which they communicated the most riotous secrets. Frances, of course, strictly forbade such heathenish babblings at her tea parties, concerned about the effect on her eminently well-bred family of dolls. As the Donners moved out across the prairies on the long trail to California, Georgia and Eliza withdrew more and more into their mysterious private world. While Frances and Tamsen sat up front with one of the teamsters, or walked alongside, the two little girls burrowed beneath quilts in the family wagon, carving out caves with their arms, withdrawing like startled young animals into their cozy burrow.

Despite her healthy appearance and the merriment that dances in her eyes, something in the posture of the child on the right suggests that she stands awkwardly, and that she leans so firmly against her mother's body not merely to complete this quartet of graces, to lend it the air of a festive tableau, but in order to support her disobedient legs. Throughout childhood she will remain weaker than Eliza, and is often dependent on her younger sister's strength.

There is, indeed, a ferocious resoluteness about Tamsen's youngest daughter, and it is this, as much as the efforts of the weary rescue party, that accounts for the survival of the children during the long, frozen trek out of the mountains. It was also Eliza who sensed the generosity of the elderly Swiss couple living near Sutter's Fort, instinctively addressing the woman as "Grandma." First Eliza and then Georgia spent a week at a time being fattened and nursed back to strength on the Brunners' farm, then exchanged places, and the rotation continued until Eliza asked plaintively, "Grandma, can't you keep us both?" Far more than her sisters or her half-sisters, she understood how to get her own way, and when she and Georgia were briefly separated—one with Grandpa Brunner in Sonoma, the other with Elitha Donner, who had married and was living on the Consumnes River—it was her will that united them again. It sufficed, indeed, to persuade a passing Indian to carry her across the swollen waters of the Sonoma River, to the cousin who waited there with a pony to take her on to the Brunners. One is not surprised, then, to learn that Eliza subsequently cut a prominent figure in Washington as wife of California Congressman Sherman O. Houghton, or that at the age of sixty she would put resolute pen to paper in order to produce the definitive history of the Donners' ordeal in the mountains, though she had been only four at the time of her rescue. In a long, graphic letter, her sister Georgia then attempted to draw the narrative closer to "the dreadful truth." But none of the nine children born to Georgia and Eliza carried on the names of Tamsen and George. Only Frances would make that belated tribute.

There is, then, something fitting in the fact that the woman seated in the center of this photograph and the eldest of her daughters are wearing identical bonnets, and that their dresses are of the same plaid taffeta. The bodices are snugly fitted and closed by a row of buttons so closely set they resemble the compact grains on an ear of ripe corn. From their sheen, these buttons would seem to be made of mother-of-pearl, but they are somewhat obscured by the trailing ribbons that snug the bonnets in place, and they may be of polished ivory. The woman, unlike her daughter, wears a lace shawl about her shoulders, and there is more lace trimming the long sleeves of her dress; these are tight at the shoulder but flare from the elbow to the wrist, whereas the sleeves of the girl's dress are loosely fitted to the elbow, and stop there with a double row of ruffles of the same fabric. Georgia's dress is similar in style, but in yellow velvet with a smocked front, cut generously to allow for future growth. Eliza is entirely in white, in a long dress with an eyelet skirt that might well have served for her christening, and makes her appear even younger than she is.

One further detail about the woman demands attention, and this is the matter of the two rings on her right hand—on the first and third fingers. They appear to be identical gold bands, and they assume such prominence because of the manner in which her hand is held flat against Eliza's knees, thus putting it on a plane exactly parallel to the lens of the camera. Has she, perhaps, transferred the wedding ring from her first marriage to her index finger, to make way for George's? Or might one of these gold bands have belonged to her mother or to Colonel William? Does the one on her index finger commemorate her dead parents or her dead husband? The answer is uncertain, but there is something unmistakably assertive in this symmetry of gold, and whatever its source, it symbolizes the restoration of life which her second marriage represented, the courage to commence again to weave the threads of affection and dependence and passion and pain into the complex tapestry of matrimony. The risks she takes are immense, and the joy she receives can only seem tentative, compromised by the constant, familiar shadow of death, by the motherless children she has comforted, by the inadequate magic of the walnut medicine chest that sits on her bureau. The gold encircling her fingers acknowledges the risk, and its glow proclaims her allegiance to life, though life has given her repeated reason to doubt the terms of their contract. The hand that bears the twin rings is strong and well formed, the nails trimmed sensibly short but gracefully rounded; it is adept, ministering, capable, but though the fingers are bluntly formed, the position in which they are held across the infant's knees shows an easy elegance, and there is, perhaps, a hint of feminine vanity in their display of riches, as there is in the extravagant silk festoons of her bonnet.

Surrounded so picturesquely by her daughters, she might be posing for an engraving of "Motherhood" to appear in one of the fashionable gift books or annuals so prized by ladies of genteel persuasion. Mr. Godey himself would, no doubt, have found them a wonderfully fetching quartet.

4

ON THE 26TH OF MARCH, 1846, THE FOLLOWING ADVERTISEMENT appeared in the *Sangamo Journal* of Springfield, Illinois:

WESTWARD HO!
For Oregon and California. Who wants to go to California without costing them anything? As many as eight young men, of good character, who can drive an ox team, will be accommodated by gentlemen who will leave this vicinity about the middle of April. Come on Boys. You can have as much land as you want without costing you anything. The Government of California gives large tracts of land to persons who move there. The first suitable persons who apply will be engaged.
George Donner and others.

Despite the promise of free land and of hollyhocks that bloomed at Christmas, few young men seem to have responded to the advertisement, for it was printed again on April 12th, only three days before the departure of the Donner and Reed families. Two Germans named Joseph Reinhardt and Augustus Spitzer were signed on, and three local boys—Noah James, Sam Shoemaker, and Hiram Miller. At the last minute a gunsmith from Sheffield, England, agreed to join them, but the addition of John Denton still gave the Donners only six of the eight bull-whackers they required. Perhaps others were discouraged by the knowledge that the free land George Donner promised them was still the property of Mexico.

5

EACH DAY THE UNFINISHED CHORES HAD MULTIPLIED OVERNIGHT, until preparations for their departure seemed more demanding than any ordeals that could possibly await them on the trail. There were mounds of clothing to be washed, altered, repaired, buttons to be given an extra, securing stitch, and all must then be sorted into great Saratoga trunks labeled according to the seasons and weathers to be encountered along the way. With her eye Tamsen measured how much the girls might grow in the year before they could be settled in California, and her shears accommodated the future, creating sturdy dresses for play and ruffled ones for such social functions as the *alcaldes* of the Pacific wilderness might contrive. In gingham and linsey woolsey she carved the narrative of the months and the miles to come, as though inventing new daughters. These complex imaginary children required not only dresses and caps and bonnets and shifts and pantalets and shoes and boots, but India-rubber capes, heavy woolen cloaks, muffs and mittens. Their minds required books and slates and paper and ink and paints; their health would be protected with ointments and lotions, tonics, pills, infusions; there were salves for burns and tinctures, lint and bandages for wounds. Hogs were slaughtered to provide ham and bacon and spicy sausages to feed their growing bodies, and to these were added 150 pounds of flour for each person (including Eliza), as well as sacks of beans, salt, rice, raisins, nuts, dried fruits, sugar, coffee. This, together with tools and bedding and cooking vessels and costly bolts of lace and velvet (to be traded for Mexican land grants), had to be measured, sorted, weighed, packed and repacked. Meanwhile, there was the matter of dividing farm equipment and furniture among Mr. Donner's married children (William was charged to transport the harmonium and the great brass bedstead when he came out to join them), of securing deeds and titles and selling off some of the property, of providing sturdy compasses, a collapsible telescope, a roadometer, ropes and chains, candles and soap and oil, botanical presses, tents and harness and seed. They also laid in goods for the Indian trade: beads, tobacco, copper finger rings, handkerchiefs, cheap pantaloons, red and yellow flannel, butcher knives, mirrors, fishhooks. George rode into town almost every morning to supervise construction of the wagons, fretting over alterations, testing the grip of cleating and the seasoning of planks; he bought ox teams at auction, found fault in their gait, sold them and bought more. Meanwhile, Tamsen and the older girls and two housemaids stitched, tidied, wrapped, measured, packed, sifted, arranged, unpacked and repacked. They were weary but elated by the gaudy theatrical profusion of textures and shapes, and the girls giggled uncontrollably as they perched on the lid of a trunk while Tamsen fought to close the latch. "This is positively the last time I open it this side of California," she solemnly pledged, and within hours she would be pawing through it in search of something mislaid and now urgently required.

Matching the frenzy of their chores was a frenzy of visiting, as though the farm had become a kind of shrine to which the whole county was determined to pay homage. Some visitors, no doubt, thought them foolish and improvident to leave behind this comfortable plenty to risk the tomahawk, to gamble their futures on lands that, after all, legally belonged to the government of Mexico. But most came out of a sense of awe for the bold decision they had made, the golden horizon that awaited them, and these drew near, dawdled, gaped at the rich disarray of the house as though it held some enormous secret that life had denied them. Crops in Illinois had repeatedly dwindled and failed in recent years, and here were people going to a country where a single stalk of wheat formed seven heads and yielded up to 120 bushels an acre and never had to be seeded again after the first crop, where peaches were ripe for the picking in January, and deadly miasmic fevers were unknown. Tamsen dreaded the recurrent interruptions of visitors, many of them strangers who just happened to stop by on their way to Springfield, but she was excited, too, by their attention, their eager, envious questions, the warm and sociable bustle of these hectic, hurrying days.

Former pupils paid her ceremonial farewell calls, and many brought their children, with cheeks raw from scrubbing, to be presented for her approval. These she often asked to sit with her for a while in the parlor, the only room in the house not turned topsy-turvy, but even then her hands were rarely idle. Her workbasket contained squares of cloth pinked from remnants and from dresses hopelessly out of fashion and clothes the girls had outgrown. She had tested every inch, stretching it taut, holding it to the light that would betray any hidden imperfections. Whatever seemed stout and serviceable was cut into identical squares, and the rest into strips to be braided for rugs. As she entertained her callers, Tamsen joined the squares with tiny, brisk stitches, and when four were tightly seamed into a larger square, she pushed them to the bottom of the basket, and when there were four of these mosaics of bright calicoes, pastel chintzes and earth-hued madders, they would be joined as well, to form an even larger square. By taste, she preferred more elaborate, more fanciful designs, but the large patchwork had to be completed and then quilted before departure, and the utilitarian form could be worked more rapidly. Also, it was less likely to draw envious attention, and it was important that their California quilt seem perfectly ordinary, for between the patchwork and the interlining of cotton wadding she would secure ten thousand dollars in bank notes that George had recently received for the sale of his lots in Chicago.

The steady flow of the skeptical and the curious to the Donner farm was less surprising than the frequency with which the overworked emigrant women met together by twos and threes and fours and fives, like a secret society whose ritual exercises demanded constant vigilance. They expected to be together for months in the uncompromising intimacy of the westward trek, and might better have spent their time with friends and relatives who would be left behind, but the sense of being joined by mysterious bonds proved more compelling. Betsy Donner and Tamsen visited several times a week, and often the two called on Margaret Reed, whose invalid mother kept her housebound. The Donner wives could scarcely believe the Reed women would survive the rigors of the trail—Margaret with her migraines and her fainting spells, Mrs. Keyes with her weak heart and wandering mind. James Reed had taken over nearly all arrangements for the journey, with the occasional assistance of his thirteen-year-old stepdaughter Virginia, and he directed the operation with the same imperious efficiency that had made his cabinet works such a success. His sickly wife and mother-in-law were thus freed to contemplate the glories awaiting them in California's eternal summer.

If Mrs. Keyes was failing, the ladies took tea in her bedroom, with the old woman propped into a sitting position against the great oak headboard of her bed; dense with wooden scrolls and garlands, it had been shipped from London before the Revolutionary War. Surrounded by mounds of goose-down pillows, and with her thin legs scarcely visible beneath the embroidered white counterpane, she resembled a frail child, and her mind often strayed among the memories of childhood. Elitha, Leanna and Frances occasionally accompanied Tamsen on these visits, hoping that Mrs. Keyes would remember her amazing adventures among the Indians. During the early settlement of Virginia and Kentucky, an aunt of Sarah Keyes had been captured by the savages, and had remained their prisoner for five years before making good her escape. That fabled experience she had now appropriated as her own, recounting it with increasingly elaborate detail, and the children listened with widening eyes until it seemed that everything in the room, from the high old-fashioned bedposts to the shovel and tongs in the chimney corner, was transformed into a dusky tribe in paint and feathers, preparing for the war dance. The three mothers, all busy with their handiwork, were torn between a protective feeling that the children should not be excited by such fairy tales and their own more grisly, unspoken fears of the dangers awaiting them in Indian country.

"General Frémont says the Sioux are well disposed toward travelers," Tamsen assured them all. She bit off a thread as though such a celebrated authority disposed of all doubt.

"But the Kaws can be right bothersome," Betsy timidly ventured.

"Yes," Margaret Reed confirmed, "they are meant to be pesky, but not really dangerous." Her fingers paused in their elaborate ballet, idled over her knitting while she sought the word. "Degenerate," she finally added, and her fingers resumed their sprightly dance.

"Beggars," Betsy nodded, "and they never wash. If they get too near the wagon, you can smell them in the canvas for days."

The women bobbed their heads reassuringly over their handiwork. Dirt and beggary were conditions they could understand and, equally, deplore. Such vices were familiar, and familiarity masked the phantom images that often appeared in their dreams—images of half-naked savages, lusty, muscular, their hair heavy with buffalo fat, men not familiar with the decencies and restraints of civilization.

Their practiced needles flew in crisp, tight, disciplined lines, as though civilization itself depended on the sturdiness of their stitches, and they planted them as firmly as the palisades of a frontier fort.

Mrs. Keyes, who had been napping between chapters of her narration, suddenly sat stiffly upright in the bed, flinging offending pillows to the floor. Her white hair, freed from the bow that had snugged it in place, splayed a ragged veil across her face. "And they et up all the babies!" she shouted, pushing more pillows to the floor. "Chewed the bones, too!" Betsy gasped and sucked at the finger she had impaled with her needle. Her wide, cow-like eyes roved helplessly, seeking an escape route and finding none.

"Hush, Mama," said Margaret Reed, in a tone that consoled even while it scolded. She hurried to retrieve the pillows, smooth her mother's hair, fluff the counterpane.

"It's true," the old woman insisted.

"Now you just hush," the daughter warned, "before you scare these poor children out of their wits."

"I know what I saw," Mrs. Keyes said, pronouncing the words loudly, emphatically, and addressing them to the entire room. Her pink gums seemed to test each word before releasing it. "I. Know. What. I. Saw."

"Now, Mama, you didn't see any such thing."

"Think I'm crazy? Think. I'm. Crazy?"

"No, Mama, of course not, but maybe just a mite fanciful." As she spoke, Margaret Reed realized that a damp stain had appeared on the coverlet, and it spread rapidly. Her mother chuckled with pleasure, having found the ideal way to put an end to the silly quarrel, and with a triumphant nod to her audience she sank back into the nest of pillows. The other women in the room looked quickly to their sewing while Margaret Reed and the hired girl Eliza Williams busied themselves with the damp bedclothes. Eliza was deaf as a post, a clumsy, hardworking, even-tempered girl, and the old woman's ravings stirred no phantoms to stalk her dreams.

The entire family had tried to talk Sarah Keyes out of undertaking the long, fatiguing journey, and the minister had sat with her for hours, patiently and repeatedly emphasizing the terrible loss her going would mean to her two sons living in Springfield. Mrs. Keyes had no illusions that she would survive the trek, but she had no intention of permitting her only daughter to undertake such downright folly without motherly guidance. Furthermore, if the Lord was with her she would hold out until Fort Hall, on the far side of the continental divide, where she might see her son Caden, her baby, on his way back from Oregon Territory. And the thought of being left behind as a sick, useless, senile old woman, discarded like a worn-out shoe, sent her fierce pride reeling. No, she would rather die beneath the stars. When her mind was clear, she offered much sensible advice, gleaned from the wisps of memory of her parents' journey from Virginia into the raw plains of Illinois, and when she was strong enough to rise from her bed for a few hours, she busied herself making bundles of treats with which to surprise her four grandchildren on the western trail. She would spend the last night in Springfield baking pies for the travelers, and when her sons arose at dawn they found her stationed firmly before the smoking oven, like a vigilant captain at the helm of a floundering schooner.

The hours the women spent together were not often disturbed by concern for the unknown dangers awaiting them. Their rites were, on the contrary, intended to banish whatever reluctance or fear might remain—with talk of the rejuvenating air, the bounty and arcadian beauty of California. They exchanged advice and information, compared lists of goods and supplies yet to be procured, and earnestly discussed the merits of the Dutch oven and the reflector oven. The former was simpler and more portable, but the bread it produced was unpleasantly heavy, and it was useless for making biscuits. Tamsen felt goggles were essential for their hours in the desert, but these were reportedly available in Independence. Betsy had rooted branches of pear and apple trees from the farm, and would take them along in a wooden tub, to be reminded in their annual flowering of the home and friends she had left behind. Margaret Reed was particularly concerned that the family jewelry (including the pearls given her on her wedding day by her first husband, Mr. Blackenstoe) be properly concealed in a hidden compartment of the Prairie Palace Wagon.

It was Virginia Reed who had given this name to the great, sumptuous vehicle her stepfather had designed, and for days after it rolled majestically into the garden, the women could talk of nothing else.

"Mrs. Polk herself couldn't ride in better style," Betsy concluded, and the others murmured their awed agreement.

"You could just park it in Yerba Buena and live in it," Frances said, envying Virginia Reed this elegant portable palace.

With the aid of his most able cabinetmakers, James Reed had created a coach that would proclaim across the prairies the family's proud aristocratic lineage, and one that would snugly cushion the sickly and delicate females in his charge. Instead of the customary entrances at front and rear, the vast wagon was entered from the side, by a flight of steps that lowered on hinges. Mounting them, one was in a roomy parlor, fitted out with spring seats that had high, comfortable backs, much like the seats on a Concord coach, and upholstered in cut velvet of a deep burgundy red. The room could be warmed by a tiny sheet-iron stove, whose pipe extended through the top of the wagon, insulated from the canvas with discs of tin. There were oil lamps mounted in ormolu brackets, a Sheraton tea table, a crystal chandelier, a turkey carpet for the floor, and a Martha Washington mirror presented to Mrs. Reed by her Springfield neighbors with a warning that she not forget to keep her fine looks during the journey. Under the spring seats were compartments with tambour fronts that rolled up with a touch of the finger, and these were cushioned and fitted to hold such articles as the ladies might require at short notice: crystal flasks for medicines, boxes of lint and bandages, books and workbaskets, tins of soda crackers and sugar-drops, a tea service and lap desk. There were also rows of fitted cabinets with burled walnut doors, each inlaid with the Reed family crest. Some contained fowling pieces, powder and shot, extra writing materials, cigars and pipe tobacco, and a store of cambric handkerchiefs, but most were filled with brandy and vintage French wines. The wines were held in leather slings suspended within cradlelike containers that Mr. Reed had specially contrived to protect the bottles from the jarring of uneven ground. The Prairie Palace Wagon had both a basement and a second story. The latter, reached by a wooden ladder with leather-padded rungs mounted at the end of the parlor, held wide feather beds for the ladies and canvas bags fatly bulging with new linens. Beneath the luxurious parlor was a space large enough for the children to crawl through, with numerous compartments for storing food and clothing, as well as the tub and washboard and soap and flatirons Eliza Williams would require to keep the family laundry in order. To pull the great rolling house required four yoke of oxen, with large Durham steers at the wheel, instead of the customary triple yoke, and there were men in the town who called it "Reed's folly" and "Jimmy's ark," and wondered when the floods would come to float it to California, but for most who saw it the Prairie Palace Wagon was further confirmation of the prosperity and glory awaiting the Springfield emigrants.

When Margaret Reed first showed the ladies the wonders of her portable parlor, Tamsen asked, "Isn't it a little narrow for a cotillion?" Her hostess was not amused, but she had long since grown accustomed to Tamsen's criticizing ways, knew that at heart she meant well, and succeeded in bending her lips into an acceptable approximation of a smile. She had, for some time, suspected that Tamsen was jealous of her for having such a young and distinguished husband. Though George Donner was clearly no leader, had never displayed the gallant manliness that made Mr. Reed a hero of the Black Hawk War, he was a good man, and he doted on his womenfolks. It was wrong of Tamsen to be jealous, especially when Margaret Reed so yearned for her rosy health and her book learning. Life had given each of them compensations and blessings, and they must be grateful for them.

Trying to shore up their tiny community, Margaret Reed gestured to the plush seats and said, "You see, there's room for all of us. While we roll along we can embroider and attend to our correspondence, and Tamsen can read to us from Lord Byron and the tales of Mr. Hawthorne."

The Donner wives tested the roomy seats, and Tamsen bounced against the burgundy velvet as though the vast coach were already in motion along a rocky mountain trail. Betsy gaped, her wide eyes rolling, her tongue thickened with stammers of admiration at this never-never land to which she was suddenly transported. Though she and Tamsen were precisely the same age, Betsy seemed a full decade older. She was a large, bony, sweet-tempered woman easily perplexed by anything foreign to the plodding rhythms of domestic toil. Indeed, even crossing a familiar room she would sometimes pause, blinking as though the way were unexpectedly barred by a rigidly bolted door. Once she had dosed a child's stomach cramps with oil of cloves instead of paregoric and, when she discovered her error, she sat by the bedside staring in puzzlement at the amber vial that had, somehow, tricked her. "Will it kill me, Ma?" Solomon Hook had asked. "W-w-w-well," she finally stammered, "I sure hope not, son." Of the three women who sat now enjoying the imperial elegance of the Prairie Palace Wagon, it was Jacob Donner's wife Elizabeth, Aunt Betsy, who was least prepared for the unaccustomed trials of the coming months. Even Margaret Reed, fashionably frail and constantly pampered, had more of the quickness of mind, the tempered will, that the journey would require, and could command rich reserves of physical strength, too, when necessary.

"Recite something for us," Margaret Reed invited, and squeezed Tamsen's hand affectionately.

"Oh, please," Betsy entreated her sister-in-law, as though the familiar voice had the power to make this strange world comprehensible.

"And we shall pretend we're sailing across the prairies," Mrs. Reed added. She tossed her head, shook her dark, heavy braids like a playful child.

"Very well," Tamsen agreed, and to the imagined rhythm of the great wheels, the swaying plod of the oxen, she chanted one of the verses her older pupils had learned by rote from Mr. Longfellow:

> Ye voices that arose
> After the Evening's close,
> And whispered to my restless heart repose!
>
> Go, breathe it in the ear
> Of all who doubt and fear,
> And say to them, "Be of good cheer!"
>
> Ye sounds, so low and calm,
> That in the groves of balm
> Seemed to me like an angel's psalm!
>
> Go, mingle yet once more
> With the perpetual roar
> Of the pine forest dark and hoar!
> Tongues of the dead, not lost,
> But speaking from death's frost,
> Like fiery tongues at Pentecost!
>
> Glimmer, as funeral lamps,
> Amid the chills and damps
> Of the vast plain where
> Death encamps!

Filtered by dense canvas, the dim light that entered the wagon glowed on marquetry and brass, crystal and lacquer, made the looking glass a deep, liquid pool, and struck reddish glints from the heavy wedding bands the three women wore. The air was perfumed with the smells of oiled leather and varnish, freshly planed wood, horsehair and hemp and kerosene. As Tamsen rhythmically chanted, her listeners felt the chill that laced the spring air, and hugged their shawls tightly around their shoulders.

6

NETTLE CLOTH WAS STRETCHED TAUT ON THE GREAT QUILTING frame, covered with dense rows of fluffy cotton wadding like drifts of virgin snow. Tamsen folded each of the stiff new bank notes twice, doubled and redoubled them, and spaced them into a bold checkerboard, islands of bare earth locked in a bright, frozen landscape. Then she covered the notes with another snowy layer of wadding and over it laid the bright patchwork. She tugged and smoothed it, patted the edges into place, adjusted right angles, and drew it into a taut plane that her stitches would marry to the layers beneath, forming plump cocoons where the bank notes were concealed. Her fingers sought their outlines, fenced their invisible boundaries, buried treasure to be excavated for her children on the shores of an ocean so different from the cold, rocky promontories of her own childhood. Bending over the rainbow squares, searching for the secrets they concealed, she felt herself grow tipsy with the riot of color and texture, the drag of tweed and the glide of satin. Yellow chintz flourished with the bright slashing of green, the severed tip of the leaf. Her shears had pruned away the rest, but its swollen silhouette, thinly framed in yellow, had found its own place in a field of earth-hued madders. The chintz had been a bargain, imported direct from Paris (or so Mr. Bradford had claimed), but the dress she made gave her the look of an upside down buttercup. It was better with the green sash borrowed from last year's muslin tucked snugly about her waist, though a trifle gaudy, perhaps, for an apprentice schoolteacher. Still, it would do for a picnic if she was careful of grass stains, and if Edward didn't give her another lapful of his mother's bread-and-butter pickles. Why should he bother, everyone wondered, when everyone knew he would rather be courting one of the lads from the upper form, and him with his scent of violets and worried eyes and heroic Latin verses. But at least it was perfectly safe, perfectly respectable company, and there would be no blackberry-picking charades that ended in sudden hot arms and watchchain-snagged buttons.

She wondered, bent over the sloped quilting frame, that she still remembered Edward's name, the piney tang of Carolina woods, the very buttons she had used for the chintz dress. There were six in all, ivory roses bought by her own mother from a sailor peddling exotic souvenirs from door to door, and strung together now at the bottom of her work basket, bunched like grapes on a single thread, waiting.

As her fingers firmly buried one treasure, others came to light, until the quilt blazed with memory like some magical garment in a fairytale. Stroking a square of soft cambric, she remembered Eliza's urgent, painful birth. She was the fifth child and the others, especially the boy, had been larger, but only this impatient daughter had threatened to split her open like an overripe melon. The stubborn determination recalled stories of sister Elizabeth, so bent on being in the parlor with the grownups that she hammered her head against the cast-iron bedstead until she was unconscious, and was, of course, promptly carried to the parlor. When their mother died, Elizabeth was only sixteen, but with a docile beau who sported a mustache that reminded Tamsen of an ailing caterpillar, Elizabeth became lady of the manor, vigorously bossing the housemaid morning and night, until the girl threw a pail of clabbered milk on her and departed. And as Tamsen's own fifth child thrust and shouldered its way into the saving air, she thought, "If it is a girl, I will name her for Elizabeth. Eliza Poor."

Somber gray twill recalled the Sugar Creek schoolhouse and a scrap of paper passing between the aisles, passing again, then fluttering to the oiled floor under her mock-stern gaze like a wounded messenger bird. Tongues tumbled the continents, the seas, the presidents all in a row (with two named Adams), the Declaration of Independence, European capitols, fractions and ounces, pecks and rods and miles. Bedsheets transformed even the most untamed of her pupils into Christmas angels, the ceiling sparkled with golden stars, and parents squeezed knees-up behind the desks to gape at the procession of candles, verses, carols and mistletoe.

It was summer when Mr. Donner appeared there, waiting without a word of excuse or explanation or even a mumbled "by-your-leave." Silver filigreed his coal-black hair and beard and he was handsome and tall and rich, but it shocked her to think that this suitor was nearly as old as her own father had been when he died. She quickly learned that George Donner wore his age as lightly as he wore his substantial fortune. The latter, like the former, was the natural and inevitable result of a life of industry. He had worked the earth with his own hands, often clearing land that no other white man had ever seen, then selling it not so much for the hundred-fold profit accrued by his husbandry as for the chance to tame yet another corner of wilderness. For later settlers, those less daring and resolute, he unveiled the promise of sprawling orchards and meadows, the tilled fields and spacious barnyards that lay sleeping beneath tangles of hackberry and scrub oak. Most of his profits were returned to the earth, assuring richer and richer harvests for himself, his children, his grandchildren. Such multiplication was the way of nature, he reasoned, and not a thing for a man to get all high-hatted about.

Her eyes smarting, Tamsen rose to trim the wick of the lamp, savoring the luxuriant, unaccustomed stillness of the house. More than a week remained before their departure, but each night she found some further, urgent task that would not wait until dawn, and while her family slept she claimed possession of emptying rooms whose aspect changed with each hurried day. Her vigil honored the steady dismantling of an accustomed world whose tangible forms surrendered so easily to shadows. Only a smudged and skeletal silhouette remained as proof that a clock had once stood on the kitchen mantlepiece. A trailing strand of cobweb was sole testimony to the harmonium that had once loomed so massively that the parlor might have been built around it. By day she could scarcely pause to read the fragile text their lives had inscribed here, and she was determined to omit no single phrase. She had purposely saved the California quilt until the last, knowing the familiar routine would soothe her, the compact symmetries give shape to the hectic disorder of their leave-taking.

Tamsen drew the lamp nearer to the quilting frame, stretched to relieve the dull ache in the small of her back, and began to stitch a square of blue-and-white gingham into place. For weeks the girls had tittered and whispered behind doors suddenly closed, fiercely guarding their secret yet scarcely able to contain it until her birthday. Their quick fingers hurried her own, plucking away the paper that wrapped the gingham apron with their names embroidered in plump apples of red felt appliquéd across the skirt: Elitha, Leanna, Frances, Georgia, Eliza. There were other children, other names that would never ornament a birthday apron of sky-blue gingham, and Tamsen braced herself against this unexpected threat to her quiet reverie, sidestepped memory as cautiously as she might have avoided a damp, shaley turning on a steep hillside path. She reminded herself to buy caustic soda the following morning, to find a heavier flask for vinegar, to look for white gloves for Elitha. Mr. Donner's Sunday braces needed mending, there were letters to be mailed, and they must find homes for the last of the puppies. She also had to make a final call on Reverend Proxmire's mother and take her a jar of her favorite quince jelly, though it would scarcely cheer an old woman so angry with her own body for wearing out too soon.

As she consciously recited to herself the chores that still demanded her attention, Tamsen's fingers brushed a square of taffeta, as silken and fine as the glow of down on Tully's eager, boyish arms. Startled by the sudden, rude intrusion of her first husband, she flung back her head so violently she bit her tongue, wincing at the pain, the sudden salt taste in her mouth. Then, sternly reminding herself that there was no time for namby-pamby foolishness, she bent again to her work. Cretonne and piqué, velvet and shalloon, madder the color of holly, and again the yellow chintz, this time divided by a green stem reaching upward for a vanished rose.

7

THOUGH THEY ONLY PLANNED TO MAKE THE FEW MILES INTO Springfield an April 15th, then camp there for an afternoon and evening of farewells, George Donner insisted they rise at sunup and be off by noon, but the sun had already slipped past the meridian when Jacob's three wagons came rattling into the farmyard, timbers creaking and cooking pots hammering together like a blacksmith's forge, oxen bellowing, hounds baying, children shouting over a din so loud Tamsen heard it even before the wagons crossed Sugar Creek. They were followed by a farewell parade of buggies and farm wagons, men and women on horseback and on foot, stray dogs and barefooted children and a bucking, walleyed mule. With Betsy beside him tightly clutching the baby and plunging her legs for balance, Jacob drove the lead wagon, sitting high and majestic and with his grizzled beard parted into twin pennants by the wind. Joseph Reinhardt and Augustus Spitzer drove the others, shouting instructions in a guttural German that the oxen seemed, somehow, to translate into "Gee!" and "Haw!" and "Whoa!" Noah James was herding the extra oxen, beef cattle and fat milch cows. Driving for George were the Springfield boys Sam Shoemaker and Hiram Miller, with the little Sheffield gunsmith John Denton riding herd and clearly having problems holding his seat when his horse shied to avoid a lumbering ox. There was too much loose stock to be guided, goaded, prodded along behind the wagons, and George's son William had agreed to accompany the clan as far as Independence, where other hands could be engaged, young men hungry for California but without families or wagons of their own.

George Donner had already sent his two supply wagons into town—one loaded with the necessaries of camp life, the other densely packed with merchandise and articles that would first be wanted in California. He lifted Georgia and Eliza over the tailgate and they tumbled, giggling, from his grip into the cavernous shadows of the family wagon. Frances, Elitha and Leanna rode with their father on the buckboard, arms twined around each other, heads leaned together like a cluster of morning glories, both proud and shy of the enthusiastic audience below them. Tamsen climbed the spokes of one of the rear wheels, like the steps of a drunken ladder, and entered the back of the wagon. From here she could almost touch the heads of the two horses tethered to feed boxes hung from the tailgate, and from here she could have a final glimpse of the orchard before the vast wheels slurred around a muddy, rutted curve and began the last sloping mile into Springfield. She knelt with her arms on the tailgate, crouching like a child intensely peering into a forbidden window, but not out of any sentimental yearning to breathe farewell to the land that had lulled her with plenty, where her three daughters had been born as testament and proof of her own return to the living. All that she had studiously put away, locked securely, drowned the key. She watched more as she might have watched the turning of the final page of the final chapter of the third and final volume of a novel that had amused her through a long, snow-bound winter—sad that it was finished, pleased with injustice righted, evil punished, identities restored, the tangled skeins untangled and wound neatly, compactly, into a ball.

Her reverie was exploded by Eliza's cries, sharp alarms of panic and fear that froze Tamsen's heart, and she held the child pressed tightly against her, rocked her to the rocking of the wagon, but still the terrified screams continued. "Does it hurt you, dear? Show Mama where it hurts." The child shook her head, screamed more furiously, and even the saddle horses shied from their oats, dragged against the restraining bridles. "Shush, child, shush," Tamsen whispered, as Eliza's body bucked violently against hers, the legs furiously slashing the air. "Shush." And when exhaustion finally began to dim the volume of her cries, the breath notched in sobs that told the mother it was ending, Tamsen looked up and realized she had missed the final turning. They had vanished—house, orchards, barns, fields —all vanished, and she wondered if anyone would secure the loose plank on the kitchen steps or soap the window sash that had jammed again with spring damp. Anger mounted stiff and bitter in her throat, and she wished they had fired it all, bent it to the embrace of flame, set torches to barns, fields, orchards, the gaping empty house stripped of laughter and the smells of bread, where balls of lint chased each other like mice through the vacant rooms. She was ashamed of the unfamiliar, unwelcome anger, and then so angered by her own needless shame that she reflexively clutched the sobbing child more tightly, and the sudden force of her grip startled Eliza into silence.

In Springfield the nine wagons were drawn up into a corral on the edge of the common, not far from the statehouse. Arms reached up to swing the children down, and Tamsen was watching Eliza and Georgia being passed overhead, laughing at the acrobatic game, when she felt herself lifted, whirled, turned head over heels. Before she could cry out, her feet were planted firmly in the wet, ankle-high grass of the common.

"Pardon me, ma'am," John Denton gasped, "I thought you were one of the children. I'm awfully sorry."

"The baggage seems to be in order," Tamsen remarked, tugging down her shirtwaist and brushing her rumpled skirt. She liked this young man with his hooked nose and shy good manners, the worried look about his eyes. It was said he wrote poetry, and she thought him all in all an unlikely bull-whacker. "But you're a mite stronger than I would have guessed," she added.

John Denton crimsoned, rocked back on his heels in the soggy grass, but was clearly pleased with the compliment. "They say the West can make a fellow strong as an ox," he ventured.

"Don't tell Mr. Reed that, or he'll hitch you up to his palace wagon. Besides, California doesn't just need strong backs, Mr. Denton. It needs a few poets to tell the muscles what to do—or what they've done."

"And maybe a few schoolteachers," he added. She realized she had used the kind of tone with which she had once kept her older pupils under control. Even if she happened to be old enough to have borne him, she already thought of him not as a child or a pupil and certainly not as a hired hand, but as a comrade, a co-conspirator.

"Someday you must tell me all about Sheffield, Mr. Denton."

"With pleasure, ma'am." He rocked again on his heels, timid and pleased.

"But now I must try to find the children. And if you persist in rocking back and forth in this marsh, you'll soon be up to your knees in it. We'll have to bronze you and put a memorial plaque around your neck."

John Denton looked down at his muddy boots, pulled first one and then the other slowly out of the muck. The noise made Tamsen think of a thirsty cow at a water trough.

"At least they rhyme," she told him.

"Indeed they do," he agreed, and his quick laughter reminded her that she really must locate the children.

As she left she lightly touched his sleeve and said, "Thank you for the whirligig ride, Mr. Denton."

Tamsen found the older girls sitting in the palace wagon with Virginia Reed, receiving visits from their envious schoolmates and friends. She marveled at their grown-up airs, the ladylike distinction they borrowed from the splendor of the coming journey. Virginia firmly excluded the younger children, whose prying fingers might have disturbed the wagon's neatly ordered interior, and she laid a strip of burlap before the door so that muddy shoes would not soil the new carpet. Her back poker-straight, hands folded neatly in her lap, and bestowing the occasional bounty of a patient, tolerant smile, she seemed the image of her mother, and Frances was clearly following the genteel example.

"Excuse me, ladies," Tamsen interrupted, "but has anyone seen Georgia and Eliza?"

"They *said* they were going to make pancakes," Frances answered, an empress responding to an inquiry about the diet of aborigines in one of her far-flung colonies.

"Oh, mercy, not that!" Tamsen hurried down the steps and followed the sprawling oval of the wagons, peering under them, calling the girls, pausing to accept yet again the voluble good wishes of the townspeople. Inside the makeshift corral the oxen, cattle and horses shifted nervously, pawed the ground, unaccustomed to such close confinement under the open sky, made restless by the continuous clamor of voices. Tamsen found the girls under one of Jacob

Donner's wagons, with Patty Reed and Betsy's daughter Mary. Each of the girls was carefully patting a ball of mud, squeezing and flattening it into a pancake to add to the damp pile that rose between them.

"Children!" Tamsen shouted, but at first they did not hear her, each busy tamping a sticky mass into shape. "Children!" she repeated.

Georgia looked up, smiled, and said, "Hello, Mama."

"Children, come out from there this minute."

"Not finish," Eliza complained.

"This minute," Tamsen warned.

When the four had crawled out, Tamsen sent Patty and Mary to their mothers, then stood looking at her own mud-streaked daughters.

"I thought we were leaving the piglets with William," she scolded, but when she saw Eliza's plump bottom lip begin to tremble, she drew her skirts up and crouched down beside the child. "Now, Eliza," she began, "and Georgia. You must try to keep your dresses clean. We don't know when we'll stop to do the washing, and we don't want you to get to California looking like two pecks of dirt, do we?"

Eliza looked at her hands and began to wipe them on her dress.

"Eliza, don't!" Tamsen pleaded. "Come, we'll find some water and clean you up, and then you can help me with supper. All right?"

Both girls nodded eagerly.

"Good! But no pancakes, if you please."

Eliza and Georgia cooed together in the brief, arrested melodies of their secret language, while Tamsen led them to the pump on the common and repaired, as best she could, the damage to their traveling dresses.

While the men adjusted harness and running gears and fed the stock, they continued the old debate about the best point for crossing the Mississippi—at Nauvoo, which lay west by northwest, or St. Louis to the south. Nauvoo was closer, the river narrower there, but to reach it they would have to cross the Illinois, and it could be treacherously high with the spring rains. If they traveled down the eastern bank they could cross two rivers in one at St. Louis and be done with it, but there the Mississippi was more like a great muddy sea than the rivers they knew, and some felt it wrong to head south in order to begin the journey to California. They wanted to feel the sun warming their backs as they departed, to see it set over the bobbing yokes of the oxen. In the end, only Jacob Donner held out for St. Louis, but he did so less out of any geographical conviction than the knowledge that Betsy would quake and tremble until Nauvoo was well behind them. The Mormons had been driven out, seventeen of their dead saints thrown into a well, but there were said to be some of the devils still skulking in the woods near the river, and they kidnapped Gentile babies, sacrificed them like the old Hebrews used to sacrifice lambs. Jacob could not put Betsy's womanish fears against the arguments of the other men, and even though Milt Elliot supported him, he finally conceded defeat. They would leave for Nauvoo at dawn.

THEY COULD HAVE HAD THEIR PICK OF SUPPERS WITH A DOZEN Springfield families, but the Donners and Reeds cooked their own farewell meal over a large campfire and ate picnic style. Only old Mrs. Keyes was absent, spending the final night with her sons. All were wearied by the excitement of the day, ready for bed and yet impatient to be off, to bring their long beginning to an end. They had exchanged trinkets with friends left behind, made earnest promises to send letters back at every opportunity, sighed and embraced and exclaimed, but now seemed unable to leave the glowing fire to seek their beds. Milt Elliott took out his mouth organ and began to play "Rock of Ages," but the mournful air brought a groan of protest from the group, and he rapidly slid into the merrier strains of "Charlie Is My Darling." Mr. Francis moved around the circle, making a final list of the travelers' names and ages to publish in the *Sangamo Journal,* and cronies of James Reed arrived with a bottle of fine Scotch whiskey. He promised to open it on the 4th of July and look east to drink a toast to friends in Illinois, while they drank his success from an identical bottle, their faces turned to the west. They would raise their glasses precisely at noon, and systems for determining the difference in time were solemnly analyzed. Margaret Reed leaned exhaustedly against her husband's protective shoulder, from time to time drawing a filigreed vinaigrette from the ample pocket of her dress and deeply inhaling its restorative vapors.

Tamsen held Eliza on her lap. The child was excited, fretful, her eyes heavy with the sleep she stubbornly resisted. Bending over her, the mother softly hummed a lullaby, repeated it again and again until she felt the child's breathing grow deeper and more regular. Then, rising in slow, careful stages so that Eliza would not awake, she carried her to the tent George had pitched beside the wagon, bedded her down and tucked the blankets and quilts snugly about the sleeping child, to prevent her kicking free of them in the night. As Tamsen dropped the flap of the tent, a figure suddenly loomed before her, materialized out of the gloom—dark, threatening, clutching her in the dense shadow it threw from the campfire.

"*Excusez-moi.* I trust I do not startle you."

"Mrs. Lincoln," Tamsen acknowledged, thinking how typical it was of the strange, moody woman to appear like this, unannounced, and turn her hair gray with fright.

"I had hoped my husband could join me, but he has not returned. He was obliged to attend to urgent business for the circuit court in Tremont."

"Of course," Tamsen replied. It seemed to her clever of the man to arrange such frequent extended absences. Tamsen did not like Mary Todd Lincoln, had known her even before her hasty marriage to Mr. Lincoln, and had not liked her then. It was said by all her neighbors that she was a devoted wife and mother, but Tamsen found her frightening, and wondered if she were not actually somewhat mad, as her brothers and sisters were rumored to be. Perhaps that was the reason the Lincolns never entertained, though they were seen often enough in local society and were, of course, great favorites of James and Margaret Reed, since the men had served together in the Black Hawk War. Strange things were whispered, however, of their domestic life. There was something about the drawn-out vowels, the exaggerated Kentucky accent, the peppering of French phrases, the self-consciously genteel manners of Mrs. Lincoln that made Tamsen impatient, as did the way the stout woman always sought to conceal her large, clumsy hands in the folds of her dress.

45

"My husband and I want to wish you and your family a good journey." Tamsen imagined herself transcribing the words on a slate: "Mah huzbund ayund ah wawant to wiyush you an yoah fammuly a goowud juhney."

"How very kind."

"We shall pray for you."

"We can use your prayers to good advantage, I'm sure."

The woman was muffled in a long black cloak, and only her hectic eyes were visible, like those of a famished bird alert for unwitting prey.

"Won't you . . . won't you join us?" Tamsen asked, gesturing to the group still gathered at the fire, softly singing now to Milt's accompaniment. They seemed, suddenly, a desperate distance away.

"*Mais non,*" Mary Lincoln protested, and drew further into the black drapery. The fabric rustled like the flapping of wings. "I should not wish to disturb. But please convey our best wishes to your husband and to the Jacob Donners and the Reeds."

"Certainly."

"I do envy you," the woman said, but in a dry, broken whisper.

"Why, anyone can go to California, Mrs. Lincoln. It seems to be quite the fashion these days. We expect to find hundreds of emigrants gathered in Independence."

"That is not what I mean. I envy you your courage, your *espirit.*"

"It was not my decision," she replied, and immediately regretted that the remark might suggest domestic conflict, or that Mr. Donner had somehow compelled her to follow him into the wilderness.

"*Bien sûr.* But you might have refused."

Tamsen hesitated. "Yes, I could have refused," she admitted, and for the first time knew that this was true. Yes, she could have taken the children to William's farm, perhaps gone back to her schoolroom, let the older girls accompany their father, joined them later if all had gone well, waited to receive them if it had not. Indeed, she had options the simple Betsy and the frail Margaret Reed both lacked.

"It must be so wild, barbaric," Mary Lincoln pressed on. "Even

Springfield seems wild to me when I think of Lexington and Ellerslie. *Sauvage!*"

"Then we shall have to tame it," Tamsen said. "Kentucky, too, was a wilderness when Mr. Donner first saw it."

"And the flower beds were all lined with whitewashed bricks," the other woman added, as though the irrelevancy held some coded wisdom only the two of them could comprehend.

"I really must tend to the girls, or they won't have a wink of sleep the whole night. They're so terribly excited." She started to move away, but Mary Lincoln reached out, held her with a powerful grip.

She drew near, seeming to fold Tamsen into the shadowy cloak, and her peppermint breath drawled again, "I do envy you, Mrs. Donner. *Comme je vous envie.* I envy you the courage to accompany your husband wherever destiny leads him. It is not easy for those of us who have known another life."

"I could have refused," Tamsen answered, and realized that the curious visitor had taught her at least this much, and that it was a lesson worth remembering. Though at first she had opposed the scheme, in the end she had accepted it, made it her own. "It was my choice as well," she amended.

"*Exactement!* And only by choosing could you show true courage. I do not envy those who blindly follow their husbands because they have stood up together uttering vows. That is the loyalty of horses and dogs and pickaninnies."

"But I have had certain privileges," Tamsen began.

"*Moi aussi,*" the other woman interrupted. "We must never forget them. Never!" She turned away then, without a syllable of farewell.

II

SPRINGFIELD

·TO· INDEPENDENCE

1

GOVERNOR THOMAS FORD ADDRESSED THE DEPARTING EMIGRANTS
from the broad granite steps of the capitol building, reminding them
solemnly of the blood and bravery of the pioneers whose vision had
led them into the Illinois Territory in the twilight years of the last
century, when its mighty forests knew only the tread of wild animals
and savage Indians. They had carried with them the tender spark of
a young democracy, fanned it with their courage and labor, and now
the families of James Reed, Jacob Donner and George Donner
would bear the torch of civilization across the great prairies and the
forbidding mountains, to the bay of Francisco on the ocean named
peace. It was a great day for Springfield, a great and historic day in
the annals of the sovereign state of Illinois. Reverend Proxmire
delivered prayers for the divine guidance and protection of the
emigrants, for their safe arrival in the bountiful promised land of
California, and then his rich baritone reached out to embrace and
lead them as they recited together: "The Lord is my shepherd, I shall
not want. . . ."

James Reed pulled out first, the Prairie Palace Wagon lurching
into motion as he cracked the long bullwhip and shouted, "Giddap!
Roll out!" The canvas cover was drawn up on the sides like a theater
curtain, revealing the set of an elegantly appointed drawing room
that might have served for a Restoration comedy, complete with the
eccentric mother-in-law, the invalid wife, the lissome daughter, each
well schooled in the role she was to play. Though the spring seats
occasionally bounced them dizzily into the air, they maintained their

theatrical composure, waving demure farewells first left, then right, and nodding acknowledgment to familiar faces. When Reed's supply wagons had passed, George Donner urged his own teams into motion, and Jacob followed. Tamsen sat beside her husband, clutching his arm, feeling the muscles stretch, grow taut, flex as they guided the team into a curve, slacken as the animals found their own rolling pace, held it. Now that they were at last in motion, the town thinning and then rapidly disappearing, Tamsen felt a vast relief. Whatever labors remained unfinished, they were behind her now, together with the last lingering hesitations and misgivings, and the boundaries of her world had contracted to the three wagons moving slowly past John Mather's farm. The dancing green of Mather's ample pasture was as remote, suddenly, as the noisy wharves of Newburyport or the tight wooden cube of the Sugar Creek schoolhouse with its heavy, unvarying perfume of chalk, ink, paste, paper. Like a city on wheels, a planet, a universe, the wagons carried all the stuff of her life: husband, children, food, clothing, books, medicines, mementoes, treasures. A rich man's portion was stitched into the California quilt, gold was secured in a cleat in the bed of the family wagon, and she and George each wore buckskin girdles strapped around their waists, heavy with gold eagles and half eagles to meet unexpected expenses along the way. This sudden shrinking, the abrupt concentration of her world, made Tamsen Donner aware as never before of its amazing abundance. It was sumptuous, princely, and she was its undisputed mistress. Leaning against her husband, she marveled at his boldness and vision, at the energy which had set this extraordinary expedition in motion, concentrating their fate and fortune into this single, intense moment. Again he had shown her the resoluteness with which he had sung Arabian Leopard to victory, with which he had appeared so abruptly at her schoolhouse and summoned her back to life.

George turned to her with eyes that glittered like those of a mischievous boy. "We're on our way to California, child."

"So it would seem, Mr. Donner." She fumbled for her pocket compass, aligned the dial and studied it with self-conscious seriousness. "Yes," she then concluded, "I do believe you're right!"

The nine wagons moved due west along the Berlin road, then

angled slightly northwest, circling a low range of wooded hills. After pausing for a lunch of ham, biscuits and coffee, Tamsen and Betsy walked for a time beside the wagons with the older children, gathering bouquets of wildflowers.

"It sure helps a body to stretch her legs a little," Betsy observed, wobbling still from the effort to keep her balance on the joggling wagon, and Tamsen agreed. Even Margaret Reed joined them briefly, until Mrs. Keyes woke from her nap and complained of being abandoned by her ungrateful, unloving daughter.

Later, sitting with the girls in the back of the wagon, Tamsen showed them how to weave the wildflowers into garlands, carefully knotting pliant stem to blossom, then plaiting the single strands together to form a dense blue-and-yellow rope, which they strung between the curved stays of the wagon. From time to time the dogs set up a barking, baying chorus, and hied off across meadows, crashed through underbrush, on the trail of rabbits. The Reeds had six dogs with them, and Jacob Donner's family had five. George Donner had brought along a pair of his best hunters, and Elitha had at last coaxed him into allowing Coalie to come as watchdog, despite the fact that the slightest threat sent him slinking for cover, tail between his legs, and he was known to bark only at the promise of food. There were, then, nearly as many dogs as children.

James Reed had handed the reins of the palace wagon to Milt Elliott, with a warning to take the curves wide, and rode ahead on Glaucus; he was accompanied by his stepdaughter Virginia, whose pony had grown skittish after being tethered all morning to the back of the wagon. The two brought back enthusiastic reports of an ideal campsite for the night, in the lee of a hill, where a creek bubbled with clear, sweet water. They made more than fifteen miles the first day, in a mood of festive high spirits that resembled a Sunday-school outing more than the beginnings of a bold continental migration.

When they had pitched their camp, watered the animals and set them to graze, the hired hands gathered fuel and the three wives set up improvised kitchens. Tamsen had to cook for ten, Betsy for twelve, and Margaret Reed stirred up a batch of batter bread, even though she had Eliza Williams along to prepare the meals. The men were full of admiration for the women's efforts, pronouncing the feast one of the finest and tastiest they had ever imagined, praising their ingenious womenfolk and then praising the sturdiness of the wagons, the wonderful strength of the oxen, the ampleness of their provisions, the surprising mildness of the spring weather. They filled pipes and sucked at them thoughtfully, contentedly, gathered now before a central fire, while the women carried dishes to the brook to rinse them in the swift, icy water.

"If we keep to this pace, I reckon we'll make Independence in maybe two weeks," Jacob Donner mused.

George Donner blew out a thin, aromatic trail of smoke and said, "Three, I'd guess, but that's soon enough. We're in good time."

"Don't forget there's a couple of mean rivers to get over," Milt Elliott reminded them. He was a lanky, muscular young man, conscientious and precise in his appraisals, who had quickly risen to the position of foreman in Reed's cabinet works.

"Rivers!" George responded, and fanned the smoke away impatiently, as though disposing of all such ridiculous obstacles. He and Jake knew a thing or two about rivers. Thought they knew it all until the Red River in Texas territory, bubbling with orange mud, taught them a hard set of lessons after the heavy snows had melted.

Indeed, it is true that the brothers know much of rivers and much about the signs the earth makes to announce an early winter, and they can smell rain coming when the sky is blue as a robin's egg. They can also judge the age of a horse by stroking its flanks, and check the teeth only as an afterthought, and because it belongs to the ritual. An instinct tutored for more than sixty years tells them where to sink a well, announces that the heavy frosts have finished, that the time has come for tilling and seeding, and this same instinct has given them a kind of easy carelessness, treating the earth as a familiar tool worn glossy and smooth to their grip. The rolling plains have taught them their geographical alphabet, and taught them well, but they know little of deserts or mountains, whose signs are written in a language they have neither read or imagined.

"So long as we're there by mid-May," James Reed added. "The caravan won't pull out before then, because the prairie grass isn't high enough for the stock. It takes it that long to get through last season's dead cover." He spoke with the amiable authority with which he would have described the preferred technique for decanting silted wine—as casually confident, indeed, as George and Jacob Donner, though he was a city man who had never followed the blade of a plow. He stretched his legs, admired the sheen of firelight on the oxblood leather of his new riding boots. They had been specially made for him in Philadelphia, and had arrived by express coach only the day before, together with a matching saddle and bridle for Glaucus.

"There'll be some hard traveling ahead," James Reed conceded, "but we can take our time now, let the women and children get used to things."

The other men consulted their glowing pipes and seemed to agree with him. The last light faded, concentrating the homey, protective glow of the fire, and from the creek came the clatter of tin plates, the high, melodious voices of children at play. Warmed, content, with full bellies and minds lulled by their auspicious beginning, the men failed to hear the approaching horsemen until they had turned from the road and gained the outskirts of the campsite.

It was the two Germans, Reinhardt and Spitzer, who heard them first, scrambling to their feet and shouting, *"Indianer! Indianer!"*

The women hurried from the creek, rapidly drying their hands on their aprons and shooing the children before them like a flock of unruly chickens.

The brief panic was ended by Baylis Williams, Eliza's brother, who announced, "It's Mr. Francis!" The simple, thick-tongued boy was an albino, and spent most of the day trying unsuccessfully to protect his pale, pinkish eyes from the sunlight, but by night he had the unerring vision of an owl.

The editor of the *Journal* reined his horse and sprang down into the circle of light, clearly pleased with the brilliant drama of his arrival. With him were the sons of Mrs. Keyes and several members of the reading society, who had spontaneously decided it would be a wonderful lark to ride out and spend the first night on the trail with the emigrants. They embraced, pumped hands, slapped backs, exclaimed and marveled at the surprise as if they had been exiled from

civilization for months, though beneath their excitement the travelers all felt a vague undertow of regret, to think they were still so near
home that relations and friends could ride out with the ease of
paying a Sunday afternoon call.

James Reed disappeared into the palace wagon and returned
carrying a bottle of brandy and two fitted wooden cases, velvet lined,
holding monogrammed snifters. "Gentlemen," he declared, "this
calls for a bit of the grape. It's not often that our humble fireside
is graced by such eminent visitors from the East."

"How's the weather back home?" George Donner asked.

"Not half so fair as here," Mr. Francis answered. "Makes a man
feel ten years younger!"

"Any news from Texas?"

"General Taylor seems to have the devils under control, but
there's still talk of war."

"Can't imagine who'd want to fight over that godforsaken,
no-account piece of dirt."

"It's the principle, sir, the principle, and many of our citizens
have interests there. We have claims that run clear the way back to
La Salle, and the pride of our great nation forbids that they be
abused by ignorant savages with no respect for the decencies of
civilized behavior."

"Gentlemen," James Reed interrupted, "we have far more
important matters at hand." He raised his glass. "To California," he
said, "and to the great and sovereign state of Illinois!"

Even Baylis Williams received a ceremonial thimbleful of the
amber liquid, enough to send him retching into the shadows beyond
the campfire, followed by his clumsy, flat-footed sister, moaning with
helpless motherly compassion.

2

Beardstown, Illinois
Sunday, April 19th, 1846

I have resolved to keep this journal that my daughters may have a record of their journey to California, together with such particulars as memory may obscure, but which may eventually prove of interest to them and to their own children. Inasmuch as I have resolved to make botanical notations and to prepare despatches for the newspaper in Springfield, I am attempting no daily record. The jolting of our vehicles makes it impossible to write while on the road, and when we have camped there is little time remaining after the chores, cooking, etc. But I will attempt to utilize Sundays or any other days when we may happen to lay by or to make camp early to record such details of our progress as seem pertinent.

We are camped today on the western banks of the Illinois River, near the little hamlet of Beardstown. Though awash with the swollen river, the bridge was intact and nobly bore the weight of our wagons and teams. Our party set out from the capitol building of Springfield, Illinois, on the morning of April 16th (a Thursday), following official speech-making and prayers for our safe journey. We are comprised of the following individuals, with their ages:

James Frazier Reed (46)
Margaret Reed (32), his wife
Sarah Keyes (70), her mother
Virginia Reed (13), daughter of Mrs. Reed's
    first husband, Mr. Blackenstoe, but having
    adopted her stepfather's name.

The children of Mr. and Mrs. Reed, being Patty (8),
    Jimmy (5) and Tommy (3).
The Reeds are accompanied by Milford Elliott (28),
    a teamster but former carpenter, Walter Herron (25),
    likewise a teamster, Baylis Williams (24?
    isn't sure), who herds the loose stock,
    and his sister Eliza Williams (25? also isn't
    sure) to cook and do laundry and help care for
    the smaller children.
Jacob Donner (65)
Elizabeth Donner (45), his wife
Solomon Hook (14) and William Hook (12), sons from
    her first marriage.
The children of Mr. and Mrs. Jacob Donner, being
    George (9), Mary (7), Isaac (5), Samuel (4) and
    Lewis (3).
These are accompanied by two teamsters, Augustus
    Spitzer (30) and Joseph Reinhardt (30), of
    Germany, with Noah James (20) herding.
George Donner (62)
Tamsen Eustis Donner (45), myself
Elitha Donner (14) and Leanna Donner (12), daughters
    of Mr. Donner's second wife Mary Blue Donner.
The children of Mr. and Mrs. George Donner,
    being Frances (5), Georgia (4), and Eliza
    Poor (3).
These are accompanied by Samuel Shoemaker (25),
    teamster, and Hiram Miller (24), teamster,
    with John Denton (28) from Sheffield, England,
    herding.

We thus comprise 17 adults and 16 children (not counting
Mr. Donner's son William, who accompanies us only as far as
Missouri), but expect to engage additional hands when we reach
Independence and commence the more onerous stage of our trav-
els. Each family is equipped with three wagons, two of them being
hitched together in the manner of railway coaches, as well as

numerous livestock and dogs. We thus make considerable racket when we pass through the peaceful countryside. The mild spring weather has favored us, and the girls and I walk for a part of each day alongside the wagons, in search of botanical curiosities. Today, growing near the river in marshy ground, we found a variety of groundnut previously unknown to me, but delicious in taste, together with a species of wild narcissus that exudes a particularly intense perfume. Of the latter we gathered a considerable quantity to sweeten the bedding, but the groundnuts found no favor.

Since leaving Springfield we have made nearly twenty miles a day, which the men agree is most satisfactory, and expect to reach Nauvoo by mid-week, where we cross the Mississippi and catch, perhaps, our first glimpse of the Latter Day Saints. Most of the Mormons have moved on into Missouri and beyond following the recent disturbances, but a few are reported to remain. Some are said to have as many as twenty wives, and I should not like to be the unfortunate one assigned to do the cooking! All in our party are mercifully well, free from aches and bruises, though our milch cows show signs of the sniffles. Even Mrs. Keyes, who was rapidly failing before we left home, evidences blood in her cheeks once more. The air is very reviving.

Only our kitchen accommodations present difficulties, but these will be overwon with practice. The pot or skillet required always rests beneath a heap of things not required, and ash is liable to blow into the biscuits. Also, there is never anywhere to drain the dishes when they are washed, though luckily we have brought tin and not queensware like the Reeds, for much of it was broken on the first day, being carelessly packed by the servant girl Eliza Williams. If these, however, remain our principle complications, we shall be the most fortunate of fortunate pilgrims. The girls all find sleeping in a tent a grand adventure. We have two of these, one for the children and one for their parents, though Eliza Poor is certain to crawl in with us during the night.

I ought to add here at the beginning that the principal reason of our joining the Great Overland Caravan is the fevers which are indigenous to the Illinois geography. They have spared us, but they come without warning and then sometimes take away entire families in a matter of days. Many others, fearing this, would have joined us on our expedition but that the outfitting is so dear. My brother William Eustis is for like reason contemplating removal with his children to the territory of Wisconsin. Agues and fevers are said to be entirely unknown in California, and the land especially fertile, requiring only a minimum of labor to yield the richest crops. During the recent winter we read and discussed all available reports on the country, and even if some are only gilding the lily, it must still be quite a noteworthy species of the genus *Lilium,* and worthy of closer scrutiny. In a few months we shall find out for ourselves.

It is late now, and the river sings me bedwards.

3

FROM THE ILLINOIS THEY ADVANCED ALONG A LITTLE STREAM called the La Maine—hardly a river even in its spring abundance, but clear and swift-moving, ideal for watering the stock and supplying their nightly campsites. North of Colmar the waters forked, then forked again, splayed across the land like an outstretched hand, now scarcely more than a network of brooks that trickled together to form the meandering river they left behind. Two of these bent sharply westward before vanishing into the earth a few miles east of Nauvoo. The Reed and Donner families camped at the source on the evening of April 23rd, and the husbands rode forward on horseback to make arrangements for ferrying the wagons and stock across the Mississippi the following morning.

The ferry was a flat-bottomed rectangle, nearly as broad as it was long, and blackened with a glistening coat of tar. To port and starboard were windlasses turned by mules that slowly drew up the ropes guiding the clumsy vessel across the river. When it reversed its course, port and starboard effortlessly switched positions. The ferry's barefooted captain, who issued monosyllabic orders to the crew, was an ancient Peoria Indian wearing a battered stovepipe hat and frock coat and named Burning Oak. The crew consisted entirely of his wife, who responded quickly to his growling commands, but punctuated each renewed effort by shooting a stream of tobacco juice into the water. The children all felt the bronze pair announced the edge of civilization, and were crestfallen to learn they would camp for the night within walking distance of the settlement of Montrose.

Only a single wagon at a time could be accommodated aboard the ferry, with wheels chocked and running gears removed and stowed beneath, so that it took nearly the entire day to propel teams and wagons and loose stock to the western bank, reassemble the wagons and draw them to high ground. It was slow, tedious work, and even the drama of seeing the ferry hang in midstream, braked and suspended by the force of the current, ropes arcing and complaining at the strain, soon lost its fascination. The elaborate procedure had cost them an entire day, but when they reached the opposite shore they had left behind them not only the state of Illinois; they had left behind the United States themselves. They were in Iowa territory now, landscape that James Reed knew vaguely from skirmishes with the Black Hawks, but to the rest an unknown wilderness, the real beginning of the West. On Friday the 24th they forded the Des Moines and knew they had returned, for two or three weeks, to the States, but Missouri was also slave country and thus seemed foreign, exotic to them all, and the very earth was altered —lighter in color, coarser and rockier than the loamy soil of central Illinois. They forded the shallow Fox River, feeling increasingly confident of the reliability of wagons and teams, and were late in pitching camp near the Wyaconda by the thin, luminous light of a new moon.

The emigrants were up at six the following morning and breakfast was finished by seven. After a week of practice the women's motions were brisker, more economical, as they roasted coffee and then ground it, set strips of bacon to fry in cast-iron skillets, brought dried fruit to a boil, stirred batter that must suffice for the nooning as well. Afterwards, the older children helped wash and stow away dishes, while the hands yoked up the oxen, the fathers struck the tents, furled them around the ridge poles. By 7:30 the cry went up: "Roll out!" Each day a different family took the lead, and on Saturday the 25th Jacob Donner's wagon pulled out first, driven by Augustus Spitzer. It had proceeded no more than five miles when the animals began to balk, moaning and rolling their heads from side to side. The saddle horses, too, jerked their heads, eyes bulging wildly, and moved only with vigorous goading. The drivers were baffled by this sudden mutiny.

James Reed, who had ridden forward on Glaucus, forced the animal about and headed back to the stalled train. Every few yards the horse stopped, stiffening its forelegs, and Reed had to force her on.

He passed the wagons driven by the two Germans and reined up beside George Donner's family wagon. George and his wife sat forward, and the man was having trouble controlling his own team as well.

"Something's spooked the animals," Reed said.

"Maybe they're sick," George Donner suggested. "Maybe there was somethin' wrong with the water." That their animals might fall ill from eating poison weed or drinking the wrong water was a fear haunting all emigrants, for this could strand them helplessly with their vast, overburdened wagons as unmovable as beached whales.

"But we drank the same water, and we're all fine. And there was plenty of good clover for grazing," Reed countered. Glaucus whinnied sharply, flung her head as though trying to free herself from the bridle, and Reed reached forward, slapped the horse's neck. The animal was as lathered as if she had just run ten miles. By now, all the oxen had come to a standstill. The loose stock lagged far behind, and despite the shouts and goading of the four men herding, could only be persuaded to move in tight, nervous circles, as though they had lost all sense of bearing. The dogs huddled together whining.

The cloudless sky had darkened slightly, as if a thunder storm were in the making, but there was no smell of rain and no distant lightning and no wind stirring the trees.

Tamsen clapped her hands suddenly and cried, "The birds!"

"What birds?" Reed asked.

"Listen carefully," she instructed.

Both men listened, but beyond the low, frightened moans of the animals, they heard nothing. The landscape seemed drained of sound.

"I don't hear a chirp," George said to his wife.

"Or a peep," Reed added.

"Precisely," she agreed, then stood on the wagon seat and, shielding her eyes, peered into the sky.

"Well, what is it? What do you see, child?"

"Mr. Donner, we are having an eclipse of the sun."

"An eclipse?"

The word was shouted back along the train and forward to Jacob Donner. The curious children spilled out of the wagons, all wanting to know if the Indians were coming.

"It's only an eclipse," Betsy Donner said to Solomon and William Hook, in a tone meant to console, but her voice trembled and broke with the effort.

"Mrs. Keyes always has an almanac to hand," Tamsen said. "If you'll just fetch it, Mr. Reed, I can tell you how long this is likely to last."

James Reed slid instantly from the saddle and ran back to the palace wagon, where his wife and mother-in-law both sat as rigidly as pillars of salt. Without asking their assistance, he found the almanac in one of the tambour compartments and carried it to Tamsen. Most of the party had now gathered at George Donner's family wagon, looking up to the former schoolteacher as though only she knew the formula that would save them. While she leafed quickly through the yellow book, the sky grew perceptibly darker, not with the deepening indigo that succeeds twilight, but as though dirty gray veils were being lowered over it one by one.

"Here!" she said at last, and then paused for a moment. "No," she then added, "we won't have the worst of it, but Newburyport will be dark as a coalhole." The thought seemed to please her, but left her listeners unsatisfied. Some stared in disbelief at their hands, as though seeing them through a pool of murky water.

"It won't get any darker," she reassured them, "or not much. It's only a partial eclipse, and we'll not have the worst of it." She would have known it was due, have welcomed it, had there not been so much coming and going in the last months, and she would have made of it a grand adventure for the children.

"Sure spooked the animals," Jacob Donner said, and Betsy bobbed her head in rapid, bewildered agreement. "How much longer you reckon it'll last?"

Tamsen ran a finger along the tables, did rapid calculations with her lips. "About an hour," she concluded.

The group mournfully echoed her, mouthing the word "hour" as though she had told them they would be stranded here for weeks.

Seeing the bewilderment on the upturned faces, hearing the younger children begin to fret, she suggested, "Why not have an early lunch? Then we can still get in a fair day's travel. You won't get the animals to move before, unless you want to beat them half to death. The poor dumb things probably think it's the end of the world!"

The others laughed at such downright foolishness, and some clapped the frightened animals reassuringly on their trembling flanks. Then they gathered tin plates and baskets from the wagons and, with Tamsen taking the lead, spread their picnic on a great, tablelike slab of rock. Earlier travelers had apparently used it for the same purpose, as it was scarred with crudely formed initials and dates, some carved, others painted with tar.

The children were calmer now, but all turned their eyes upward from time to time, as though fearing the sky might collapse, and they only picked at their food. When Tamsen had repacked the baskets, she said to Elitha, "Would you fetch me my knitting things?"

"Yes, Mama." But the girl held back, perhaps reluctant to leave the protecting circle of the group.

"Are you afraid, child?"

"Oh, no," she answered quickly. "We studied all about eclipses."

"Then what is it?"

"Nothing, Mama," she answered, but with a catch in her breath that made Tamsen fear she was ill.

"Are you poorly, Elitha?"

"No . . . no," the girl replied, and as though to avoid further questions, dashed off to the wagons.

"It's in the canvas pocket on the side!" Tamsen called after her.

When Elitha returned, Tamsen stood Eliza in the center of the sloping rock and handed her a bright yellow ball of yarn. "You," she announced, "shall be the sun!" She lifted the child's arms, and Eliza held the glowing ball overhead, the gloom of the last hour banished by this new adventure.

"You," Tamsen said to Georgia, "must be the earth," and gave her a green ball to hold. "Now, walk very, very slowly in a big circle around Eliza. That's right!"

She called Frances to her and lifted the girl up behind Georgia, groaning dramatically at the child's unexpected weight. "You must be the moon, and walk in a circle around the earth." Frances held a ball of blue yarn overhead. "Georgia has to go a little slower, Frances just a mite faster. Don't let the moon run away from you! That's right!" The other children leaned against the rock, enthralled by the mysterious pantomime. Georgia took tiny, careful steps, unsure of her balance on the uneven surface, and Frances passed her on the right, moved beyond, began to circle back.

"Stop!" Tamsen called. "You're a perfect planetarium, and you've just made the most wonderful eclipse. You see," and her finger moved from yellow to blue to green, "when the moon gets in the way of the sun, all three in a straight line, no light comes through. It makes a big shadow on the earth, and that's called an eclipse of the sun. If the earth gets in the way, it can cause an eclipse of the moon." She exchanged the blue and green balls, demonstrating. "Isn't it interesting that the animals knew it was happening even before we could see it? How do you think that could be?"

"Maybe they read Mrs. Keyes' almanac," Frances suggested, and hid a smile behind the ball of yarn.

"Child, what a peculiar thought!"

"Mr. Reed says Glaucus is smart enough to read," Frances

volunteered, then laughed at her own joke, and the others joined her. Only Virginia Reed found the humor misplaced, and let it be known that she must tend to her pony.

Relieved that they had forgotten their fear, Tamsen gathered the balls of yarn, nestled them in the canvas pouch, then swooped Eliza up, swung her around as the child giggled breathlessly. "What a wonderful sun you are! Who would have thought a chubby giggle of a daughter could be such a sun!"

Light seemed to leak through the veils of the sky, brightened and shimmered on the air, and bird song exploded from the nearby woods.

"Come, children, we must be on our way to California!" They scrambled from the rock and raced toward the wagons. Tamsen walked slowly, letting Elitha catch up, and put an arm around the girl's waist.

"Won't you ride with your father and me?"

"Yes, ma'am."

"That would be nice for us old folks!" She tightened her arm and felt the unaccustomed stiffness in Elitha's body.

"What is it, dear?"

"Nothing." But she trembled slightly and seemed to lean against Tamsen's shoulder for support.

Despite their unexpected delay, the Reed and Donner party covered nearly twenty miles in the afternoon, and set up camp in unusually high spirits. The darkening of the Missouri sky, the sudden warp of the natural world, they took not as an omen of foreboding but as additional proof of their own wonderful resilience. It was another test they had passed, as their wagons and animals had passed the test of rivers. Such natural obstacles only confirmed the bold grandeur of their enterprise, made it tangible, muscled, and gave them renewed confidence in their own ingenuity.

While John Denton gathered the wood for the kitchen fire, Tamsen took Elitha aside. The girl had been uncommonly quiet throughout the afternoon, and her eyes seemed strangely sunken, clouded. Shortly before they halted to make camp, Tamsen noticed her stepdaughter press a clenched fist against her stomach and thought, "The poor child is also in the shadow of the moon," wondering why it had to happen here, with the wagon jolting her and making the cramps worse. If it had only commenced before, at home, she would have put Elitha to bed, wrapped her warmly, given her a few drops of laudanum to relax her tensed muscles. Then, when she awoke from her nap, there would be a steaming beef broth and later a rich egg custard to strengthen her blood.

"Come with me," she said to Elitha, and the girl followed as Tamsen strolled casually away from the wagons, as if to take a turn in the evening air. But when they were shielded by a little copse of trees, she halted and placed her hands on the girl's shoulders. Elitha was taller than her stepmother, and Tamsen had to look up to study her worried face.

"Do you have cramps, child?"

The girl nodded.

"And are you bleeding?"

Elitha sobbed and looked away.

"Now, Elitha, it's just as I told you, and it's not a thing to fear. It means you're a woman now."

"I don't want to be a woman," she whispered. "Not if it hurts."

It is only the beginning, Tamsen thought, of so many hurts, and she would protect this motherless girl as she would protect her own from the deepest, cruelest of them, from those that stabbed and left you bleeding for months, for years afterward, trying to seal the wound but feeling the blood trickle from you, such a terrible quantity of blood, finding fresh outlets just when you thought it finally stanched.

"But you *are* a woman," Tamsen gently insisted, "and the cramps won't last long. You'll see!" She stroked the girl's hair, drew it back from her face admiringly. "And you will be the loveliest woman. I can see it already in your eyes. They're different than they were yesterday. Even the sun was surprised, and blinked when he saw you!"

Elitha sobbed again, but the hesitant flicker of a smile lighted her face.

"Ah, she gets prettier every minute! Now, you wait here while I fetch some things. All right?"

When she returned to the wagon, John Denton was already

lighting the fire. "I'm obliged to you," Tamsen said. "Elitha's a little poorly, but maybe Leanna could help you get things laid out. I won't be long."

She had rolled a length of gauze and a pair of fresh pantalets into a tight, inconspicuous bundle, which she took now to Elitha, together with a pail of water and a cloth with which the girl could wash herself. When it was done Tamsen reached up and kissed her stepdaughter lightly on the forehead. "How nice it is to have another woman in the family," she said. "And I must remember not to call you 'child' any more. If I do, you must correct me. Promise?"

Elitha nodded.

"And since you're a woman now, I thought you should have these." From the pocket of her apron she drew a pair of earrings, each a circle of gold with a tiny ruby suspended from it in a star-shaped mounting. "They were your mother's," she added.

Tears glazed Elitha's cheeks as she carefully lifted first one earring and then the other, then stared at the traceries of ruby and gold nestling in Tamsen's palm.

Ignoring the tears, Tamsen suggested, "Don't you want to try them? Come, let's see how they suit you." She fastened them in place, then rapidly dabbed the girl's cheeks with the hem of her apron, and stepped back to admire the effect. "You should see how beautiful you are. My, they *do* become you! I ought to have brought a mirror, but there's plenty of time for that later. We don't want you having an attack of vanity on top of the courses, do we? You can wear them to the first party in California, with the new moiré dress, and be the belle of the ball. I shall be terribly jealous because all the handsomest men will want to dance only with Miss Elitha Donner of Springfield, Illinois, and I shall be a perfect wallflower. And I do so love to dance!"

Tamsen lifted her skirts slightly, spun around, and made a low curtsy. "But now," she said, "you must take them off and put them very carefully away, or the other girls will all be wanting presents, too, and they wouldn't understand. For now it will be our very own secret. All right?"

Elitha reached up, and her fingers questioningly traced the outlines of gold. "Yes," she breathed.

Tamsen bundled the soiled pantalets, emptied the pail and dropped in the damp cloth. "Come along," she said. "We've supper to cook, child."

"I'm not a child," Elitha responded, but her voice lifted the statement into a question.

"Well, of course you're not. You're my dear, beautiful Elitha."

With that she turned again toward the wagons, leaving the girl to remove the earrings and hold them up to strike fire from the light of the moon. Tamsen found John Denton with his arms plunged into a sticky mass of dough. Each time he tried to pull an arm free he lifted the entire pan, and he struggled unsuccessfully to brace it with his flour-dusted knees.

"Why, Mr. Denton," she exclaimed, "I had no idea it was time to caulk the wagons again!"

4

Little Fabius River,
Missouri
Sunday, April 26th, 1846

Though Mr. Reed was for pushing on, the majority expressed a strong yearning to remain in camp today, not for religious reasons but from general weariness and the powerful wish to sleep twice in the same spot. It is also thought good to rest the oxen from time to time. For the two-legged creatures it could not exactly be called a day of rest, however. The men have been busy with repairs and adjustments to the wagons and have shifted loads to make a better balance, while the women have baked, mended, washed, aired the bedding and scrubbed the grime of the road from the children. One chore, at least, has been lifted from us, thanks to the discovery that the bouncing of the wagons is not only good for removing loose teeth but an excellent system of churning butter. When I have milked in the morning I cover the bucket with damp sacking and tie it in place, then hang it under the wagon. By the time we have settled on a camping place for the night there is a nice golden pat of butter freshly churned for our supper.

On the 24th of April we crossed the broad Mississippi River without mishap, though the current was so powerful it seemed certain to part the slight ropes fastened on either shore. For all the children this was a great adventure, not because of the hazards of the crossing but because the ferry was captained by a giant and very antique Indian named Burning Oak. He was assisted in his labors by Mrs. Oak, who could kill flies at twenty paces with a squirt of tobacco juice. Our presence seemed a considerable inconvenience to both of them. Since the Mississippi we have crossed several smaller streams, some no more than brooks though often esteemed on our map with the designation of river. Of these there are several called Fabius, seemingly branches of a single stream, all lazy and meandering, which would not count as a river in either Massachusetts or Illinois. Did Fabius actually roam about here after defeating Hannibal, or just some belated admirer of his? There is a Hannibal in Missouri as well, but considerably to the south and east of us. We are now aimed west by southwest, and so cannot pay him a visit. Though Latter Day Saints are rumored to be camping hereabouts, we have seen not a hair of them, also none in Nauvoo, and no Indians except Mr. and Mrs. B. Oak. The name Nauvoo is claimed to mean "beautiful place," but we found no considerable beauty there, the town consisting primarily of abandoned houses rapidly being reclaimed by mother earth.

There was great excitement and bewilderment among our party (and especially among our poor frightened oxen) yesterday. By mid-morning all the animals seemed spooked and most refused to pull or be driven but stood rooted like great trees. The cause of this was established to be a partial eclipse of the sun, becoming visible around ten in the morning and reaching its darkest point shortly before eleven. It had cleared completely by midday, and we took advantage of the animals' reluctance with an early nooning. The darkness was never complete, but more like an ordinary cloudy day except that there were no clouds to be seen. If the skies had been overcast we might have taken no note of it whatever. Nonetheless, it seemed at first some terrible visitation, and our poor Germans were on their knees praying—whether to Martin Luther in heaven or the Pope in Rome remains unclear but the message seems to have been delivered.

All of us are well though Elitha has felt a little gone for the last few days and I have given her a strengthening tonic at morning and evening. It is composed of 2 oz. each of Cinchona, Colombo, Gentian, and Quassia, mixed well. It is best to dilute the mixture with water to prevent the acids from damaging the teeth.

The landscape locally is somewhat rocky but with good topsoil and much is under excellent cultivation. We are for most of each day out of sight and sound of habitation but frequently see fields and orchards on a very large scale and occasionally meet farmers along the way, but they have few words for poor travelers, perhaps from fear of Mormon invaders. The roads are good, water plentiful for the stock, and the streams we pass are too shallow to give problems, though Mr. Reed's family wagon sank to the hubs in the mud of the Fox River and our team was unhitched to pull him out. We have seen a wonderful quantity of *Cercis,* sometimes known as flowering Judas, and the *Cornus florida* or flowering dogwood is just commencing to open its buds, both in far greater quantity and reaching a considerably greater height than I have witnessed elsewhere.

Margaret Reed and her mother seem to grow stronger and healthier each day and will soon leave the hired girl Eliza Williams little to do. Even Mrs. Keyes has taken to having a short stroll alongside the wagons from time to time. The children are well behaved and do all they can to help me, perhaps because it is easier to see what has to be done than it is in a house. Mr. Denton is also a great assistance, and we never tire of hearing his accent. One evening Leanna said to him, "I believe you've dropped something, Mr. Denton," and he looked to his feet. "What?" he asked, and Leanna answered, "Your H's, Mr. Denton." He found it a fine joke and repeated it to the whole company the following morning.

We expect to reach the Missouri by the end of the week, and will follow the southern bank to Independence. Everyone agrees we are making very good time.

5

THE ROAD THAT LED DOWN TO THE SHALLOW FORDING AT BLACK Creek was blocked by a mud slide, and the wagons turned east to search for another, since the way west was blocked by a series of low but wooded hills. At points the water of the creek was narrow enough for the men to jump across, but the banks were thickly lined with willows, and felling enough to make a passage on both sides would have taken most of the day. For the first time they were reversing their course, betraying the compass with prows pointed east, and it took most of the morning to make the frustrating detour. Even then the opening in the trees and dense underbrush lining the creek offered a crossing thick with rough boulders, but Jim Reed had scouted for miles ahead and reported it to be the best fording. Several of the boulders were too large for the wagons to clear, rocky islands around which the brook bubbled, parted, joined again. Wading in the chill water, the men shouldered some aside, prized others from the creek bed with staves and toppled them from the path. One had to be looped with ox chains and dragged away.

While the men labored to create a passage, General Zachary Taylor was fortifying his improvised camp near Matamoros on the Rio Grande River, taking such emergency measures as might convert his ragged, dispirited Expeditionary Force into a fighting army. The total company numbered fewer than four thousand, weakened by the fevers that had besieged them at Corpus Christi and their later march across a bleak, searing landscape in which only chaparral and rattlesnakes and mirages seemed capable of survival. On April 25th, when the Reed and Donner families were halted briefly by a

72

partial eclipse of the sun, General Taylor had responded to increasing rumors of hostile Mexican troop movements by sending out Captain S. B. Thornton and two companies of dragoons to reconnoiter the surrounding countryside. They rode nearly twenty-five miles along the blockaded river before receiving information that General Anastasio Torrejon had been seen in the district with part of his sixteen-hundred-man cavalry contingent. Thornton and his second-in-command were skeptical of the report, since it came from a Mexican peasant, and sought confirmation at a nearby rancho. There they entered a large enclosure thickly walled with chaparral, knocking courteously at the door, and were answered with a murderous volley from Torrejon's troops. Thornton took a bullet through the shoulder, sixteen of his dragoons were killed or seriously wounded, and the survivors were all made prisoners of the Mexicans. On April 26th, when the Springfield emigrants were laying by on a branch of the Fabius River, General "Rough and Ready" Taylor drafted a grimly uncompromising letter to President James K. Polk, informing him that "hostilities may now be regarded as commenced," and calling upon the governors of Texas and Louisiana for five thousand volunteers. It would take his urgent message nearly two weeks to reach Washington via the Southern mail, only two days for the president to persuade Congress to declare war in retaliation for the outrage, asserting that "Mexico had invaded our territory, shed American blood on American soil," thus with a phrase deftly annexing the disputed lands between the Nueces and Rio Grande rivers.

Meanwhile, on the day the Donner and Reed families, together with their wagons and stock and hired hands, were ferried across the Mississippi, President Polk was empowered by Congress to press a territorial demand that had played a central role in his election campaign—namely, the annexation of Oregon. The president himself felt war with Great Britain far more imminent than war with the impoverished Mexicans, whose ill-equipped forces were already strung along a series of strategic frontiers. For months his secretary of state, James Buchanan, had sought a gentlemanly compromise that would grant the Americans all territory south of the 49th parallel, but the president had campaigned with the slogan "54°40' or fight"; spurred on by a chauvinistic press, he renewed his determination to see American control extend north of the Columbia River to the border of the Russian holdings. In a special message to Congress he therefore called for an end to the joint occupancy treaty the United States had signed with Britain in 1818, and which could be ended on formal notification one year in advance. Arguing that the Union had "reached a period when the national rights in Oregon must either be abandoned or firmly maintained," he concluded with the assertion that "they cannot be abandoned without a sacrifice of honor and interest." This was clearly war talk, and mass meetings of support were held throughout the country, government departments and congressional committees charged to draw up war strategies. Despite the clear popularity of the president's stance, the resolution floundered for more than two months in Congress, while political intriguers and potential presidential candidates jockeyed for power. On April 23rd the House of Representatives and the Senate finally compromised on a phrasing that would authorize Polk to abrogate the joint-occupancy convention, but which simultaneously fissured his own volatile party and gave the opposition fresh tactics for future campaigns. The stress of these vast territorial undertakings also severely weakened Polk's health, and though he was the youngest president to occupy the White House, he would die soon after his term was completed.

As much as Texas and Oregon occupied Polk's thoughts in April of 1846, he secretly nourished an even more lavish territorial dream—the annexation of all of California. Others before him had urged the same scheme, including the sober and aristocratic John Quincy Adams and Polk's own temperamental, hard-bargaining patron, Andrew Jackson. Andy Jackson had tried to purchase California from the Mexicans, and when he failed his envoy advised him to take it either by guile or by force. Like most Americans, James Knox Polk had only the vaguest notions of California, which in 1846 had not yet been dependably mapped, but the sprawling land was an essential step in his expansionist program, his passionate commitment to a continental imperative for the American nation. Furthermore, like George and Jacob Donner, he was from North Carolina, the son of a farmer, and understood something about both the real and the psychic values of land itself. Polk and his contemporaries knew a few details about Monterey because of the old Yankee trade there in hides and tallow, and Richard Henry Dana's gripping *Two Years Before the Mast* had given the robust seaport a vivid place in the popular imagination. The Bay of San Francisco, too, had become a familiar and colorful port for American sailors and merchants after the Russians withdrew, but virtually nothing was known of the land that stretched eastward from the coast. In contrast, Oregon had been extensively explored, mapped, described by numerous missionaries, trappers, traders and settlers, and the Willamette Valley was being rapidly tamed by American citizens. There were, to be sure, a few reports on California gathering dust at the War Department, and there were three or four books of dubious accuracy, but Polk had read none of them. One of those books, the first treatise on the fabled region of California to appear in English, was written by an elderly Scot who had never been there, but did not allow that omission to inhibit him in offering *A History of Upper and Lower California*, "from their first discovery to the present time, comprising an account of the climate, soil, natural productions, agriculture, commerce, etc. A full view of the Missionary Establishments and condition of the free and domesticated Indians." Even without benefit of such authorities, Polk knew that it was America's "Manifest Destiny" to spread to the golden shore of the Pacific. The phrase was increasingly on his lips, punctuating cabinet meetings and peppering public addresses. It had appeared in the press the previous summer, and been used thunderingly in Congress for the first time the day before the president called for repeal of the joint-occupancy agreement.

Sending General Zachary Taylor to provoke a confrontation with the Mexicans on the northern bank of the Rio Grande was thus part of a larger scheme, an elaborate feint and parry, in which he would deflect attention and resources from the greater prize of California and justify a blockade of the Pacific ports. His sole fear was that the Californians themselves might seek a protectorate status from the British, or that old John Bull might actually invade the area to strengthen his threatened position in Oregon. Polk had thus caused a secret communiqué to be sent to the commander of the

Pacific Squadron, instructing him to seize without delay the harbor of San Francisco in the event of war being declared with Mexico. Brevet Captain John Charles Frémont of the U.S. Topographical Engineers, heading his third expedition to explore the Rocky Mountains, was also alerted to give support to any concerted activity on the part of the local populace to declare their independence from Mexican rule. The president's most elaborate tactic, however, consisted in encouraging his shrewd consul at Monterey, the merchant Thomas O. Larkin, to miss no opportunity to encourage local unrest; he should, indeed, use all means at his disposal to fan the discontent to such a point that the residents of the country would revolt in order to detach themselves from Mexico. Both Larkin's wealth and his official position gave him considerable opportunity for such manipulations. Furthermore, as half brother of the celebrated novelist James Fenimore Cooper and father of the first American children born on California soil, he was already well on his way to becoming a legendary figure in Monterey. The president's confidential instructions to Larkin were dispatched on the frigate *Congress*, which was to convey them round Cape Horn to the Sandwich Islands, and from there to California. A copy of the urgent orders was entrusted to a Marine Corps courier who proceeded by sea to Vera Cruz and carried them across Mexico; he then sailed from Mazatlán to Honolulu, where he took passage on the U.S. sloop *Cyane* for Monterey, arriving there on the day the Donner and Reed families departed from Springfield, Illinois. The courier, who presented himself as an invalid traveling for his health, had been under way for more than six months.

6

Arrow Rock, Missouri
Sunday, May 3rd, 1846

I have known again the amazing and quite unexpected luxury of sleeping in an actual bed with headboard and footboard and downy mattress! It stands not on the earth but on a floor of sweet-smelling pumpkin pine, and with a firm, leak-proof ceiling overhead. In place of the tent-flap there is a door with brass knobs and a lock with a key to fit it! This miracle is situated in the second story of the Arrow Rock Tavern, property of Judge Joseph Houston. Never mind that there are two other beds in the room, or that all are as packed with weary females and children as peas in a pod, for we were uncommonly fortunate to find such noble accommodation. Only the early departure of a group of Tennessee travelers accounted for the unexpected vacancy.

We arrived here shortly before dusk on Saturday, having crossed on the ferry and watered our livestock at a spring near the boat landing, where we encountered the first true crowds of men and animals since our departure from Springfield. In recent days we have seen other emigrant wagons, but in no great numbers. Here, however, we join the route followed by the Santa Fe traders as well as travelers bound for St. Louis in the east and Independence in the west. This, together with the river traffic, gives Arrow Rock a most lively appearance, and it therefore seemed unlikely that sleeping space would be available at the Tavern. The gentlemen of our party, however, are compelled to pass the night in tents a short distance from here—not just because we have made of the bedrooms such giggling hen-coops, but also to guard our goods and animals, for there is said to be much thievery in such river ports. Certainly there is a good deal of noise, the worst of it from a

77

fiddling competition that lasted much of the night and threatened to shatter our looking glass.

The beds are clean and food in the tavern tolerably good, though Mr. Reed claims the store of Kentucky whiskey is only suited for pickling skunks. Judge Houston is a genial and helpful host, a native of Virginia, who caused the tavern to be constructed after the model of an inn in Albemarle County. He also availed himself of the labor of slaves in burning the bricks and planing the timbers, as it was not only architecture that he imported from the land of his birth. There are many poor slaves hereabouts, and one might guess the entire town, from gutters to weathervanes, to be the fruit of such labor, though their own quarters are not great testimonial to their skills. Or to the charity of their owners. Judge Houston informs us the community takes its name from nearby bluffs named "pierre à fleche" by French explorers, who noted the popularity of the flints there for the making of Indian arrowheads. We have also heard Arrow Rock pronounced Airy Rock by some of the Westerners. The town is smaller than Springfield, though the large quantity of itinerants makes it seem almost larger. There are a number of fine, stately houses, most built according to the English muse, and in one of them we took a pleasant lunch today, consisting of calf-head soup, pork with ketchup sauce, smothered breast of mutton, pickles, horse radish, boiled potatoes, and a dessert of sago pudding.

This feast was served to the members of the George Donner family by Dr. John Sappington and his wife, to whom we brought a parcel from friends in Springfield. I had availed myself of Dr. Sappington's fever pills since first arriving in Illinois, and was curious to meet their inventor, who was the first to propose the effectiveness of quinine (obtained from conchona bark) in treating the malaria that is a curse of the southern frontier. He is sometimes called "Daddy of all the Pills" by the local citizens, but they intend him no disrespect, and he has dosed them all with his bitter nostrums and possets. Although a full three-score-and-ten (just the age of Mrs. Keyes), the doctor is a very adroit and singularly eccentric character, jocular and lively and rather quizzical, possessing a high degree of hospitality and gentlemanly demeanor. He is a large, fine-looking man about six feet tall with a heavy suit of hair white as a fresh fall of snow. His beard is equally white and makes a large bib to spread over his chest, from which he regularly picks any crumbs that are nesting there. Dr. Sappington presented me with an autographed copy of his famous "Treatise on the Treatment of Fevers," for which I hope there shall be no subsequent occasion, but it makes an interesting remembrance of our enjoyable afternoon. Mrs. Sappington is a pleasant, agreeable lady who appears much her husband's junior, but they have raised a numerous family together. Two of their married daughters were present during lunch and a son, William B. Sappington, who used to assist his father in making his medicinal preparations. The latter has prospered through his large plantations of hemp and caused to be built a great mansion christened Prairie Park, southwest of the town. We have been invited to view this residence, together with the owner's lead coffin, which he has provided for the occasion of his own departure from the earth (or into it). This worthy object, he states, is stored beneath his bed, where it provides a handy container for apples and nuts.

Also present at lunch was Mr. Caleb Bingham, a former Arrow Rock resident and now representative in the Missouri Legislature, who has made a wide and distinguished reputation as a painter. Hereabouts it is said to be as uncommon not to have a Bingham on the wall as it is not to have a Bible on the center table. Some of Mr. Bingham's colorful productions hang in the Sappington parlor, with another in the dining room of the tavern, and I cannot think a more skillful hand or eye could be found even in the academy at Dusseldorf. Though a trifle shy and nervous, he is a most charming man, but somewhat distracting in conversation on account of the constant adjustments to the wig he wears, and which Georgia found most fascinating. With each stage of the meal it seemed to sit in a renewed position, and my chubby daughter once tried to remove it entirely. We were lucky not to see it fording a bowl of calf-head soup!

Mr. Reed was busy today at the Masonic Temple, but we must not inquire too precisely what errands he was about. His womenfolk spent their time calling on the ladies of the Marmaduke family, and seem to have found many topics of common interest. Mr. Denton got himself a sunburned nose from lazing on a raft with young men of the town. I am writing this by the light of a lamp, which causes some disturbance to my chamber-mates, and so I must extinguish wick and quill for another night of downy dreams.

7

SUDDEN, BRIEF RAINSTORMS HAD ACCOMPANIED THE REED AND Donner party for several days before they reached Arrow Rock, and rain had weighted the canvas wagon tops, making the hoops that supported them protrude like the bones of gaunt prehistoric skeletons. The weather cleared shortly before they crossed the Missouri on May 3rd, but early on the morning of the 5th the emigrants awoke to a fierce downpour that rapidly overflowed the gutters of the town and left wagons and stock stranded in a shallow, murky lake. The men struck their tents and took refuge in the tavern, hoping to wait out the storm, but by noon there was no sign of the torrent easing, and they reluctantly decided to postpone their departure until the following day. On Tuesday, their nine mud-splattered wagons mingled with the bustling traffic that made the trail from St. Louis to Independence a major highway. From Arrow Rock the route struck diagonally northwest toward Malta Bend, through hummocked Missouri country thick with clumps of oak, willow, hackberry and scrub. From Malta Bend, the road closely followed the coppery windings of the river, offering frequent glimpses of steamboats crawling slowly against the current with their heavy freights of goods for Independence, Santa Fe, and the western forts.

In the spring of 1846 traffic to Independence was thinned somewhat by the troubles brewing with England and Mexico, which caused many to postpone their journeys west until such time as the border controversies were resolved, but the Reeds and Donners were rarely out of sight of other prairie schooners, lumbering Santa Fe wagons, pack trains and farm wagons. Attacks by Texas freebooters and aggressive troop movements in New Mexico had led General Santa Anna, president of Mexico, to reimpose the ban on American commerce with Santa Fe and Chihuahua, but many caravans continued to exploit the rich trade route. The Army of the West, under the command of Colonel Stephen Kearny, remained sufficiently visible to warn the Mexicans of the foolhardiness of attempting to prohibit the trade entirely.

James Reed's rolling palace no longer seemed out of scale in comparison to the traders' wagons bound for New Mexico, each loaded with five thousand pounds of goods and drawn by eight or ten mules. For the Illinois travelers there was a shock of strangeness in these great vehicles and in their arrogant, boisterous drivers, all cracking great rawhide whips and shouting constant, unintelligible messages to the straining animals. The toil and danger of their route had toughened them, welded them into an intimate fraternity, a brotherhood whose mysterious language and signs were as foreign to the emigrants as those of some cabalistic religious order. The experience was both exhilirating and bewildering. Though they had not yet reached the edge of the wilderness, had not jumped off into the unknown stretches separating Independence from California, they seemed to have traversed an invisible line where new energies, new laws of motion were observed. From Springfield to Arrow Rock they had experienced a strengthening of resolve, a growing confidence in their own physical control, but in comparison to these aggressive teamsters, they suddenly felt clumsy and incompetent. Mud dragged at the wheels of the wagons, splattered the osnaburg cloth that had gleamed like a banner only two weeks before, and prevented them from descending to take refreshing walks beside the trail. At night, the damp wood of their campfires burned irregularly, and it was impossible to put up the tents, so they were compelled to sleep crowded uncomfortably together beneath bedclothes that increasingly smelled of dampness and mold. It took nearly five full days to cover the eighty-five miles to Independence, and only there did the real journey to the West begin.

They would not meet and join forces for more than a month, but William H. Eddy and his family were already traveling within sight of the Springfield emigrants. A carriagemaker from the town of Belleville, Illinois, a few miles southeast of St. Louis, Eddy had left home ten days before, heading for the Pacific with his wife Eleanor, his small son and infant daughter. A brawny young man of twenty-eight, he had learned his trade well, but lacked the capital to set up the kind of works that could have competed with the other carriagemaker already well established in Belleville, or with the more elaborate businesses that flourished in nearby St. Louis. Most of his time was thus spent making routine repairs to crude farm wagons— dull, repetitious work that called for few skills and brought at best a scanty income, but it was better than providing sweat and muscle for another man's business. Eddy had often considered moving to St. Louis, but hesitated to expose his family to the vices of the raw river town, and for more than a year had thought increasingly of Oregon as an alternative. A skilled hunter and woodsman who had grown up on the Kentucky border, he was powerfully drawn to the idea of a wilderness landscape, unspoiled and untamed, and felt certain the young settlements to the west would have ample need of his professional skills. Unable to afford hands to assist him, Eddy traveled with a single wagon, an extra yoke of oxen, and a pair of milch cows. He had brought ample supplies, but had less than forty dollars in cash after outfitting, and the stores would have to suffice for the entire journey, perhaps supplemented from time to time by fresh game when he could manage to borrow a rifle on shares. He transported no bright baubles to pacify hostile Indians, no brocaded silks with which to barter for tracts of virgin forest. His fortune rested entirely in his inventive mind, his fierce will, his broad, muscular shoulders. At the time Eddy departed from Belleville his destination was Oregon, but along the way he heard frequent praise of California's milder, healthier climate, and began to weigh such reports with increasing interest; a final decision, however, would not have to be made until Fort Hall, when the trail forked.

William Eddy was a patient, soft-spoken man, whose limber, loose-jointed motions indicated an easy confidence in his own physical strength and ingenuity. His dedication to his small family was fiercely intense, and concern for their well-being was the dominating passion of his life—the sole passion, indeed, that could provoke his generous spirit to anger. In the coming months he would threaten to commit murder for a cupful of brackish water to slake their terrible thirst, and he would kill a wounded grizzly with his bare hands to save them from starvation. When that supply of meat was nearly exhausted, he walked for a month across the snow-covered Sierras on frozen feet that at one point left a heavy trail of blood six miles long and, when he had finally reached safety, almost immediately reversed his steps to accompany the first relief party halfway up the mountains.

Eleanor Eddy shared her husband's gentle, selfless disposition, but she lacked his amazing physical vitality and his occasional capacity for rage. Even as their wagon drew near Independence, she felt weary with travel, depressed by the relentless rain, and was constantly concerned about the year-old daughter she was nursing. The infant had been colicky ever since they left Belleville, and often spit up yellowish clots of soured milk. Neither the discomforts she suffered now nor the agonies awaiting her in the deserts and impassable mountains would cause her to doubt the wisdom of her husband's decision to go west, for she knew it was his intense love for her and for their children that drove him to seek a better world for them all. The mounting troubles they encountered, the suffering, were the fault of nature or of fate or of God, and perhaps all three working in cruel conspiracy. When William Eddy left the camp of death in the Sierras, she secretly slipped most of her own remaining ration of bear meat into the bottom of his pack, wrapped in a note that read: "My dearest husband, I believe that you will find this gift when you need it. You must save it until the last possible moment. I believe it will save your life and help you hurry back to us for we need you so. Your own dear Eleanor."

William and Eleanor Eddy, with their children James and Margaret, arrived at Independence on the afternoon of May 9th, only a few hours after the wagons of Jacob Donner, George Donner, and James Reed had climbed the long, tortuous rise into Independence. The town square rang with the incessant hammering and banging of a dozen frantically busy blacksmith shops, but the deafening chorus itself was frequently drowned by the clank of wagons, the crack of bullwhips, the sounds of cattle lowing, horses whinnying, dogs barking, riders whooping as they galloped their swift ponies theatrically through the mud, voices shouting and greeting and protesting and bargaining in Spanish, French, German, English. The children's impatience to see authentic Indians in authentic costumes was instantly satisfied by blanketed, feathered, painted Shawnees and Kansas, many of them proudly wearing presidential medals; but there were even more exotic figures milling about the noisy square. Both George Donner and William Eddy called their wives' attention to a great African slave, his skin gleaming like polished onyx, who drove a six-horse team of matched bloodred bays, swaying from side to side and singing loudly, with a large iron ring piercing one ear and dragging the lobe down nearly to the shoulder. A group of dark-skinned Spaniards lolled against a wall of the brick courthouse, indolently aloof from the turmoil, puffing deeply at fat cigars. Each wore a conical hat with a red band and a bright blue roundabout trimmed with rows of small brass buttons; their duck pantaloons were slit above the knee, revealing ruffled white drawers that brushed the top of their low half-boots. A diminutive French-man in a snug black velvet suit and beret, bullet pouch dangling from one hip, bowie knife from the other, tried repeatedly to mount a mule that waited patiently until he had one foot in the great wooden stirrup before letting his heels fly. Busy drovers and self-important merchants hurried through the streets, mingling with grizzled mountain men in buckskins, hunters expensively outfitted as though about to leave for a grouse shoot in Surrey, the toughened bull-whackers of the Santa Fe trail, soldiers on leave from Fort Leaven-worth drunk on forty-rod, rivermen and roustabouts and black-faced stevedores and light-fingered gamblers. Many of the emigrants merely stood gaping at this unimaginable frenzy, while others rushed from shop to crowded shop, shaking heads in bewilderment as they compared the scalpers' prices asked for a bag of flour or a pound of saleratus, and scarcely pausing to answer the question they heard from strangers a dozen times a day: "Are you for Oregon or Califor-nia?" The smaller children fretted, screamed, and harried mothers sought unsuccessfully to comfort them while shouting constant warnings to the older ones to stay out of the reach of flying hooves and iron-shod wheels.

Emigrant campsites sprawled in a radius of five miles around the town, wherever the spring grass had not been too badly over-grazed. The Donner and Reed families planned to remain for a day or two, making final purchases, hiring additional hands, and gathering information about the organization of the great overland caravan. William Eddy also intended to pause for a while in Independence, in the hope of finding odd jobs to augment his modest cash reserves. The new arrivals quickly learned that more than twenty smaller trains had already departed from Independence, Westport, and St. Joseph, and there was concern among all the men about whether the browse remaining after their passage would suffice for the stock. The largest single contingent had left only a few days before and would camp at Soldier's Creek, a tributary of the Kansas River, to await latecomers. The advance party included former Missouri Governor Lillburn Boggs, locally celebrated for his fierce resourcefulness in driving the hated Mormons out of the state and slaughtering many of those who refused to move quickly enough to suit him.

As soon as camp had been established, Margaret Reed and Tamsen Donner washed, dressed their hair, and changed their soiled clothing to accompany their husbands on a visit to Jessy Quinn Thornton, a journalist for Horace Greeley who was traveling to Oregon from Quincy, Illinois. Thornton hoped the pure mountain air would revive his invalid wife Nancy and provide a cure for his own asthma. Pious, genteel, unimpeachably respectable, the journalist was keenly proud of his Virginia ancestry and the gentlemanly education he had received in London, and was pleased to think of having such well-bred companions for the journey across the bleak plains. He and James Reed, furthermore, were mutual friends of Stephen Douglas. The Thorntons knew from the *Sangamo Journal* that the prosperous Springfield emigrants had set out on April 16th, and had postponed their own departure from Independence in order to receive them. Jessy Thornton cautioned the newcomers that they should not delay unduly if they wanted the protection and companionship of the main party bound for Oregon and California.

"It is reported," he warned in a thin, rasping whisper, "that the Kansas have held a war council and are resolved to slaughter all whites who dare to cross their territory. The Mormons, too, are determined to make trouble, and there are thousands of them, all armed to the teeth. They even have ten brass field pieces at their barbaric command. And then there are the British troops," he hinted, but broke off with a dry, embarrassed cough, as though reluctant even to imply that the flower of Anglo-Saxon civilization might seek to impede their noble and necessary progress. "It would," he concluded, "be unwise to travel without the protection of an ample company. We have, of course, already sent an express to Colonel Kearny at Fort Leavenworth to request the protection of his troops, but their jurisdiction is limited."

"We ourselves are well armed and all tolerably good shots," James Reed assured him.

"You are fortunate to have the strength to defend yourselves and your families. I fear the health of my wife and myself would not be sufficient to such exertions." As though the moment had been carefully rehearsed, husband and wife simultaneously smoothed the identical cashmere shawls with which they sought protection from the damp air, pressed them closer against their frail chests, and coughed.

While the three women sat together deploring the inclement weather that had so inconvenienced them all and discussing the sundries that still had to be purchased, the men made plans for departure on the morning of May 12th. When the final details had been clarified, Nancy Thornton served China tea in cups of translucent jasperware, and Tamsen found herself in a friendly debate with Mr. Thornton over the achievement of Robert Burns, whom her cultivated antagonist found rather too coarse in expression to be ranked with the bards of antiquity.

Later, after each family had returned to its own wagon, Tamsen remarked to her husband, "I fear I displeased our sensitive host. He seemed so used to having his opinions accepted as gospel, and cannot have had much opposition from his own poor wife."

"I should say he was pleased to find someone else who knows so much about the insides of books."

"Perhaps, but I ought not to have corrected his quotation from Spenser. Especially when he was so proud of his pronunciation."

"Never mind, child, you'll have time enough to bind his wounds with a little flattery."

"Oh, I think he's had quite enough of that sort of nursing," Tamsen said, "and any more would likely make his cough worse."

"Do you mean he's only humbugging us?"

"Well, no," she admitted, "but in comparison to his wife, Jessy Thornton's strong as an ox. Maybe he's jealous of her for being so peaky and needing so much attention."

"Then Oregon ought to be the right tonic for both of them."

"If it's really a tonic they want," she qualified. "It appears to me they've decided to have illnesses instead of babies, and they're so busy taking care of the little things they've scarcely got time to get well. It's like Mrs. Keyes. I just don't think she wants to get stronger, even if she is so set on meeting her darling Caden at Fort Hall."

"But you're the one who said the air was putting color in her cheeks."

"It was, Mr. Donner, it was. But as soon as the rains started and she was afraid of getting her feet wet, she took to bed again, and won't even leave the wagon when she needs to ease herself. She's giving up, and Margaret Reed can't do a thing for her that's right. She tries, but it just seems hopeless." Tamsen paused, clearly troubled by this cowardly, selfish surrender, and then almost aggressively declared, "It's such a fine thing to be alive, Mr. Donner, even when it's sometimes a terrible thing."

"That it is, child."

Then, knowing she was close to foolish, womanish tears, she added quickly, "As Mr. Burns would say, it's a bright and bonny braw thing, it is," and laughed at her own clumsy attempt at a Scottish burr.

George Donner reached out to fold her trembling hands in his own, lifting them as carefully as he would have lifted a fledgling with a sprained wing.

8

Independence, Missouri
Sunday, May 10th, 1846

We made camp here yesterday after being delayed in our departure from Arrow Rock by a rainstorm that would have given old Noah a turn, and left us envying the duck his waterproofed coveralls. Everything is damp and threatened with mildew—wagon sheets, bedding, clothing, flour—and though we had a few hours of sunshine to warm our arrival here and another bright hour in the forenoon today, it was insufficient to banish the damp we have stowed away in the last ten days. If the wagon sheets ever dry again they will receive a heavy coat of paint, to discourage them from functioning as a sieve when the rains are persistent.

The location of the town of Independence is beautiful, standing on a mounded elevation of land situated about six miles from the Missouri River on the southern (left-hand) side as you approach it. The surrounding country is undulating, picturesque, and with thick growths of timber indicative of a fat and exuberantly productive soil. The population of the town is about one thousand, and at this season most of them seem to be attempting the work of ten. Many of the houses around the public square are of brick, but the majority are frames, and there is a small but handsome courthouse with a most artistic fanlight over the chief entrance. There are several hotels, and the largest can provide accommodations for 400 guests, two to a bed and no cheating, which gives some measure of the ratio of itinerants to residents. The beds are all occupied, and so we sleep beneath the stars.

As well as funneling the overland parties into the prairies, Independence provides a busy rendevouz for the Santa Fe and mountain traders. They are a wild and daring troop accustomed to communicating over great distances, so that even their whispers come out like a shout. It is still not easy to understand what they say, as the whole town seems a vast smithy, busy night and day helping travelers prepare for their departure. All is a constant, clamorous bustle of lengthening girths and loading wagons, anathematizing refractory mules, jabbering in Dutch, higgling in Spanish, swearing in bad French, laughing and singing and arguing in tones unknown until Babel cleft the tongue of humanity so marvelously. One spies portly Germans phlegmatic as their own native marshes, waddling like Dutch galiots in a heavy sea, and little sallow Frenchmen skipping around beneath felt hats of parasol amplitude. Here and there is a bronze-browed hunter in a buckskin shirt, with a gaily painted hat and moccasins wrought with quills from "the fretful porcupine." The hat is usually pushed jauntily to the back of his curly head, to display the frank, devil-may-care face beneath it. Impatient of delay, he has flung himself upon the lazy mule that is to be the sole companion of his wanderings, with one foot dangling in the great, wooden stirrup ever pendant from a Spanish saddle, while he listlessly fingers his good rifle and studies the operations going on around him. The fiercest figures the eye encounters are not the painted Kansas but the Santa Fe teamsters or bull-whackers, as they are locally called— a few of them Africans but many Americans and Spaniards, and some that seem to represent all possible crosses between these various races. The Spaniard's identity is always clearly marked by his dirty poncho, which serves him as tent, blanket, tablecloth and serviette, and which he apparently wears until decay causes it to surrender and fall from his shoulders.

Many traders are now about to depart, while others who have been out to Santa Fe are returning daily, having sold their goods in exchange for gold dust, dollars and droves of mules. The dilapidated condition of their wagons and the tattered wagon sheets and the sore backs of the bony mules all give terrible evidence of the fearsome length and toil of the journey they have performed and that terminates here. In addition, many poorer emigrants are seen wandering the muddy square, dumbstruck and agog over the price of a yoke of oxen and a pound of salt, and wishing they had provisioned themselves better in Raleigh and Paducah. Most of them appear melancholy, as though the cloud has not yet passed away that came over their spirits as they tore themselves from friends and scenes around which had clustered the tender memories of the heart. The bonnets of the wives, usually lined with cardboard rather than with proper stays, already hang about their faces like wilted flowers, and add to the forlorn picture given by their troubled husbands. Such are the sights and sounds that bewilder the eye and ear in this western rendevouz, and it is a scene—an epitome of humanity—worth going far to see.

Yesterday we had the pleasure to make the acquaintance of Mr. Jessy Quinn Thornton and his wife Nancy, who are bound for Oregon from Quincy, Illinois. Mr. Thornton, who was born to one of the leading families of Virginia and educated in England from an early age, is a friend of Senator Benton and Congressman Douglas, and has been a corresponding journalist for Horace Greeley's whiggish *New York Tribune.* He is widely traveled and appears eloquently well informed on all matters of political consequence, though a trifle teetery on subjects of a more literary nature. He and his wife had obligingly awaited our arrival, which was anticipated some days before, and yesterday received us most graciously for afternoon tea, served with squares of fresh Lund cake. While they are still admirably young, both Mr. Thornton and his wife seem rather decrepit, but are persuaded that the Pacific air will reanimate their withered lungs and sluggish blood. We are now organizing ourselves to cross into the wilderness on Tuesday, and expect to catch up to the main caravan within a few days. They are expecting a few late-comers and stragglers, and will wait for us so long as prudent on Soldier's Creek.

Our present campsite is a few miles distant from the noisy town itself, so that we are mercifully spared the worst of its Bedlamish din, yet we have fresh neighbors who seem determined to recall its music to our ears. This morning, shortly before dawn, we were awakened by vigorous "Howdies!" and peeked from the tent to discover another being raised almost on top of ours by a numerous Irish clan with the patronymic of Breen. The elders of this jolly troop are named Patrick and Peggy (but called Pat and

Peg, even by their own children), and they made their way here from Ireland by way of Keokuk in Iowa, where they owned their own farm. There seem to be approximately a dozen miniatures of the father and mother, several nearly grown and one still at the breast, but they never remain still long enough to be counted, and there may possibly be no more than 8 or 10. They all seem good, well-meaning people, and Mrs. Breen has been in a constant lather of baking and fixing and amusing her little ones, while shouting all the while at the older children to be quieter in respect of the Sabbath. She carries her pretty baby girl slung on her hip like a frontiersman's hunting knife, and all her other feats—including chopping a mountain of firewood and milking six cows—are performed one-handed. Traveling together with the Breens is a quiet and kindly bachelor friend named Patrick Dolan, also from Ireland, whose principle occupation in camp is playing the violin. He insists it is not the lowly American fiddle he wields, but the music it produces is entirely of the "rend a rock and split a cabbage" variety. The Breens have three wagons, one of them a light rig with beds for the children, and Mr. Dolan pilots a wagon of his own. This energetic tribe is determined to accompany us when we roll west, and Mr. Donner agrees that the greater numbers they afford us would be a discouragement to unfriendly savages, so we will consolidate our forces.

We had intended to take on two or three more drivers and drovers here, but Mr. Donner recently returned from town somewhat discouraged in his efforts, and with only a single recruit. He is a young New Mexican named Antoine, who informs us that there is no further, family designation. His speech is a stew composed of equal parts of French, English and Spanish, in no great quantities, and from the look of him he may well have the blood of all three races in his veins, together with a little African or Indian spicing. It is to be hoped that we can locate other hands at one of the frontier forts. Meanwhile, Antoine's arrival has spared William Donner's conscience, for he was feeling guilty at abandoning us to return home, though his own cherished family will be anxiously awaiting him. He has been a great aid and comfort to us all, and I will sorely miss his companionship. He was well

91

disposed to me from the day I married his father, and has always been quick to perform little unexpected kindnesses that have recurrently brightened my life and that of my family. The children all think of him as a favorite uncle, and he has thus partly taken the place of my own brother William Eustis, who could not often enough be present. At least we can all expect a merry reunion under the sunny skies of California, and with that thought we must dry the tears of separation.

There remain now only a few necessaries to be purchased in Independence—chiefly goggles to protect the eyes during the desert crossing that awaits us in a few weeks' time. It is also said that Messrs. Wilson and Clarke, who keep a general furnishing store for western expeditions, offer a superior sort of patented India rubber overshoe, and those acquired in Springfield have not done well in competition with rain and mud. Otherwise, nothing seems to fail our party save the health of Mrs. Keyes, who took to her bed when the rains began and has remained there ever since, as fixed and determined as a nesting hen. This lack of any bodily activity thins her blood even more, so that she is unlikely to have the strength to rise even when the weather becomes more favorable. She is a source of great concern for all of us, but of course particularly for Margaret Reed, who is near distraction and cruelly fatigued by all the nursing, but Mrs. Keyes refuses to permit anyone else to tend to her needs. It took her daughter most of the morning to dribble a few spoonfuls of broth between her lips, and even then the old woman proved unable to hold them down. There is no hope, then, of getting her to swallow a tonic. She seems to have used up all her little force in willing herself away from Springfield, and we fear she cannot survive much longer. Otherwise, we are all damp but healthy, and nervous with excitement about our coming plunge into Indian country.

III

INDEPENDENCE

· TO · LITTLE SANDY CREEK

1

JAMES REED LED THE PROCESSION ALONG THE CHOUTEAU ROAD TO
Westport, followed by the wagons of Jacob Donner, those of George
Donner and the Thorntons, with Patrick Breen and his boisterous
family bringing up the rear. The weather was clear, warm and dry,
and there was a feeling of celebration as they put the mud holes of
Independence behind them to roll through green fields that sheltered vivid clumps of pink verbena, daisies, wild indigo, and brilliant
cones of lupine. At Westport they climbed down for their final view
of a town, if the word could really be applied to the raw settlement
energetically vying for the emigrant trade. It seemed a crude miniature of Independence, a cluster of hasty log structures housing the
quarters of traders, a smithy, a crowded dram shop, a hostelry and
a grocery store owned by a grandson of the famous Daniel Boone.
The town swarmed with Indians, whose muddy and shaggy ponies
were tethered by the dozen along the houses and fences. Sacs and
Foxes, with shaved heads and painted faces, Shawanoes and Dela-
wares fluttering in bright calico frocks and turbans, Wyandots
dressed in self-conscious imitation of whites, and a few wretched
Kansas wrapped in old blankets were strolling slowly about the
streets or lounging in and out of the shops and houses. The emigrants had agreed to pause for only an hour to stretch their legs, but
lingered longer in dark shops stinking of buffalo robes and tobacco
and crude homemade whiskey, scarcely believing they had reached
the western edge of the Union.

In the cluttered establishment of a Kickapoo trader, with a

single oilskin window and packed earth for a floor, Tamsen was astonished to see a volume of Milton's poetry with a revolving pistol laid across it, ominously cocked and ready for action. It spoke to her, in its blue gloss, its chipped bone handles, of a world beyond her imagining, and she recalled a favorite pair of lines from the leather-bound volume that supported the ugly weapon:

At last he rose, and twitched his mantle blue:
Tomorrow to fresh woods and pastures new.

She stared searchingly at the unexpected wedding of soaring verse with the grim engine of death, of yielding calfskin with adamant steel, trying to reconcile their presence with her own vision of the woods and pastures that must shelter them on their journey, but the vision shattered and her mind struggled to sort its sharp, splintered fragments.

Tamsen stood long in the deep, rank shadows of the trader's hut, turning away only when George lightly touched her arm and whispered, as though reluctant to disturb her meditation, "It's time to be on our way."

She was startled by his touch, jerked her arm reflexively as though brushed by something reptilian, cold, and at once regretted that she might have given offense. "I'm sorry," she apologized, "but you gave me a turn."

"Sunk in your thoughts again?"

"Yes," she admitted. "Sunk."

"The others are ready to roll out."

"I didn't mean to keep them waiting," she said, and her eyes took a final questioning measure of the swollen cylinder that gouged the book, the slender, rigid length of the deadly barrel.

Following her glance, he explained, "It's a Colt—best gun there is for a man on horseback, especially if he's got Indians to fight." His casual tone implied that fighting Indians was a commonplace, everyday occurrence.

"Colt," she repeated. The brief, crisp sound seemed to offer the unexpected answer to a riddle, so simple she should have guessed it sooner.

96

"We'll see more of them where we're headed. Some repeating rifles, too, but they're not much count." A man comfortably familiar with guns and tools, he warmed to the topic, explaining the principles of flintlock and percussion, clearly pleased to share with the uninitiated the authority of such masculine insight. It was Tamsen, then, who had to warn him that the others would be growing impatient.

"Well, let's get moving, child!"

"After you, Mr. Donner. To fresh woods and pastures new, if the mud hasn't got there first!"

Despite the fair skies under which they moved, mud slowed their progress as soon as they departed Westport, heading southwest along the first stages of the Santa Fe trail, which would eventually fork and send them north to the Kansas River. More than once oxen became mired to their bellies, and more than once teams had to be unhitched to help drag Reed's palace wagon out of a boggy trap, but some stretches of the road were firm, and there they traveled rapidly, making twelve miles before they encamped, an hour before sunset, near a blacksmith's shop and two dilapidated farmhouses. Half the surrounding countryside was prairie, covered with abundant young grass for the stock, and the remainder a tangle of walnut, oak, ash, hickory, elm, hackberry and mulberry, an abundance that seemed full of promise for the weeks ahead, for many had described the Indian territory as a vast and empty desert.

As they made camp, massive rain clouds began to pile like rough gray boulders across the horizon to the west, and the women hurried with preparations for the evening meal. Betsy Donner wailed that her dough would be turned to batter again, but the rain held off until the tin plates had been scraped of their last morsels and vigorously shined with wedges of bread. The fierce downpour, with drops the size of buckshot, sent them all scurrying to the shelter of the tents, from which they emerged only briefly for a reassuring look at the group of wagons that came rattling into camp and took up positions near their own, but it was morning before they exchanged handshakes and names and the routine question, "Are you for Oregon or California?"

The newcomers, all for California, consisted of two affluent

97

German families, the Kesebergs and the Wolfingers, and a short, stocky hand known as "Dutch Charley" Burger who worked as teamster for Keseberg. The Wolfingers were proud and remote, the wife meticulously dressed in a costly silk gown and wearing jewels that would have become an imperial court; she often darted bewildered looks into the distance, as though the carriage charged to bear her to the levee had inexplicably taken a wrong turning. Perhaps the Wolfingers feared attacks from jewel-thieving highwaymen, or perhaps the middle-aged couple only seemed aloofly withdrawn because their command of English was still so rudimentary. Keseberg was another matter entirely—a tall, blond, garrulous man in his early thirties who could bargain and curse and flatter and philosophize with equal ease in four languages. He was an agreeable companion until some change of plan, some unexpected obstacle or resistance disturbed his orderly mind, and then he would become sulky and morose, occasionally launching out in fits of violence that seemed, then, to purge and make him sociable again, though he never made apology for his outbursts. When mutual effort was called for, he was cooperative enough, yet seemed to keep extensive mental records of accounts payable and receivable. Borrowing a length of rope or a lump of axle grease, he would elaborately explain that this had now cancelled some prior indebtedness which the lender had, in most cases, thoroughly forgotten. Asking for help in rounding up a stray ox, he would just as meticulously point out, "I am in your debt," and immediately begin searching for an occasion to repay the worrisome obligation. His bookkeeping was rigid and precise, and he neither asked nor offered favors. If such behavior cultivated no friendships, it also made him no enemies. His treatment of his small daughter was another matter. He beat her almost daily, for the good of her blighted soul or to teach her manners, and it was not long before the other travelers had reason to suspect he occasionally administered the same discipline to his timid, wide-eyed wife, yet it was a firm rule of the trail that no one interfered in family disputes unless they threatened the general welfare.

Where the Wolfingers remained reticent about the history that had brought them west, or what private dream awaited fulfillment in Eldorado, Johann Ludwig Christian Keseberg readily began with details of his birth and childhood in Berleburg, Westphalia, the son of a learned pastor of the State Protestant Church and a mother who claimed descent from minor nobility. He had been educated in the best schools and early learned the uncompromising discipline of the Prussian infantry, though he demonstrated no great capacity for leadership. Widely traveled, he knew the leafy boulevards of Paris almost as well as the cobbled streets of the market town where he was born, though frequent journeys across the border brought him under the suspicious eye of state authorities who feared the importation of revolutionary foreign ideas. Nonetheless, Keseberg seemed embarked on a brilliant commercial career when he wrecked career and reputation and family alliances beyond repair through his marriage to Phillipine Zimmerman, a vivacious Catholic girl nearly ten years his junior. The Protestant pastor's son was immediately ostracized, and in the spring of 1844 sailed for America with his wife and their year-old child Ada. After a brief pause in New York, where his name was transformed to Lewis Keseberg, he proceeded to Ohio, but the move failed to fulfill the ambitious immigrant's glittering expectations of a new world, and the German communities there seemed as cramped and conventional as the one he had left behind. Thus, in 1846 he bought two wagons, oxen and supplies, and departed for the rendevous in Independence, though Phillipine was pregnant for a second time and fearful of the unknown dangers and toil of the far journey.

By now Keseberg had frequently shown his defiance of convention. There was nothing radical or even calculated in such behavior, for at heart he was a rigidly, stubbornly conventional man; his flaunting of accepted codes of behavior seemed rather to spring from a deep perversity of spirit, an instinctive impulse that seized him periodically and left him astonished at its results. His courtship of Phillipine Zimmerman, for example, was no rapturous star-crossed romance in which Montague defied Capulet, but an impulsive desire to sample the forbidden. Since Phillipine abandoned her religion and adopted his own, Keseberg was first amazed, then bitterly resentful of his parents' tight-lipped disapproval of their union, and when clients took their business elsewhere he was not appalled by their provincial bigotry but enraged at their lack of commercial wisdom.

What began as perverse impulse, aggravated by the compulsion to command attention, ended in angry defiance, but the anger was in part directed at himself for disturbing the clean and systematic neatness his Prussian temperament demanded from experience.

Somewhere between St. Louis and Independence, Keseberg had grafted the Wolfingers onto his party, though they were so clearly lacking in the resilience and physical skills the journey required that most travelers would have regarded them only as a hindrance. A common nationality may have pleaded their case, and Keseberg would not have been unimpressed by their obvious wealth or the tempting carelessness with which they displayed it. He treated them deferentially, but in his deference was a mild edge of contempt that grew steadily sharper as the journey progressed. The helpless bewilderment of the Wolfingers provided a convenient whetstone for his arrogance. On the morning after they joined the wagons of the Donners, Reeds, Thorntons, and Breens, it was Keseberg who made the presentations and Keseberg who announced, as though conferring prerogatives of inconceivable magnitude, that his little party had consented to join the others.

"Pleased to have you along," George Donner assured him, and James Reed told Keseberg that his own two wagons should file out after Jacob Donner's. The Wolfingers could follow him.

"Each morning a different family takes the forward position," Reed explained. "I usually scout ahead on Glaucus, to check the condition of the trail, and to locate the best campsite."

"As you wish." Keseberg's response was accompanied by a brisk bow that acknowledged Reed's position of leadership and Keseberg's own pleasure at finding himself part of such an orderly troop.

The expanded emigrant train set out in a light rain that soon swelled to a drenching thunderstorm. Shortly before noon they caught sight of the last fixed abode of a white settler, a small log shelter partially enclosed with a decaying sod wall, standing like a lonely sentinel at the border of Shawnee territory. As the wagons passed it, eyes stared wonderingly from beneath the soaked canvas, as if the one-room shanty with its sloping roof of interlaced boughs covered with oilskin were a turreted, castellated palace. Throughout the day they could hail occasional wagons returning from Santa Fe, and for a time rode parallel to a group of thirty Indians, who at first alarmed them but never drew close enough for real concern. In the afternoon they overtook the wagons of Governor Lillburn Boggs, the relentless scourge of the Mormon community, together with other emigrants who had painted their destination in huge crimson letters on their wagon sheets. The two groups paused to exchange greetings, to compare plans and rumors, and each man took rapid measure of the other's wealth and status in the elaborateness of his outfit and the number of hired hands assisting him. Together, they covered another ten miles before stopping to make camp in the open prairie, where there was little wood for fires and the only available water was murky and bitter with rotted grass and leaves.

WITHOUT YET KNOWING IT, THE REEDS AND DONNERS HAD already sketched the pattern that would mark their route to Little Sandy Creek—not merely the wearying pattern of rising at dawn, preparing breakfast, gathering the stock, chaining up and rolling out, nooning and more travel and then the search for a campsite with adequate fuel and water, pitching the tents, grazing the animals when graze was available, cooking and washing and mending and sometimes visiting, sometimes singing and occasionally even dancing together, then almost invariably stumbling to their improvised beds with exhaustion, but the pattern of joining and dividing, regrouping, parting, assembling, and finding the essential, sometimes monotonous, sometimes perilous rhythms of their lives intimately twined with those of others. People who would not have paused to give greeting on the streets of Quincy or Joplin, would never have crossed each others' threshholds or occupied the same pew in Springfield or Durham, shared a pail of water or a cooking fire, tended each others' children, gathered fuel, fought mud, dust, heat, cold, wind, rain, hunger, thirst, rattlesnakes and swarms of mosquitoes, exchanged life histories, boasted or complained of the homes they had left behind, alarmed each other with tales of Indian and Mormon ravages, calmed and consoled, paid witness to births and deaths, trembled at the soprano howling of coyotes, envied each others' goods and shared them freely or grudgingly, occasionally stole them, quarreled and cursed and threatened, prayed together, discussed politics and reincarnation, debated the relative merits of Oregon and California, shouted oaths at sluggish oxen, joined teams to pull steep grades, traveling as intimately, vitally linked as Siamese twins, and then the link was suddenly broken and almost as suddenly forgotten, as a family dropped behind with a cracked oxbow, laid by to search for strayed cattle or to shoe horses or dry flour that was beginning to rot. They were joined in turn by others, often men chronically suspicious of strangers, fearful of being burdened by the slow-footed or exploited by the greedy or made to seem ignorant, laughable, by those whose English was more fluent, but even more terrified of traveling the wide, desolate prairies alone. These formed a new, impromptu group, and were soon sharing a stew of squirrel or prairie dog, lamentations over their misfortunes and raptures about the health and fortune awaiting them at the end of the trail, all the while searching for some link, some coincidence of place or name or religion or origin or destination or acquaintance that would ratify their young alliance. Together, wives stooped wearily beside creeks and springs and muddy rivers to wash dented tinware and frayed clothing, some complaining of husbands, others praising them, but the younger ones too shy to do either and only listening, reddening at intimacies bluntly revealed. Many remained together for weeks and months, others for only a day or two, and then new parties formed, elected a leader, took a different fork in the trail, refused to budge on the Sabbath, split apart, were left behind, caught up, overtook, outdistanced, lolled for a day or two by a shady creek and fattened their oxen, sought a rumored cutoff or bypass the others didn't trust, waited for torrents to subside, struck off on the path of a mirage, and a few, discouraged, turned back to seek the protection of the rising sun.

More than a dozen families were now moving together across the Blue Prairie, but only five of those would remain together, with occasional breaks and brief separations, to the end of the trail. The Donners and Reeds remained throughout a unified, closely knit party, to which the Breens, Wolfingers, and Kesebergs had now tenaciously attached themselves, a little awed, perhaps, by the richness of their outfits, comforted and inspired by the patriarchal dignity of Jacob and George Donner. If James Reed annoyed them with his aristocratic flourishes, awakened jealousy of his ample estate, they did not underestimate his alacrity of mind or his physical stamina, and knew such qualities could spell their survival. For the foreigners, German and Irish, these educated and prosperous Americans held some key to success that they were desperate to possess for themselves, and hence they stuck with an uncommon tenacity. If the Reeds and Donners argued for a change of route, for pushing on harder or for slowing their pace, the Breens and Wolfingers and Kesebergs might quarrel and grumble over the decision, but almost invariably adopted it as their own.

Three days after their departure from Independence, the Reeds and Donners caught up with the main overland caravan that, as Thornton had promised, was encamped to await them—not on Soldier's Creek, as expected, but stretched along the banks of the Waukaruska. The group had already appointed an official guide, voted for administrative officers, and elected Colonel William H. Russell as captain. A tall Kentuckian whose distinctive hallmarks included a luxurious, heavily waxed mustache and a broad panama hat with an oiled-silk cover, he was a thundering orator who fought for his most recent election with the same noisy, congenial affability he had practiced on the hustings in Kentucky and Missouri, and won easily over his less eloquent opponents. Officially he became Captain Russell, but many still called him Colonel, and intimates knew him as "Owl." Legend recorded that one dark evening as he drifted to sleep beside a campfire he heard an owl hooting from the woods, and mistaking the who-whooing for the inquiry of a potential voter, jumped to his feet and roared into the darkness, "Colonel William H. Russell of Kentucky—a bosom friend of Henry Clay!" Russell had promptly taken an official census of his rolling constituency, listing 72 wagons, 130 men, 65 women, 125 children. The newcomers were nominated for membership by Russell himself, and after a unanimous vote in their favor, James Reed mounted a stump to deliver an acceptance speech that rang with praise for the captain's vision and then rose in a stirring crescendo of tribute to the enlightened patriotism of the western migration.

When Reed had completed his address, Captain Russell

stepped forward and pumped the newcomer's hand. "Exceedingly delighted," he roared.

"We're much obliged to you, sir," Reed responded.

"Exceedingly delighted," he repeated to George and Jacob Donner, then to Jessy Thornton, who wheezed an asthmatic "Thank you, Colonel."

"Yes, I'm most exceedingly delighted," Russell continued, gripping Pat Breen's hand so firmly the little Irishman's face drained of color, and he was too breathless to respond to Peg's sharp elbow in his ribs or her whispered insistence that he make some reply.

"Exceedingly delighted," Russell assured Keseberg, who clicked the heels of his mud-covered boots together and bowed quickly from the waist, like the flick of a whip.

"Exceedingly delighted," the captain roared at the reticent Wolfinger, who replied with a stumbling, "Whole my side, *danke.*" Russell paused briefly, as though weighing a suitable reply, then patted his luxurious mustache and continued down the line of his richly expanded constituency.

THE REEDS, THORNTONS, AND DONNERS BROUGHT WEALTH AND authority to the caravan for those already assembled under Russell's command, and their arrival thus gave additional confirmation to the nobility of their search for the promised land. The group contained few of the squatters and poor whites and butcher boys who would swell in proportion as the costs of the western trek dwindled, but consisted largely of farmers who had sold their lands at a generous profit, outfitting themselves handsomely for the journey; with them were lawyers, journalists, teachers, two ministers of the gospel, masons and carpenters, botanists, a doctor, a jeweler, a gunsmith, several merchants and blacksmiths—a rich and varied nucleus for the germ of civilization they were conveying to the Pacific. Well suited as they seemed to colonize the wilderness, few of these greenhorns possessed any of the particular skills or the clear, quick judgment that life on the trail would require, and though they had at once provided themselves with an organizational structure that was reassuringly familiar, the duties of the captain and his officers were vague, and even their most ardent supporters frequently exercised the noisy privilege of criticism and dissent. Most were still bewildered by the strangeness of the landscape, made jumpy by the presence of Indians, and this had much to do with the sprawling disorder of the encampment near the Waukaruska. Jessy Thornton, quick to reduce the unknown to tidy metaphor, described it as resembling a Methodist revival, with a constant chorus of sound that mingled the neighing of horses, the braying of mules, the excited voices of men locked in earnest debate, little knots of women laughing and gossiping, children crying or piping merrily from the nearby woods. The tents were new and clean, gleaming like vast prairie blossoms in the moonlight, the cattle were numerous and fat and strong, the food abundant, and most of the party seemed in high spirits—some, indeed, almost boisterous in their mirth. Nearly all were strangers, and made a special effort to give the most favorable impression to others. Suffering, privation, anxiety and drudgery had not yet blunted their energies and their optimism, frayed their tempers, excited violent jealousies, and yet already there were signs of dissension beneath the exuberant surface. It was visible in the wagons drawn up irregularly along the bank of the creek—some with "California" painted on them, others inscribed with "Oregon" or "The Whole or Nothing" or "54° 40′," and factions had already begun to form, quarrelsome, stubbornly opinionated, and frightened.

Colonel Russell had scarcely urged his unwieldy train into motion, strung out for almost five miles across the prairie, before the problems began to erupt. Almost immediately two men were expelled for attempting to drive a herd of 140 cattle with them, on the grounds that such numbers would threaten the forage of the working oxen in the desert country ahead, and that so much walking beef was too tempting to Indian raiders hungry for steak. But most people were also having trouble herding their own stock—the oxen stubborn and stupid, the mules recalcitrant, the horses diabolically alert to slip away and return to the settlements, the milch cows constantly wandering from the trail in search of restful pasturage. This unavoidable four-legged confusion was only aggravated by such a large herd, and its owners were plainly no longer welcome; they were also resented by some because of their refusal to slaughter the calves that slowed their progress—a supply of fresh meat that would have been welcomed. The names of Baker and Butterfield were not the only ones struck from the official census. No sooner was the sprawling train in motion than the Reverend Mr. Dunleavy, offended at the coarse language of some of his comrades and the frequency with which jugs of Kentucky mash were tilted to the sky, dropped back in the hope of encountering more sober and pious companions. Mr. Gordon became impatient with the cumbersome pace set by the captain, and persuaded a total of thirteen wagons to strike out ahead. Meanwhile, hysterical rumor was almost as common as the long, muddy swells that laced the prairie: Mormons had been sighted up ahead, all thirsty for the blood of Governor Boggs and prepared to slaughter the entire train; British soldiers were massing on their flank, close enough for the wind to carry the sound of rattling sabers; Indians were shooting cattle in the rear of the train; a child had a raging fever that was certainly the deadly cholera.

There was often no visible trail to guide them, and they set their course by occasional parallel lines slashed in the damp earth by previous wagons; those were widely separated, so that the caravan fanned out across the landscape, as often traveling parallel as in orderly file, and more and more resembling a routed army. People grew edgy, impatient, and concealed their mounting fears with anger—at the stumbling animals, at the earth, at each other, and above all at the elected leaders who failed to protect them from these frustrations. Within a matter of days unrest had reached such a boiling point that Governor Boggs, James Reed, Jessy Thornton, and George Donner held a council to propose emergency measures, but before they could present them to the group a hearty democrat took to the stump, and with fiery oaths and a fist invoking Jehovah, denounced Russell and his lieutenants as incompetents. When others joined him to accuse them of misfeasance and malfeasance, the governing body resigned en masse, only to be reinstated to vigorous applause an hour later, and the train resumed its uneven pace. There were fewer trees now, except those lining the banks of infrequent creeks, and the vast prairie stretched before them like the green swells of an uncharted sea. It grew increasingly difficult to find fuel for their fires, and the water was often brackish. Though the air was still mild, one ox had already become overheated and died of exhaustion, its tongue lolling black and swollen as it slumped heavily to the ground, grinding the heavy wooden yoke into the neck of his bellowing partner.

2

near the Kansas River
Sunday, May 17th, 1846

We are encamped for the night (not the day!) on a small, well timbered creek a few miles distant from the Kansas, which we expect to cross tomorrow by ferry. While many were opposed to travel on the Sabbath, most had no such scruples, and the will of the majority prevailed. On Friday last we caught up to the main caravan at the Waukaruska, awaiting stragglers, and were accepted into the party by unanimous voice vote. We find ourselves under the vigorous captaincy of Colonel William H. "Owl" Russell, a tall and forceful Kentuckian who had a distinguished political career in his native state before carrying his oratorical skills and his splendid mustaches into Missouri, where they also claimed many devotees.

A further star in our political firmament is ex-Governor Lillburn Boggs of Missouri, who is much consulted for his insight into the Mormon threat. Following outrages not unlike those perpetrated at Nauvoo, the governor ordered the expulsion or extermination of the "Destroying Angels"—a decision that nearly cost him his life. One of the Sons of Dan crept up to a window of the Governor's house and shot him, but his wounds were not fatal. I cannot think all the angels such bloodthirsty villains as the Governor allows, but his opinion will not be swayed, and most of our party are in concurrence with his judgment.

Governor Boggs travels with his wife, Panthea, a granddaughter of the legendary Daniel Boone. Three other descendents of the eminent frontiersman are with them, and from this something of the general composition of our party may be inferred. We have many prosperous farmers in our midst, but also ministers of the gospel and lawyers and successful merchants. We even travel with our own watch-maker, but he has little trade, as the sun punctually regulates our days. Mr. Edwin Bryant, who was once a student of medicine and for some years edited his own newspaper in Louisville, is among the scribblers of our group, and Mr. Charles Stanton of Chicago is an ardent botanical researcher. Including children, our caravan is more than 300 strong, and the majority are plain, honest, substantial, enterprising and virtuous. They are, for the most part, estimable persons, superior to those who usually settle a new country, and the loss of their society will be felt by friends and loved ones left behind.

The landscape through which we have traveled since leaving Westport is remarkably rich and fertile, and the rolling prairie abloom with larkspur, geranium, verbena and indigo. Along creeks and other water sources it is heavily and variously wooded, but for long stretches there is no sizable timber, and we have suffered some scarcity of fuel. The water is often bitter but somewhat improved by boiling with a pinch of saleratus. We have been fortunate to gather a quantity of delicious wild strawberries, as well as sassafras and slippery elm for making infusions.

Rains have continued to hamper our progress and dampen our beds, but these have become less frequent and of shorter duration. When there are no clouds to deck the night sky, the stars look so near one could easily reach up and pluck a bushel.

Yesterday we learned that a company of American dragoons has been attacked near the Rio Grande, and all either killed or taken prisoner by the Mexicans, leaving their commander General Zachary Taylor in a most perilous situation. This news was brought by a horseman hurrying to catch up with a train ahead of ours, who brought with him a copy of the St. Louis *Republican* containing a lengthy report of the hostilities. The distressing information was confirmed a few hours ago by Mr. Webb, editor of the Independence *Expositor* and a Mr. Hay, who arrived in camp a little after dusk, having come direct from the settlements to communicate to us the last intelligence we should receive before arriving at the Pacific. The letters and papers brought by them gave us additional information concerning the commencement of regular hostilities, together with the reactions of Congress. Mr. Reed is of the opinion that this unhappy development will lead to an increased vigilance of all troops stationed at the frontier forts, and consequently give us greater safeguards. Others fear Colonel Kearny's batallions and those at Fort Laramie will be deflected to the south, leaving us more exposed to Indian and Mormon depredations. Most, however, are of the opinion that we will be little affected, and manifest great confidence in General Taylor's ability to bring the unfortunate conflict to a rapid conclusion. Mr. Donner has no special fondness for Texas, but feels the General will extricate himself in a manner honorable to the American arms, and one that will bring additional luster to a name already greatly endeared to his admiring countrymen.

We are frequently visited by members of the Cow or Kaw or Kansas tribe, as they are variously called—a miserable, degraded looking people who continuously beg for "hog," by which they mean bacon. Many look to be on the edge of starvation, and seem ready to eat anything that doesn't eat them first! When an ox belonging to some unlucky emigrant died of prostration, it had no sooner been unchained than an old Indian was at work with great vigor, skinning and cutting it up for food. He hacked away large pieces of dripping flesh and piled them on the willing shoulders of his squaw to be carried to their wigwam. The face of the old copper-skin was lighted up in a manner that showed how elated he felt at this miraculous wind-fall. Yesterday evening some of us spied a small company of Indians in the valley upon our right, and went there to pay a call, having the honor of being received by Hachingo, a Kansas chief, together with two warriors and their squaws and children. They all sat cross-legged upon platforms raised about two feet from the ground and draped with smoke-colored skins. The chief cradled an ancient rifle against his chest, but seemed not to understand the use of it very well. His face was painted red, and his hair entirely shorn away save for a small scalp-lock at the top. He wore a showy medal of Jefferson suspended about his neck; this, his rifle and a few shaggy ponies seemed to constitute his earthly estate, but he was obviously revered as a leading citizen. Hachingo looks to be about 50 years of age, with a strikingly handsome profile, yet without the nobility of Mr. Cooper's Mohicans. The squaws and children were filthy and miserable looking beings, and one of the mothers was busy plucking lice from the heads of her children and cracking them between her teeth. These are, apparently, a prairie delicacy, for she gave frequent grunts of satisfaction while she dined.

Mrs. Keyes is rapidly failing, and Margaret Reed is no longer able to attend properly to her needs, as she suffers terribly from one of her migraines, which shows no sign of abatement. Virginia Reed has proved herself a thoughtful and surprisingly able nurse for the pair of them, and Mr. Bryant has applied his skill to their sufferings. His medical study was limited, however, and he chiefly believes in the herbal applications, which can do little good to a woman simply worn out by her long life, and unwilling to see it continue. The remainder of our immediate acquaintanceship and our own relations remain in good health, though the children have had a fit of costiveness that required ample doses of Epsom's salts. A German woman, Mrs. Keseberg, must soon be delivered of a child, and endures great discomfiture through the jolting of the wagons. The poor woman has already one small child to care for, and I made some effort to distract the pretty little thing, but Mr. Keseberg let it be known that this was his wife's exclusive obligation. He is a proud man, and his squaw has much to bear from him.

Where we are presently encamped, the water is fresh and plentiful and makes a pleasing music to soothe us to sleep. The green-coated frogs are heard in great numbers among the plashy pools and reedy margins of the stream, and the voice of the whip-poor-will runs along every nerve of my body, even to my finger ends, like the vibration of a harp string. From the rich melody he pours forth, I guess he is seeking a wife, and I have advised him to proceed no further without a mate, as brides are said to be scarce in California, and he will want one to work for him, keep his nest and bear his young.

3

near the Blue-Earth River
Sunday, May 24th, 1846

Again we have had a Sabbath with no rest for man or beast, traveling today over broken country but with numerous streams and good, abundant grass. The weather is clear and warm, and two cattle have died of the heat.

Last Tuesday, shortly before dawn, an event occurred which is worthy of being chronicled—namely, the birth of twin boys to Mrs. Wallace Hall. Luckily, there was an attending physician, as Dr. Rupert of Independence had ridden out for a last few days with a brother, a consumptive invalid, who is attempting to make the journey to California with the hope of being improved in his health. Dr. Rupert gave his name to one of the new-born, and the name of our worthy leader, Colonel William H. Russell, was bestowed upon the other. We were unable to partake in the celebration of this event, however, for while the twins were making their appearance a number of our cattle strayed off into the prairie, and when the main body moved out we were obliged to remain behind to seek them. Mr. Burns, a blacksmith, also wandered into the prairie and got himself plentifully lost. Distances are singularly difficult to reckon in these treeless stretches, and swells in the land can instantly cut off familiar landmarks. When taking a turn about the garden, one is advised to keep a compass by his side!

After gathering up our wandering cattle we traveled hard to catch up with the caravan, making camp only late at night near Soldier's Creek, where we had originally expected to rendevouz when we left Independence. The stream is called Soldier's Creek from the circumstance that several years before the time of our encamping there, a party of Indian traders and trappers had smuggled into the country a quantity of whisky. They were pursued by a company of U.S. dragoons, who overtook them at the place we were then at, and knocked in the heads of the barrels. If was for that reason, according to some of our party, that the fishes there were unable to swim in a straight line.

All had expected to reach Soldier's Creek sooner, but crossing the Kansas had consumed most of Monday, for it was deemed imprudent, in consequence of a threatened rain, to attempt a fording. The only available ferry boat, whose captain answered to the name of Tall Charles, could accommodate but a single wagon at a time, and it was tedious work to get our large party across. The task was somewhat diminished by the fact that a few hours before this Mr. Dunleavy, with a large company of wagons, had resolved to remain behind in consequence of being dissatisfied with the organization of the company. The ferryman's wife was a Kansas squaw who seemed to possess far more intelligence than most Indian women. She had been taught to read and to write a little at a Methodist mission, although the knowledge she had there acquired, she had for the most part forgotten. We saw many other Kansas about the ferry, some of whom were dressed in savage finery and geegaws, but the most of them appeared to be very poor, filthy, and covered with mud. They had all brought their eternal hunger with them.

We have recently passed a deserted village of the Indians, situated about a quarter of a mile from the usual traveled way. The huts were constructed of the bark of trees, secured to upright poles, with cross-timbers running up like the rafters of a house. Externally, these habitations were not unlike some of the humble and low-roofed cabins occasionally seen on the borders of our Western States. A few miles farther we sighted a similar group of dwellings, but this time thickly occupied. One of the local citizenry was proudly disporting the scarlet uniform of a British soldier, and it was not thought prudent to inquire too precisely how he acquired it, or to ask after the health of its previous owner. A little girl who was perhaps his daughter had on a scarlet blanket with two shades of pink ribbon stitched on it, leaving a little of the blanket to appear between the stripes. The edges of this colorful garment were ornamented with green ribbon, and the whole looked very well.

For some days we have had a permanent troop of Kansas at our side and at our heels, with a constant chorus of "Hog! Hog! Hog!" One of them has repeatedly tried to bargain for Mrs. Thornton's favorite parasol, but has only a pair of stiff and badly made moccasins to offer in exchange. The Reeds had a shock upon determining that the braves trying to strike a trade for Virginia's pony expected the pretty maiden riding it to be included in the bargain. She is now confined by day to the safety of the Reeds' capacious family wagon. Our bronze companions are very poor and some of them wont to steal what they are not given, so that we have seen fit to employ an agent to keep them under control. This good gentleman is called Ki-he-ga-wa-chuck-ee, and he receives a daily ration of flour and bacon for his services. Through him and his plump, jolly wife we have learned a taste for a farinaceous prairie root with a flavor more agreeable than that of the potato. It is especially delicious when buried in the fire to roast, then peeled of its charcoal skin.

We have experienced several refreshing showers along the way, which made the green of the prairie grass flash with the rich light of emeralds, and the wildflowers seemed all to turn their faces up to receive the cooling spray. On Thursday, however, we confronted a storm of alarming proportions, the kind which can sweep across the prairies with the swiftness and force of a typhoon at sea. In a brief period the sun was obscured far more thoroughly than during the modest eclipse which visited us early in our journey. A green haziness began to fill the atmosphere and the whole distance between the moving clouds and the earth, throwing a sort of disastrous twilight upon everything below. Blinding explosions of lightning, followed by sharp peals of thunder, were observed at length to leap from cloud to cloud, like the advance columns of approaching armies. A murmuring sound of an extraordinary nature was heard in the west, which became each moment more distinct, as of marshalling hosts rapidly preparing for dreadful attack. In a very few minutes, a brilliant flash of lightning and a deafening crash of thunder gave the signal for a general and terrible engagement. The wind blew a tremendous blast, which laid the weeds and grass prostrate to the earth, and immediately the air was filled with flying leaves and twigs, swept before the rapidly advancing tempest. As the winds passed on, heaven's artillery at once seemed to open from every cloud, and the earth was deluged with pitiless torrents of rain. Flash followed flash in rapid succession, casting a lurid glare upon every object; and thunder warred with thunder in a manner that awed every faculty, hushed every emotion and feeling but that of the sublime. The clouds rolled majestically forward and at length passed far away to the east— the thunders becoming less and less distinct, until they were only heard in low, rumbling sounds, although the lightning at intervals was still seen sparkling along the frayed selvages of the clouds. The declining sun at length re-appeared, and a most beautiful rainbow hung over it, as a symbol that the elemental strife was at an end and the heavens once more at peace. In the country through which we travel, the ways of nature often give cause for wonder at their breathtaking variety.

We have lately passed pleasant hours with Mr. Alphonso Boone, a grandson of the celebrated Daniel Boone, and a brother-in-law of ex-Governor Boggs. At his inspiration many of the men have been amusing themselves by target-shooting with the rifle, in preparation for the buffalo. A group of Rocky Mountain trappers who passed us recently, heading east with their rich store of pelts, informed us that on the Nebraska, some 200–300 miles ahead, we should see immense herds of the bison (as they are properly called) and live on the fat of the land. This would, indeed, provide a welcome variation on our routine bacon, biscuit and beans.

Our party has dwindled again, with the loss of 13 wagons, near half of which belonged to Mr. Gordon, of Jackson County, Missouri, who separated from the main caravan on the grounds that the company was too large to move with the necessary celerity. We are considerably behind the recommended schedule, but it is hard to imagine pushing the poor oxen any harder, lest even more drop in their tracks.

We find fewer flowers now, but I have gathered a curious specimen of lady-slipper *(Cypripedium pubescens)* whose blossom

114

is divided into two equal parts by a membraneous partition. Mr. Stanton agrees that it is a noteworthy oddity of the Western wilderness, and took care to preserve several specimens of his own.

With the exception of Mrs. Keyes and her daughter, all the Springfield emigrants are well, but many in the train are sick, perhaps due to drinking unclean water, and the services of Mr. Bryant are much in demand, especially now that Dr. Rupert has bid farewell to his brother and returned to Independence. We are encamped on the open prairie with very little fuel, and much of that too damp to be fired. About a mile distant from here Mr. Denton found a dead elm, which was cut up and distributed among our friends. Elitha has acquired an adoring beau in the eldest son of Patrick and Peggy Breen. He is a handsome, sturdy boy of 14 who can already do the work of a man, and is often obliged to, as there are so many in his family to be provided for. Despite our unaccustomed and often very wearisome circumstances, the rhythms of life continue to regulate themselves as they are wont to do elsewhere.

4

WHERE THE KANSAS JOINED THE BIG BLUE, THE WATER HAD RISEN nearly twenty feet with the spring flooding, and the ford looked more than two hundred yards wide. Colonel Russell and George Donner had ridden to the edge of the bluff and stood staring down at the bloated stream.

"We'll never roll across," Colonel Russell said. In his voice was more than dejection at encountering this sudden natural obstacle to their line of march. There was also the weariness that came from wrestling with the dissensions and strife that repeatedly flashed like wildfire along the train, just when harmony seemed to have been reestablished. He was accustomed to lead, became more and more expansive as the sphere of his authority increased, but was unaccustomed to having his decisions put to such quibbling tests by any mother's son who could raise $21.67 for a yoke of oxen.

"Maybe we could caulk the wagons and swim them across."

Russell shook his head. "No, the current's too strong, and a lot of the oxen are green. They'd panic and capsize the whole shebang, lock, stock and barrel. We'd lose half the wagons, sure as shootin'. Half the teams, too."

"Then we'll just have to wait until she goes down."

"That could take a week or two, and like as not we'd have us a real mutiny on our hands by then. We ought to be to the Platte by now, and a lot of folks are itchy already." He stroked his great mustache, curled the tips between finger and thumb, seeking reassurance from the luxurious growth.

A damp wind raced up the bluff, but the noon sun scorched the men's faces, and George Donner mopped his forehead with a linen handkerchief. "What if we built a raft?" he asked.

"A raft?"

"Our own ferry. It couldn't take more than a couple of days, and it beats sittin' bellyachin' around until the water goes down. Keep folks busy, too."

"Them as can," Russell qualified. "There's a lot of sick folks among us." He was thinking aloud, weighing the notion, testing its chances for ratification.

"It won't take that many," George Donner assured him. "Jacob and I could do it alone, with a few younger fellows to haul timber for us. Fell a couple of cottonwoods and hollow them out like Indian canoes, then build a platform between them to hold the wagons. We're lucky there's so much good timber." He pointed to the riverbank below them. "Look over there. There's cottonwoods near forty feet high, and they're easy to work."

"Well," Russell hesitated, "I reckon we could maybe give it a try." He was divided between his own instinct to give a good plan his immediate endorsement and the knowledge that there were members of the company who would oppose whatever idea was put forward, out of pure and unadulterated contrariness. Furthermore, they expected to have their say about every bend in the trail. "But we'll have to put it to a vote," he reflected.

"Why not? And those that don't cotton to the idea can grow wings and fly across."

Russell laughed. "Some's got enough hot air to make it without wings."

"Then more power to 'em, I say."

"Mr. Donner, you're the kind of man I like. We'd get to California a damned sight sooner if we had more like you and your brother and Mr. Reed and less of these dadblamed Jacksonians."

George Donner was flattered by such a compliment, a little awed that this respected politician would single out the Springfield emigrants for special praise. He stammered his acknowledgment.

"Well, we'd best be heading back, Mr. Donner. Folks will be wanting some report." When the two men had mounted their horses and turned from the bluff, Colonel Russell added, "I think I'd better do the recommending, sir. That'll give it more weight."

IN CAMP, THE WOMEN TOOK ADVANTAGE OF THEIR DELAY TO catch up with the washing that had accumulated for weeks. Copper pots and zinc tubs were dragged from the wagons, filled with water hauled a bucket at a time from the nearby creek, and set to boil. By late afternoon clothing and bedding were spread out to dry on every bush and grassy hummock within a hundred yards of the camp, like a shattered rainbow.

Two men exploring a few miles to the west discovered a swarm of bees in an oak near the river, and built a fire to smoke them out. They returned to camp with singed eyebrows and three buckets of wild honey. Mr. Bryant picked several bushels of prairie peas and distributed them among some of the women, together with spices for pickling. He rapped lightly at the entrance to Reed's palace wagon, in case the ladies of the family were napping.

It was Tamsen Donner who appeared, and the deep lines between her eyes told him that the situation was still acute.

"Mrs. Reed is feeling a little stronger," Tamsen told him, "but her mother cannot last much longer."

"Can I be of assistance?"

She shook her head. "They are both sleeping, and I will watch with them. But you might see to the Thorntons. Both seem to have caught a chill during the night."

"I left some peas and pickling spices with one of your pretty daughters," Bryant said.

"I'm much obliged to you." She smiled, and Bryant was struck by how young she seemed then—scarcely older, in fact, than the girl with whom he had just spoken at the Donner encampment. Though she was certainly not plain and her features were well formed, Mrs. Donner could never have been called pretty. On the other hand, when her eyes brightened as they brightened now, she was suddenly transformed, as though a spell had been lifted, and her beauty then was remarkable. Mr. Bryant tipped his hat, not merely in farewell, but in tribute to this singular metamorphosis.

THE MEN WORKING ON THE RAFT CHRISTENED IT THE BLUE River Rover. When the river continued to rise, the turbulent current seething with driftwood, they abandoned their efforts, but when the water fell fifteen inches overnight, they voted to resume them again.

FRANCES POURED WATER INTO TIN CUPS AND PASSED THEM TO her guests.

"The tea is a little weak today," she said, and dropped a piece of loaf sugar into the murky liquid. Patty Reed immediately scooped hers out and popped it into her mouth.

Offended at such ill-mannered behavior, Frances said, "Your Gran is dying."

"She is not," Patty shrilled.

"She is. Everybody knows she is."

"She is not. She's going to stay with the angels." Patty hugged her wooden doll tightly and sucked noisily at the sugar lump.

"You have to *die* to go to the angels," Frances explained.

Patty had begun to cry, and the other children grew restless. Seeking to give them a more neutral topic of conversation, Frances raised the wagon sheet and peeked out. "I do declare," she sighed, "It's going to rain again. I do find the rain most *boring,* don't you?" Her cousin Mary nodded and grabbed for another lump of sugar, while Eliza emptied her cup on Georgia's head. "Rain!" she shouted.

WRAPPED TIGHTLY IN HIS CASHMERE SHAWL, JESSY THORNTON hunched over his journal and in a fine, sloping hand completed his description of the terrible storm that had visited the camp the preceding night. "Eventually the rain slackened," he wrote, "and the thunder became less and less distinct, dying away in low sullen growls, far off to the southern horizon, and leaving me with a sense of my own infinite nothingness. When I considered the Deity as careering upon the storm, and riding upon the wings of the wind, while the terrible lightnings seemed to struggle, that they might escape from his hand and descend upon a guilty world, I was tempted to think, for a moment, that I was too insignificant, as compared with the immense objects that concern the Deity, and engage his attentions, to receive any portion of his observant regard."

MILT ELLIOTT RESTED HIS HEAD LIGHTLY ON HIRAM'S CHEST, and could feel the warmth of the sun radiating from his skin. Hiram reached down to pull a slender blade of grass from Milt's hair, pressed it to his lips and tried to blow a tune, but the grass split and the rude noise made them both laugh.

"You're a nice partner," Milt said, "a mighty sweet partner."

"Think so, do you?"

"I'd not be goin' to California with you if I didn't think so."

"Maybe you was expectin' to spark some pretty girls along the way," Hiram teased.

"What do I need pretty girls for?" Milt asked.

"Maybe to wash your socks?"

"I'll wash my own, thank you very much, and boil my own beans if I have to."

"Mine, too?"

"If you treat me right."

"How's that?"

"Just the way you been treatin' me, partner. Just don't ever stop." Milt rolled his head to the side and drank in the heavy perfume of sun and sweat and grass. "I'd like that just fine," he added.

WHILE HIS WIFE LOOKED HELPLESSLY ON, HER HANDS KNOTTED rigidly in her lap, James Reed held the old woman's writhing body to the bed, wondering from what dark and secret reserves she had commanded this fierce animal strength, this ultimate defiance. She might have been wrestling with the angel of death, her body arching like a strip of tensile steel, arms and legs flailing murderously at her assailant. Her eyes were clenched shut and no sound escaped her lips, no energy was wasted that could be marshaled for this mortal combat. She would, from time to time, pause in the struggle, and when James Reed felt her muscles slacken, he eased his grip, but she was only gathering her strength, perhaps seeking to trick her invisible enemy into thinking she was defeated, and then she lashed out at him with fresh fury. When the old woman was briefly still, Tamsen leaned forward to rub her forehead and temples with a cloth soaked in a mild solution of witch hazel. From where she sat, the face of Mrs. Keyes was inverted, and when her toothless mouth clamped in bitter determination, it seemed to be smiling coyly. Then, as Tamsen watched, the mouth collapsed inward, with a great rush of foul-smelling air. Slack and wasted, it resembled an empty leather purse or a crumpled, discarded glove.

"SCHNELLER," KESEBERG DEMANDED. "FASTER!"

Phillipine clawed at his knees for balance and he clamped her shoulders, jerked her crouching body forward.

"Tiefer!" he ordered, but released her shoulders when she made choking noises and then began to gag.

JESSY THORNTON SHARPENED THE NIB OF HIS PEN, MIXED MORE ink, and completed the entry: "The morning dawned clear, cloudless and peaceful, and every living creature seemed to offer thanks to the gentle heavens. The wood thrush, a hermit of the thick and tangled forest, poured forth its wild, sweet notes from the border of the stream, overshadowed by the dense foliage of boughs, so thick and dark, that the rays of the summer's sun seldom penetrated there. With the genial warmth and the verbal breeze there mingled the songs of countless other feathered choristers, including the cheerfully clownish mockingbird. Prairie hens cooed merrily along the hillside."

THE GRAVE WAS DUG AT THE TOP OF A GENTLE SLOPE CROWNED by an oak tree, sixty yards from Alcove Spring Creek. A few days before, James Reed had carved his name in a boulder near the bubbling spring, and now he carved the name of his mother-in-law into the living oak. Milt Elliott and Hiram Miller fashioned a coffin from the trunk of a cottonwood, the joints tightly beveled, and John Denton cut a stone that was securely planted at the foot of the grave. The crude but bold lettering read "Mrs. Sarah Keyes D I E D May 29, 1846, *Aged* 70." Tamsen Donner assisted Margaret Reed in washing the corpse, then clothing it in a black silk dress, and they made a fragrant cushion of wild flowers against the pale wood before the body was lowered into the coffin. At two o'clock in the afternoon the funeral procession advanced slowly from the wagons to the rise where the grave gaped rawly in the earth. The Reverend Mr. Cornwall reminded the mourners seated on the grassy hillside that the deceased had been born, like the nation itself, in 1776, and that the journey on which they were embarked was a fulfillment of that historic moment, even as the loving children and grandchildren of Sarah Keyes were the fulfillment of her earthly life. But, he admonished them all, they must not neglect to seek for another and better country, where neither sickness nor death could hold dominion. That evening Jessy Thornton wrote in his journal, "Death in the wilderness—in the solitude of nature, and far from the busy abodes of men, seemed to have in it more than the usual solemnity."

5

Big Blue River
May 31st, 1846

Our Springfield company has suffered a sorrowful diminishment in the death of Mrs. Sarah Keyes, the mother of Margaret Reed. Her mortal remains were laid to rest on Friday, May 29th, 1846, in a simple but touchingly beautiful ceremony delivered by the Reverend Mr. Cornwall. There can have been but few among us who did not think of loved ones dear and departed and now left behind to rest unattended in their beds of clay. Mrs. Keyes was born in Virginia in the same year as the American Republic, and richly fulfilled her three-score-and-ten. Her sylvan grave is situated on a hillside a short distance from the customary trail, beneath the sheltering boughs of a magnificent and ancient oak tree. Here the iron wheels of later travelers will not disturb her resting place, but it will be visible to all, and may perhaps afford to some a timely reminder of the perils that await us all on this earthly journey. Mrs. Keyes had failed steadily for the last three weeks, and during that time was a great trial to her daughter, but those who knew her well will remember her wonderful spirit and her innumerable kindnesses. It was the desire to assist her daughter and to be reunited with her youngest and cherished son, Caden Keyes, that sustained her. She had hoped to encounter him on his return from Oregon.

At the time of Mrs. Keyes' final agony we were encamped near a crystal stream that flows into the Blue just above the fording. Exploring its mazy course Mr. Edwin Bryant encountered, approximately a mile from camp, a large spring of water, as cold and pure as if it had just been melted from ice. It gushes from a ledge of rocks which compose the bank of the stream, and its waters fall ten feet into a natural basin. It is sheltered by a shelving rock, over which tumbles a beautiful cascade of water, and it was this unusual natural formation which led Mr. Bryant to give the place the name of Alcove Spring.

The solemn experience we have recently endured has diminished our spirits, and nature has not greatly alleviated them. Our march to the Big Blue was very fatiguing, with the wagons frequently stalling in mudholes and crossings of the small branches. Three or four hours were strenuously occupied in fording a single diminutive tributary. The banks on the eastern side were so steep that the wagons required to be let down with ropes and the teams were doubled, sometimes quadrupled, in order to draw them up the other side. No sooner were these labors behind us than we received reports that the usual fording place on the Big Blue River (where it flows together with the muddy Kansas) was completely flooded out, and we were in camp for most of five days while a raft was constructed. This sturdy and jolly bark was christened the Blue River Rover, and it roved not a little with the fierce current. Yesterday, one of the first wagons to be ferried across was nearly capsized when the Rover struck a submerged log. Today, the men have been in the icy water since early morning, assisting to get the remaining wagons and the animals across, and I fear many more will be taken with chills and fevers in consequence. In the late afternoon the weather turned uncomfortably cool, with a raw wind from the northeast. This is especially distressing to the women and children, most of whom are thinly clad and ill-prepared to resist the effects of such sudden changes.

We have also had a series of severe thunderstorms, but these occurring chiefly in the night, when they create a most awe-inspiring pageant in the heavens and fill the air with a sulphurous stench. The contrariness of the weather has reawakened agues that most travelers thought they had left behind in Ohio and Indiana. Many are indisposed, and many more are ill-disposed as a result of the perpetual vexations, the long time in camp, and frequent dissatisfaction with the organization of the company. Tempers are wont to erupt, and today two men fought by the riverbank as the result of a simple confusion (easily remedied) about the sequence of the crossing—attacking each other first with words, then with fists, and finally with knives. They were separated by friends without serious injury to either, but their battle has not helped the general mood. We are camped now a little more than a mile from the Blue, the last wagons having made the crossing shortly before nine o'clock in the evening, and hope to have a good day of prairie travel tomorrow, which should relieve some of the frustration suffered by the impatient.

Since we entered Pawnee country the soil has become more sandy, and the landscape is of unsurpassed loveliness. There are few trees, but the earth is lushly adorned with a heavy coat of green grass, and in the bottoms along the Blue River there was an abundance of wild grapes, though far too green yet to be eaten. Wolves often howl about the camp at night, and a cowardly pack so severely chewed at the legs of a little calf that it was necessary to put the poor animal out of its misery. On the open prairie we have sighted large numbers of tawny antelope, and several hunters have given chase, but the creatures are fleet as the wind and quickly outdistance the horses. Apparently we must wait for the buffalo to supply us with fresh meat, unless someone can provide a recipe for making the humble mosquito into a tasty repast. Some say they have killed ones big as turkeys, but with my own eyes I have seen none larger than ordinary sparrows, and scarcely worth the trouble of stuffing and roasting.

6

BEFORE THE WAGONS WERE EVEN UNDER WAY, THE TWO MEN WHO had fought the previous day by the river had resumed their violent quarrel. They had traveled together from eastern Kentucky, bickering and squabbling without interruption for an entire month. One owned the wagon, and felt this entitled him to make all the important decisions, since it contained their worldly goods and supplies for the trail. The other, who owned the oxen, claimed priority because without his teams those same goods and supplies would not be rolling west.

The owner of the oxen now refused to chain up. "These here oxen are my inalienable right," he claimed, "and they'll not be pullin' no damned wagon 'til it's clear who's boss of this outfit."

"Ain't no doubt," the other told him. "I'm boss of this little outfit."

"Then you can pull your own wagon."

"It's too heavy!"

"Well, ain't that a purty mess."

"And it's too heavy 'cause it's got so much of your rubbishy truck in it."

The owner of the wagon began to heave boxes up and tumble them onto the ground. He threw after them a pile of soiled clothing and a cracked whiskey jug.

"Keep your filthy hands off my private property!"

"Keep your greasy mitts off my wagon, you motherless bastard!"

Knives flashed again, and James Reed sprinted from his wagon to wrestle the weapon from one of the men, while George Donner pinned the other's arm behind his back.

"There'll be no more of that," George whispered in the struggling man's ear. "No more of that, do you hear?" The calm, low whisper seemed to deflate the man's wrath quicker and more effectively than a shout.

"He was messin' with my private property," the man whined, but when George released his arm, he spun about and said with a snarl, "Besides, nobody give you the right to play sheriff!" The man's rancid breath, like that of a panting hound, sprayed George's face.

"Gentlemen!" James Reed warned. "You will keep your quarrels to yourselves."

"We've got an inalienable right to do what we damned please. Ain't nobody got the right to go interferin'."

"You've not got any rights," James Reed cautioned him, "when you start throwing knives around in the middle of a crowded camp. May I remind you that there are women and children present?"

"It's nobody's business . . ."

"It's everybody's business," George Donner interrupted, "and if you don't like it you can strike out on your own."

"Or you can stay here," Reed suggested, "and cut each other to ribbons for all we care. You can eat each other alive, but you'll not be disturbing the peace of honest folks who just want to get on with things."

"Me, I wouldn't like to have to get through Pawnee country alone," George added. "I wouldn't like to see my hair hanging from some savage's belt."

The two combatants looked uneasily at each other. "Tryin' to scare us?" one of them asked.

James Reed shook his head. "No. Just trying to make sure you understand the rules."

"What rules would those be, I'd like to know?"

"The rules that are necessary to ensure the general welfare of the company. The rules that give decent people the right to protect themselves from shenanigans like this. Those are the rules I'm talking about, and you can take them or leave them, gentlemen." His forced politeness made clear that it was growing harder for him to keep his own anger in check, and as he spoke he flicked his glossy boots with a riding quirt.

For now, at least, the two Kentuckians seemed to prefer to accept Reed's rules. They continued to swear at each other, almost out of habit, but moved together to chain up the oxen.

Tamsen was frying thick slices of ham when Frances came running toward the fire, her voice shrill with fear as she shouted, "Mama! Mama!"

Pushing the skillet aside, Tamsen made a circle of her arms, held Frances tightly against her and felt the child's heart race with terror.

"What is it, Frances? Tell mother what's wrong."

The girl's breath jerked as she said, "Two dead babies!"

Tamsen held her at arm's length, her hands resting protectively on the child's shoulders, but her face showed she had little patience for foolishness.

"Have you been dreaming?" she asked.

"No, Mama, there's two dead babies in the woods." Her eyes seemed vast, and they had begun to fill with tears.

"Now, Frances, you children must stop making up tales and frightening each other with them.

"It's *not* a tale," Frances whined. "It's not!" She stamped her foot, twisted away from her mother's hands. "Two dead babies this big," she insisted, and stretched her arms to make the measure. "Ask Aunt Betsy."

Tamsen looked up to see Betsy Donner approaching, her youngest child clutched against her chest like a bag of flour. She had been running, and panted with exhaustion.

"It's the saddest thing," she announced. "Oh, the sorriest, saddest thing, Tamsen." Betsy let Lewis slide to the ground, and the boy immediately raced for the woods again. "Come back here!" the mother shouted after him, then sighed in resignation and sat heavily on a stump.

"Whatever is the matter?" Tamsen demanded.

"Nothing," Betsy answered, and held her chest while she caught her breath, the loose skin on her neck trembling like a turkey's wattle. "It's just so sad," she added.

"Betsy Donner, will you stop your babbling, please, and tell me what in creation you're talking about?"

"Back there," she explained, and gestured over her shoulder. "The children found them."

Tamsen felt a sudden chill, imagining some unspeakable horror, perhaps the bloodied remains of an Indian massacre or some wicked Mormon rite.

"*What* did the children find?"

"Two graves," Betsy said, with a long, shuddering gulp of air. "Two itty bitty graves. Fresh ones. The younguns found them and set up an awful ruckus."

"Graves," Tamsen echoed, relieved to think the children had not been confronted with mangled corpses, scalped heads.

"Two dead *babies*," Frances insisted, and began to cry.

"Now, child," Tamsen comforted her, "it's just like Mrs. Keyes. She died and we buried her, and it wasn't anything to be afraid of, was it?"

Frances shook her head, sniffled. She had insisted on wearing her best bonnet and gloves to the funeral, and had seemed to accept the event as a necessary, even pleasant, social observance.

Tamsen turned to Betsy and asked, "Will you keep an eye on the ham for me so Coalie doesn't steal it?"

"Yes, if you'll tell my Lewis to come here at once. He's gotten stubborn as a mule."

"Now, come along Frances. You must show me what you've found."

She took the girl's hand and on the far side of the campsite they entered a dense thicket of oak and haw and dogwood. Bushes and a few smaller trees had been uprooted to make a circular clearing that held two graves. Clumps of wild flowers were planted on both but had withered now and drooped against the dried clods of earth. At the head of one of the small graves stood a clumsy cross made of barrel staves hacked apart with an ax, the two pieces secured with bent nails and a length of rusted wire that wound about them like a pea vine. Over the second a stone had been placed with the simple inscription "May 28, 1846" crudely hacked into the porous rock. While Mrs. Keyes was dying, then, the earth beyond the Blue River had been opened to receive these nameless children, and the trees had silently witnessed those who turned away from them, sorrowing and depleted, to continue their weary journey. On Saturday the men under Captain Russell's command had been finishing the Rover, and the corpses planted here belonged to no friend or companion of the trail whose grief could be weighed or shared or perhaps eased with a kind word. Yet the very fact that she did not know and perhaps would never know the identity of these lost children made the clumsy cross and tiny tombstone appear even more pathetic, more feeble in their homely effort to give dignity to death, to distinguish it from simple rot. She wondered suddenly if the children were lying in caskets. If not, the wolves would certainly dig them up again for a midnight feast. Tamsen grappled suddenly, unprepared, with the horror she had checked and subdued as she watched Mrs. Keyes' final agony.

"Frances, dear, why don't you see if you can find some fresh flowers?"

The child seemed at first reluctant to leave, as though sensing the turmoil her mother fought to contain.

"Please," Tamsen coaxed. "The others look so wilted and sad. I'll wait for you. And if you see that naughty Lewis Donner, tell him he must go back to his mother at once."

Tamsen knelt before the parched mounds of earth, tore away the drooping flowers and flung them aside, thinking that those lining Mrs. Keyes' coffin would now be just as wilted, their colors bleached, their perfume drained. She had been grieved by the old woman's death, but it had touched no vital part of her. She remembered Mrs. Keyes' passionate affection for her grandchildren and their friends, the delight she took in telling them stories, in knitting for the infants and advising new mothers on how to cope with colic and teething. In a box near her bed there had always been bright bundles of sugar drops or cookies, tied up in scraps of calico, with which she surprised younger visitors. Tamsen remembered all this, and remembered the dignity with which the old woman hobbled along, her back stiffly erect, with her hands clutching the huge silver handle of her cane; it represented the head of a greyhound with the ears folded sleekly back as though it raced the very wind, and it had been brought from England by her husband, who had also braced shuffling old age with its firm stock of polished ash. Even in the last months, when Mrs.

Keyes had frequently been as disagreeable as a spoiled child, when her mind had wandered indiscriminately through halls cluttered with fraying memories and outrageous fantasies, Tamsen felt for her the sort of patient affection she might have felt for her own mother. The old woman had often combined the grace of contented old age with the mischievousness and waywardness of a child. When she was feeling crotchety, she would rattle her heavy cane against the window of her bedroom to startle the birds she herself had lured there with lumps of suet. Those recollections had flowed vividly in Tamsen's mind as she sat at the dying woman's bedside, reminding herself that the life that was here ending had been full, enriched and enriching, and that a necessary cycle was now being completed. Yet even a few weeks before she could not have imagined sitting so calmly and witnessing the last agonized struggle, with Margaret Reed helplessly remote, sealed away in her own pain, and James Reed for all his self-assurance so clearly in need of a woman's assistance. Even less could she have imagined raising the frail, lifeless arms and legs, sponging and drying and lightly powdering them, and feeling them begin to stiffen. She had held the corpse cradled in her arms while Margaret Reed fumbled to secure the long row of buttons that marched down the back of the rustling silk dress, and the wrinkled cheek against her own was cool and gossamer, a gentle embrace of flesh on flesh. She had not flinched or looked away as the body was lowered into the flower-strewn coffin, the lid shoved into place and nailed shut, the sound of the hammer hideously familiar in its recitative. Whether the spirit that had animated this flesh had ascended to some gentle paradise, as the Reverend Mr. Cornwall had claimed, was irrelevant. That she did not know, could not know, but she knew it was no longer here, for they had buried only the broken vessel that once contained it. The sureness of this conviction astonished her. Life was with the survivors, and an excess of grief would drain the energies they all required to endure the trials ahead. The dead must not drag the living with them into the grave as they had, once, nearly dragged her. Of that much she could be sure, she reasoned, as she watched the pale cottonwood coffin being swallowed by the damp earth like a ship sinking beneath the sea. Her conviction wavered now, stumbled over these anonymous twin graves in the tiny clearing that would soon be reclaimed by brambles and saplings, for here was no necessary cycle completed, but one torn brutally apart, and she felt the return of the desperate anger she had felt weeks before when Mrs. Keyes abruptly surrendered the will to live. When the old woman fought so fiercely in the last hours of her life, Tamsen had to suppress a shout of joyful victory for the renewed struggle. The ragged cross and the rough lump of stone, the size to chock the wheels of a wagon, mocked that joy, and she hammered with her fist at a clod of dried earth, then another, splitting them apart as though each had personally offended her, and with this fury she damned her threatening tears. For tears are salt, she thought, and no amount of them will stir the slightest seed buried here or give back what death has stolen and devoured without pity or discrimination and not even with malice but admitting no resistance, making no exceptions, no smear of blood over the threshhold to turn him away. This she accepted, but the knowledge was not surrender; appraising her opponent's ruthless, uncompromising dominion only nurtured her defiance. He would have to fight for his victories: this was the message she hammered with clenched fists into the raw earth.

"LEFT AND ONE AND TWO. NOW RIGHT AND ONE AND TWO. That's it. Arms a little higher. Turn and one and two. Turn again. Give me your arm now. Left and one and two. Right and one and two and turn."

With one hand Elitha lifted her skirt a few inches, held it to the side and flourished it to emphasize the turns.

"Wonderful!" John Denton said. "Wonderful!" He was breathless, but there was a merriment in his voice that had not been present since they left Independence. "Don't forget now. That's it. Left and one and two. Give me your arm."

Milt Elliott's harmonica wailed the simple melody over and over, while the dancers' feet kicked a swelling cloud of dust into the air. It mingled with smoke from the cooking fire, until they seemed to be dancing through a bank of fog.

The refrain came to an end, and John Denton bowed low to

his partner, then remained hunched over his knees, catching his breath.

"Again?" Elitha asked.

"I think I'm getting *old,*" John Denton moaned.

"Please?" she begged. "Just one more time."

"Well, if Milt Elliott's lungs can hold out, I guess my poor old legs can, too."

Milt said, "I'm just fine, buddy," and gave him an encouraging wink. "Show us your stuff, Johnny-boy!"

The harmonica wheezed again in brisk 4/4 time, and John Denton took Elitha's arm. "Left and one and two and right and one and two and turn." From the corner of his eye he watched Milt's curly head bob and sway to the bucking rhythm of the music.

THE KENTUCKIANS CONTINUED THEIR QUARREL, AND OTHERS BE-gan to take sides with one or the other, until the whole camp threatened to be divided by their feud. Few really cared how the matter was resolved or which of the two was in the right, but the conflict provided a pole around which their own dissatisfactions could gather—frustrations about the weather, about illness and natural obstacles and the failure to agree on any consistent plan for determining whose turn it was to camp near the water.

Colonel Russell called a general meeting to discuss the problem. "It sticks in my craw," he declared, "to think civilized folks can't make a better job of gettin' along together." But he also admitted that with grass and fuel growing scarcer, it was time to think about reorganizing, and proposed the wagons divide into two groups. The Kentuckians were bound for Oregon, and if the Oregon emigrants pulled out ahead, formed a train of their own, it would be easier to keep the troublesome pair under control.

When no one voiced an objection, Russell asked, "Who'll make it into a motion?"

Jacob Donner raised his hand and drawled, "Do so move."

"I'll second that," called out a lanky farmer bound for Oregon. He'd be glad to be shut of the California lot, who were always going on about the awful winters up north.

The motion carried by unanimous vote, and twenty wagons pulled out in advance of the rest. Among them were Jessy Thornton and his wife Nancy.

Keseberg managed to leap free as his wagon overturned, but Phillipine and Ada were carried with it and then spilled down a muddy ravine in a tangle of boxes and bales and cooking utensils.

"*Lieber Gott!*" Keseberg screamed, and began to kick at the oxen, who bellowed as they struggled to remain upright against the pressure of the twisted chains. "*Scheiss Tiere!*"

James Reed pulled up alongside and quickly surveyed the damage. "My dear fellow," he said, hoping to calm the man's hysteria, "you're lucky to have a broken wagon tongue. Otherwise, the oxen might have been thrown into the ravine, and their legs are a mite harder to mend."

"Wagon tongue?" the German repeated. "*Ach, Du lieber Gott,* where do I get a wagon tongue in the middle of nowhere?"

"You don't," Reed said bluntly. "You repair the old one or you cut a tree and make yourself a new one."

"I am not a carpenter," he moaned.

"You will learn," Reed assured him.

Margaret Reed raised the wagon flap and called out, "Is Mrs. Keseberg all right?"

"*Maria und Josef,*" Keseberg swore, and scrambled down into the ravine, where Phillipine sat clutching the trembling child tightly against her, the pair of them too stunned to utter a sound.

"My little ones," Keseberg wailed. "What is with you?"

The woman tried to rise, but the child weighted her down, and she sank back into the mud.

"Is something *kaputt,* broken?"

She shook her head.

"Then why are you sitting on your *Arsch* in the mud?"

Keseberg extended his hand to help her, but at the same moment seemed to transfer his wrath from the animals to his wife.

"We have work to do. We have no time to sit around and enjoy the beautiful trees!"

She winced as he drew her up, and pressed a hand against her swollen stomach. Keseberg instantly relented. *"Liebling,"* he said, and wiped a smear of mud from her forehead. "Little darling, my darling little ones," and swept his wife and his child in his embrace, terrifying them with the suddenness of his motions but ending their stupefied shock. Ada began to cry noisily, and Phillipine wailed in sympathy.

"How are they?" Reed shouted from the trail.

"Good, good," Keseberg answered him. "Silence!" he roared to his wife and daughter. "We have much work to do."

The German asked no assistance from the other emigrants, and no one offered it. His teamster, Dutch Charley Burger, cut a tree and worked it into a passable wagon tongue, while Keseberg directed Phillipine's efforts to clean the worst of the mud from their supplies. They caught up with the others late the following evening.

THE ROUGH GROUND TOOK ITS TOLL ON ALL THE WAGONS. Spokes became as loose as rotted teeth, and sprung tire irons made the wheels wobble so badly that cleats loosened and planking pulled apart, but no one stopped for repairs so long as the wagons still moved. Edwin Bryant, like Keseberg, had no choice, for his axletree split like a piece of dry kindling, and he had just unhitched the teams when William Eddy's wagon came into sight.

"Can I be of help?" Eddy asked.

"If you know anything about fixing wagons."

"I reckon I do," Eddy said proudly. "I'm a carriagemaker by trade. William Eddy's the name. My missus and me are from Belleville, Illinois."

The man extended his hand, and Edwin Bryant shook it enthusiastically. "Just the fellow I was waiting for," Bryant told him. "I'll make it worth your while, sir. Just name your customary fee."

"I'm not lookin' for business," Eddy assured him, and his pride seemed offended by the suggestion of payment for helping a traveler in distress.

"But, Mr. Eddy, I'm accustomed to give professional wages for professional services."

"Well . . . ," Eddy hesitated, "I guess we could use the money."

"Then that's all settled," Bryant pronounced, and smiled with relief as he watched the stocky man set to work.

"Should I ask Mr. Bryant to have a look at you?" Tamsen asked Margaret Reed.

"Oh, no," she answered quickly. "It's . . . it's just a female kind of thing, and it will pass." The woman was as pale as bleached flour, and clearly in pain.

"But you need your strength," Tamsen urged her, "and you're not getting any stronger. You get weaker every day."

"I'll be fine," Margaret Reed said, but her voice shook, and Tamsen feared she would begin to weep again. With her long, dark braids and her wide-set eyes, she resembled a frightened child.

"If you will not consent to see Mr. Bryant, then you must accept my doctoring," Tamsen scolded.

"But—"

"I'll hear no argument from you, Margaret Reed."

"Very well," the woman sighed, but seemed relieved to acknowledge Tamsen's domination.

"You will have to show me exactly where the pressure is greatest."

"Here," Margaret Reed whispered, and laid a hand cautiously against her abdomen.

"All I can see there is a lot of black challis wool, and that will have to go."

"But . . . but I couldn't," she stammered. "I really just don't think I possibly could."

Tamsen planted her hands firmly at her waist and said, "Don't be a silly goose. I'm not some bull-whacker or wild man come galloping down out of the mountains. I'm your friend, and I insist you raise your skirts and show me exactly where you feel the worst pressure."

Margaret Reed reluctantly obliged then, timidly lifting the hem of her dress as though about to cross a puddle of water, but looking away when Tamsen pushed the skirt higher and tugged at the mazes of her underclothing.

"Have you been wearing all this the whole time? Ever since we left Springfield?"

"Of course." Her voice made it clear that the question was a foolish one.

"All of it?"

"It's what I always wear," Margaret Reed insisted.

"You've got on more harness and trappings than a circus pony!"

Margaret Reed pushed her skirts down violently, reflexively, and Tamsen ducked from beneath them. "Oh, dear," she said, and stood to hold the trembling woman in her arms. "Oh, dear, dear Margaret, I should never have said such a terrible, wicked thing." She tightened her embrace and waited a moment before adding, "I shouldn't have said it even though it's true," and felt Margaret Reed suppressing her laughter. Then she suddenly laughed aloud, and Tamsen joined her. The wagon seemed to rock as their mirth exploded again and again, leaving them both breathless, gasping for air, and then falling into new fits of laughter as they saw the strained expressions on each other's face.

"I just don't believe it," Tamsen said when they had finally suppressed their hilarity. "Why, you're gussied and gunnied within an inch of your life. It's no wonder you're feeling a little gone."

"But it helps hold the organs in place," Margaret protested.

"The wrong place, maybe. Now get out of all those contraptions and let me have a proper look at you."

When it was done, Tamsen said again, "Now show me exactly where you feel the pressure."

Margaret Reed lifted her skirts, bundled them around her waist, and pointed to a spot a few inches above her groin. Tamsen pressed it lightly with her fingers, and was answered with a sharp cry of pain.

"Are you wearing a pessary?"

"Yes."

"When was it inserted?"

"About three years ago—a few months after Tommy was

born," Margaret Reed whispered. "My womb was still dropped."

"It will have to come out," Tamsen said. "You cannot bounce around on a wagon all day with a pessary inside you and a corset cutting you in half and expect to feel comfortable."

"But my womb . . . ," she started to protest.

"Your womb is probably ulcerated from the pressure, and that's part of what's causing you the pain. Have you been bleeding?"

"Bleeding?"

"Has there been any blood between the courses?"

Margaret Reed hesitated, chewing at her lip, and then blurted, "Well, no, not really blood."

"Well, what then?"

"Just a kind of fluid."

"What *kind* of fluid?" Tamsen persisted.

"Yellowish," Margaret finally answered. "But no blood," she quickly added, and brushed her skirts out as though this closed the subject.

Tamsen ignored the gesture and said briskly, "First you must have a good dose of laudanum. Then we will remove the pessary and check the womb for ulcers. If there are any, they will have to be burned a little with a borax pencil, to seal them. And after a good night's sleep you'll feel reborn."

"But . . ."

"Otherwise, the pain will get worse and you will be even weaker than you are now, and your husband will be worried to distraction and your children neglected. Besides," Tamsen added, "if they have to eat any more of Eliza's biscuits, they'll all turn to stone."

Margaret smiled, but tears streamed freely down her pale cheeks and Tamsen held her again in her arms, rocked her as tenderly as she would have rocked a child wakened by the phantoms of nightmare. "It will all come right," she consoled. "You'll see."

7

We are camped now near a chain of clear pools mercifully left over from the rains, having departed the Little Blue River yesterday to cross the dry stretches to the Platte. Our party has been reduced by 20 wagons in consequence of the separation of the Oregon emigrants, who have formed their own train. It grieved us to part with new friends, who had quickly come to seem like old ones thanks to the shared trials and intimacies of our journey. We shall particularly miss the Thorntons, who offered us many hours of pleasant companionship, but expect to see them from time to time, as they are no more than two or three miles in advance of us. This division in our ranks became necessary because of conflicting interests between the Oregon and California pioneers, and due to the increasing scarcity of fuel and water. We have been compelled to make our first experiments at cooking with so-called buffalo chips, the dried dung which we find scattered in abundance on the prairie, and which produces intense heat when burned. Mr. Thornton caused much amusement when he insisted on classifying this emergency fuel as *bois de vache.*

The soil of this region has grown increasingly sandy since we left the river, and I recently encountered two species of *cacti.* I also observed and took samples of a beautiful five-petalled flower of a deep crimson color, growing upon a creeping vine. Its shape is that of a hollyhock *(Althaea rosea),* but more rigid and more brilliant in coloring. I find no mention of it in Mr. Torrey's catalogue of Western plants.

Pawnees are particularly thick about the area and have a bad reputation for stealing horses and cattle from the emigrants, when not in sufficient force to attack them openly. For this reason, guards are posted near the animals each night. Two handsome braves galloped their swift ponies into camp yesterday, giving some of us a great shock, but it was a peaceable mission after all. One of them spoke tolerable English, and indicated that he and his companion wished to trade buffalo robes for guns and ammunition, but we sent them away unsatisfied, save for a little bacon. Today we were visited by a much larger, fiercer delegation, consisting of 23 warriors mounted on horseback and armed with bows and arrows. As the sun was about to set behind the hills, they appeared upon the top of a distant eminence, between us and the declining light. After reconnoitering our position for a few minutes, they came sweeping down the slope at a quick charge. Despite this threatening approach, there was something in their appearance not exactly warlike. It bore, rather, the insolent assurance of bandits, whose eyes brightened on sight of the spoils they already regarded as wrested from the hands of defenseless emigrants. The men all armed themselves with rifles and went out to meet the raiders, which they ought not to have done, as it would have been far more prudent to make a breastwork of the wagons and await them there. But all went out, with Colonel Russell bravely in the lead, and though the men with arms were somewhat outnumbered, their show of determination and courage did indeed alter the conduct and aspect of the chief of these roving robbers. He instantly changed from the cruel expression he first wore to one of bland and pleasant friendship, made signs that he came in peace, and embraced Colonel Russell. A half-breed, wearing a new hat and a surprisingly clean shirt, then explained in imperfect English that they were a buffalo-hunting party, and had had no success at the chase. They looked much better than either the Kansas or the Shawnee Indians, but were just as troublesome in their begging solicitations for food.

Several of our party have had misfortunes with their wagons. Mr. Keseberg overturned and broke his wagon tongue, requiring nearly two full days to catch up with us again. This morning Mr. Bryant was stalled by a broken axletree, and we feared for his safety at the hands of the Pawnees, but he came into camp shortly before our savage visitors appeared, bringing with him a poor couple from Belleville, Illinois, who had overtaken him as he was about to begin his repairs. Their names are William and Eleanor Eddy, and they have two small children with them. The wife is shy and perhaps rather frightened by the perils that surround her, but the husband is a frank and jolly man, full of self-assurance and manly courage. He is a carriagemaker, and we can all make good use of his skills.

8

south bank of the Platte River
Sunday, June 14th, 1846

Since Monday last we have been following the curving south shore of the Platte River, which the Indians know as the Nebraska. In their tongue, this means "shallow river," and indeed there seems no point at which a man cannot wade across and still keep his knees dry. When first viewed from the bluffs, it appears a mile wide and a foot deep, and the first impression is not so deceptive after all. The water of this stream is so filled with earth and sand that it seems to flow with its belly up, and is scarcely fit for man or beast. After being left to stand for a few hours, it improves somewhat, on account of the yellow sediment falling to the bottom of the bucket, but still remains cloudy and somewhat bitter to the taste. Some say it has to be chewed.

The constant rolling up and washing about of sand effects constant changes in the bed of the stream, and also in the depth of the water, so that entire sandbars can appear and disappear overnight. Yesterday, in the dusk of the evening, several women went a short distance eastward for a dip in the river, even if the water was somewhat thick for such sport. At that point there was scarcely any bank, but tall bunch grass and increasing darkness provided sufficient protection against a "Peeping Thomas," had there been such a one in camp. The sensation of stepping into the stream is one that will not easily be forgotten, for when the foot touched bottom, the bottom began to fall away and there was a hasty scramble for terra firma, with vivid recollections of dreadful stories about quicksand and its unhappy victims. It was only the most courageous (or the most foolhardy) who dared stay in the water and hang onto an anchor of grass. We made a queer looking swimming party, no doubt, as we peered along the river bank, and were reminded of the song:

> Hang your clothes on a hickory limb,
> But don't go near the water!

The river is paralleled with sandy hills known as the Coast of the Nebraska and thinly covered with grasses, but otherwise supporting no vegetation save the hardy cactus, in delightful variety of color and form. At the level of the river itself there is a flat prairie from 2 to 4 miles in width, with saline and alkaline efflorescences whitening the ground in low situations. The soil appears rich despite its unpleasant odors, though timber is thinly confined to the margin of the stream and the numerous islands that interrupt its course. One of these, the so-called Grand Island, extends for so many miles that when we encamped opposite it, neither end was in sight. Beyond the western tip of this mass, the river expands into a broad and shallow stream of nearly two miles in width, but utterly unfit for purposes of navigation. We encountered a miserable party of trappers attempting to transport their costly pelts on bull boats, but they spent most of the time harnessed to the vessels like oxen and dragging them over the resistant sandbars. Some had suffered terribly in their faces from the effects of frost, and one had lost two of his fingers to the fierce winter they had endured.

We have passed numerous sprawling communities of the industrious prairie dog not far distant from the bank of the Platte, occupying from one to 500 acres. Two of the creatures were shot and brought into camp by Mr. Breen, who was curious to have a nearer view of them. In general shape they resemble a puppy, with the head formed like that of the bull dog, but the teeth, feet and tail show strong resemblances to the squirrel. Their color is a dunnish, reddish grey and their size about twice that of a fox squirrel, with whom they also share a remarkable alacrity. Their principal food is said to be prairie grass. Like rabbits, they burrow in the ground, throwing out heaps of earth and often large stones, which remain as a bulwark at the mouth of the tunnel. The entrance to their snug burrows is about 4 inches in diameter, and runs obliquely into the earth about three feet, when the holes ramify in every direction and connect with each other on every side. Milt Elliott and Hiram Miller experimented at pouring water into what seemed an isolated burrow, in the hope that the inhabitants would bolt for dry land and one could be trapped as a pet, but after nearly a hundred bucketfuls they abandoned their efforts. Some kind of police seems to be observed among these sociable creatures; for when human beings approach too near, one of the dogs will run to the entrance of a burrow and, squatting down, utter a shrill bark. At once, the more diminutive of the community (perhaps the wives and children) disappear into their holes, while numbers of the larger dogs squat, like the first, at their thresholds and unite in the barking. A nearer approach causes even this sturdy chorus to disappear in a twinkling, as though turning summersets into their holes. It is singular but true that the screech-owl and the fearsome rattlesnake keep them company in their burrows, rather like hotel guests. I have frequently seen the owl in their midst, and the trappers we encountered informed us that it is common to discover all three in the same hole. The little prairie dog is eaten by the Indians with great relish, and sometimes by the mountaineers, whose famous motto is "Meat's meat."

No one in our party can comment on this Western delicacy, but yesterday we enjoyed our first buffalo, thanks to the skill of Governor Boggs and Mr. Grayson in bringing down two choice cows, whose meat they shared around the camp. It is rich in taste, not unlike that of mature beef, and surprisingly tender considering the animal's rocky appearance. We roasted our steaks over a trench filled with buffalo chips, at which we have now grown very expert. To cook a meal requires about a bushel of dry chips, which burn with an intense, even heat, much like charcoal. They are white as cotton and light as feathers, and some appear to be at least 50 years old.

We have spent today in camp, to give a much-needed rest to the weary and footsore. Many of the two-footed creatures are poorly, and the four-footed have suffered greatly in the last week. The grass is poor in the Platte bottoms, owing to the large buffalo herds that have grazed here, often creating wide paths worn into the soil as smoothly as if cut with a spade. The grass is, in any case, rather sparse, and having been burnt by the sun presents sharp stubs which wear and irritate the feet of the cattle. The men have been busy today treating these afflictions by washing the foot with strong soap, then scraping or cutting away the diseased flesh and pouring tar upon the exposed sore. This operation seems to give the poor beasts considerable relief from their discomfort.

Colonel Russell has been visited by a malarial fever which he has carried in his veins for many years, and two new officers have been elected to his staff. These lieutenants form an emergency committee which is empowered to take command in the event of his being at any time too disabled to make decisions for the company at large. One of these proud new officers is Mr. George Donner of Springfield, Illinois!

Others in our group also suffer from agues and fevers, some from drinking bad water, and the trains ahead of ours seem to be no better off. At noon a horseman rode into camp to make urgent request of Mr. Bryant's medical attentions at one of the forward companies, where a young boy suffers from a badly broken leg.

As the Platte rolls its broad and shallow sheet along the margin of our camp, the setting sun has turned it the color of liquid gold, and the islands around which it ripples are graced with aspens that tremble in the cool breeze that announces the advent of evening. Were the mosquitoes not so tirelessly attentive, the poetry of the little scene would be quite complete.

9

EDWIN BRYANT RECOGNIZED AT ONCE THAT THERE WAS NOTHING HE could do for the dying boy, whose leg had not simply been broken but crushed and mangled when a wagon wheel rolled over it. Swollen and putrefying, with its stench filling the wagon, the leg was wrapped in a strip of faded blue cotton ripped from a woman's skirt. When Bryant unwound it, he saw that the torn flesh was crawling with maggots, and immediately covered it again.

"There is nothing to do but make the boy comfortable," he said to the mother. "He can't last much longer, poor fellow."

"But you're a doctor," she protested, and her voice mingled a whining, pleading tone with a clear note of accusation.

"No," Bryant informed her, "I have studied a little homeo-pathic medicine, and I know something about elementary surgical practices. It is not much, but it is sufficient to tell me your son is dying. I would be better advised to spend my time doctoring your husband." From the horseman who rode out to fetch him, Bryant learned that the boy's father had been prostrated for four weeks by rheumatic fever.

"It's just one of his spells," the woman insisted. "He'll get better. It's my Jamie you've got to help."

"I can't help him," Bryant said. "No one can help him."

The boy was only half conscious, and he gasped noisily for air, as though some invisible weight pressed upon his thin chest. The accident had occurred nearly two weeks before, and the pain and infection had so drained his strength and wasted his body that Bryant was astonished to learn the child was nine years old. He would have taken him for no more than five.

The hysterical woman ignored Bryant's explanation, on her

knees before him and pleading hysterically that he amputate the infected leg.

"It would kill him."

"Cut it off, doctor. Cut it off!"

"Madam, I will not be your son's murderer."

"They had to cut off my brother's leg, and he was good as new," she whined, and then, as though her strength suddenly failed, her head slumped forward against Bryant's knees.

He pulled her roughly to her feet and looked into her twisted face. Distorted by grief and powdered with alkali dust, it might have been the face of a corpse.

"Cut it off," she moaned.

"I will not be your boy's murderer," he repeated in clipped, emphatic syllables, and in response she began to wail like a wounded animal.

A crowd had gathered around the wagon, including several men from trains camped nearby, who had ridden over to visit with friends. One of them pushed his way forward and climbed onto a rear wheel to look into the wagon. He nodded and cheerfully announced, "I can do it."

Bryant looked at the grimy speaker in astonishment. "And who might you be?" he demanded.

"Someone what knows somethin' about operations."

"But the gangrene has spread into the boy's body. There's no surgeon on earth who could save him now."

"I reckon it's worth a try. All he can do is die, and he's doin' that already all by hisself."

"Then why put the poor chap through such unnecessary suffering?"

" 'Cause there's always a chance he might get well. No chance otherwise."

Bryant protested, but the bereaved mother had now transferred all her hopes to this unexpected relief, and she would tolerate no objections. The would-be surgeon, as Bryant heard from his proud, talkative friends, was a French Canadian who worked as drover for one of the families bound for Oregon, and he had once been employed as an orderly in a hospital. He meant well, perhaps, but Bryant did not trust the ardor with which he sharpened the worn blade of a butcher knife, whistling noisily, while his friends lifted the boy from the wagon and strapped him to a packing case. A woman tried to force laudanum into his slack mouth, but it coursed down onto his shirt, and someone suggested holding camphor to his nose. The drover inserted the knife just below the knee, and the tip released a thick gush of pus, but the boy made no sound, and then the man seemed to reconsider, probed the flesh with his fingers, and asked for a length of cord. This he looped around the leg and tied firmly just above the knee. Then, halfway up the thigh, he made an incision with the butcher knife, slicing down to the bone, and set to work with a handsaw. The saw was so dull that the total operation required nearly two hours, and the stump was being wrapped with a flap of skin when the boy died.

Bryant stepped past the weeping mother and reentered the wagon to examine her husband, leaving the man some attenuated solutions and advising him to take them as they were, one at morning and one at evening. He had seen enough of those afflicted with similar diseases on the trail to know they often devoured medicines as the starving devour food, in the belief that greater quantities must produce a speedier cure. He then visited a woman who had dosed herself so heavily with Epsom salts, as a cure for what she called "intermittent fever," that she was completely dehydrated, her skin like brittle parchment. Bryant also consulted with a young man whose ailment he diagnosed as heart disease, leaving him with the faint hope that the Western air might effect a cure. There were others, less seriously ill, for whom he prescribed, and when he had seen the last of them, he decided to accept Jessy Thornton's invitation to visit his former companions at their camp.

The Thorntons were both in exceptionally good spirits, serving him a delightful supper on a white damask tablecloth Nancy Thornton had carefully spread on the grass. In addition to roast antelope and stewed buffalo with wild onions, the feast included the choicest savories she could provide from her rolling larder. After the leisurely meal, the three friends proceeded to the tent of another Oregon emigrant, where the Reverend Mr. Cornwall married Mr. Lard's thirteen-year-old daughter Mary to young Mr. Riley Septimus Mootry. The women of the company had somehow contrived to bake a wedding cake, which they ornamented with slender tapers, and all had put on their choicest finery. The men had even shaved for the festive occasion.

Jessy Thornton could not wholly approve. "It looks so much like making a hop, skip and jump into matrimony," he whispered to Bryant.

The part-time doctor, on the other hand, felt much relieved by the merrymaking, and when a trio of fiddlers struck up a vigorous tune, he asked Mrs. Thornton for the pleasure of a dance.

She pressed her chest and made a vague remark about respiratory congestion, but then accepted the invitation with a girlish smile and a curtsy.

IN HIS JOURNAL ENTRY FOR JUNE 14TH, JESSY THORNTON NOTED that in the several trains scattered within sight of each other along the south bank of the Platte there had been a birth, a death, and a wedding all in one day. On the same Sunday a group of eager American revolutionaries that included William Todd, the nephew of Abraham Lincoln, marched on the tiny cluster of adobe dwellings composing the town of Sonoma, California, and proclaimed it American territory. From the chemise sacrificed by one revolutionary's wife and a petticoat dedicated by another, Todd fashioned a flag consisting of red-and-white stripes, a red five-pointed star, and a bear that most observers took for a hog. There was, however, no mistaking the letters he drew in pokeberry juice, boldly proclaiming the new "California Republic."

It was also on June 14th that Brigham Young arrived at the bank of the Missouri River, near Council Bluffs, with an advance troop of Mormon pioneers; they knelt in prayerful thanks for deliverance from their Gentile persecutors, and entreated the Almighty to continue to safeguard the little nation of Israel. Here the faithful would await the other refugees struggling across the Iowa plains, many of them ill and pushing their depleted supplies in wheelbarrows or handcarts; and their Apostle would deliberate, gazing out over the muddy river, whether it would still be possible to send the first party to Zion in the summer of 1846. Meanwhile, there were repeated alarms about bloodthirsty posses of Missourians on the move to the south, bent on total extermination of the Angels, and about a troop of soldiers detailed to intercept Brigham Young at Mount Pisgah. In fact, the lone officer and three troopers with him came not to massacre but to solicit the Mormon leader, with a deference he was not accustomed to receiving from the government, to lend the strength of his followers to the holy cause of Mr. Polk's quarrel with the Mexicans.

The president had recently concluded that a batallion for the defense of California could be assembled from Mormon volunteers, to strengthen Kearny's Army of the West that was preparing to march to Santa Fe. Polk had come to view New Mexico as the key to California, and a military presence once designed to protect the rich Santa Fe trade was now ordered to produce another bloodless conquest for the Republic. Brigham Young was happy to collaborate with the territorial scheme, for the fees his followers were promised would enrich the Saints' depleted coffers and put an advance party into the western territory while he was waiting for the tardy to catch up. Slowed by an epidemic of mumps, ill-trained, chronically short of supplies, and divided over the degree of loyalty they owed a Gentile commander, the Mormon Batallion lagged far behind Kearny's First Dragoons, and by the time they reached Santa Fe, rebellious and dispirited, Kearny was already marching toward San Diego. His commission had finally been signed, and he answered now to the title of General.

President Polk felt increasingly confident about the success of these diverse territorial maneuvers. To the south, General "Rough and Ready" Taylor and his troops sat securely in Matamoros, on the southern bank of the Rio Grande, having trounced the disciplined army of Manuel Arista at Palo Alto, and the American flag waved an unmistakable warning over a foreign city. Polk was certain the Mexicans would relent in the boundary dispute, as the British had done in Oregon, though the terms of the settlement there threatened to cause the White House acute political embarrassment. The Marine Corps band was entertaining the president and his guests when dispatches arrived with the news that Her Majesty's government was now willing to settle the Oregon boundary at the old 49th parallel, but the heated oratory of "54°40'" threatened to block the compromise. Polk privately acknowledged that his new, extensive commitments in Texas, New Mexico, and California meant that the extreme position would have to be abandoned, and had prepared a contingency plan that would permit him, on the considered advice of his Cabinet, to submit any such proposal to the Senate for their deliberation. The only thorn beneath the rose was his perverse secretary of state, James Buchanan, who now argued as passionately for "54° 50'" as he had once pleaded for a gentlemanly compromise on the 49th parallel. The breeze of presidential ambition had brushed him—the same breeze that General Taylor felt stirring balmily on the Rio Grande. Nonetheless, when Richard Pakenham, the British minister, drove under the White House portico with an official proposal in hand, Polk received him with uncommon enthusiasm, duly forwarding the document to the Senate, where war hawks shrieked but a solid majority instructed the president to accept the offer. On June 15th, when the Donners and Reeds left their rest camp on the Platte, the Secretary of State and the British minister officially signed the convention that concluded the long and often bitter Oregon dispute. With Taylor securely encamped in Mexico, the president could now concentrate his energies on California.

10

THE DONNERS AND REEDS WERE NOONING TOGETHER ON JUNE 16TH when they were joined by seven men who had left Oregon City on March 1st, and were now headed for Independence. The men had gone to Oregon the previous year, and one was a close friend of Caden Keyes, who was reported to have traveled south to California. Despite the obvious sufferings they had endured on their own journey, the men gave an encouraging report of the territory ahead. They had seen few Indians and those all peaceable, and there were plentiful herds of bison. The men had met the advance Oregon caravan west of Fort Laramie, and counted in all more than four hundred wagons for Oregon and California. Tamsen Donner took advantage of the meeting with the eastbound travelers to draft a letter to the *Sangamo Journal,* which Mr. Francis shared with his readers on July 23rd:

> near the junctions of the North and South Platte
> June 16th, 1846
>
> My Old Friend,
>
> We are now on the Platte, two hundred miles from Fort Laramie. Our journey so far has been pleasant, the roads have been good and food plentiful. The water for part of the way has been indifferent, but at no time have our cattle suffered for it. Wood is now very scarce, but "buffalo chips" are excellent; they kindle quick and retain heat surprisingly. We had this morning buffalo steaks broiled upon them, that had the same flavor they would have had upon hickory coals.
>
> We feel no fear of Indians, our cattle graze quietly around our encampment unmolested.
>
> Two or three men will go hunting twenty miles from camp; and last night two of our men laid out in the wilderness rather than ride their horses after a hard chase.
>
> Indeed, if I do not experience something far worse than I have yet done, I shall say the trouble is all in getting started. Our wagons have not needed much repair, and I cannot yet tell in what respects they could be improved. Certain it is, they cannot be too strong. Our preparations for the journey might have been in some respects bettered.
>
> Bread has been the principal article of food in our camp. We laid in 150 pounds of flour and 75 pounds of meat for each individual, and I fear bread will be scarce. Meat is abundant. Rice and beans are good articles on the road; cornmeal too is acceptable. There is so cool a breeze at all times on the plains that the sun does not feel so hot as one would suppose.

We are now four hundred and fifty miles from Independence. Our route at first was rough, and through a timbered country, which appeared to be fertile. After striking the prairie we found a first-rate road, and the only difficulty we have had has been in crossing the creeks. In that, however, there has been no danger.

I never could have believed we could have traveled so far with so little difficulty. The prairie between the Blue and the Platte rivers is beautiful beyond description. Never have I seen so varied a country, so suitable for cultivation. Everything was new and pleasing; the Indians frequently come to see us, and the chiefs of a tribe breakfasted at our tent this morning. All are so friendly that I cannot help feeling sympathy and friendship for them. But on one sheet what can I say?

Since we have been on the Platte we have had the river on one side and the ever varying mounds on the other, and have traveled through the bottom lands from one to two miles wide with little or no timber. The soil is sandy, and last year on account of the dry season the emigrants found grass here scarce. Our cattle are in good order, and when proper care has been taken none have been lost. Our milch cows have been of great service, indeed. They have been of more advantage than our meat. We have plenty of butter and milk.

We are commanded by Captain Russell, an amiable man. George Donner is himself yet. He crows in the morning and shouts out "chain up boys—chain up," with as much authority as though he was "something in particular." John Denton is still with us. We find him useful in the camp. Hiram Miller and Noah James are in good health and doing well. We have some of the best people in our company, and some, too, that are not so good.

Buffaloes show themselves frequently.

We have found the wild tulip, the primrose, the lupine, the eardrop, the larkspur, and creeping hollyhock, and a beautiful flower resembling the bloom of the beech tree, but in bunches as large as a small sugar-loaf, and of every variety of shade, to red and green.

I botanize, and read some, but cook "heaps" more. There are

four hundred and twenty wagons, as far as we have heard, on the road between here and California.

Give our love to all inquiring friends. God bless them.

Yours truly,

Mrs. George Donner

There was no mention of agues and fevers, of the death of Mrs. Keyes, of prairie graves and terrified children and crippled oxen, of drenching rains and winds that flattened the tents, of brackish water or none at all, of quarrel and dissension, of the crumbling authority of Captain Russell, of mud or swollen rivers or gullies where the wagons had to be lowered on ropes and windlassed up the opposite bank, of mosquitoes or rattlesnakes or wolves or coyotes, and there was no reference to the stinging alkali dust that grew increasingly dense as they moved westward along the Platte. In part, Tamsen screened herself from the steadily increasing difficulties of the trail; in part, too, she was calculatedly providing her Springfield audience with the kind of jolly travel report they expected to find in their weekly *Journal,* and which would allay any fears they might have for their distant friends. But in using the exorcism of language to neutralize the horrors that lay behind them, she was also seeking to still her mounting anxiety about what lay before, particularly if they took the unknown route that Mr. Hastings so enthusiastically recommended. "Indeed," she had written, "if I do not experience something far worse than I have yet done, I shall say the trouble is all in getting started." Yet she secretly feared far worse.

The horseman who carried Tamsen Donner's letter also took with him two closely written pages from James Reed to his brother-in-law James W. Keyes, which gave the gentleman's view of their adventures:

South Fork of the Nebraska

Ten Miles from the Crossings

Tuesday, June 16, 1846

To Jas. W. Keyes, Esq. from James F. Reed

Today, at nooning, there passed, going to the States, seven men from Oregon, who went out last year. One of them was well

152

acquainted with Messrs. Ide, and Caden Keyes—the latter of whom he says went to California. They met the advanced Oregon caravan about 150 miles west of Ft. Larimere, and counted in all for California and Oregon (excepting ours) four hundred and seventy-eight wagons. There is in our train 40 waggons, which makes 518 in all; and there is said to be twenty yet behind.

Tomorrow we cross the river, and by our reckoning will be 200 miles from Fort Larimere, where we intend to stop and repair our wagon wheels; they are nearly all loose and I am afraid we will have to stop sooner if there can be found wood suitable to heat the tires. There is no wood here, and our women and children are now out gathering "Buffalo chips" to burn in order to do the cooking. These "chips" burn well.

So far as I am concerned, my family affairs go on smoothly, and I have nothing to do but hunt, which I have done with great success. My first appearance on the wilds of the Nebraska as a hunter, was on the 12 inst., when I returned to camp with a splendid two year old Elk, the first and only one killed by the caravan as yet. I picked the Elk I killed, out of eight of the largest I ever beheld, and I do really believe there was one in the gang as large as the horse I rode. We have had two Buffalo killed. The men that killed them are considered the best buffalo hunters on the road—perfect "stars." Knowing that Glaucus could beat any horse on the Nebraska, I came to the conclusion that as far as buffalo killing was concerned, I could beat them. Accordingly yesterday I thought to try my luck. The old buffalo hunters and as many others as they would permit to be in their company, having left the camp for a hunt, Hiram Miller, myself and two others, after due preparation, took up the line of march. Before we left, every thing in camp was talking that Mr. so and so, had gone hunting, and we would soon have some choice buffalo meat. No one thought or spoke of the two Sucker hunters, and none but the two asked to go with us. Going one or two miles west of the old hunters on the bluffs, and after riding about four miles, we saw a large herd of buffalo bulls. I went for choice young meat, which is the hardest to get, being fleeter and better wind. On we went towards them as coolly and calmly as the nature of the case would permit. And now, as perfectly green as I was I had to compete with old experienced hunters, and remove the stars from their brows, which was my greatest ambition, and in order too, that they might see that a Sucker had the best horse in the company, and the best and most daring horseman in the caravan. Closing upon a gang of ten or twelve bulls, the word was given, and I was soon in their midst, but among them there was none young enough for my taste to shoot, and upon seeing a drove on my right I dashed among them with Craddock's pistol in hand—(a fine instrument for Buffalo hunters on the plains)—selected my victim and brought him tumbling to the ground, leaving my companion far behind. Advancing a little further, the plains appeared to be one living, moving mass of bulls, cows and calves. The latter took my eye, and I again put spur to Glaucus and soon found myself among them, and for the time being defied by the bulls, who protected the cows and calves. Now I thought the time had arrived to make one desperate effort, which I did by reining short up and dashing into them at right angles. With me it was an exciting time, being in the midst of a herd of upwards of a hundred head of buffalo alone, entirely out of sight of my companions. At last I succeeded in separating a calf from the drove, but soon there accompanied him three large bulls, and in a few minutes I separated two of them. Now having a bull that would weigh about 1200 lbs., and a fine large calf at full speed, I endeavored to part the calf from the bull without giving him Paddy's hint, but could not accomplish it. When I would rein to the right where the calf was, the bull would immediately put himself between us. Finding I could not separate on decent terms, I gave him one of Craddock's which sent him reeling. And now for the calf without pistol being loaded. Time now was important—and I had to run up and down hill at full speed loading one of my pistols. At last I loaded, and soon the chase ended. Now I had two dead and a third mortally wounded and dying. After I had disposed of my calf I rode to a small mound a short distance off to see if Hiram and the others were in sight. I sat down, and while sitting I counted 597 buffalo within sight. After a while Miller and one of the others came up. We then got some water from a pond near by, which was thick with mud from the buffaloes tramping in it. Resting awhile the boys then wanted to kill a buffalo themselves. I pointed out to them a few old bulls about a mile distant. It was understood that I was not to join in the chase, and after accompanying the boys to the heights where I could witness the sport, they put out at full speed. They soon singled out a large bull, and I do not recollect of ever having laughed more than I did at the hunt the boys made. Their horses would chase well at a proper distance from the bull. As they approached he would come to a stand and turn for battle. The horses would then come to a halt, at a distance between the boys and the buffalo of about 40 yards. They would thus fire away at him, but to no effect. Seeing that they were getting tired of the sport and the bull again going away, I rode up and got permission to stop him if I could. I put spurs to Glaucus and after him I went at full speed. As I approached the bull turned around to the charge. Falling back and dashing towards him with a continued yell at the top of my lungs I got near enough to let drive one of my pistols. The ball took effect, having entered behind the shoulders and lodged in his lungs. I turned in my saddle as soon as I could to see if he had pursued me, as is often the case after being wounded. He was standing nearly in the place where he received the shot, bleeding at the nostrils, and in a few seconds dropped dead. I alighted and looped my bridle over one of his horns. This Glaucus objected to a little, but a few gentle words with a pat of my hand she stood quiet and smelled him until the boys came up. Their horses could not be got near him. Having rested, we commenced returning to the place where I killed the last calf. A short distance off we saw another drove of calves. Again the chase was renewed, and soon I laid out another fine calf upon the plains. Securing as much of the meat of the calves as we could carry, we took up the line of march for the camp, leaving the balance for the wolves, which are very numerous. An hour or two's ride found us safely among our friends, the acknowledged hero of the day, and the most successful buffalo hunter on the route. Glaucus was closely examined by many today, and pronounced the finest nag in the caravan. Mrs. R. will accompany me in my next buffalo hunt, which is to come off in a few days.

The face of the country here is very hilly, although it has the name of "plains." The weather rather warm—thermometer ranging in the middle of the day at about 90, and at night 45.

The Oregon people tell me that they have made their claims at the head of Puget Sound, and say that the late exploration has made the northeast, or British side of the Columbia, far superior to the Willamette valley, in quality and extent of territory.

Our teams are getting on fine so far. Most of the emigrants ahead have reduced their teams. The grass is much better this year throughout the whole route than the last.

Respectfully your brother,
James F. Reed

Reed was so enthused over the thrills of the buffalo hunt and the superiority of his beloved Glaucus to all other horses in the train that he neglected to tell James Keyes that his mother had died just over two weeks before. Like Tamsen Donner and many of the other emigrants, he was still so dazzled by the novelty and the adventure of their undertaking that as its grimmer realities began to appear he thrust them away, left them at the side of the trail like unwanted baggage abandoned to lighten the load in the wagons.

11

THEY HAD ALL EXPECTED TO ENCOUNTER TREACHEROUS QUICKSANDS, but the lower crossing of the Platte proved surprisingly firm, though fear of sinking into the bottom kept all the wagons moving at a brisk, steady pace. Only the herd animals seemed reluctant to cross the mile-wide channel, and some bolted, seeking the fastnesses of the sand hills behind them. No sooner was the entire party across than a new source of strife divided them. Since striking the south bank of the Platte they had rotated camping places north to south, so that those located nearest the river on a given night would shift to the south side of the corral when the next camp was made, giving the more favorable position to others. Now there were those who maintained the compass still regulated the company, and having camped to the north the previous night, insisted it was their turn for the southern position, which would give them two consecutive nights near the riverbank. Others stormily asserted it to be a foolish notion, and that it was water, not the compass, that established the pattern.

In the turmoil that followed, Colonel Russell tendered his resignation. He was weakened by the malarial fevers that alternately boiled and then froze his blood, and heartily disgusted by the continuous squabbling among the emigrants. Since nearly all of them, whether they followed the dictates of compass or river, blamed the commander for their cumulative misfortunes, the resignation was instantly accepted, together with those of his officers. Governor Boggs was elected as Russell's successor, but there was little enthusiasm in the brief speech he made to the assembly.

Edwin Bryant felt scant confidence that a new administration could function better than the old. He had no partiality to Russell's brand of hell-fire oratory, but thought he was probably a better than average captain, and that no one could be expected to deal effectively with such a rowdy troop, whose bickerings delayed the whole company. For weeks he had been troubled by the fact that they seemed to lag farther and farther behind the schedules recommended in the guidebooks he carried, and which all warned that snows could come early to the mountains that lay across their route. With each slow mile he yearned more for the green valleys of California, but they seemed nearly as remote as they were in Independence. As early as May 24th Bryant had complained to his journal, "I am beginning to feel alarmed at the tardiness of our movements and fearful that winter will find us in the snowy mountains of California or that we shall suffer from the exhaustion of our supplies and provisions. Many have no conception of the extent and labor of the journey before them. They seem to be desirous of shortening each day's march as much as possible and once encamped reluctant to move on."

Bryant confided his concern to James Reed, but referred only briefly to the dangerous mountain crossing, for Reed had no choice, with his numerous family and wagons and hired hands and livestock, but to stick with the main company.

"I guess I'm a little impatient," Bryant said, "and ought to push ahead on my own. There seem to be a few who might be willing to join me—other men without families."

"But I doubt the oxen will stand a faster pace."

"Oh, we'll have to give up the luxury of wagons," Bryant explained. "We ought to be able to trade teams and wagons for a string of good mules at Fort Bernard or Fort Laramie, and pack the rest of the way."

"We will miss your good company, sir," Reed said, and the expression was genuine, for he admired the transplanted Yankee's gentlemanly bearing and his thoughtful judgment.

"And I will miss yours, but at least I can prepare a welcoming reception for you in California."

"We should all be much obliged for that, Mr. Bryant."

"I doubt," Bryant cautioned, "that we can provide wines to equal your famous cellar, but we will make our best effort."

Later in the day eight men rode away from the train with Bryant, pushing rapidly westward to the forts in hopes of striking a speedy bargain for trail-savvy mules, while their teamsters followed with the wagons.

James Reed was disturbed by Bryant's departure, by the man's obvious fears that they were already too far behind schedule to complete the journey safely. It was, he thought, a typical example of exaggerated Yankee caution, but he had read the guidebooks as well, and could easily enough reckon that they were more than two weeks behind schedule. Confident that the time saved through Lansford Hastings's new cutoff would easily cancel the difference, Reed was still uneasy, somewhat irritable, and thus reacted more harshly to Keseberg than he would have done otherwise.

On several occasions since reaching the Platte, the train had passed the corpses of Indians wrapped in buffalo robes and placed on scaffolds where they would be safe from scavengers. In the confusion that followed Russell's resignation and the election of new officers, Keseberg dropped behind, and when he entered camp that evening he proudly displayed a dusty buffalo robe.

Reed was the first to confront him. "May I ask how you acquired that, Mr. Keseberg?"

"It is my concern," Keseberg answered, and the arrogance in his voice was matched by that in his eyes.

"Perhaps it is," Reed granted, "but it may affect the rest of us as well."

"My property is not your concern."

"That, I think, is for the whole group to decide. I will ask you one more time how you acquired this so-called property."

"I traded for it for beads and some sugar."

"Mr. Keseberg, there have been no Indians within sight the entire day. Except dead ones," he added.

Keseberg quickly abandoned the lie and adopted a new tactic. "A dead man has no use for such things," he asserted, as though the matter were too obvious to permit further discussion.

"There you are correct, sir. They are only of interest to the living—like most burial customs. The Sioux are not kindly disposed to travelers passing through their territory, and will certainly not take well to having their dead disturbed."

"I did not disturb. I was very quiet," Keseberg said in a whisper, pressing a finger against his lips. Then he laughed shrilly.

"My God, man, don't you understand what you've done?"

"Yes, I've got a nice soft bed for my Phillipine to wrap herself in when the new baby comes." Reed's anger had unsettled him, and reference to the baby that would soon be born was meant to placate his aggressive opponent.

"If you need more blankets, I'll give them to you, man. I'll give you a feather bed as well, if you want one. Damn it, you don't have to rob the dead!"

Keseberg paused, stroked his long face as though considering the merits of such an eccentric proposition. "The dead don't care,"

159

he pronounced finally. "It's the living who must look out for themselves."

"It's worse than trying to talk the skin off a mule," Reed said, but half to himself. "Will you return that robe or not?"

The German shrugged helplessly. "I don't remember where I found it."

"Then I have no choice but to propose you be banished from the train." Reed turned briskly on his heel and strode off to consult with George and Jacob Donner. The two agreed with his judgment, not out of any sense of sacrilege in the theft, but because they feared bloody reprisals by the Sioux. Tamsen was unhappy, for she felt Mrs. Keseberg would need assistance in her delivery, and with two men and a child to care for, she already had a difficult time.

"Don't concern yourself," Reed advised her. "They can wait for the group that's moving up behind ours."

"But that could take days," she pleaded.

"That is Mr. Keseberg's problem. He can still choose to return the robe where he found it."

"He won't do that," Tamsen said, shaking her head. "He's much too proud for that. He will have to show you his will is stronger than yours, and it is his wife who will suffer for it. And that just isn't fair, James Reed."

"No, of course it isn't fair," he admitted, "but the choice is his, and the alternative is to endanger all of us. We have the strictest instructions from Colonel Kearny to take particular care not to offend the Pawnee and the Sioux, and not to give the slightest indication of an intention to settle in their lands."

"I know," Tamsen told him, but it was clear that the knowledge gave her no comfort.

Reed canvassed the entire company, and the unanimous decision was that Keseberg would have to leave. Without Reed's forceful arguments, a few might have dissented, but in the end he succeeded in bringing even the Wolfingers around to his opinion. When Keseberg learned the group's decision, he immediately rechained his teams and, without a word, pulled out a mile to the west. The dusty buffalo robe was wrapped conspicuously around his shoulders.

Ash Hollow, where the emigrants began the crossing to the North Platte, was the steepest grade that had confronted them on the trail. Brakes were set and front and back wheels chained together, but there was still a danger of the wagons sliding forward so rapidly the animals would be crushed, and everything was done to slow the murderous drop. Pine trees were felled and the tops secured to rear axles to increase the braking action. Picket ropes were also attached, and the people who held them got down the hill as best they could, some standing and straining against the plunging weight, others sitting and being dragged down the hill, legs stiff and heels scarring the earth, alert for cactus in their path.

At the foot of the treacherous half-mile grade, the danger they had passed seemed trivial compared with what lay ahead. Here they encountered several families that had survived a Pawnee raid and were putting their outfits together again, abandoning their bulkier possessions and combining teams. A huge mahogany bureau stood beside the trail; the drawers had been removed to feed cooking fires, and the spaces they had filled were a dozen gaping, sightless eyes. Women and children sat listlessly in the inadequate shade of frayed tents, while the men continued the salvage operation. A pair of wrecked wagons were being cut down and converted into carts and others had already been stripped to provide spare parts for the trail ahead. The scene was even more desolate than the grim landscape in which it was set.

The wagons under Governor Boggs's command were scarcely in better shape than those of the Pawnee victims. As they revolved, the brittle axles shrieked incessant protest, and the wheels had been so shrunk by the thin, dry air that the iron banding them sometimes sprang away to wobble its own erratic course through the sagebrush. Spokes pulled out of hubs, and often the hubs themselves locked for want of grease. Had there been enough wood for a proper fire, they could have laid by for repairs, cutting out a section of the tire and welding it together again, drilling new holes and pinning it to the wheel. Otherwise there was nothing to do but hammer in a few more whittled wedges between the tire and felloe, and then hope they would not be jolted out by the rough ground. William Eddy doubted whether even half the wagons would make it to Fort Laramie, where there was reportedly a blacksmith who could do the job for them.

As the land sloped imperceptibly but relentlessly upward toward the continental divide, the air grew thinner, and many had prostrating seizures of nausea and violent headaches. Lungs strained increasingly against the dust blown up by the ceaseless winds, and a few emigrants began to spit up handfuls of blood. The biting alkali and the glaring light reddened and swelled the eyes of those not wise enough to have equipped themselves with goggles, and several were nearly blind. They washed their eyes repeatedly with solutions of zinc sulfate, but it only temporarily relieved the corrosive action of the alkali, and it did nothing to combat the fierce glare that sprang from shimmering deposits of salt that often seemed to fill the plain with broad sheets of water. Some could not accept the alluring deception, and stumbled off across rough ground in search of a cooling bath. Lips ached, swelled, split open and bled, and licking them only aggravated the raw sores that formed. A few of the women stuck strips of paper there, but suffered worse when it was peeled away. Heavily coated with the burning dust, they sometimes had difficulty recognizing each other, and mothers confused their own children. The fine white powder plastered their faces and hair, stopped their ears, scalded their throats, sifted through tight collars and cuffs and chafed wherever clothing rubbed, raising painful blisters on the skin. And it coated the bedding, filmed drinking water, settled on frying meat, invaded the pages of books and ledgers, worked its way into trunks and tins and tightly sealed jars, as though it were a medium as universal as air itself. When the train was in motion, it traveled under a dense grayish canopy visible for more than ten miles.

TAMSEN SAT ON A BENCH-LIKE SLAB OF ROCK THAT THRUST OUT OF the sand, and her knees balanced the oblong drawing board. At her feet spread a cactus plot that might have been arranged by an eccentric gardener, with the plants clumped together in ragged strips whose outlines were determined by the vivid coloring of the blossoms: a sulfurous yellow, carmine red and magenta and an intense cornflower blue, like jeweled ornaments on the fat, prickly stalks of the plants themselves. Some hugged the earth like crouching animals, while others thrust boldly upward in defiance of the blazing sun. Tamsen held the sketch at arm's length, tilted her head to one side and then the other as she studied it, and seemed pleased with the results. Then she made notations that would guide her later in filling in the colors, realizing as she did so that the very earth, which at first seemed such a drab and uniform tone, held sparkles of silver and topaz and brilliant ochre, and she was noting these, too, thinking how she could dot them in with a fine brush, then suffuse the whole with two or three thin layers of wash, when she was startled by a sudden movement at her feet. Always alert for the rattlers that often coiled by a mound of buffalo chips or slithered beneath the most tightly pegged tent to seek the warmth of quilt and counterpane, she became as immovable as the rock on which she sat. This defensive lesson she had learned well, knowing that any sudden, startled movement could provoke an attack, and knowing what the results would be, for she had also seen the deep channels cut into a man's arm in hopes of draining the poison before it reached his heart. She froze but carefully searched the ground with her eyes, and discovered what seemed a gossamer mass of silk, a delicate membrane writhing and twisting in a frantic dance to music her ears could not perceive. Her instinct was to leap up, to flee to the safety of the wagons, but the agitated dance compelled her attendance, and when the silken mass remained still for a moment, the thudding of her own heart seemed to set the tempo as it began to gyre and spin again, throwing fine sprays of sand into the air, pausing again for a moment and then launching even more vigorously, more hectically, into its frenzied dance. Then, as though it had thrown aside constricting veils, a form appeared, thrust forward and split the fine covering, rending it and flinging it aside, and the taut triangular head of a sand viper lifted itself from the discarded costume. The eyes blinked, the jaws opened testingly, and a forked tongue lanced the air. The body stretched, taking the measure of its own length, and the tail flipped away the shriveled membrane—

arrogantly, as a dandy might have rejected a suit of shoddy, ill-fitting clothes. Slowly the length of the body lowered onto the sand, tugged itself forward, rose again to display its brilliant suiting, and the mouth opened wider now, the tongue flicked left, then right, and the eyes concentrated the brilliance of stars. The creature was no more than six inches in length, but the imperious glare dominated its rocky kingdom, commanded tribute and obeisance, brooked no impertinent opposition. Again its tautly muscled body lowered, slid forward across the sand as swiftly and effortlessly as lightly skating drops of mercury. It was only then that Tamsen saw the parent snake, coiled nearby in proud attendance at the birth, its broad head cocked attentively as the miraculous offspring flowed to her like a curling satin ribbon drawn rapidly across the sand. The head was covered with ten regularly formed scales like an armored cap, and on either side of the body a yellow stripe extended from the base of the skull to the tail; another yellow stripe stretched along the spine between parallel lines of intense orange, and these bands of color shimmered and vibrated as though the strength of the parent flowed out to animate the newborn, impelling it forward. The parent snake was nearly two feet in length, and it uncoiled, raising itself to rigid attention as the smaller one drew near, and their cloven tongues lunged again and again in greeting. Tamsen willed her eyes away from the slithering embrace of their firm bodies, but her eyes would not obey, and she stared at the meaty coils folding and unfolding, stroking and caressing, until the two shapes suddenly darted across the sand to vanish beneath the rock on which she sat. The delicate lines of her desert sketch were blurred and smeared beyond recognition by the sweat from her palms, which she had pressed rigidly against the shield of the drawing board.

EACH EVENING KESEBERG HALTED HIS WAGONS A FEW YARDS CLOSER to the main camp, until he and his family were within plain view. Phillipine moved heavily as she bathed the dust from Ada's face, tended the cooking fire, carried heaping plates of beans to the hungry men. Her shoulders were tensed against the pendulous weight of the child she was carrying, and it was clear that her time was due. Less than a week after his banishment, Keseberg pulled his two wagons directly into the camp, and none had the heart to turn him away.

12

We made camp in the late afternoon within sight of a great natural curiosity situated upon the south side of the Platte, consisting of a huge isolated cliff or bluff which rises abruptly and dramatically from the even plain. It gives the natural appearance of an enormous building, somewhat dilapidated in condition, but with its mighty walls intact, together with the roof, turrets, embrasures, dome, and the very windows themselves. A few rods in front of the main building stand what appear to be stout guard houses. These antique structures look scarcely more than a mile distant, and Messrs. Reed, Elliott and Denton set off on horseback to give them a closer inspection, only to discover the true distance to be closer to seven miles. Others, who had set out on foot, returned after an hour to complain that the elusive wonder kept retreating as they advanced. This deception was owing to the pure atmosphere through which it was viewed, together with the want of comparative objects by which accurate ideas of distance can be acquired without measure. If he will not lose all sense of judgment, the traveler through these regions must exercise great and continuous vigilance.

Mr. Denton estimates the mass of the bluff to be about 300 feet in height and some quarter of a mile in length, by 200 yards in breadth. Its outlines and general proportions are such that it is difficult to look upon it and not believe the hand of art had something to do with its ingenious construction. Trappers have given the formation various names, indicative of its approach in form to different structures in civilized life, including both "Court House" and "Cathedral," and for many it shows resemblances to the famous capitol in Washington, representing a main building and wings surmounted by domes. "Court House" is the most favored, though for me it might also have been viewed as the ruins of a great castle, perhaps the former citadel or stronghold of a populous kingdom. Other bluffs can be seen in the far distance, and tiny but strikingly exact on the horizon at setting sun was the famous Chimney Rock, a soaring tower that perhaps once supported hanging gardens of perfumed plants. The observer might easily imagine that around and about the plain were the dwellings of a numerous people, a civilization that had been a nursery of the arts and sciences, the seat of great inland commerce. What sanguinary foe swept them all away, giving no quarter to young or old? Certainly no soul escaped the ensuing slaughter, and their history has been given to the winds, leaving no trace of their former existence save these remains of architectural grandeur and magnificence that now lift up their heads amid the surrounding desolation.

Such melancholic reflections are easily produced by our locality, but are also given inspiration by the recent ardors of our journey. The dust along the North Platte is so light it needs only a breath of air to set it floating in clouds, and the very oxen are sometimes quite obscured to the driver. I fastened a curtain across the front of the wagon and opened the cover in the back, in an effort to secure air thin enough for the children to breathe, but this had little effect. Sage tea with borax and sugar gives some relief to raw throats, but the effect is only temporary. We have often wondered what is supposed to happen to a mortal who swallows twice his allotted peck of dirt, and that in the course of a single day, yet the outdoor life seems to render us impervious to what could kill a stationary resident of the States. Only the other day I chanced to see Mrs. Breen warming over some rice that had been previously cooked and left to stand in a brass kettle. There was a thick rim of verdigris all around the edge, but she briskly stirred this in as well, and none seemed the worse for it, but this jolly family does seem in all things to have an enviable talent for survival. Dropped from a cliff, they would probably bounce like India-rubber!

While crossing from the South to the North Platte we made our most perilous descent, along a hill that seemed nearly a mile in length and which leads into Ash Hollow. All hands were set to work at breaking the precipitous fall, and even the poor children were drawn into service, clinging for dear life to picket ropes that had been attached to the wagons. None were hurt in the effort, but the experience did no good to our vehicles, which are ever more sadly in need of repair. Encamped in Ash Hollow were several emigrant families who had survived a raid by the fierce Pawnee, whose warriors drove off most of their cattle and horses. Two men were murdered when they proved so foolhardy as to demand the return of their teams, but they were powerless to move on without the animals and therefore saw no other recourse.

Both Mr. Donner and Colonel Russell have resigned their executive responsibilities, due to continuing disputes within the party, and new officers were duly elected, with Governor Boggs at their head. Colonel Russell continues to suffer from malarial attacks, but was clearly more indisposed by the ill humor of his constituents than by the fever itself, to which the years have made him painfully accustomed. Mr. Bryant has ridden ahead to the forts in the hope of trading wagons and teams for a string of pack-mules, with which he and his impatient companions will then proceed at a more rapid pace to the Promised Land.

Our table (which these days usually consists of a simple rubber sheet spread on the earth) has been graced recently not only with juicy buffalo steaks but also with plentiful hares and sage hens. The latter are in every respect like our domestic hen, excepting the head is somewhat smaller in relation to the body, and the color is much the same as that of the pheasant. The meat is dark-colored and surprisingly tasty, and the hare is quite as finely flavored.

The excitement of chasing the buffalo has proved a popular diversion from the monotony of the day's toil, and we have seldom been out of sight of immense herds, some of them extending over the plain for several miles. When the fiery hunter dashes in among them, the dense masses open left and right before him, but he selects his target carefully, concentrating on the eager pursuit of a young cow that finally receives his shot and falls. While such sport is plentiful, it requires no little courage and dexterity to move within the flashing hooves, select a victim, and aim accurately from a joggling seat, then to reload and continue the chase. The difficulties are patent even to the distant observer, but not to Mr. Lansford W. Hastings, whose guidebook is so esteemed by many in our party. He gives the following description of the ease of securing fresh steak for supper, and it as clear an idiocy as one might hope to find within the pages of a mere book:

"Having been a few days among the buffaloes, and their horses having become accustomed to these terrific scenes, even the 'green horn' is enabled not only to kill the buffalo with expertness, but he is also frequently seen driving them to the encampments with as much indifference as he used formerly to drive his domestic cattle about his own fields, in the land of his nativity. Giving the buffalo chase for a few minutes, they become so fatigued and completely exhausted that they are driven from place to place with as little difficulty as our common cattle. Both the grown buffalo and the calves are very frequently driven in this manner to the encampment and slaughtered."

Either Mr. Hastings left his wits behind him in Ohio, for safe-keeping, or they strayed out among the sagebrush and lost their direction.

There has been little time for botanizing in the last weeks, but along the river I discovered some purple *Liatris scariosa* and several asters as conspicuous features of the scant vegetation. I was pleased to recognize among specimens collected near the forks the fine, large-flowered *Asclepias speciosa,* described by Mr. John Torrey in the preface to his catalogue of plants, and which Mr. Geyer also found in Nicolet's expedition. It seems to be the same species described and minutely figured by Sir W. Hooker under the designation *A. douglassii.* Growing very abundantly near our camp is a plant about one foot high which in many respects resembles buckwheat. The stems from which the leaves grow all spread from a common stem near the ground, and the flowers are in large clusters upon a stalk, shooting out of the center, some of them of a straw color, while others are pink. The most common vegetation is the sagebrush *(Artemisia tritentata)* which fills the air with a strong smell of turpentine. It burns too rapidly to be of much desirability as a cooking fuel, but a quantity added to the buffalo chips gives roasting meat a delicious, tangy flavor.

We expect to reach Fort Bernard and then Fort Laramie by the end of the week, and will have a chance to make good the damages our wagons have suffered through the dry air and the uneven roads. Mr. Eddy, who is a carriagemaker by trade, says that half of them are not much good for anything but kindling.

We are generally entertained at night with coyote concerts (admission free), but as the usual thing are so fatigued that we say our prayers backwards, roll over once, and are asleep before they get from the verse to the chorus.

13

Fort Laramie
Sunday, June 28th, 1846

From Court House Rock to the Laramie River our trail led us past numerous curiosities of nature which the continuous action of wind and rain have carved into the soft, marly rock of the region, and which did much to relieve the tediousness of our journey. At the celebrated Chimney Rock, where we paused for nooning, several brave and hearty explorers climbed part way up the conical mound to engrave their names and their greetings to later travelers, but none ventured up the so-called Scott's Bluff. They were discouraged not only by the forbidding appearance of the rocky fortress, but also by the mournful tale attaching to its history. A party of Rocky Mountain trappers in the employ of the American

Fur Company was attempting to return to St. Louis by boat, but when the water became impassable at this point, the boats were abandoned together with Mr. Scott, the leader of the little expedition, who was extremely ill and physically helpless to continue unassisted. His companions claimed on their arrival in St. Louis that he had died and been suitably buried, but some time in the following year another party found the dead man wrapped in blankets and with clothing and papers that proved his unhappy identity. He had recovered sufficiently to drag himself up the bluffs and attempt to make a rough shelter before he died, so that his treacherous companions were effectively given the lie. The thought of this deserted creature, slowly starving and alone save for the howling wind, moved some nearly to tears, and we were glad to put the somber scene behind us.

After fording the Laramie River, we paused briefly at little Fort Bernard, which consists both principally and entirely of a two-room log cabin chinked with mud. We lost but an afternoon and evening in exploring its diversions, though we were happy to encounter Mr. Bryant, who had succeeded in persuading Taos traders to give him seven mules and packsaddles in exchange for his wagon and oxen. All his comrades had made similar terms, and were now awaiting us to come up so they could fulfill their side of the bargain. During our brief pause at Fort Bernard we also made the acquaintance of an interesting young literary gentleman from Boston, looking most handsome and distinctly un-Bostonian in his wonderful fringed buckskins. His name is Mr. Francis Parkman, and despite frail health he has survived many exciting adventures among the Ogalala Sioux, accompanying them on hunting parties and actually sleeping in their lodges. So great is their respect for him that he was offered a *bona fide* Indian princess as his bride, but modestly declined the auspicious union.

Agreeing to continue our interesting conversations at Fort Laramie, we pressed on for the few remaining miles and were awarded a tumultuous greeting—first, by the heavens, that opened up with the most violent storm we have encountered in weeks, and then by what appeared to be the entire Sioux nation, encamped about the fort and working themselves into noisy ecstasy at the gift of rain. At least 600 lodges are pitched here, with wild and savage bucks whooping everywhere and shaking rattles borrowed from passing snakes, hammering skin drums and galloping their hard little ponies. They are for the most part a handsome, graceful people when seen close up, and surprisingly fair for Indians, but far too many are drunk on whiskey traded from the American Fur Company in exchange for buffalo and beaver and antelope skins. The company's officials would prefer not to deal in such volatile stuff, but argue that the independent French traders would otherwise claim all the business. Even the women, some of them quite delicately beautiful, with elegantly rounded limbs, are not immune to the effects of "fire water," and it is said they would sell their last possession to obtain it. Because this is something of a holiday, most of the Sioux are dressed in pale buckskins ornamented with the finest and most elaborate beadwork we have seen, but some are covered only by dirty blankets, which they keep fastened by a miracle, for there is otherwise nothing to effect the closure, neither pin nor string. I have traded a pair of mirrors for a lovely pair of buckskin moccasins, wonderfully supple and of a deep, golden tan color. A piece of scarlet broadcloth edged with several rows of white beads decorates the top, and from either side of this extends around the top of the quarters a drop-curtain effect, delicately fringed by making fine cuts an inch deep around the edges. To fasten securely on the feet, they are tied with a string run through little slashes cut in the top.

The Indians' horses have so stripped the grass around the fort that we could only make camp six miles beyond, but then rode back to dine with the "bourgeois," as the head man is called. We were served a satisfactory meal of corned beef, biscuit and milk, but there were no vegetables available, and they would have offered a welcome variation from our prairie diet. Colonel Russell was so enthusiastic in sampling the traders' whiskey that he could only be got back to camp tied across his saddle, and somewhere en route said farewell to his wonderful hat with the oiled-silk cover. He has lately been loud with complaint to all who will listen about the mutiny of envious small men that turned him out from his rightful post. In the local language he might fairly be described as being "drunk as a pigeon" much of the time, but claims it does his malaria a world of good.

The imposing Fort Laramie is built upon a rise of ground about 25 feet above the Laramie River, a bold mountain stream of clear and refreshingly cool water. The fort is a quadrangular structure of 180 by 120 feet, and its lofty whitewashed and picketed walls look appropriately formidable. It is principally constructed according to the Mexican usage of adobes or large sundried bricks, but reinforced with log buttresses. The whole is said to have cost the American Fur Company more than $10,000, although most of the building materials were to be had for the taking, which gives a measure of how highly they value the trade carried on in these parts. The chief entrance to Fort Laramie fronts the river, covered by the soaring square tower that guards its inhabitants, and which affords a pleasant nook where the idler can sit and enjoy the evening breezes. Further defense is offered by two sturdy bastions, and on the interior are numerous houses, one or two stories high. These are plastered like swallows' nests against the walls, to permit an open court about 130 feet square in the center. Only those Indians in the direct and regular employ of the fur company are permitted through the double gate into the heart of the fort itself, but many of the men have taken squaws as their temporary wives, and a flock of half-breed children whoops night and day through the busy court.

There are estimated to be about 3,000 whites in the immediate vicinity, many of them traders and trappers, but the most are emigrants bound for Oregon or California. The number also includes a most woebegone company of travelers all returning from those lands and bringing evil reports of their experience there. They maintain that the country is wholly destitute of timber and that wheat can scarcely be raised in sufficient quantities for bread. These unlucky voyagers have spent their entire substance, and are now returning to commence the world anew, somewhere in the vicinity of their former homes. Among the Oregonians is a young man entirely blinded by dust along the way and being taken back to the States in the hope of restoring his sight.

Our hearts sank in our breasts on hearing such ill reports, but luckily we have superior authorities in our midst. One of them is Mr. James Clyman, who has just returned from California in the company of Lansford W. Hastings, whom he left at Fort Bridger preparing to guide a caravan across the mountains. Mr. Clyman and Mr. Reed were comrades at arms during the Black Hawk War and were as pleased to see each other again as long-lost brothers. Mr. Clyman, who was once captured by hostile Indians, has crossed the continent many times, and guided the first permanent settlers into the Oregon country. He would be a useful man to have at our side, but can remain only a short time, as urgent business awaits him at St. Louis. This experienced traveler thinks little of the Hastings cut-off that is being advertised far and wide, and says it is probably unfit for wagons.

The Thorntons came into camp at noon today, and agree it would be pleasant to rest here for a time, but such relief is not to be granted us. The bourgeois warns in the strongest terms that Indian tribes in the area (especially the Sioux and Cheyenne) are in an aggravatedly hostile mood to the whites and restrain themselves from attacking emigrants only because they fear the military force of the United States. A large and ferocious war party is nonetheless gathering in the hills, and we have been urged to move on at once rather than delaying until Tuesday, as originally planned. The situation is aggravated by a conflict brewing between the Sioux and their old enemies the Crows, which makes them all sulky and cross, like powder kegs waiting for the igniting spark.

With this unwelcome abbreviation in our itinerary there has been a great bustle to repair wagon wheels and re-shoe horses in preparation for tomorrow's departure, and the cottonwoods are all blossoming with the copious washing we have done. Each in our drooping company might truly take for himself Mr. Longfellow's tribute to the sturdy blacksmith:

> Toiling,—rejoicing,—sorrowing,
>   Onward through life he goes;
> Each morning sees some task begin,
>   Each evening sees it close;

Something attempted, something done,
Has earned a night's repose.

14

"I'VE BEEN BOTH WAYS, AND I'M TELLIN' YOU SURE AS I'M SITTIN' here that the old route from Fort Hall is the best," Jim Clyman repeated, but he was growing tired of hearing his own voice.

"There is a nigher route, and it is no use to take such a round-about course," James Reed persisted.

"That's right," Jacob Donner said, addressing his words to the entire group gathered around the dying camp fire. He waved a worn copy of *The Emigrants' Guide to Oregon and California*, the una-voidable and sovereign evidence of the printed word, black on white.

"I don't give a hang what it says in books," Jim Clyman told him, and spit the last word out like a mouthful of mealy peas.

"Just listen," Jacob insisted, "right here on page 137." He cleared his throat and read slowly, giving each word equal emphasis, "The best and most direct route, for the California emigrants, would be to leave the Oregon route, almost two hundred miles east from Fort Hall; thence bearing west southwest to the Salt Lake; and then continuing down to the Bay of San Francisco . . ."

"Rubbish," Jim Clyman said. "That takes you through the meanest country I've ever had the misery of seein'. You'll lose half your wagons and stock tryin' to get through the desert. Go by way of Soda Springs and Fort Hall, or you'll likely find yourselves shov-elin' snow in the mountains all winter."

"Now, Jim," James Reed said, "why would Hastings be so anxious to promote a trail nobody can get across? It'll save us more than three hundred miles. You just came across it yourself, and you don't look much the worse for wear."

"I was on horseback, you darned fool, and wasn't pullin' a wagon big as a barn."

The allusion offended James Reed. He had, in fact, been astonished by the way mountain life had roughened Jim Clyman, coarsened his tongue. What he had once admired as frankness in this lank, broad-shouldered comrade now seemed an unnecessary bluntness verging on bad manners. He wondered if Lansford Hastings had perhaps felt the same repulsion, and if the two had developed some quarrel that now led Clyman to attempt to discredit the author. If so, Reed thought, he should be careful of taking his petty revenge at the expense of the innocent.

Jim Clyman felt an obligation to the emigrants, and ever since Bear River had been conscientiously trying to persuade every group he met to avoid the dangerous cutoff. He made a final try now.

"I'm tellin' all of you one last time that I've just traveled that route, and it's as rough as anything I've ever laid eyes on. You've got the Wahsatch with canyons too narrow for a cat to squeeze through, and the biggest piece of salt desert that's goin', and a stretch of mountains where the closest thing to a trail is a path about a foot wide that the Indians have made, and that trail's goin' for game, not for California. You're all plumb crazy if you try. You're late already, and the snows could catch you. It's barely possible to get through if you go by Soda Springs and Fort Hall, and it may be impossible if you don't."

"May I ask you just one question, Jim? I don't believe you've yet answered it to the general satisfaction." James Reed's voice had become nasal with the effort of maintaining a polite tone to suppress his irritation at Clyman's mule-headedness.

"Shoot."

"Precisely what has Lansford Hastings got to win for himself by telling us that the shortest distance between two points just happens to be a straight line?"

"I'd like to know that myself," George Donner added.

"A hell of a lot," Clyman answered, and yet it was partly guesswork, partly seasoned intuition that made him suspect Hastings's high-pressure salesmanship. "For a start, he's chargin' dear for takin' wagons across that godforsaken route, and his buddy Gabe Bridger is buildin' himself a nice trade on the Bear River. Maybe Hastings has got a deal or two goin' in California, too. The man's got so many irons in the fire you can't see the fire anymore. Why, when he wrote that good-for-nothin' book he hadn't even laid eyes on the Wahsatch or the Great Salt Lake. You can't trust a fool just because he's learned his alphabet."

Those who had grown weary with the quarrel stirred to attention, lifted their eyes from the crumbling coals of the fire. They were, for the most part, men who had been taught all their lives to honor the sanctity of the written word, to regard it as the irreplaceable and invaluable key that could open to them the treasure troves of the republic, and here was a crude mountain man with a beard liberally streaked with tobacco juice, trying to tell them that the very institutions that made a protective barrier between civilization and savagery were not to be trusted. A few believed what Clyman told them—Jessy Thornton, for one, but since he was bound for Oregon, he withheld his opinion. Owl Russell also inclined to the established route, but as he was giving serious consideration to adding his seasoned authority to the discussion, a jug of whiskey passed his way and stilled his tongue. Edwin Bryant, on the other hand, thought the man a bold-faced liar, exploiting the situation for his own purposes, whatever those might be, but he didn't say as much. Instead, he simply announced that he and his company would follow Hastings's instructions, and Clyman admitted that with only horses and mules, they might save time with the cutoff.

"We're obliged to you for your advice," James Reed said, drawing a ceremonial end to the meeting.

"And damned if you'll follow it," Clyman muttered.

"I can only speak for myself, and perhaps for the Donners," Reed insisted, and the two brothers nodded their consent. "In our judgment Hastings has the best answer. No offense, old friend, but we've got important appointments in California, and are bound and determined to get there the quickest way we can." He smiled nervously, a little apologetically, in an effort to restore something of the damaged spirit of their reunion. "Besides," he added, "we've still got a few weeks to think about it before we leave the old trail."

"I'd sure think about it hard," Clyman suggested, but knew the case was lost.

As THEY LEFT THE FORT THE WAGONS ROLLED PAST AN ENTIRE VIL-
lage of the dead crowning a low hill. Much of the scaffolding erected to lift the Indian corpses up to heaven was decayed and partially collapsed, so that the angular silhouette against the clear morning sky resembled the ruins of a half-finished town, with joist and girder and balustrade sagging toward the earth. Decayed buffalo robes flapped loudly in the wind, like garments hastily discarded when the former residents abandoned the town, but some had not escaped in time, for the ground was strewn with bones that had bleached to incandescent whiteness in the sun. It was here, then, that the wolves had howled so loudly and longingly throughout the night.

For several miles the straggling emigrant caravan was accompanied by its own Indian escort. Some estimated there were as many as three hundred of them urging their ponies up and down the train, most with their faces fiercely painted, but if they were dressed for war, their intentions seemed peaceful enough. Many of the braves clenched green twigs between their teeth, which Jim Clyman had said was a sign of good intentions, and they vigorously, repeatedly shook the hands of the emigrants to confirm their desire to be friends, perhaps enlisting future allies against the Crows. Or perhaps they only wished to demonstrate their pleasure in seeing the unwelcome visitors depart.

After a few miles, most of the colorful escort dropped away to return to the fort, but a small band remained with them as they moved parallel to the Platte, crossed the gray, powdery bowl of an extinct volcano, and paused to rest at a spring that trickled from the cleft in a ledge of rock that looked as though it had been split apart by a blast of lightning.

While Tamsen was bringing coffee to a boil, a young Indian woman knelt beside her and extended her hand in greeting. Tamsen was surprised by its softness and coolness, which made her realize

177

again how chapped and toughened her own skin was by alkali dust and sun, even though she had worn half-mitts most of the way to protect them.

"Hello," the visitor said, then covered her embarrassment with a silvery gush of laughter and tucked her pretty face against her shoulder.

"Hello," Tamsen replied, but the greeting seemed to deplete the young woman's store of English, for she simply repeated it again.

"Hog?" Tamsen asked. The sound apparently carried no meaning, so she raised a thick strip of bacon and pronounced the word again.

The Indian's eyes brightened and her head nodded rapidly.

"Very well," Tamsen said, and was about to skewer the pork on a twig, to roast it over the fire, when it was snatched from her hands and disappeared down her visitor's throat.

"You will give yourself a dreadful tummy ache," Tamsen warned her.

"Hog?" The word sounded more like "haw," but Tamsen recognized an unusually quick pupil, and thought it better to reward than correct. This time she held the bacon to the side, out of the woman's reach, until it had been skewered, and then dangled it over the fire.

"Cook," Tamsen pronounced.

"Cook," came the reply, followed by the wonderful silvery laughter.

"Cook hog," Tamsen explained, pointing at the strip of pork that curled and dropped its noisy juices onto the fire. The other nodded as though some immense, weighty mystery had suddenly been made clear.

Tamsen fanned the meat to cool it, repeating the word "hot" several times, before extending it to her guest. This time the young woman ate more slowly, nibbling small bites and chewing carefully, no longer afraid the precious prize would be denied her. When she had finished, she carefully wiped the corners of her mouth with the tips of her fingers, in a gesture so dainty and so modest that Tamsen could scarcely believe she had not learned it at some exclusive academy for young ladies. Then she took from her waist a buckskin

178

pouch, untied the thong that held it shut, and spread it on the earth between them. The treasures it contained consisted of dried leaves and plant stems and roots that were all strange to Tamsen's eyes, save for one closely resembling the wild onion they had gathered on the Blue Prairie.

The Indian woman lifted a pale white tuber, held it to her lips and made chewing motions. "Hog," she declared, and handed it to her hostess.

Tamsen sniffed at it before taking a small, testing bite from the tip. The smell was musty, somewhat bitter, but it had a rich, nutty flavor, and while her new friend watched in fascination, she took a larger bite, making noises that she hoped would express her appreciation.

The young woman gestured then to the water that bubbled from the great cleft rock. Thinking she might want something to drink after the salty strips of bacon, Tamsen drew the bucket near and was about to dip in a tin cup when the cool hand stopped her with a quick, light touch. It pointed again to the spring, then to the bucket, and drew a wandering line in the earth.

"It grows near water," Tamsen said. "Of course! It grows near the water," and dipped water out onto the ground, placed one of the white tubers beside it.

Her instructress nodded rapid approval, but held her forefingers closely parallel and sighted along them, looking down at the damp spot between them.

"Yes . . . ," Tamsen followed her, "it grows along streams or brooks—near narrow waters."

Inscribing a circle with her arms, the Indian woman identified spicy fern-like plants gathered from the shores of a lake. These were not "hog," but seemed intended for some kind of medical treatment —a poultice to remove swelling from the joints. When this point had been established, a gnarled root was held up, silvery and knobbed like a miniature piece of driftwood. A finger pointed upward to indicate it could be found in the hills, and more signs clarified it should be boiled before eating. The pantomime continued with the hands clutched together, fingers entwined and pointing downward, to show what had been dug from between the

179

roots of a tree. An arm held erectly, the elbow planted against the ground, finally identified the edible fruit plucked from a cactus. This one was harder, became clear only when the woman touched the upraised hand with a finger and jerked back as she came in contact with one of the prickles.

"My dear girl," Tamsen finally said, "if you would only come with us, we should eat like kings, and have a spell of good doctoring too, I should guess."

Seeming to understand that she had been paid a compliment, the Indian woman again hid her face against her shoulder, and Tamsen thought her in that moment the loveliest, most graceful creature she had ever seen.

PHILLIPINE KESEBERG HAD BITTEN INTO HER LOWER LIP FOR SO long to still her own screams that two runnels of blood streamed down her chin, and Tamsen wiped them away with a soft cloth.

"Scream," she told her. "Scream if it helps you, Mrs. Keseberg."

"My husband," the woman murmured apologetically, and bit again into her lip, loosing a fresh flow of blood.

"Your husband is of no concern at the moment," Tamsen insisted, and looked up at the man who loomed over them, throwing his angular shadow across the pallet that had been arranged with buffalo hides and quilts. "You may leave now, Mr. Keseberg."

"My little Phillipine—" he began, but Tamsen cut him short.

"There is nothing you can do for her now. Your job is done, and your wife's has started. She is not having an easy time, as you can see, and you are not making it any easier for her or for me." Again she urged the agonized woman, "Scream if it helps you, Mrs. Keseberg."

"No!" Keseberg roared. "It is the coward who screams."

"Well, Mr. Keseberg, I happen to be a coward, a natural-born coward, one of the most famous cowards ever to draw breath, and I shall scream myself if you do not leave this minute. I shall scream so hard it will clabber milk."

"Very well, very well," Keseberg muttered, and withdrew to the other side of the camp fire, where he enthroned himself on an empty barrel that served the family as a dining table, and began to pare his fingernails.

Tamsen watched him retreat and thought that if anything were to go wrong with the birth, the man would probably murder her on the spot. She pushed Mrs. Keseberg's skirts higher, tucked them about her waist and said, "Press down, Mrs. Keseberg. Push against me when you feel the pain is reaching its peak. And feel free to scream if you like."

A soft voice inquired from the shadows, "How is she, Tamsen?"

"She's having a hard time," Tamsen said to Betsy Donner. "It looks like her baby wants to wait until she gets to California." Phillipine Keseberg had relaxed again, her body slack between the painful contractions, and Tamsen bathed her forehead and arms with cooling witch hazel, then sat watching her, waiting for the next contraction to come. The woman's face was so blackened by sun and wind, the features were so pointed by her pain, that the face more nearly resembled a lump of anthracite than anything human. Her soft thighs, plump and creamy white, bore no relation to the haggish face surrounded by brittle hair ruthlessly stripped of life and color by the alkali dust.

The woman moaned again, a long hollow sound like the wind exploring an abandoned house. "Press down, Mrs. Keseberg," Tamsen urged her, while Betsy turned and ran, stumbling over clumps of sagebrush, to her own wagon.

"That's right," Tamsen encouraged. "That's right, it's coming now, just keep pressing."

Betsy returned, flatfooted and breathless, and something gleamed in her hand, flashed a reply to the moon.

"It's too soon for that," Tamsen said, seeing the blade of the knife.

Betsy shook her head. "Put it under her," she panted.

"Under her?"

"Under her. It cuts the pain."

"Betsy Donner, that's the worst nonsense I've ever heard in my whole life."

"It's true," she insisted, and there was an uncontrollable sob in her voice.

"Oh, very well," Tamsen said, relenting. "Give it here, then. It certainly can't hurt anything." She took the knife, slipped it far beneath the buffalo robe, where there was no chance of its injuring the woman.

Betsy's hands hung limply before her like a pair of animals strung from a trapper's belt. She herself began to moan as she watched the woman writhe, try to brace her feet, collapse with the weary effort.

"Will she be all right, Tamsen?"

"Of course she will!" Tamsen leaned forward, stroked the sweat again from the woman's face, and then stood beside Betsy. "The problem," she said, speaking softly now, "is that it's the shoulder and not the head."

Betsy's startled eyes filled with helpless tears. "But it'll break its little neck," she whimpered, "or get strangled in its own cord."

"It will have to be turned," Tamsen told her.

"Turned? Oh, Tamsen, do you think you ought to do that?"

"No," Tamsen answered, "definitely not. What I ought to do is send you for a doctor, but it's a long way back to Independence, and the wolves sound hungry tonight."

"Tamsen!" Betsy scolded. "Don't be such a mean old thing."

"I'll stop being such a mean old thing if you'll bring me my medicine chest from the wagon. George can show you where it is."

"Oh, of course, Tamsen. Right away!" And Betsy set off importantly on her errand.

There was nothing in the medicine chest that could help, but at least it would give Betsy something better to do than standing around and frightening herself half to death with another woman's pain. Tamsen knelt again beside her anguished patient, and the melody of her voice rose and fell, rose and fell, as she repeated, "It will all be all right, Mrs. Keseberg. It will all be just fine."

GOVERNOR BOGGS WAS INCLINED TO SPEND THE DAY IN CAMP, and as he moved among the travelers to consult their opinion, he found that most agreed with him. Many were crotchety from being denied the rest they had expected at Fort Laramie, and others were eager to get up a hunting expedition.

"The teams could use a rest, too," George Donner added, "and the graze and water are the best we've seen since we left Laramie. They're not much count, but we're not likely to find better for a spell."

"Also," Tamsen added, "Mrs. Keseberg had a very hard delivery, and travel over this rough ground will be a torture to the poor woman."

"Well, that seems to settle that!" Governor Boggs cheerfully announced, and tipped his hat to the Donners.

The captain had proceeded only a few yards when a horseman entered the camp, bringing news from Fort Laramie about a large group of emigrants who had just arrived there. One of their party, a Mr. Trimble, had been butchered by the Pawnees, and the Sioux were thirsty for their share of the white blood. Governor Boggs ordered camp to be broken without delay, and the California emigrants moved on through the desolate landscape of the Black Hills. Laramie peak was in full view on the horizon, unless it was obscured by the swarms of grasshoppers that frequently rose like angry storm clouds to blacken the air.

WILLIAM EDDY'S WAGON WAS BRINGING UP THE END OF THE train when it was overtaken by one of the strangest contraptions he had seen since leaving Belleville, Reed's palace wagon included. It had apparently begun life as a simple farm wagon, but a second bed had been raised above the first, extending at least a yard over the sides of the original vehicle, and with the familiar white top raised above that. Doors had been let into the sides of the old wagon bed, for storing supplies, and ropes and kettles and harness dangled from the overhanging platform. The driver had no box to sit on, but simply dropped his legs over the front edge of the raised bed, perched high above the backs of the oxen.

"Halloo," the driver shouted as the wagons pulled parallel to each other. "Are you for Oregon or California?"

"California!" Eddy shouted back. He had finally made his decision, and less out of any consideration of politics or geography than because he felt more at home with the California emigrants, especially the other folks from Illinois.

"Us, too!"

Only then did Eddy realize that the driver smiling at him so broadly was a woman, wearing a man's clothing and a broad straw hat that had frayed so badly it hung around her face like a clump of dried prairie grass.

"Murphy," she called. "The Widow Murphy."

"William Eddy," he answered, "and this is the missus, Eleanor. Two little tykes in the back." He gestured with his thumb.

"Mighty pleased to meet you. This is my daughter Harriet," the driver said, reaching an arm around the young woman who sat beside her, cradling an infant in her arms. "That's her husband Bill Pike on the sorrel, and the fellow driving the cart's named Bill Foster, married to my Sarah. He's not much use, but he was about the best we could get in a hurry. The crazy one up yonder's my oldest boy John Landrum. Got about as much sense as his daddy, God rest his soul." A boy who looked to be thirteen or fourteen was riding the wagon tongue, straddling it and balancing himself with one hand on the rump of each of the wheel oxen.

"That's fine, ma'am," Eddy replied, unable to catch much of the catalogue of names she continued to sing out over the rattle of the wagons. He thought he heard the names Mary and Catherine, but was not sure about the rest.

"Seven kids, two in-laws and three grandbabies," she summarized, and Eddy whistled appreciatively.

Lavina Murphy and her troop had decided only that morning to pull away from the Oregonians and set their sights on California. It had taken them much of the night to come to an agreement, and their discussion was so vigorous that Jessy Thornton termed it "an offense to the nocturnal ear of Nature." Apparently there had been frequent changes of destination, for the words "Oregon" and "California" had been painted over each other so many times that hardly any of the original cloth of the wagon sheet was still visible.

For all her brashness and the booming voice she sent across the

184

wilderness, Mrs. Murphy was a gentle, big-hearted woman who had adopted the clothing and, occasionally, the rough manners of her late husband because it seemed the only way to keep the family together, and she saw that as her sacred duty. Mr. Murphy had been a farmer in Tennessee, not far from Nashville, until talk of the rich soil of Missouri and a string of bad crops at home persuaded him to pull up stakes and head west. He was breaking the first field when he died, and Lavina found him propped stiffly between the handles of the plow, like something put there to frighten the crows away. While the older girls were washing their father's body, she finished the field for him. The land was rich, but after putting in the first crop they all realized there wasn't enough acreage to feed thirteen mouths, and more sure to come. With what they could get from the sale of the farm, they could put together a nest egg for the West, and somewhere along the trail they would decide where to point their wagon tongue. It gave them, at least, a lively topic of debate each night while they made camp, and they quarreled good-naturedly about the merits of north and south, until finally the widow wearied of the topic and said her destination was New Helvetia, and they could come along if they liked.

Since she was the only woman to lead her own contingent along the trail west, Lavina Murphy always stirred speculation and gossip among the emigrants. Some believed her a Mormon refugee whose husband had been slain at Nauvoo, while others knew beyond the shadow of a doubt that she had worked as a laundress in St. Louis and had never seen her name on a certificate of matrimony. In fact, there was nothing hidden or mysterious in her history of fifty years, and there was no attempt to draw attention to herself, no calculated eccentricity, in wearing her husband's clothing. She had few dresses good enough to pack, and those she would need to make the right impression when they arrived at their destination. She frugally saved them for the end of the trail, or for the rare Sundays and holidays when they were not moving. Dressed in severe widow's weeds, she was indistinguishable from a legion of doting grandmothers, and when she wasn't cracking the whip to urge the oxen on, she seemed shy and somewhat unsure of herself. Trail life demanded a leader, however, and though she was as fond of them as she was of her own children, Lavina Murphy didn't trust her daughters' husbands to take command. But her physical reserves were far less than William Eddy would have guessed when she pulled up beside him and thundered her bewildering chorus of introductions.

Edwin Bryant and his companions had made good time, but now one of them began to have second thoughts about Jim Clyman's warnings, deciding he would rather not risk the unknown cutoff after all, but proceed southwest to Fort Hall and wait for a caravan to form there. Accompanied by Owl Russell, Bryant turned east again to rejoin the main party and seek a replacement to help manage the mules, chafing at the further delay but pleased at the prospect of spending Independence Day with his friends.

Like most of the women, Tamsen had initially been modest about relieving herself with strangers looking on, and had always sought the shelter of bush or tree, even if it meant walking some distance from the wagons. Later, as the vegetation thinned, she often had to settle for the inadequate cover of sagebrush, and then even that became a luxury, while the fear of rattlers and wolves made her ever more reluctant to venture far from the protection of the camp. Some of the younger men took the problem as a sport, having contests to determine who was more gifted at writing "California" or "Oregon" in the dust or who had the better aim, and one of the teamsters had developed the habit of standing on the wagon box, holding the reins in his teeth as he unbuttoned and sent a spray out over the trail, until a sudden gust of wind cured him of the practice. The women tried to maintain other standards, but soon abandoned their efforts to control the younger children, and then gave up insisting on marking off one area for themselves and another for the men. As the route became more arduous and tedious, a few would stroll beside the wagons, chatting, and then stop to hoist their skirts, never pausing in the conversation, while wagons and stock lumbered past them. Tamsen tried to wait for the nooning, or until camp was made for the night, but it was not always possible, and more than once she complained to her husband, "I think my teeth are about to float away."

The moon was near the full and they were camped in a little hollow whose phosphorous rock glowed as though lighted from within, and every shape stood out in vivid silhouette against the luminous terrain. It was late before the children were bedded, the tent flap securely fastened to discourage intruders, and by then George had already slipped into the bottomless sleep of exhaustion that washed over him every night as soon as he had finished his evening meal. Taking with her a spare hardwood spoke for protection, Tamsen left the circle of the wagons and started up the rise, pausing every few feet to test the ground and thrust her weapon cautiously into threatening shadows. She turned and looked back at the camp below and imagined it as Mr. Bingham might have painted it, with the gracefully bowed wagon tops, the thin ribbons of smoke rising from dying fires, the huddled backs of the animals rolling and shifting within the circular corral, and all of it mingled in a mist of silver and gray that the moon struck from the pale rocks, with the shadows a deeper, liquid purple in contrast.

She moved higher up the hill, carefully checking her footing, treading so softly that she could hear only the soft whisper of her own breathing, and turned for another look at the sleeping camp. It was an enchanted kingdom waiting for the magic incantation, the touch of a wand, that would stir it to life, and the view held her while she bunched her skirts and squatted, balancing the heavy wooden spoke across her knees. There was neither sound nor movement to divert her attention, yet something drew her, and as she slowly turned her head, she knew there would be other eyes waiting to greet hers, and she met them without flinching, though she trembled as if struck by a gale. Seeking to hold unknown terrors at bay with the tensed muscle of her own will, she locked her gaze with that turned toward her, staring brightly from the shelter of a ragged outcropping. Neither moved, even when a coyote sent a single mournful note reverberating from the hills, but remained as fixed and rigid as if hewn from the rocky landscape. Only when Tamsen's legs began to cramp did she dare to shift her heels slightly, clutching her clumsy weapon even more firmly, so that she felt the coarse grain bite into her palms, and when this slight movement brought no response, provoked no lunging attack, she allowed her eyes to shift as well. They showed her at first a tangle of white, smoothed and rounded shapes that flowed in and out of shadow. It might have been the remains of some elaborate form carved in purest alabaster and polished to a rich gloss, inert and inanimate, had the eyes not glowed so intensely from a dark circle, a well of shadow that blended with the outcropping above it. How long she remained there Tamsen could not have said—perhaps not more than a minute or two, but it seemed much longer before John Denton's sunburned face separated from the shadow, before the figure stretched beside him became, distinctly, Milt Elliott, with his head of great tousled curls cradled on Denton's shoulder, apparently asleep. She stood then and brushed out her skirts, felt her knees about to buckle and commanded them not to abandon her now, while her gaze remained for an instant longer locked with that of the reclining man. Perhaps she did not understand it all, but she understood the pleading look in his eyes, for she had seen it there before, when he came to seek her assistance or her approval, and she had grown fond of the tender, boyish appeal. Hoping he would know how to measure her response, she nodded once, briefly, before she turned and moved back down the slope.

JULY 4TH WAS THE HOTTEST DAY THE ARMY OF THE WEST HAD faced on their straggling march toward Santa Fe, and because the baggage train lagged behind, delayed by difficult fordings, the men were all on short rations. Most had a cup of whiskey to wash down their scant breakfast, but the mood it produced was far from festive. One recruit noted that if contact with the commissary wagons could not be made soon, "we shall have nothing to eat but our own horses."

General Taylor's army, on the other hand, was by now comfortably and familiarly at home in the little river town of Matamoros, and found the conquered Mexicans amiable companions, who added their own colorful pageantry and cookery to the Independence Day celebrations. In the officer's mess, draped with bright cotton banners, the general raised his glass and delivered a stirringly patriotic toast to the Republic of Texas and the mighty union of the United States of America. He was already consciously rehearsing for a presidential campaign.

Before the town of Monterey, Commodore John D. Sloat had anchored the flagship *Savannah* in line with the *Cyane* and *Levant*, the stout trio clearly announcing to the British squadron the folly of attempting to interfere with American interests in the area. News had arrived of the war with Mexico, but Sloat was old and feeble and so cautious about taking the weighty responsibility of seizing a foreign province, that almost a week would elapse before the American flag waved over the little customshouse. But the glorious Fourth was observed with rumbling salutes fired from the three ships riding at anchor in Monterey harbor.

The emigrant trains bound for Oregon and California that had drawn up together along Beaver Creek ushered in the day with a volley of rifle shots followed by a wavering trumpet rendition of "The Star-Spangled Banner." A spare wagon pole lifted the Stars and Stripes over the festive campground, where the emigrants paraded stiffly in their Sunday clothes, and throughout the day a series of orators mounted stumps, water barrels and wagon tongues to sound the praises of the nation. Colonel William Henry "Owl" Russell was the popular favorite, and many wondered how they could ever have doubted his brilliant leadership. James Reed gathered the Springfield contingent together and with solemn ceremony opened the bottle of whiskey he had received as a parting gift nearly three months before. The men all faced east to lift their glasses in tribute to the friends they had left behind.

Touring the noisy camp, Edwin Bryant found his recruit in George Donner's able teamster, Hiram Miller, who had quarreled with his partner Milt Elliott. For a time, the two had kept a diary together, beginning with their names and the words "left home together." They had also made a joint investment in goods for the California trade, to be carried in one of the Donner wagons in lieu of the usual wages the teamster would have earned. No one knew the source of the disagreement between the two men, but the sulking Miller seemed determined to push out on his own, and

Bryant so persuasively argued his need for another man to manage the mules that George Donner finally relented.

Bryant's party proceeded rapidly to Fort Bridger and moved out along the vague route that Hastings sketched for them, repeatedly losing their way in the narrow, boulder-strewn canyons of the Wahsatch, and consuming most of their supplies. In the treacherous Salt Desert the mule that carried the remaining food wandered away in search of water, and precious time was consumed in finding it again. Nonetheless, they succeeded in making what was normally a two-day crossing in only thirty-one hours. Exhausted, half-blind, dehydrated, skinny as their own starving mules, they had survived the worst trials the cutoff had to offer, and when they rode into New Helvetia, John Augustus Sutter greeted them with the announcement that the fort was now a military outpost of the United States of America.

15

North fork of the Platte River
Sunday, July 5th, 1846

Since leaving Fort Laramie we have continued to advance westward along the thinning Platte River, and expect to cross to the Sweetwater in a few days. If the water there is indeed sweet, it will be a great boon to thirsty travelers, for most of what we find along the way is very bitter. The creeks and smaller streams emptying into the sandy river flow over ground containing a great quantity of mixed salts which, in addition to their unpleasant taste, do little to relieve the continuous thirst of men and animals.

We had not been long on the road after our abbreviated stay at Fort Laramie when Mrs. Keseberg commenced her labor, and the unfortunate woman spent many hours in great pain, as the terrain over which we were then passing was singularly uneven, and the threat of attacks by the Sioux made all cautious of stopping to make camp early. It was near midnight, however, before her baby appeared, a healthy boy with stout lungs who was at once named Lewis Sutter Keseberg by his proud father. Without stating it directly, Mr. Keseberg encourages people to suppose the founder of New Helvetia to be a personal acquaintance, but I guess he is only preparing a calling card for California. Mrs. Keseberg is very weak still, but Margaret Reed has persuaded the father to allow little Ada to travel with her family. Since I have no nursling of my own, I often have the infant Maggie Eddy with me during the day. She is a sweet-tempered child with wonderful blue eyes and hair the color of copper, a kind of miniature of her pretty mother, who is sorely weakened by dysentery and unfit to care for two small children. Mrs. Eddy is altogether much too feeble to ride the wagon box beside her husband, as she is otherwise accustomed to do, and he plainly misses her tender companionship through the long, tedious days.

We passed the birthday of the Declaration of Independence in an encampment on Beaver Creek, where there was much festive merry-making, including patriotic orations and singing and a dance in the evening that a little resembled a buffalo stampede. Mr. Bryant passed the day with us, having returned together with Colonel Russell in search of a new recruit to replace Mr. Kuykendall. These visitors resumed their westward course late in the day with our former teamster Hiram Miller. He was quiet and sometimes moody, but a good and loyal worker, whose departure greatly diminished our strength. The decision to leave us was partly owing to the impatience many feel at our slow progress, but was also sparked by a disagreement with his friend and partner, Milt Elliott. Perhaps they will make up their differences when they meet again in California.

The creek where we celebrated the 70th anniversary of the Union takes its designation from the many energetic beavers that have built their residential dams across it. William Eddy killed one of the creatures and brought it into camp, giving us an opportunity for a close examination of this singular and sagacious animal before putting it into his soup pot. It resembles almost exactly the common muskrat in the appearance of the head and body, though the specimen I saw was over two feet long without his tail and half as broad across the back. The tail, which serves both as paddle and steering oar, was over a foot long, about 5 inches broad, flat and hard and scaly like a fish or some parts of an alligator's hide. The teeth resemble those of the squirrel, but are exceptionally long and powerful, set in jaws whose strength is indicated by the deep cuts they can make in hardwood. The whole animal seemed far stronger in proportion to its compact size than anything I had ever conceived of, if one can judge by the masterworks of engineering they create. I visited one of their dams and was astonished by the ingenuity and calculation exhibited in its construction. It was thrown across the stream where 2 projecting points in the bank formed abutments, and a bar in the middle provided the requisite support. The whole was constructed of willows, with which the banks are lined, varying in size from 1 to 3 inches in diameter, all cut off as clean and smooth as though felled by the skillful stroke of a hatchet. Bushes had been laid with great regularity parallel with the course of the stream, piled layer upon layer with sticks placed among them to bind the whole and thus form a very strong and durable breastwork. Above this dam the beavers had thrown in moss and leaves which, catching the silt and sand the stream pushed along, had completely stopped the water and raised it four feet. The dam was some forty feet long and altogether more stoutly constructed and resistant than the one Mr. Donner erected on Sugar Creek! I do not wonder that the superstitious Indians are said to ascribe a soul to the beaver, for the evidences in his favor are sufficient to overset the theory about "instinct alone."

We find no relief from the abrasive and burning alkali dust. A coating of buffalo grease helps somewhat to protect the exposed skin, but the smell is so rancid that few can suffer it for long. The increasing difficulty of the trail allows scant time for botanical expeditions, but Mr. Stanton has gathered a number of interesting specimens, and shared some of these with me. They include the *senecio rapifolia,* the *lippia cuneifolia,* and the *sheperdia argentea* among the most frequent specimens, as well as several interesting *Chenopiacaceaem.* One of these was first discovered by Dr. James during the famous Long expedition, but ours appeared to be a new genus, and we regretted it could not be formally described for want of the ripe fruit.

The landscape through which we have been passing consists principally of agrillaceous sandstone, sometimes cut by wind and rain into formations resembling the pyramids of old Egypt. There are also many large cubical granite rocks, often entirely exposed and rising to a height of 100 feet and more from the plain, and these sometimes laced with beautiful serpentine, semi-transparent and of a deep-green color not unlike emerald. I have added a few samples to the geological traveling cabinet I have made by sewing pouches against the inside of the wagon cover.

Several cattle have died, and there was not time to stop to dress the meat, though the Indians have given us a good lesson as to how this can be accomplished on the prairies. They cut buffalo meat into long strips, plait these together, and after dipping them in brine suspend the whole from four stakes over a trench filled with burning chips. The procedure produces a large black lattice of meat, very tough and dry but so perfectly preserved as to remain edible for many months. Despite certain unfortunate tendencies, many of which they have borrowed from the whites, the western Indians are provident in their use of nature's available resources, and we could learn much from their ingenious practices. I think, however, that I could never develop a stomach for the little hard cakes the Sioux women cook in buffalo grease, or for the grasshoppers they consume. These swarm about in regular clouds, but when they alight they can blend perfectly with a stalk of prairie grass, and then they are detectable only by their thread-like legs hopping about. Some are the size of a small frog, and I can easily understand how Indians are said to live from them when game is unavailable, for one would make a good mouthful.

There are still vigorous debates among the Californians about whether to proceed via Fort Hall or Fort Bridger, and I begin to wish Mr. Hastings had stuck to his career as a temperance lecturer and not gone in for exploration. Mr. Donner, however, is much persuaded by his arguments, and Mr. Reed will not hear a word against the wisdom of the cut-off.

It will soon be Frances's birthday, and I must think of some trinket that will give her pleasure in the wilderness.

16

After leaving at last the "chewable" Platte, we passed through an inexpressively dreary country, without the slightest diversity of color or form. The earth was iron and the heavens brass, a wide waste of desolation where even the winds had died, and which began to vary its aspect only as we drew near the celebrated Independence Rock. This formation owes its name to the circumstance of a number of patriotic Americans once pausing there to celebrate the anniversary of the nation. The great rock resembles nothing so much as the scarred and weathered shell of a gigantic black turtle, stranded in the midst of the plain, and so many names have been carved into its porous surface that it comprises a veritable register of the desert. Colonel Frémont offers the following description of the natural curiosity: "This is an isolated granite block, about 650 yards long and 40 in height. Except in a depression of the summit, where a little soil supports a scanty growth of shrubs, with a solitary dwarf pine, it is entirely bare. Everywhere within six or eight feet of the ground, where the surface is sufficiently smooth, and in some places sixty or eighty feet above, the rock is inscribed with the names of travelers. Many a name famous in the history of this country, some well known to science, are to be found mixed among those of the traders, and travelers for pleasure and curiosity, and missionaries among the savages. Some of these have been washed away by the rain, but the greater number are still legible."

It was at this place some years ago that Mr. Lansford Hastings and his companion Mr. Lovejoy, having lingered behind the main party to inscribe their names, were taken by a savage band of Indians, who inflicted many painful indignities on their helpless captives. Through a Canadian half-breed who spoke a little English, they were ultimately able to persuade the aged chief that their intentions were peaceable, but then found themselves unwilling recruits of a war party bent on attacking the wagons of their friends. Luckily, Mr. Hastings's facile tongue did not desert him, and through his interpreter he was able to persuade the chief of the folly of such an attack, and to bargain for the freedom of himself and his companion with the promise of gifts to be fetched from the wagons. These consisted of several twists of tobacco, with which the Indians seemed satisfied, for they gave up their aggressions. I wonder if the adventurer was pleased with the cheapness of his bargain, or if he felt dismay at seeing the worth of his life measured out in a few puffs of smoke.

In the scanty soil around Independence Rock there were a number of bushes, in general appearance like the common gooseberry, with yellow fruit tasting much like the ripe persimmon, but somewhat less tart. While gathering these desert delicacies, the children chanced upon a pair of bloody trousers with a bullet hole through one leg and a pipe stuffed with fresh tobacco in the pocket. It is feared the owner, perhaps a straggler separated from his party like Messrs. Hastings and Lovejoy, was killed by the Indians while snacking on the pleasant yellow fruit. Thus can the most innocent pastimes turn deadly in these bleak and barren regions, and often quite without warning. Rattlesnakes are also thick about the base of the great rock, and the strictest caution is necessary when first approaching it.

Far more majestic than Independence Rock is the Devil's Gate, situated about five miles distant, and consisting of a steep, narrow gorge through which the Sweetwater River wends its sparkling course. This spectacular cleavage, which varies from 300 to 500 feet in height, confines the river passage to a mere thirty yards, and the shadows cast by the encroaching walls do indeed give the picturesque spot an awesomely "devilish" appearance. With a single stride the visitor can move from blazing desert heat into the deepest chill of winter, that penetrates in an instant to the very marrow of the bones. Beyond Devil's Gate the valley of the Sweetwater is about five miles wide, bounded by wooded mountains on the south. An arid, barren, sandy plain, with little growing upon it save for the odious *artemisia tridentata,* presents the appearance of a brown heath stretching off from near the right bank of the river to the foot of the desolate-looking mountains to the south. From the left bank, however, this brown heath and sandy plain is exchanged for rich meadows, from the greensward of which crumbling granite masses rise abruptly in sterile grandeur to the height of 1500 or 2000 feet, terminating in a line of broken summits. Their heads are not covered with mountain ash, nor are their gray sides harmonized by mosses, lichens, and yew trees. Occasionally a hardy pine has succeeded in rooting itself to a precarious ledge, but otherwise they are destitute of vegetation. They are precipitous, and bear on their sides fragments of rock, which in the distance look like ruins of buildings that have either fallen down or are rising up from the plain, amidst deep verdure and a profusion of flowers.

On the upper stretches of the river, and near the dividing range, Mr. Stanton collected several species of *castilleja; pentstemmen micrantha,* Nutt.; several *gentians;* the pretty little *androsace occidentalis,* Nutt.; *solidago incana,* Torr. and Gr.; and two species of *eriogonum,* one of which was new. The grass of the region is abundant and tolerably good, but some of the animals have drunk so much alkali water that their stomachs reject it, and I fear yet more of them will die.

The humans have also had some amusing variation in their diet, apart from the wild gooseberry. Approaching Independence Rock we encountered a large pond so strongly impregnated with carbonate and bi-carbonate of potash that the water would no longer hold it in solution. Along the edges of the pond it was found in broad and perfectly white sheets, from 1 to 2 inches thick, like a coat of freshly fallen snow. That taken up from the bottom of the hoary pond was indistinguishable in texture from fine salt, and was collected to be used for the purpose of making bread light and spongy, at which it succeeds even better than processed saleratus. On the day following this discovery we encountered a low and grassy swamp on the right side of the road that proved to shelter a thick layer of crystal-clear ice. The men dug up enough to fill all the water kegs, which afforded us the luxury of ice-water all through the heat of the day, and this was a great relief to parched throats. The dust is still with us, and several of our goggles have broken.

We have viewed our first desert rabbits, clumsy-looking beasts that from the distance might easily be confused for small mules, and numerous soaring eagles. At some distance back on the road I observed a very large eagle flying backward and forward, in a half-circle, in front of an immense rocky precipice where she had built her nest. At length I saw that she was not seeking prey but endeavoring to induce her newly-fledged eaglets to leave their lofty home and take to the wing. She frequently fluttered over the nest, upon the edges of which the eaglets were sitting, after which she gracefully and majestically circled upward, evidently endeavoring to encourage them to imitate her aerial sweep. This she did frequently, and the eaglets often extended their necks to gaze after her, but in consequence of timidity or fear of leaving the nest, they declined following. At length, after various unsuccessful attempts to induce them to come abroad, she appeared to be very angry with them for clinging to their nest as though it was the only place in the world, or even the best one. She then darted at it fiercely and threw it together with her own children down the sheer face of the wall. In a moment, she was below them with outstretched wings, as though to break their plummeting fall. Very soon, however, the young birds, who had demonstrated such an inordinate attachment for the little pile of brush, learned both the fact of their having wings and the manner of employing them. They began to rise, at first slowly and rather heavily. Soon the parent bird led the way, describing gradually enlarging circles as she ascended, while her young ones followed. Upward still the noble family arose, until the eaglets became mere specks upon the sky, and then disappeared, and soon the parent bird itself was lost in heaven's pure depth of blue. Their destination is unknown, but certain it is that they will arrive there with far more ease than what we experience, tied to the earth far below them.

At dusk today, while we were still busy making dinner, a lone rider came into camp and introduced himself as Truman Bonney, lately of Oregon, and carrying a letter from Lansford Hastings addressed to all the California emigrants. This document was composed "At the Headwaters of the Sweetwater," and contained the unsettling communication that, due to the hostilities with Mexico, the indigenous California authorities might seek to restrict the entry of emigrants. We have been urged to form one large party for defense, and to save time, strength and effort by using the new road from Fort Bridger over the south end of the Great Lake to Mary's River. The author himself will await travelers and give them his personal guidance over the cut-off, which additional assurance has won over several who had remained skeptical of the author's intentions.

Mr. Denton has suffered an attack of mountain fever, but is a cooperative patient and should soon mend. The other Springfield delegates are in middling good health, but all complain of blistered feet, for the brittle grass is nearly as unyielding as stone, and takes a high price of shoeleather.

17

TRUMAN BONNEY, WHO HAD ARRIVED WITH THE OMINOUS WARNINGS from Lansford Hastings, volunteered to carry with him any letters destined for the States, but most of the emigrants were too weary to take advantage of the offer. Many, as well, found increasing difficulty in reconciling the ardors of the trail with the sprightly travelogues their friends and relatives would expect to receive. Only thirteen-year-old Virginia Reed was capable of rising to the challenge, and in her frank, random style she also acknowledged both the death of her grandmother and the threatening Indian wars, two unpleasant themes which the adult correspondents of the party had studiously avoided.

Independence rock Julyth 12 1846
To Mary C. Keyes from Virginia E.B. Reed
My Dear Couzin I take this oppertuny to Write to you to let you know that I am well at present and hope that you are well. We have all had good health—we came to the Blue—the water was so hye we had to stay there 4 days—in the mean time gramma died, she became speechless the day before she died. We buried her verry decent We made a nete coffin and buried her under a tree we had a head stone and had her name cutonit and the date and yere verry nice and at the head of the grave was a tree we cut some letters on it the young men soded it all ofer and put Flores on it We missed her verry much every time we come into the Wagon we look at the bed for her. We have come throw several tribes of Indians the Kaw Indians the soux the shawnies, at the Kaw viliage paw counted 250 Indians We diden see no Indians from the time we lefe the Kaw viliage till we come to fort Laramy the soux Indians are going to War with the crows we have to pass throw ther Fiting ground, the Soux Indians are the pretest drest Indians there is, paw goes bufalo hunting most every day and kils 2 or 3 buffalo every day paw shot an elk some of our compian saw a grisly bear We have the thermometer 102°—average for the last 6 days We celebrated the 4 of July on Plat at Bever crik, severel of the gentmen in Springfield gave paw a botel of licker and said it shoulden be opend till the 4 of July and paw was to look to the east and drink it and they was to look to the West and drink it at 12 o clock paw treted the compiany and we all had some lemminade, maw and paw is Well and sends their best love to you all. I send my best love to you all. We have hard from uncle Cad several times he went to california and now is gone to oregon he is well. I am going to send this letter by a man coming from oregon

199

hisself. He is going to take his family to Oregon We are all doing well and in hye sperits so I must close your leter, you are for ever my affectionate couzen

Virginia E.B. Reed

18

THE CALIFORNIA EMIGRANTS HAD BEEN FORCED TO MAKE CAMP IN the open plain, for the Sweetwater had sealed itself away behind narrow, perpendicular cliffs. While the men watered the panting oxen, the women searched the ground for buffalo chips, spreading in widening circles from the cluster of wagons, for the giant herds rarely traveled the higher plateaus. Tamsen and Elitha held the bushel basket between them, and Frances moved ahead, calling out proudly each time she found a little fuel, but waiting for the others to come up before she ventured to lift any of the dried chips. Her mother carried the familiar wagon spoke as protection against rattlesnakes and giant spiders that might happen to be nestled nearby.

The three were nearly a half mile from camp when Frances shouted, "Mama, a hole!"

The girl was standing at the edge of a great bowl-shaped rock when Elitha and Tamsen arrived with the half-filled basket swinging between them. The shallow stone bowl tilted away from them, and at the base of the incline was a narrow opening like the mouth of a storm cellar sliced into the earth.

"It must be a lava spill," Tamsen explained to the two children. "Look how porous it is. You can see how the rock bubbled and cooled." She leaned down to feel the coarse, abrasive surface, and was surprised by the warmth it had retained from the sun.

"When did it happen?" Frances asked.

"Oh, a long time ago, child."

"How long, Mama?"

"A thousand years, maybe, or a thousand thousand."

"So long?" Frances' eyes widened with astonishment at the inconceivable measure.

"Maybe longer. Maybe this is where time began," Tamsen answered, and as she stood her heels sent a spray of fine black pebbles skating down across the sloping depression in the rock. Balancing carefully, she started to follow their path, but turned to the two girls first and said, "Now you wait here, while I have a look."

She had not appreciated the steepness of the slope. From where they had looked down, the depression seemed to fall away gently from the crenellated edge, but as she stepped out Tamsen felt the sudden lunge of gravity. She stiffened her legs, leaned backward and extended her arms to the side, braced against the fierce downward pull and moving ahead slowly, one cautious foot sliding before the other like a novice tightrope walker. As she inched forward, the opening at the base of the incline seemed to expand and swell, revealing an enormous cavern scooped from the porous stone. Her feet discharged another blast of pebbles that flashed before her, were sucked instantly into the black opening.

"Tamsen, please don't go nearer," Elitha shouted.

"Come back, Mama," Frances begged.

With a little wave of her hand she tried to reassure them that there was no serious danger, but her entire body began to tremble as she moved one careful step nearer, and then another. Each advance showed her more of the real dimension of the gaping wound torn in the rock, and she could feel against her face the chill air that emanated from the impenetrable shadows. She listened attentively, thought for a moment that she heard the distant rushing of a thousand startled wings, and then realized with a faint, nervous smile that she had heard her own brittle hair against her cheeks. The silence from the cave was as vast, as impenetrable, as the darkness, and both assumed a mass and texture, like something crouched beneath the scalded earth, waiting. From the pocket of her dress Tamsen drew one of the carnelians she had collected during nooning, took careful aim, and flung it into the mouth of the cave. No sound measured the fall, no echo completed the experiment, though she strained to catch the faintest, most distant note. Panic turned her, drove her against the ruthless drag of the earth, and she stumbled, fell, clawed at the unyielding rock as she jerked ahead on her knees with the clumsy motions of a crippled insect. When she had moved a few yards up the steep incline she felt the panic ebb as suddenly as it had come, and her body hugged the warm stone in a long, shuddering embrace. Then she climbed slowly to her feet again and composed a reassuring smile for the two girls who waited above her, with a chalky pallor laid like a coat of whitewash across their sunburned faces.

AFTER HIS FRUSTRATING EFFORTS TO PERSUADE THE CALIFORNIANS to avoid the Hastings cutoff, Jim Clyman continued his journey to the States, arriving at the east bank of the Blue River on July 15th. When camp was made he sat Indian-fashion on a folded buffalo robe and, feeling uncommonly philosophical, made the following entry in his journal:

This stream affords some rich vallies of cultivateable land and the Bluffs are made of a fine lime rock with some good timber and numerous springs of clear cool water here I observed the grave of Mrs. Sarak Keys agead 70 yares who departed this life in may last at her feet stand the stone that gives us this information. This stone shews us that all ages and all sects are found to undertake this long tedious and even dangerous Journy for some unknown object never to be realized even by those the most fortunate and why because the human mind can never be satisfied never at rest allways on the strech for something new some strange novelty.

FOR WEEKS THE EARTH HAD BEEN LIFTING IN IMPERCEPTIBLE stages, tilting them toward the rocky spine of the continental divide, where waters began their trickling flow toward the Pacific. The guidebooks the emigrants carried gave them some rough measure of the elevation they had reached, and what they diagnosed as mountain fever was, in fact, the body's painful protest against the rapidly thinning air they breathed. Still, there was little in the landscape to announce that they were now climbing the ridgepole of the continent, though the glittering snow line that capped the peaks of the Wind River Mountains was in plain view, and the Sweetwater had narrowed and then divided into a series of brisk mountain streams. When they thought of the South Pass, most of the emigrants awaited some dramatic view of a canyon or narrow defile through the Rocky Mountains, slicing between sheer precipices that would form a lofty ceremonial gateway to the lands of the Pacific. But the pass itself was a gentle valley almost twenty miles wide, and the ascent so gradual as to seem indistinguishable from the dozens of rocky plateaus along which they had toiled, heads down, since their hasty departure from Fort Laramie. They had left behind the grassy plain of the Sweetwater and rolled across ancient gray rock that hammered viciously at the loose wagon tires, the constant metallic din reinforcing the unrelieved solitude of the landscape.

Then, as gradually as they had begun the ascent, they rolled down the western side of the pass and made camp at the shaded oasis of Pacific Springs. For hours men sat crouched beside the bubbling source, watching the thin ribbon of water flow westward toward the ocean, in seeming defiance of the rhythms by which their lives and the lives of their fathers had been regulated. They dropped in blades of grass to watch them spin away, to be fed to larger streams that would marry into the rivers swirling and plunging into the distant Gulf of California, and they repeatedly dipped roughened hands into the chill water to drink ritually, wonderingly, from cupped palms.

THE LUSHLY ABUNDANT GRASS AT LITTLE SANDY CREEK ENCOURaged both the Oregon and the California emigrants to linger there for a while, resting the oxen and cattle and making final decisions about the route ahead. Some would decide for the old established trail to Fort Hall, while others preferred to take Greenwood's or Sublette's cutoff, a forty-mile dry drive that could save them two or three days of hard traveling. Some of those bound for California were determined to strike out southwest to Bridger's Fort and pick up the Hastings cutoff, though there was some dismay that the explorer had not appeared to guide them, since his letter to the future Californians had been addressed from the upper reaches of the Sweetwater, which they had passed days before. James Reed had been confident they would meet him there, or at Pacific Springs, but at Little Sandy Creek they learned he had already departed for Fort Bridger with a party more advanced than theirs, so their meeting would be delayed for a few days. In fact, as the Reeds and Donners decided to cast their lot with Hastings, he was already leaving Fort Bridger as official guide to the Harlan-Young Party. Bryant's mule train also headed west from the fort on that July Sunday, but the transplanted Yankee had left concerned letters behind him to warn his friends of the folly of attempting the same route with their heavy wagons. Old Gabe Bridger perhaps guessed their contents, for he declined to deliver them when the emigrants arrived at his crude wilderness trading post.

Jessy Thornton and Governor Boggs, both bound for Oregon, cast their lot with Greenwood's cutoff to Fort Hall, as did some of those with "California" emblazoned on their tattered wagon tops. The Donner brothers and James Reed, however, maintained their faith in Hastings's vision of a shorter, easier trail. Others were inclined to follow their lead, persuaded less by the force of their rambling and repetitive arguments than by the obvious breeding and prosperity of the Springfield families. Silent and rigid, Tamsen Donner sat with a sheet of paper pinned to her drawing board and composed an official roster of the party that would set out at dawn for Bridger's Fort:

> George Donner, his wife Tamsen, and 5 children
> Jacob Donner, his wife Elizabeth, and 7 children
> John Denton
> Noah James
> Samuel Shoemaker
> Antoine
> Charles Tyler Stanton
> James Frazier Reed, his wife Margaret, and 4 children
> Baylis Williams and his sister Eliza
> Milford (Milt) Elliott
> James Smith

Walter Herron

Patrick Breen, his wife Margaret (Peggy) and 7
    children

Patrick Dolan

William Eddy, his wife Eleanor, and 2 children

Lavina Murphy, widow, with 5 unmarried children
    and 2 married daughters with their husbands—
    William and Sarah Foster and 1 child, William
    and Harriet Pike and 2 children

Lewis Keseberg, his wife Phillipine, and 2 children

Karl (Dutch Charley) Burger

Mr. Hardkoop

Joseph Reinhardt

Augustus Spitzer

Mr. and Mrs. Wolfinger

With the exception of the Springfield travelers, who had always presented a united front, the shape of the new company was the product of accident and coincidence that stretched for hundreds of miles across the wilderness, that reached beyond the wilderness to farms in Missouri and Tennessee, towns in Ohio and Illinois, and then beyond the ocean to Belgium, Holland, Ireland, Germany. Illness and death, financial reverses and unexpected windfalls, a newspaper editorial or congressional debate or territorial hunger or a sprung wagon wheel had eventually brought them here to sing out their names for Tamsen Donner's census. Most of the members knew the others intimately, as part of the sprawling emigrant train that had spent more than two months hauling from Independence to the Little Sandy, often drawing their wagons side by side to make camp, then losing sight of each other for days or weeks, hailing friendly greetings as they were reunited. Old Mr. Hardkoop, a plump Belgian merchant who had lived briefly in Cincinnati, was an exception, for his English was so fragmentary that he communicated only with Keseberg, and the rest of the party never even learned his first name. His life would thus make no more sense to them than his lonely and mysterious death in the salt desert, where his body was left unburied and unmourned.

Shortly after she had finished composing the official roster, Tamsen added to it the name of Luke Halloran, a young Missourian who was plainly dying of tuberculosis, and who feared being deserted by the friends with whom he was traveling, for he was too weak to sit his horse, and there was no room for him to ride in the wagon. He had found a vague connection to George Donner through a mutual acquaintance in Vandalia, Illinois, and it was sufficient to make his polite introduction to the family, though it was Tamsen to whom he addressed the plea that he be allowed to pay for his continued passage in one of their wagons. While he told his story, his long, emaciated fingers formed a lattice before his face to hide his frightened tears. There was no more a question of the Donners taking money for their assistance than there was of abandoning the consumptive man with his cultivated manners and soft-spoken eloquence.

JESSY THORNTON WAS FEEBLE, FEVERISH AND ILL TEMPERED, FOR his drivers had deserted him and he lacked both skill and strength to control his own teams. His journal entries became briefer now, his effusively picturesque interludes more rare, but on July 20th he took particular pains with his entry, for it signaled the final parting from friends he had learned to respect and trust on the trail: "The Californians were much elated, and in fine spirits, with the prospect of a better and nearer road to the country of their destination. Mrs. George Donner was, however, an exception. She was gloomy, sad and dispirited, in view of the fact that her husband and others could think for a moment of leaving the old road, and confide in the statement of a man of whom they knew nothing, but was probably some selfish adventurer."

19

Little Sandy Creek
Sunday, July 19th, 1846

We have passed across the dreary hump of barren rock that divides the North American continent into two shelving planes, and find ourselves now on the western slope, from which waters begin their flow to the sunny Pacific. All had eagerly awaited this moment, but the road through the South Pass proved singularly disappointing, and not at all romantic. The path itself is generally a smooth champaign country, about 19 miles wide, commencing at the rough broken ground at the foot of the Wind River chain of mountains and terminating at Table Rock, where the rough and broken country may be said again to commence. On entering this broad valley there is nothing in sight to merit the name Rocky Mountains—no crags or overhanging precipices, nor any other thing our former geography led us to believe was there. As we took leave of the waters running toward the homes of our childhood, we began an ascent so gradual as to be almost imperceivable, along a road leading through a desert of upright stones. Only these everlasting gray rocks lifted up their forms to relieve the naked sterility, the gloomy vastness and awful emptiness of the place. Slowly we advanced into the region of the clouds, whose gloomy masses rolled thickly before our eyes, and when these finally parted and dispersed, we beheld far below a scenery sublime and grand, which in some measure relieved the disappointment of our initial expectations. High, rugged, cold blue mountains towered far up on either side, into a misty region where all save the voice of the storm is hushed, where all is cold and lonely and chill as death.

Our first camp on the western slopes was at Pacific Springs, and from there we proceeded to the broad, shallow waters of Little Sandy Creek, where we have enjoyed several pleasant reunions with travelers pausing here to recruit themselves and their animals. Mr. Thornton is among the gypsies, and his health has severely deteriorated since we saw him last, both from the increasing rigors of the journey and from the unaccustomed exertions he has had to make in consequence of the desertion of his treacherous drivers. We have said a final adieu to these loyal friends of the trail, for they are to proceed now to Oregon via Fort Hall, while we make our way to Fort Bridger.

Our party comprises 35 adults and 35 children, the tidy symmetry having been completed by Mr. Luke Halloran, a consumptive from the state of Missouri who had rightly grown to suspect the goodwill of his traveling companions, and begged that he and his trunk might be accommodated in one of our wagons. Due to the lateness of the hour and the preparations for departure still remaining, the election of a captain was postponed until tomorrow. It seems likely that the choice will go either to Mr. James Reed or Mr. George Donner, though Mr. Reed's aristocratic disposition has alienated the hearts of some of his companions. The foreigners, in particular, find him a trifle "fancy" for their taste.

Since approaching the source of the Sweetwater, we have each day expected to encounter Mr. Lansford Hastings, who offered his services as our guide through the wilderness ahead, but we have seen neither hide nor hair of him. Yesterday we learned that he has already proceeded to Fort Bridger with an advance party. This fact gives further evidence of the tardiness of our own itinerary, and many are eager to remedy this by taking advantage of any available shortcut. I fear that if Mr. Hastings knows no more of geography than he does of the habits of the bison, we may end by doing some of his exploring for him, for his description of the wonderfully straight line running west from the fort contains nothing by way of recognizable points of orientation for the passage through mountains and deserts. These reservations I repeatedly communicated to Mr. Donner and Mr. Reed, but they were unanimous in dismissing them as womanish fears unworthy of deliberation in the councils of the wise. Such councils are principally ruled by the adage that "A woman should be seen, not heard," and sometimes by the motto:

> Ask a woman's advice, and whate'er she advise,
> Do the very reverse and you're sure to be wise.

That this is not a necessary circumstance of life is bravely demonstrated by the Murphy family, which travels under the able leadership of a widow-woman who makes all essential decisions for the most numerous party in our midst. It is true that in doing so Mrs. Murphy sacrifices a measure of her feminine charm (together with her petticoats), but more moderate versions of her decorum are surely not unthinkable. On the other hand, it ought to be noted that this excellent woman takes no objection to Mr. Hastings's rhetoric, and I pray her motherly instincts are correct. Perhaps I am only feeling a little out of spirits, yet I fear that in following the recommendations of this adventurer, we shall find ourselves sheared, shaven, polled, scraped and pared.

IV

LITTLE SANDY CREEK

·TO· TRUCKEE MEADOWS

1

THEIR BODIES WERE STILL JOINED, THE MUSCLES OF HIS THIGHS still tensed against hers, when he plunged into sleep like a stone dropped from a mountain precipice. Tamsen edged free of the slack weight, careful not to disturb him, though she knew only the wildest pandemonium would intrude on his corpselike slumber. For an entire night his back had rested on a stone whose razor-sharp edge sliced through two doubled blankets, his waistcoat and shirt, and gouged a ragged wound in his back. His nightly surrender to weariness, which often seized him before the evening meal was finished, had frightened her at first, made her feel helpless and tearfully vulnerable to the sounds that laced the darkness—to the moans and scratchings, the sudden clatter of stones, the brisk flap of a wing, the startled whistle of the horses. She tried to dismiss her fright as the kind of addle-pated weakness better suited to the heroine of a novel, predictably fainting at the sight of a drop of blood, and remembered her repeated assurances to the children that the darkness was nothing to be feared, but more than once she had awakened to find herself gripping a wagon spoke so tightly it had planted splinters in her hand. Often it was only the ceaseless soprano wail of the wind that had startled her.

She sat up and dragged a brittle buffalo robe over George's shoulders, wincing at its sour smell as she pushed the edges beneath her husband's body, wedging them in place with the same brisk, unconscious movements she might have used in bedding one of the children. Then she pulled down the heavy flannel chemise she wore

213

as protection against the chill air, tucking it like Turkish trousers about her legs. With a blanket snugged beneath her arms, a shawl wrapped around her shoulders, she watched the delicate dance of shadows on the wall of the tent—the restless silhouette of aspens lining the Big Sandy River, where they had camped in the thin but radiant light of a new moon. They were late in arriving, for they had remained in camp that morning to elect a leader, and there had been much discussion of the qualities demanded by such a weighty post. Most of the men had surely talked only for the pleasure of hearing their own voices, for only two names—those of James Reed and George Donner—were ever seriously proposed. Mr. Eddy might have been a better choice, she thought, for he was full of youthful energy, well liked by all the company, and resourceful in coping with the physical problems of the journey. But Eddy was not a man of property. Though somewhat withdrawn from the group, perhaps too shy in his manners, Charles Stanton was the kind of sturdy, clear-thinking personality to inspire trust, but a bachelor traveling without dependents might be suspected of taking unnecessary risks. Thus, the only serious candidates were James Reed and George Donner, and Reed's aristocratic flourishes finally told against him. When George received a weighty majority, Reed graciously proposed the vote be made unanimous.

Her eyes shifted from the flickering light irradiating the wall of the tent to the sleeping form of her husband, Captain George Donner, and her hand sought his as though to offer apology for having entertained disloyal thoughts. She was proud of his captaincy, and he had richly, rightly earned his new distinction. No man of the party was more careful or more fair in his judgments, and he and Jacob knew more of journeying than all the rest combined. Yet his unquestioning faith in the wisdom of Lansford Hastings troubled her. He would brook no syllable of criticism raised against the explorer's claims; their wisdom had become his anchor, and it seemed to her a perilous mooring in the trackless sea that lay ahead. Tamsen felt no disloyalty in opposing his judgment, for George had never wished her to be docile and subservient, as Betsy was to Jacob, but perhaps she should not have disagreed so publicly, put her foot down so emphatically, and sulked over her drawing board as she recorded the names of their companions. It was not for herself that she resisted him, not to pit her will against his in some contest which both, ultimately, would lose, but for the children whose very existence might hang on the fragile thread of a moment's decision. Of the fifteen children he had fathered, ten had survived, and though he doted with an almost grandfatherly affection on the three daughters she had given him, there was something remote in his feeling for them.

For him, she thought, they are a bounty, but for me they are the pledge and very seal of life itself. She felt again the heavy milk with which she had nourished them, remembered the veins coiled blue beneath the ache of skin, the brittle crust of its seepage coarse fine sand before the damp relief, the easing flow of a deeper spring that had been blocked in the moment she watched three hasty coffins, hard wooden lozenges, descend into the promiscuous rot of earth. Of all this, the man beside her could know nothing. Plunged in his bottomless, oblivious sleep, he suffered no alarms at the scrabbling noises, the rush of invisible claws, that summoned her to rigid wakefulness. Often she rose in the night to pass swiftly to the tent where the girls lay in tangled sleep, and often the hammering of her own heart obliterated the thin melody of their breathing.

Tamsen clamped her eyes against the contorted pantomime of shadows on the wall of the tent, tried to imagine the vertical geometries of a house rising sturdily from a foundation of earth-colored bricks. But this time the ruse did not succeed. Fancy could not blot out the acrid presence of the buffalo robe or the coarse perfume of the eternal sage. Its deformed branches and penetrating stench had become synonymous with this pitiless landscape, with the secret menace it held for her and her daughters. Dried, stinking, hideous sage, growing in warped hopeless vacant blind travesty of growth that gives no shade or comfort or nurture or beauty or relief its roots seeking no hidden cooling spring but only dust its twisted branches decked with dust some monstrous crippled insect stranded rooted in torment companion only to the fat writhing coils of the rattlesnake occasionally visiting with slimy accidental embrace click and chatter of the scorpion scrabbling through the mock shade swaying in the effort to spill no drop of its poison on the poisoned ground the nurture of poisoned crippled creatures vengeful murderous in the glare of light that raises boundless lakes refreshing streams where there is only dust shale the stinking sage and the busy murderers that scratch and slither tense and coil beneath the luminous ghastly white of a bleached skull bones stripped to unknown nakedness by wolf and buzzard sudden tracks rapid fleeting stamped on the earth beginning nowhere ending nowhere vanished pursued or pursuer dry unbroken dance of death mosaic of bones crumbling to more dust a cushioned powdery bed for murderers soft mute with the unreadable passing alphabets of claw and coil erased by the faintest gust of suffocating air that thickens the gray velvet pall on sage and rock hunter and prey silts wagon ruts the mockery of a trail vanishing leaving only the dwarfed forest of unending unborn undying sage.

A wolf howled defiance at the slender crescent of the moon, and Tamsen tensed against her husband as she listened for the shrill, nervous response of the horses tethered nearby. The buffalo hide scraped her cheek like a rough hand, and its stench brought an acid churning to her stomach. "Captain Donner," she whispered, testing the words, then repeating them like an incantation to hold back the darkness.

2

Black's Fork
Sunday, July 26th, 1846

We are encamped tonight on a slight, meandering affluent of the Green River known as Black's Fork, whose banks are lined by the quaking and musical aspens. This picturesque resting place was chosen by our new Captain, Mr. George Donner, formerly of Springfield, Illinois. A unanimous vote entrusted him with the weighty decisions of the coming weeks and miles, and he accepted the referendum in proud but sober knowledge of the increased burden placed on his broad, capable shoulders. He will more than ever require the ministrations of the doting womenfolk who accompany him.

The barren upland country through which we have passed in recent days is scarcely worth a skinny paragraph. On the open plain the dun-colored monotony is relieved only by the persistent sage, which has grown hateful to us all. Along the mazy river courses there are occasional grassy meadows, largely burnt to brittle straw by the fiery sun, and sheltering aspens are often rooted along the banks. The sole variants in this tableau are provided by rare clusters of stout, showy lupine, and by stampeding "herds" of mosquitoes.

On Thursday we crossed the Green River, which takes its name not from the color of its waters, as generally supposed, but from the member of Ashley's expedition who first sketched its path, and reported on the curious wealth of fossils studding the banks. Though the river proved too shallow to dampen even the beds of the wagons, we followed its mazy course for a day. This compelled us to take an unwonted eastward swing, but the grass was superior to most we have lately seen, and all were anxious to strengthen their teams for the barren stretches ahead. A clue to their bleakness was provided yesterday in a tedious dry drive from the Green River to Black's Fork. This sluggish but clear-running guide will conduct us to Fort Bridger, which we expect to reach on Tuesday. The trading post offers the last habitation we can expect to view before arriving at Sutter's California settlement of New Helvetia. At Fort Bridger we also expect to encounter Mr. Lansford Hastings, and to learn further particulars of the celebrated cut-off with which our lot is now cast.

Tonight we share our campsite with a guest of most terrifying visage. With his sprawling beard and tangled hair, his clothing hanging about him in unclassifiable shreds, he somewhat resembles a domesticated grizzly bear as he shambles about tending his footsore herds. For leggings he wears strings of dirty scalps that sway hideously when he moves, and which he personally stripped from the heads of Digger Indians. He is proud of their number, but cannot utter the word "Digger" without spitting furiously at the earth, as though this freight of human hair were insufficient editorializing. It is, however, not just this habit of "dotting the i's and crossing the t's" which makes it ill-advised to stand downwind of him.

Our visitor answers to the name of Joe Walker, and informs us proudly that he acted as guide to Frémont's mission, leading the main expeditionary force into California. The legendary Kit Carson was one of his companions in this undertaking, and Mr. Walker boasts that they were the first to have struck a trail directly across the vast Salt Desert that lies athwart our path. He speaks very ill of the Hastings route, but with such a rush and splutter of violent profanity, like some ceaseless waterfall of filth, that his opinions on all matters are dismissed as those of a "croaker" and a "puke," to use the western terms for a man of unredeemably vile character. Such judgment is strengthened by the suspicion that the large herd of horses and mules he is driving east could only be the fruit of rustling among California ranchers, for the prices he asks are but a fraction of the established rates, and he seems perhaps a trifle too eager to be rid of them. Despite the unpleasant "air" of our visitor, we were pleased to have fresh communications about Mr. Bryant, whom he encountered at Fort Bridger making final preparations for the crossing. Our Yankee friend seems as determined as ever to follow the Hastings route, though two of his companions have resigned in favor of the established trail that runs via Fort Hall.

Apart from the strains and scratches and bruises, the mosquito welts, chapped lips and blistered feet to which we have got so accustomed we will surely miss them in California, all save one member of the Donner Party enjoy unquenchable good health. The exception is the newcomer Mr. Halloran, who coughs steadily and becomes ever more pitiably gaunt, though he takes a strong broth several times a day, with generous quantities of bread soaked in it. We learn little of his more private history, for conversational effort always brings on renewed coughing, and his lungs are so strained that we constantly dread a hemorrhage. His manners, however, are so gentle and refined that he clearly comes from no commonplace background, and it is not unusual for the sickly sons of better families to seek a renewal of health in these regions —like our fastidious Boston acquaintance, Mr. Parkman. The curative effects of the dry air, however, are scarcely to be noted in our own invalid charge, and we greatly fear the strain of the rough journey, which tosses him about like an autumn leaf, will further weaken the acutely aggravated tissue of his lungs.

My captain orders me to douse the light, and I must set the remainder of the company a good example in honoring his judicious commands!

3

Eddie Breen had one foot wedged into the massive wooden stirrup when the bronco bolted and the boy's leg cracked with the brittle snap of a dried branch halved across the knee. The bucking pony dragged him across the corral before the twisted foot slipped free, flopped like that of a rag doll into the dust.

"It'll have to come off," Jim Bridger announced to the crowd that quickly gathered in his cabin. "Just below the knee." The trapper rubbed his calloused palms together in a rapid scrubbing motion, as though preparing himself for the operation.

"No, it won't!" shouted Peggy Breen. In the dense, whiskey-smelling air her voice was a bludgeon, and men who had faced avalanches and wounded mountain lions without flinching winced now at its raw power.

"Now, Peg . . . ," Patrick Breen began, but her fury lashed him, sent him cowering into the shadows.

Only Jim Bridger and his partner Louis Vasquez stood their ground, facing her across the crude bench where the thirteen-year-old lay with one arm clamped rigidly over his face. His pants had been cut open to expose the twisted leg and the jagged point of bone protruding through the flesh.

Without pausing for breath, Peggy Breen shouted for the Virgin's intervention, cursed the universal stupidity of men, railed at the boy for his carelessness, and demanded a gun so that she could personally put a bullet through the bronco's head.

Bridger watched her with faded gray eyes as shiny and hard as polished agates, and when the torrent of her rage seemed to slacken, he repeated his words in a voice scarcely more than a whisper. "It'll have to come off. Just below the knee." He had seen more than his share of mangled arms and legs, and had once amputated a man at the hip with a blunted hunting knife, then stopped the bleeding by cauterizing the stump with a red-hot bullet mold. And years before he had let Dr. Whitman cut a three-inch iron arrowhead out of his own back, without making a sound to betray the pain he felt or give any satisfaction to the onlookers. Life was like that in this part of the world, and a screaming female wouldn't change it. She could shout the mud from the chinks between the logs, but that wouldn't change a blamed thing.

"He's right," Louis Vasquez confirmed. "What he says is true. Otherwise, your son will certainly die from the infection, the poison in his blood, and he will suffer terribly." There was sympathy for the hysterical mother in his melodic, oddly cultivated speech, and while he spoke he dipped a rag in a tin cup of whiskey, reached forward to squeeze a few drops into the boy's gaping mouth.

Peggy Breen's arm lashed out with the speed and deadly accuracy of a coiled rattler, sent rag and cup flying across the cabin. "You'll not be makin' a drunkard of him, too! A drunkard and a cripple! Fillin' him with your devilish likker, choppin' off his leg! I'll not have any boy of mine made half a man. I've got enough of those already to suit me," she added, and glared into the corner where her husband had retreated.

Jim Bridger scrubbed his hands together once more, then shrugged in a way that said the noisy controversy had begun to bore him. He was used to foolish emigrants who thought they knew better than the men who had opened up the country, and who were too dumb and too ornery to know how fast it could make you dead. Local wisdom held that the only treatment for a broken leg was amputation, and Jim Bridger was as full of local wisdom, whiskey, and wanderlust as any man in the West. "T'ain't none o' my business," he concluded.

"Now you're talkin' the truth for once," Peggy spit at him.

"Let the boy die if'n you want. Ain't none o' my kinfolks." The trader walked briskly out of the cabin, and Vasquez followed him, rubbing his arm.

Peggy Breen hesitated a moment, then demanded confirmation from the boy himself. "Well, Eddie, do we cut it off or put it in a splint?"

"A splint."

"I reckon it'll hurt some."

"It hurts some now," came the faint response.

"And it'll be hurtin' a sight more takin' all the bumps in the road."

Suddenly the boy began to cry. "Don't let 'em cut it off, Peg. Please don't cut it off, Ma."

"Nobody'll be touchin' you with a knife," she promised. "Nobody's makin' my boy half a man."

"Please, Peg."

"Now, clear out!" she shouted to the trappers and the pair of Piute braves lounging against the walls of the cabin. "Clear out of here, all of you good-for-nothin' layabouts! Pat Breen, you can bring me a piece of cloth and two stout planks, and then you're gonna help me pull this leg back where it belongs."

As she waited for her husband to return, clutching Eddie's cold hand, her lips jerked in rapid, ceaseless prayer.

TAMSEN AND MARGARET REED WERE CONVINCED THAT EDDIE Breen's accident was partly the fault of Old Bill Williams, the wild-eyed mountain man who roared about the fort, swearing and boasting and exciting all the children. A few days before their arrival, the old trapper and guide had paid an emigrant twenty dollars for what looked to be a fine rifle, but when he first drew a bead and pulled the trigger, it exploded with a roar of splinters and spun him head over heels. The two Indians who carried him to the fort took him for dead, but Jim Bridger raised the corpse with a cup of whiskey, and now Old Bill boasted loudly to anyone he passed, "Since I've come to these here mountains I've been wounded a hundred times, and struck by lightnin' twice, and no goddam mean rifle can kill me!" His face was pitted with sores from the explosion, and he scratched at them constantly, as though to keep vivid the proof of his resurrection.

The man's rough, swaggering ways made Joe Walker, their recent cattle-rustling guest, seem almost gentlemanly in comparison, and the mothers were frantic in their efforts to keep their own children away from the excited pack of half-breeds and dogs that trooped behind the man wherever he walked.

"I do believe he could do all the swearing for our army in Mexico and then have a surplus," Tamsen said.

"Mr. Bridger claims he was once a Methodist preacher," Margaret Reed confided. "Surely no man of the church could ever descend to such depravity."

"I should think him more likely to have been a medicine man to the Shoshone, complete with paint and feathers. He'd have a necklace of teeth he pulled with his own fingers from the jaw of a mountain lion."

Margaret Reed hesitated, her own fingers plucking birdlike at a loose thread in her skirt. "Do you think the stories about him are true?"

"Which stories?" Tamsen countered, but knew even better than Margaret Reed the bloody tales that circulated around the camp fire. "Do you mean the horrors? I'd believe almost anything about the man."

"But not that." Margaret Reed shook her head in disbelief. "Surely . . . surely not that." Her voice trailed away, as though she had stepped back, physically removing herself from the unthinkable prospect, as she might have drawn her skirts away from a foul-smelling mudhole in her path.

"You've seen the man with your own eyes, Margaret Reed, and you know he's a savage. Why, he makes a Digger look high-toned. I don't mean that I blame him," she added quickly. "Maybe he couldn't help it. It's the terrible life he's led—the things he had to do to survive. Things we can't imagine."

"But his own wife?"

"His own squaw," Tamsen corrected. "That's not quite the same as a wife. You've seen the loads they have to carry. They're more like mules, and I guess most men would kill and eat their mules if they were starving to death. If it was the only way."

"But a woman . . ." Margaret Reed faltered while her lips worked soundlessly to complete the sentence, and panic twisted her delicate features.

"Stop picking at your skirt," Tamsen told her, "or it won't be good for anything but wadding."

The woman clamped her hands tightly between her knees and forced a laugh at her own absentmindedness. "I guess I'm just a big scaredy-cat."

"No, you're not," Tamsen assured her. "You're just a little nervous—like the rest of us. It's a bitter dose to find Mr. Hastings gone on without us after all his promises. And then poor Eddie Breen, and that wild man stirring up the children something terrible. It's no wonder everybody's feeling a mite skittish."

Margaret Reed seemed to ignore the distraction, her mind continuing to probe its terror like a dog gnawing at a wounded paw. "They say that after three whole months without food, he came back alone, all plump and sassy, like he hadn't missed a single meal."

"Well, maybe he ate the air, promise cramm'd, like the Prince of Denmark. It's thick enough to eat sometimes, if you could find a way to cut a piece off. Besides, you can't believe half the ranting and raving you hear from those men. Half's bad enough," she admitted, thinking of the tale Mr. Donner had brought her that morning, while she was putting away the breakfast things. He told it with such a deep, belly-shaking laugh that he had to repeat it twice before she understood the final line: "And Kit Carson says in starving times ought no man walk in front of Old Bill Williams on the trail."

With a catch in her voice, Margaret Reed admitted, "Sometimes I think it's a good thing mother died when she did, near that pretty little spring with the shady alcove. This would have killed her. All this." She gazed vaguely around her, first at the open plain, then at the crude palisades of the fort.

"What a naughty thing to say! Mrs. Keyes never complained

about her life, and it must have had its horrors, too, when she first went to Illinois. Or," she corrected, remembering the daughter's own suffering during her mother's illness, "she never complained until the end, when she was so poorly. She loved her children and she loved her life too much to let the horrors get the whip hand of her. You're cut from the same cloth, Margaret Reed, only sometimes you forget it!"

"Please don't scold, Tamsen."

"Was I scolding?"

"Yes."

"I'm sorry. I just don't like to see you always making such misery for yourself." And, she thought, what is written in your troubled face is a knife that probes high beneath my ribs, sinks and twists its poisoned tip in my heart.

"I know," Margaret Reed finally admitted. "I know you mean well, Tamsen."

"Then you stop being a scaredy-cat and I'll stop being a scold, and we'll just be friends instead!" Tamsen briskly pulled her knitting from the canvas bag she had slung from her shoulder when she sat beside her friend on the steps of the Reeds' great family wagon, and the yarn raced through her fingers, spilling dense hieroglyphs of pale yellow wool.

"Are you not sometimes afraid yourself?" Margaret Reed wondered after a moment.

Tamsen paused in her knitting, as though to weigh the unexpected question. She looked up, stared into her friend's wide hazel eyes and saw her own face suspended, doubled, in their glossy depths, saw her cheeks blackened by sun and wind, her hair stripped brittle and colorless by the fierce alkali dust. The twin hags mocked her apparent superiority, her cool and level-headed discipline, her hateful and unavoidable charade.

"I am," she pronounced with great care, "always afraid. I fear everything. Sometimes I fear the wind, sometimes a falling leaf. But more than all the rest, I fear the children may guess how I feel. Or Mr. Donner."

"Not you, Tamsen." She laughed nervously, as she would have

laughed at a joke only half understood. "You can't expect me to believe . . ."

"Whether you believe it or not, it is the truth," Tamsen insisted. "I am not trying to make you feel brave. What I have told you is the solemn and absolute and unvarnished truth."

At Fort Bridger four names were added to the roster of the Donner Party—those of two men, a woman, and a child. The men could not have made a more comic contrast, for one was dark and diminutive, the other a giant of a man measuring nearly seven feet with his boots off, with the powerful shoulders of a workhorse and a head of shaggy, coppery curls that made him look even taller. The giant's name was William McCutcheon; he had recently celebrated his thirtieth birthday, and he had traveled from central Missouri in a simple farm wagon with his wife Amanda and their year-old daughter Harriet. His past seemed to consist principally of "a yellow-bellied forty acres not worth the powder to blow it to hell," and like William Eddy he had a breezy confidence in the future he could provide his family through muscle and will. Soon after his arrival at the fort, a fever carried in his blood since childhood sent McCutcheon plunging into a coma, and when he became conscious again, he learned that the Harlan-Young Party, with Lansford Hastings as their guide, had departed without him. His peppery speech caused some initial distress to the ladies, but his easy, mischievous smile disarmed them, and in the months to come his obliviousness to personal danger or distress made him at crucial moments a symbol of hope for the entire party.

The fourth addition to the official roster was Jean Baptiste Trubode, hired to take the place of the Donners' departed teamster, Hiram Miller. Trubode claimed to be the son of a famous French trapper and a Mexican mother, but George Donner described him as "a feisty little mongrel," and from his appearance he may indeed have carried Indian and Negro blood as well. A short wiry man with the strut and bustle of a fighting cock, he had swarthy skin, close-set black eyes that never seemed focussed, and a drooping mustache meant, no doubt, to make him look older than his twenty-three years, though it succeeded only in giving him the woeful air of a clown. The New Mexican spoke broken English, broken French, and broken Spanish, and professed to know several Indian languages, as well as something of the geography through which the Donner Party now had to pass. At times sulky and withdrawn, at times childishly animated, he proved thoroughly ignorant of geography and wonderfully adroit at shirking responsibility, but the survival of Tamsen Donner and her children would ultimately hang on the thin thread of his stubborn, grudging loyalty.

WHILE THE DONNER PARTY LINGERED AT FORT BRIDGER, the women busy with washing and mending, the men making repairs to wagons and harness, Major John Charles Frémont seized San Diego in the name of the Republic, Brigadier General Stephen Kearny arrived at Bent's Fort, and Major General Zachary Taylor conquered the unresisting town of Camargo in northern Mexico. On July 29th, freshly commissioned as head of the Navy Batallion of Mounted Riflemen, Frémont disembarked from the flagship *Cyane* with a band of freebooters dedicated to the liberation of California, all staggering with seasickness following the colossal drunk that had launched the voyage from Monterey. Leaning perilously to windward, they advanced through the sleepy streets of San Diego and raised the Stars and Stripes in proclamation of another bloodless victory.

On the following day, General Kearny's ragged Army of the West, weakened by scurvy, dysentery, and measles, straggled into the shelter of the massive adobe walls of Bent's Fort. Here the general reorganized his troop, leaving most of the infantry to dull their weariness with the fort's icehouse, billiard room, and jugs of Taos Lightning, while he and the Dragoons set out on the final stage of the march to Santa Fe. Before departing, he issued a stirring declaration that the province of New Mexico east of the Rio Grande was now United States territory.

Dressed in freshly starched attakas pantaloons, the victorious Major General Zachary Taylor had idled for weeks in the shade of his tent fly, basking in the solicitous attentions of the newspaper correspondents who called to interview him. Further aggressive action would be both costly and superfluous, he crisply informed them, and Polk fumed to his diary over Old Rough and Ready's relentless conspiracy to overthrow him in the next presidential election. Meanwhile, so many volunteers had arrived that the general now commanded more than twelve thousand troops, made restless not only by the chronic shortages of supplies, but by their continuing inactivity. Oblivious to any contradiction of his dove-like statements to the gentlemen of the press, Taylor finally determined to move the best of his men into northern Mexico. On July 31st, as the Donners rolled away from Fort Bridger, Taylor made his first conquest—the small, unresisting, insignificant town of Camargo, which he immediately determined to make his new base of operations, though it huddled in the center of the most pestilent region his ailing troops had yet encountered.

JAMES REED BOUGHT TWO YOKE OF OXEN AT FORT BRIDGER to replace those that had died on the trail from drinking poisoned water. He and George Donner talked frequently with Jim Bridger and Louis Vasquez, repeatedly questioning them about the Hastings route, and receiving repeated assurances of the pleasant landscape ahead. Reed was at first suspicious of Bridger's roughness, but so reassured by Vasquez's cultivated manners that in the letter he sent back to Springfield he praised the partners for their honesty and pronounced them both "very excellent and accommodating gentlemen." He then composed a lyric description of the final stage of their journey:

The new road, or Hastings' Cut-off, leaves the Fort Hall road here, and is said to be a saving of 350 or 400 miles in going to California, and a better route. There is, however, or thought to be, one stretch of 40 miles without water; but Hastings and his party are out ahead examining for water, or for a route to avoid this stretch. I think that they cannot avoid it, for it crosses an arm of the Eutaw Lake, now dry. There is plenty of grass which we can cut and put into the waggons for our cattle while crossing it. We are now only 100 miles from the Great Salt Lake by the new route—in all 250 miles from California; while by way of Fort Hall it is 650 or 700 miles—making a great saving in favor of jaded oxen and dust. On the new route we will not have dust as there are but 60 waggons ahead of us. Mr. Bridger informs me that the route we design to take is a fine, level road, with plenty of water and grass, with the exception before stated.

Reed not only failed to interpret the shrewd but obvious propaganda Bridger was spreading to boost his own trade in the area; he almost certainly made an error in dating his letter July 31st, for on that day the Donner Party left Fort Bridger at dawn. Perhaps Reed had composed his travel report late the night before, but it is equally possible that his time sense had begun to fail, as it would soon fail the other travelers. As though some delicate mechanism had slipped noiselessly, irreparably out of control, they would first wonder, then quarrel about the date, and the pious were no longer certain which of their toiling days was a violation of the Sabbath. Even those who at first clung stubbornly to their own mental calendars began to doubt them, to make secret adjustments, then to forget whether they had added or subtracted, whether a particular wearying stage of the journey had taken four days or five, whether it was yesterday or the day before that another of their oxen had fallen to the Diggers' stealthy arrows. The pitiless sun seemed to melt time itself, to fuse hours and days into an indistinguishable mass. By then, however, most had ceased to care about such trivial measures.

4

Sulfur Springs

Sunday, August 2nd, 1846

It is two days since we departed Fort Bridger, and are now hard on the heels of Mr. Hastings and the Harlan-Young Party. Some miles west of the fort the well-worn road forked, with the clearer trail proceeding to Fort Hall and the fainter one to the southwest marking the cut-off we have determined upon. More than one head turned to cast a lingering glance at the deep ruts that diverged from us, but with such a numerous company blazing the trail ahead, we expect no grave difficulties in finding our way.

Soon after departure we commenced the ascent of a steep and mountainous terrain which led us to a lofty "butte," as it is called in these regions. The views were splendidly panoramic, but the going precarious, as the trail often plunged unexpectedly into sharp ravines or along dangerous side-hills where the wheels had to be locked and the wagons slithered down the shaly surface like overloaded sledges. The hostility of the terrain has not abated, and its rocky face has grown monotonous. Water is scant, and the only appreciable stream we have encountered ran such a startling blood-red on account of minerals that we were afraid to let the animals drink of it. Tonight we have been fortunate in making camp near a spring which bubbles merrily, though its music is more agreeable than the odor of rotten eggs it emits. The water is quite palatable when sweetened with a little sugar, but sugar has grown scant, and most prefer to risk the bubbly drink in its natural form.

The situation of Fort Bridger, where we passed nearly four days, is a pleasant one, on the bottoms where Black's Fork divides into several distinct channels. There is excellent pasturage bright-

ened like a fancy carpet by brilliant wildflowers of red and blue.
Beyond this verdant zone, however, the country is all desolation.
The so-called fort is no more than a shabby trading post consisting
of two tumbledown cabins joined by mud-daubed pickets that
serve as corral for the stock and the endless half-breed children
forever under foot. Taken all together, it bore only a faint resemblance to any human habitation, but the supplies were adequate,
and Mr. Reed was able to acquire two passably good yoke of oxen.
These seemed fairly priced, but a quire of indifferent writing paper
cost 80 cents, and peaches were 50 cents a can.

The founder of this establishment, known to all as "Jim"
Bridger, is one of the type of rough westerners we have recently
encountered, and whose dangerous escapades have often led them
to dreadful extremes. Mr. Bridger, however, was a superior sample, clean-shaven and considerably better dressed than his comrades. It is said he speaks three languages fluently, though I heard
but an imperfect English with my own ears. More remarkable is
his ability to scan the faintest moccasin track and tell the age,
weight, sex and tribe of its maker—all this, though he can read no
word of any known language, and signs with an "X." He was once
married to the daughter of a Flathead chief, killed in a massacre,
and was one of the first white men ever to traverse the South Pass.
Most of all, he is known for his bravery, the stories of which might
provide the stuff of a dozen thrilling novels. As a youngster he took
a pair of iron arrowheads in the back, and whistled calmly while
one of them was forcibly removed. He carried the other between
the ribs for many years, until Dr. Whitman operated to remove
it from his uncomplaining patient. Bridger's partner, Mr. Louis
Vasquez, is the son of a prominent St. Louis family, and one can
only wonder what vagaries of fate brought such a cultivated man
to such a cheerless enterprise. The snows about the fort are said
to be paralyzingly fierce in winter.

Mr. Donner has engaged a new teamster to replace the one
we have lost—a young New Mexican who answers to the name of
Jean Baptiste Trubode (23) and is well acquainted with the geography of this region. Our ranks are further increased by a Missouri
family who have joined us, consisting of William McCutcheon

(30), his wife Amanda (24) and their daughter Harriet (1). Mr. McCutcheon is the tallest man of our company, and he strides vigorously about beneath a veritable halo of golden hair. His speech is less than angelic, but his spirit so frank and generous that none take offense at his liberties. His powerful shoulders and manly confidence will no doubt serve us well, unless he is revisited by the fever which recently prostrated him. It was for this reason that the company ahead of ours left him behind at Fort Bridger.

Our party suffered a most unfortunate accident when the Breens' eldest child, Edward, fell from an Indian pony and badly broke his right leg. The men at the fort all agreed that amputation was essential to save the boy's life, but his mother opposed this terrible remedy, and the boy refused to let anyone come near him with a knife. Mother and son prevailed, and the bravely uncomplaining invalid now rides in the wagon, his leg bound in splints and in terrible pain from the constant jolting of the rocky road. He is the first of our party to suffer serious injury. Elitha is greatly distressed, as young Edward has been "sparking" her for some hundreds of miles, and it was their habit to walk out together (though never out of sight of the wagons) after their evening chores were completed. Many doubt the poor lad will ever properly walk again, even if he does succeed in recovering from his accident.

Mr. Halloran shows no sign of improvement, and this morning coughed up a great quantity of blood, which he sought to conceal, from a desire to protect my feelings and those of the girls. Frances has grown very fond of him, and frequently cradles his head in her lap to protect him from the rougher passages. They make a tender and delicate picture together, but one full of woe.

5

Weber River Canyon
Sunday, August 9th, 1846

Since the nooning on Wednesday we have been encamped in this mountain fastness, a few miles west of the opening to a steep canyon whose lurid red walls endlessly echo any loud noise— including a brisk clapping of the hands or a "Halloo." A single rifle shot becomes the volley of an entire infantry, and a falling stone produces the rumble of fearsome thunder rolling for whole minutes over our startled heads.

With each passing hour we more anxiously await the return of Messrs. Reed, Stanton and McCutcheon, who departed on Wednesday to fetch Lansford Hastings. He has agreed to act as our personal guide on the next stage of the journey. We entered this place after following the trail from Bear River, over a high ridge which led us to a little westward-flowing creek aimed straight as an arrow into this formidable chain of mountains. Shortly after the creek foamed into the Weber, we came upon a campsite recently occupied by the Harlan-Young Party. A letter from Mr. Hastings had been posted there in a forked stick, and its obscure contents could but fill us with confusion. The route through the Weber Canyon (which he himself was nonetheless pursuing) looked so unpromising, so full of hazard, that he doubted if his own company could get through, and urged us under no circumstance to attempt to follow. Instead, he advised that we make camp at this spot and send a messenger forward to overtake him, with the promise that he would then return and guide us by a better, shorter route. With over 60 wagons, women and children and valuable property entrusted to his judgment, it seems puzzling that he did not choose the smoother path for them.

Mr. Reed readily volunteered to ride forward, and he is the finest horseman in our company, but it was thought unwise to hazard the mountains and the threats of hostile Snakes and Utes without companions. Both Mr. Stanton and Mr. McCutcheon expressed their eagerness to join the expedition, and as the latter was without a mount of his own, we have loaned him our bay. Since the men's departure we constantly scan the valley for some sign of their return, which is now long overdue. For the sake of speed, they carried only minimal provisions, and those must be long exhausted.

Idling on the shady banks of the Weber makes a pleasant variation from the usual ardors of trail life, but anxiety dampens all diversions. Last night, in the hope of cheering the restless young folk in our company, Milt Elliott and Mr. Dolan joined harmonica and fiddle as accompaniment for a vigorous round of dancing, and the mountain walls so magnified their efforts we might have been thought to travel with our own orchestra. Elitha would take no part in the merry-making, out of respect for her injured beau, and Virginia Reed was so sick with worry for her stepfather's safety that she likewise joined the circle of wallflowers. We all rummaged in our trunks, however, and put on our civilization costumes.

I had feared the prolonged absence of her husband, on whom she so much depends, might bring on one of Mrs. Reed's paralyzing migraines, but its effect has been quite the reverse. She fairly blossoms with high color, and has never been so energetic in attending to the wants of her family. This morning she set off with Milt Elliott to search for a milch cow that had wandered away in the night, and returned an hour later driving the cow before her with a switch. She had left Milt behind at what seemed a promising spot for fishing! Mountain trout have greatly enlivened the sameness and tameness of our menu.

The two invalids have benefitted from this unexpected delay, and the poor oxen must welcome the relief to their tortured feet. Elitha and I have had a profitable spell of nursing with one of them, which seems to have been poisoned by the same noxious weed that killed two of Mr. Reed's teams. Mr. Denton reported that the poor animal was swelling frightfully and could not be bled to relieve the pressure. He was given up for dead when Elitha and I found him, but we were determined to make some effort to relieve his terrible pain. We funneled a quart of melted lard into a long-necked bottle, cut a quantity of fat bacon into strips, and filled a bucket with cold water. Those watching warned strongly that water would kill the beast, but we had no intention of permitting him to drink from it. The animal's nose was so inflamed it actually burned my hands as I sought to drench it with the lard. He seemed, however, to understand that our efforts were well meaning, and consented to let me pour the remaining lard down his throat. While Elitha stroked our patient's "fevered brow," he looked at me with such soft, docile eyes that I felt confident he would not bite, and pushed my hand into his mouth to make him swallow the bacon. We then doused him with the cold water, and he seemed to breathe more easily. The swelling had ceased, and both of us felt certain the animal would recover. This morning he was found grazing happily with his comrades, and the only sign of his earlier distress was a nose that looked as though it had been scalded.

Today I discovered a plant similar in appearance to the cattail, whose bulbous root is nutty in flavor and quite succulent when roasted. Both red and yellow currants thrive here, and though they would make an inferior comparison among other cultivated fruits, they seem a luxury provided especially for our benefit. The girls drag whole bushes back to camp and sit for hours picking off the berries and plucking the stems. I have succeeded in improvising a cobbler which is a great success served with cream, as well as currant dumplings and a quantity of jelly the color of gold and as clear as crystal. I find, however, that I have lost my taste for botanizing.

6

I<small>T WAS NOT UNTIL THE EVENING OF</small> A<small>UGUST</small> 11<small>TH THAT</small> R<small>EED WAS</small>
sighted urging his lathered horse down the canyon. Swaying with
hunger and exhaustion, he slid to the ground into his wife's embrace,
and he leaned heavily on her shoulder as she led him to the steps
of the palace wagon. He had been under way for nearly a week.

"And the others?" Margaret Reed wondered.

He gulped at the coffee she handed him, thick with brown
sugar. "The horses gave out," he explained, "and Hastings couldn't
let us have but one replacement. They'll meet us on the cutoff once
they get their mounts rested up." The way he spit out the word
"cutoff" struck the crowded circle of emigrants like an icy wind.

The answer seemed clear, but as captain of the wagon train
George Donner was obliged to pose the simple question. "Where's
Hastings?"

"Hastings wouldn't come. Said the Harlan-Young Party needed
him to get across the desert. And they're paying him for his time."

No one voiced the universal disappointment, the cruel betrayal
of those expectations that had sustained them since finding Hastings's last cryptic message. There were no words that would fill the
sudden, howling vacancy the news created.

"And how was the trail?"

"Bad."

"What's bad about it?"

"Everything," Reed replied, as he gnawed hungrily at a strip
of dried beef.

"But you did locate Mr. Hastings." Tamsen had intended to
make a simple statement, but her voice rose questioningly.

"Yes. Camped with the Harlan-Young lot on the south shore
of the lake. They were all set to pull out again."

"Then they made it!" Tamsen's voice brightened with excitement, and she smiled encouragement at her troubled husband.

"They made it," Reed confirmed. Then, after a little pause, he added, "And it came goddamned near killing the lot of them."

Margaret Reed had rarely heard her husband curse, and she started back from him, then laid a cool hand on his sunburned arm. Virginia Reed had nestled against her stepfather's knee, and he stroked her dark hair, leaned down to whisper something to her, as though the business of the day was finished and he could get on with the gentle pleasures of family life.

"Out with it, man!" a voice shouted from the crowd.

"Out with what?"

Margaret Reed felt her husband tense, and she gripped his arm tightly to check his famous anger. "We all know how exhausted you are," she began, "but we've been waiting such a long time, and we've made ourselves plumb silly with worry. Please tell us about it, Jim." Her clear, careful syllables promised they could bear whatever terrors he might disclose.

For a moment James Reed studied her face, as if trying to bring it into focus, and under his steady gaze she smiled nervously, looked away, but her hand remained firmly and protectively on his arm.

"It's impassable," Reed told his listeners.

"What's impassable?"

"The Weber Canyon."

"But Hastings got through with more than sixty wagons," came the inevitable protest.

"Just barely, and with better manpower than we can muster. At one spot it took the train a whole week to make just over a mile, with all hands at work from sunup to sundown. The canyon narrows down like a rifle barrel, and there were places where we had trouble squeezing through on horseback. The others took their wagons up over the top when that happened—windlassed them straight up into the air, and half of them were damaged knocking against the stone walls. One went over a precipice and fell nearly a hundred feet straight down. All that was left was a pile of splintered wood and shredded canvas. And even where the valley's wide enough for both wheels to run on the banks, there are huge boulders to get out of the way. Some were so big they couldn't be moved, and every man, woman, and child had to work piling up brush and rock and dirt to bridge them. It was misery, and you see the signs of it the whole hellish way."

As Reed told his story, George Donner was not alone in thinking it might be only the oversized Prairie Palace Wagon that couldn't get through, that normal wagons could maybe make it after all. He couldn't believe Reed would let such an important judgment be swayed by that kind of pettiness, but the suspicion pestered him. His question skirted the idea but gave it a nod. "If the Harlan-Young Party's got through and done that kind of improvin' on the road, oughtn't we to take advantage of it? Add a couple of improvements of our own?"

Reed shook his head. "They had plenty of good strong backs —enough to pick up a wagon and carry it if they had to. What have we got?" He intentionally looked away from the captain, focused his attention on the thoughtful face of William Eddy, who was silently weighing each scrap of information while he scratched in the earth with a stick, as though making notations. "Luke Halloran's too sick to stand on his own feet. Eddie Breen's no more than a kid, but he could do a man's work if he had two good legs. He doesn't. Hardkoop and Wolfinger can't do much more than manage their own teams. Stanton's tougher than I'd have given him credit for, and McCutcheon's strong as an ox, but Stanton and McCutcheon aren't here, and we don't know how long it'll take them to come up. The Donner brothers are tall enough and broad enough for the work," he began, then cleared his throat apologetically before adding, "but men of their age just don't have the kind of stamina it takes. That gets us down to ten, maybe twelve, who can do that kind of job, and we'd need thirty or forty."

"What's the option, friend?" William Eddy asked, still scrawling indecipherable messages in the earth.

"Hastings rode with me as far as one of the summits and showed me the way he first took. It was a scout of his who proposed the canyon route, and it's lucky Hastings didn't scalp him. I came back the original way. Part of it's an old Indian trail."

"Is it better?"

"Not much," Reed admitted, but he didn't add that he wasn't certain if the path he had blazed was actually the one Hastings intended. The man had gestured broadly with his arm, swept an easy line from east to west, pointed out a few more prominent mountains, mentioned a pair of creeks, and ridden back to the company at the lake.

"What's it got goin' for it?"

"Not much," Reed repeated, "except it keeps us out of a canyon that's got murder in its heart. If we head a little south, then west, we've still got canyons to get through, but they're not so steep, and part of the way's over level ground. We'll have to make our own trail with shovels and axes if we want to get over the top, but I think we'll spare backs and wagons that way. Stanton and McCutcheon agree." He held his cup out for coffee in a way that announced he had no more to say, that they could choose as they liked and he would abide by the decision.

"I'm for goin' over the top," William Eddy announced to the group, and Patrick Breen immediately seconded him. George Donner put the proposal to a vote and Tamsen helped him count the raised hands of the men who held property. The decision to abandon the Weber Canyon and strike directly across the mountains was unanimous.

BY NOON OF THE FOLLOWING DAY, MANY MIGHT HAVE WISHED to reconsider the vote. With Reed's wagons given nominal leadership because of his knowledge of the route, the train moved a half mile down river, then turned south, leaving Hastings's wheel tracks behind to move up a swift creek that spilled into the Weber. The narrow side-canyon was choked with aspen, willow, and serviceberry that had to be hacked away to make a passage, and at the end of the day they were camped not only within sight of the Weber, but within a stone's-throw closeness that mocked their grueling labors. On the second day they made two miles before the canyon clamped down so tightly the wagons could not squeeze through. They turned to follow a faint Indian trail up and over the divide, where they chopped and hacked a rough, winding road that looped around gigantic boulders, steep ledges of rock, and clumps of trees too dense for blunted axes. The men measured their progress by the yard, and for an entire day no wheel turned, for the weary road builders simply walked the short distance back to camp when darkness came. Many were so exhausted that the very smell of food nauseated them, and they could stomach only coffee laced with brandy or whiskey. When they finally topped the divide they faced a downgrade even more forbidding than the ascent. Often using their bare hands, they scratched and clawed a notch that skirted the open hillside, but sidehill slopes were especially treacherous for the high-wheeled, top-heavy wagons, and they could only inch along it in constant fear the nervous oxen would lose their footing. It took three days to cross the first ridge and descend into the next canyon and a creekbed whose underbrush was even more impenetrable than the first. Travelers knew it as Bossman Creek, but before its corruption it had borne the name of the plucky French trapper Beauchemin. Even if they had known of his earlier journeys through these mountains, the Donner Party would have found any suggestion of "beautiful road" a travesty of their sufferings.

The most calloused, work-worn hands grew blisters the size of half eagles that split open to reveal raw flesh that festered into running sores. The men wrapped their palms in strips of rag, but the remedy made their grip unsure, and with axes slashing constantly through the dense brush, the danger of accident was increased. Most of the men worked bare-handed, with picks and axes and shovels smeared with blood, and the younger, stronger women were soon working at their side, while the others remained in camp to care for the children, haul water, and tend the cooking fires. The first hillside had rung with curses and loud warnings as they ascended, but now no man uttered a sound, sparing his agonized breath with a silence more grim than any oath he might have shouted at the hostile mountains. Fatigue made them short-tempered and quarrelsome, but they checked their rage, intuitively realizing that any aggression that broke out now would not stop short of murder. It seemed a relief to come to swampy ground that had to be riprapped with stones, then lined again when those sank under the weight of the first wagons. There was only thin browse for the stock, and the poorer families realized their provisions were growing dangerously low. Meanwhile, Stanton and McCutcheon had still not returned, and it was feared they were the victims of Indians. George Donner would have sent out a search party, but there was not a single able-bodied man to spare.

AGAIN THE TWENTY WAGONS HAD REMAINED IN CAMP, AND THE men had advanced a quarter mile up the hillside when the improbable but unmistakable sound reached them: the rattle of chains, the groan of spokes and axles, voices shouting warning and encouragement to teams. In disbelief they looked back at the ragged scar they had left on the northern slope of the ravine in time to see three wagons lurching along it. George Donner knew beyond doubt that his party was the last to leave Fort Bridger for the season, and it was impossible that another should now be gaining on them, though the fragile line between the possible and the impossible had snapped more than once in recent days.

What he and his comrades could scarcely have imagined with their first glimpse of the tardy travelers was that the Graves family was entirely alone, that they had drifted and gawked and dawdled their way ever since Fort Laramie, oblivious to whether they had other companions or not, immune to the chronic fears of marauding Indians, careless of their shrinking supplies, indifferent to the guidebooks that told them they were now weeks behind schedule, and confident that a divine providence would mend their errors. The fact that they had survived the bloody Ash Hollow massacre, whose pitiful, ghost-like victims had struck such terror among other emigrants, made the family's cheerful nonchalance seem even more extraordinary. And they had not merely survived: they were the sole family to have lost neither life nor property to the Shawnee raiders. Quickly appraising genus and species, Tamsen at once classified them with the Breens—the enviable sort that would bounce like balls of hard India rubber if dropped over a cliff.

The thirteen newcomers were led by an elderly, perpetually

240

squinting, Vermont-born farmer from Illinois named "Uncle Billy" Graves. With him were his wife Elizabeth, a married daughter and her husband, a pretty unmarried daughter of twenty, a son of eighteen, and six small children—the youngest still a nursing infant. The unlucky thirteenth member was a handsome, cocky teamster named John Snyder, who never lost an opportunity to show his superiority at wrestling, arm wrestling, target shooting, distance spitting, poker or clog dancing. Along the trail from Independence his curly black hair and romantic profile had struck numerous sparks among the emigrant women, and his gingery temper had assured his notoriety among the men. The Graves clan received a mixed reception. The addition of three women and six children to a party already overburdened with dependents and short of supplies made some of the men skeptical, and the fact that the newcomers had used their hard-won road caused more than one to mutter about collecting a toll. On the other hand, the newcomers brought four fresh men with them, and the reinforcements were desperately needed. No vote was taken to confirm their membership in the Donner Party. There was, in any case, scarcely room for them to turn around.

On August 18th, the day after the Graves wagons seemed to drop from the blue, Stanton and McCutcheon stumbled into camp after more than a week of wandering through the trackless mountains. They had eaten so many serviceberries to blunt their hunger that their stomachs were painfully bloated, and their faces were so shredded by brambles they looked like the survivors of a bear fight.

"I'd have roasted the littl'un if there was any meat left on his miserable bones," McCutcheon said. He guffawed and slapped his knee, but two things were clear—his admiration for the city slicker who had been his companion, and the fact that both had nearly died of starvation. When pressed for details, he responded simply, "It was a pisser!"

But Stanton and McCutcheon had worse news for the Donner Party. The big mountain they had just conquered was only a divide between two branches of the Bossmann. There were more canyons, creeks, ridges and divides in their path, and the road they were now cutting would soon come to a dead end.

ONLY BLIND DESPERATION MOVED THEM NOW, AS THE EXHAUSTED men and women clawed their way through the mountains, double-teamed up steep slopes, windlassed wagons over impassable ridges, mounded earth to make a precarious passage over boulders, blundering through narrow canyons that turned suddenly, twisted and narrowed and opened into other canyons that bent bafflingly east again, ended without warning. They turned and tried again, pushed through another angle of the rocky maze later travelers would give such gently domesticated names as East Canyon, Dixie Hollow, Dutch Hollow and Mountain Dell. Finally they were heading due west again, and knew they were only a few miles from the Salt Lake Valley, moving along a likely looking canyon that the men cleared with a renewed sense of urgency, leaving stumps big around as a man's waist and so tall the wagons had to be put on blocks to clear them. Some of the men forward explored ahead and came back with the bitter news that the canyon suddenly narrowed and filled until there was no hope of getting through. Over eight thousand feet high, Big Mountain seemed to offer the only way out, and they mounted it with the aid of the windlass, dangled wagons and stock in the air, hauled, chocked, whipped, wedged, pushed, and pulled them up a slope that was almost vertical, then lowered them precariously down the other side. The following summer, Brigham Young would pause at the same spot, scrutinize the terrain, and set his men to chopping brush. Within hours the end of the seemingly impassable canyon had opened to reveal a gentle gateway to the lush green valley of the promised land. The Donner Party had spent nearly a month in traveling a total distance of less than forty miles.

7

Salt Lake Valley
Sunday, August 23rd, 1846

Two weeks have passed since my last remarks to these pages, despite a firm resolve to admit no break in my chronicle. The previous Sunday came and went unnoticed, for all hands were engaged in the wearying and seemingly endless task of road-building through the Wahsatch. I had not the heart to pen so grim an account of this desperate venture, and even now mere words seem feeble when compared with the reality. The rocky barrier of the Wahsatch is confusingly laced with innumerable canyons and side-canyons and false canyons, together with ridges and gulches and spurs and sidehills which render the passage of wagons all but impossible. The creek beds are choked with dense undergrowth where every slow inch of progress must be won with the labor of axes, and the sufferings of those who carved this passage were most pitiable. Boulders were scattered everywhere like the playthings of careless Titans, and these required to be dislodged or covered by a system of ramps composed of brush, stones and earth. Most terrifying were the precipitous ascents and descents achieved with the aid of the windlass. Somehow the fortune which otherwise frowned on our party consented to spare us any serious injury, and the sole damage to property (to one of the Reed family's supply wagons) was easily mended.

The horrors are mercifully behind us, and for two days we have rolled rapidly through the valley of the Salt Lake. The agility of the mind in sealing off the agonies of the past is made abundantly clear, for even those who suffered most terribly now begin to speak lightly of the obstacles they conquered. Mr. Denton remarked this morning, with his affection for western turns of speech, that we had recently been "between a rock and a hard place." His observation is especially appropriate for Mr. Reed, who required nearly a week to reach the Hastings company and return to us through the uncharted, hostile wilderness. Due to the collapse of their mounts, Messrs. Stanton and McCutcheon were yet more delayed, and we feared they had paid with their scalps.

Our decision to leave the Weber River Canyon and make our own course through a country where only horsemen and moccasined Indians have ever passed was based on the advice of Mr. Hastings, whose party had found the narrow valley perilous in the extreme, and lost one wagon there. As prior obligations prevented his returning to guide us personally, the explorer gave Mr. Reed a description of his own original route, and it was this we attempted to follow. No doubt both muscle and time would have been spared by improving on the improvements the more numerous Harlan-Young Party had already made along the Weber, but we could not know this without the sore lessons of experience, and the men were unanimous in choosing to strike out directly across the mountains. In consequence of the time lost, supplies have grown alarmingly scarce for the poorer members of our group, and further unwonted delays in our itinerary are unthinkable for them. Even worse than the depletion of flour and coffee and sugar is the toll taken on spirit and confidence by our recent ordeal. Though many now make light of it, as though to draw the serpent's fangs, the spiritual effects will not soon quit us.

Much to our amazement, three strange wagons hove into view in the very heart of the mountains, containing thirteen men, women and children who had traveled the entire distance from Fort Laramie without the protection of any larger company. Our party is thus increased by the following persons, with their ages:

Frank Ward Graves (57)
Elizabeth Graves (47), his wife
Their unmarried children, being Mary Ann (20),
    William (18), Eleanor (15), Lavinia (13),
    Nancy (9), Jonathan (7), Franklin Ward Jr. (5),
    Elizabeth Jr. (1)

244

A married daughter, Sarah Graves Fosdick (22),
　　and her husband Jay Fosdick (22)
These are accompanied by John Snyder (25), teamster

Though their foolhardiness gave us at first poor advertisement of these newcomers, their arrival was highly providential, as we were then urgently in need of reinforcements, especially as Mr. Stanton and Mr. McCutcheon had not returned. The family is a merry, chirruping lot, though short-sightedness gives Mr. Graves a somewhat mournful look. He was born in Vermont but had farmed for many years near Vandalia, Illinois, before the California fever took him. For reasons undisclosed, he is familiarly known as "Uncle Billy."

After fording a river which flows northward to the lake, we encountered once more the trail of the Hastings wagons, running straight as a plumb-line through open country, and have been following it for two days. The first encampment after our liberation was beside a lovely spring of pure, sweet water, with excellent pasturage. The country has grown less hospitable after passing the point of a mountain that slopes down to the shore of the salt lake. The ground of the region is marsh, and the reek of the sloughs competes with the stench of the numerous fish that lie rotting in the sun.

I have scarcely slept for two nights, as the sufferings of Mr. Halloran have required the trivial relief I could provide. His failing condition has been sorely aggravated by the ardors of our mountain passage.

8

To the members of the Donner Party, still edgy with fatigue and frustration, the sudden noise sounded like a rifle shot
whizzing just over their heads, but it was only the forward axletree
on one of Reed's supply wagons that cracked when a wheel climbed
an innocent-looking incline and dropped down the other side. Reed
and Milt Elliott surveyed the damage and quickly realized that
timber would have to be hauled from the Wahsatch, where they had
already cut enough for an entire fleet of prairie schooners. Shortly
before noon, the teamster set off with William Eddy to haul the
trunk of a pine fifteen miles and then work it into an axle.

When the others pulled out, Eddy's wagon and Reed's crippled
supply wagon remained behind, in a forlorn cluster with those of
George Donner. Luke Halloran had been in a coma since early
morning, and the Donners paused to ease his final sufferings.
Tamsen sent her oldest daughter away with the words, "I'll sit with
him now," and Frances reached down to touch the patient's feverish
face before she climbed out and joined her father.

The emaciated figure Tamsen nestled in her arms seemed to
lack all weight and mass. It was a limp, feather-filled doll that flopped
helplessly whenever she shifted it, and only the rasping breath told
her it was still alive.

It was four o'clock in the afternoon when she felt the man move
against her, as though trying to sit up, and with a gentle pressure she
discouraged him. The eyelids fluttered, blinked, and the twisted
mouth gaped like that of a netted fish.

"Shhh," she told him, and laid a finger across his lips. "You
mustn't try to talk."

"I'm . . . ," he began, with a deep, gurgling sound.

"Don't," she insisted. "Please."

"I'm sorry."

"You mustn't be."

"For the bother," he finished, and the blood rushed from his lips in a warm crimson stream that flowed as swiftly and freely as a mountain brook.

Instinctively, foolishly, Tamsen pressed her hands against the torrent, attempting to stanch the perilous rupture, and the blood jetted between her groping fingers, bathed her arms and soaked the front of her dress. When it was over, she cradled his head for long minutes against her breast, pressed it to her as if she would give him back the precious life that had flowed from him. There was a pool of blood in her lap, and she felt it seep through her dress, trickle along her thighs, and would have wept with the insistence of its warm embrace had she not found that her tears were dry.

The Donner wagons rolled into camp with Halloran's body shortly after sunset, halting beside the same jutting black rock where Reed had encountered Hastings three weeks before. The death of a near-stranger brought little response from the exhausted travelers, and none volunteered to assist with a burial. Halloran had bequeathed his horse, saddle, bridle, and a small, worn trunk to the Donners. When the trunk was opened it was found to contain $1,500 in silver coin and the insignia of a Master Mason. James Reed shared the high Masonic office, and had soon organized the other Masons to prepare a suitable burial. In deference to the ceremony, the party decided not to travel on the following morning, but only to shift the camp to a better location. Each Masonic brother donated a plank from his wagon to construct a coffin, and a grave was dug alongside that of John Hargrave, who had been buried near the barren lake by the Harlan-Young Party. James Reed recited the ritual service, then dropped into the grave a pine branch trimmed from the trunk Eddy and Elliott had dragged back, yoked to their saddle horns. Again Tamsen sought the cleansing release of tears, but they would not come. "Perhaps," she thought, "there is already too much salt in this desolate earth."

ALL THAT GUIDED THEIR COURSE WERE THE TWINNED WHEEL marks of Hastings's wagons, already partly silted over with dust and sand, and in rocky stretches vanishing completely, to reappear as much as a mile later, as if the entire train had been swept up in the talons of a giant bird and set down again. For miles they traveled swelling dunes that lined the crusted shore of the briny lake, then swung into a range of hills to avoid the stinking marshes where slippery gray earth balled around the feet of the oxen and plastered the wheels of the wagons, slowing them to a crawl. Even on higher ground there were traces of ancient sandy beach, the surface rippled as though a cooling wave had just dashed over it and sighed away. Rounding the point of a hill, they began to descend, and the crude map scrawled in the earth took them south from the lake, with more hills hunched to the west, a plain flat as a tabletop to the east, with nothing but sage rooted there.

Eddy had pulled out to the right of the train, in hopes of sparing Eleanor and the children from the choking spray of dust of the wagons ahead. With his wife handling the reins, he walked alongside to spare the straining team, and almost at once had the feeling of being watched, of a dozen pairs of curious, intruding eyes following his every footstep. He glanced right across the dwarfed forest of sage and saw nothing, yet knew that invisible witnesses held him as firmly in their gaze as he would have held the curving golden back of an antelope with the bead of a rifle. Without breaking his pace, he revolved, surveyed the vacant track behind him, and was turning again when he saw the other train, nearly a half mile out on the plain and moving parallel. There were twenty wagons, all a bleached, ghostly white, and beside each plodded a man in a slouch hat like his own. All moved in such orderly file, with such mathematical precision, that without their ragged emigrant costumes, he would have taken them for a disciplined troop of soldiers. Perhaps they were Mormons, for it was said the Latter Day Saints all knew the strictest regimentation. He paused to survey them more closely, and the men paused as well. He lifted his hat and waved it in the air, and as the file of wagons moved on, passed them, the men stood waving theirs in response. When he turned to lope forward to his own wagon, the other emigrants did the same, as though mocking him. Suddenly angered by their mimicry, he swept off his drooping hat and flung it to the earth, but they had anticipated the gesture, stood like him with legs astride, hands on hips, staring through the rippling curtain of heat. He slowly lifted one arm, and when they did the same, he knew that he had been tricked by a mirage, that the fata morgana that had seduced so many of his companions into visions of sparkling streams and placid, cooling lakes, had now visited him. Eddy jammed the hat on his head and dismissed the tomfoolery —pleased he had called no one's attention to the other company, yet still plagued by the uneasy feeling that the eyes of hostile strangers recorded each step he made.

It was Reed, riding ahead on Glaucus to survey the trail, who found the mysterious springs, counted them, and gave them the name of Twenty Wells. Some were no more than six inches wide, others nearly nine feet across, and each a perfect circle sliced from earth that remained hard and dry all around them. When a bucket of cool, sparkling water was hauled from one, it immediately refilled to the brim. Two, three, four buckets were lifted in rapid succession from the same small hole, and the water again rose obediently to the top, with never an excess drop to overflow onto the parched ground. Only a few weeks before, the men and women of the Donner Party would have marveled at such a curiosity, mentally shaped it into an anecdote for absent friends, a reminiscence for unborn grandchildren. Now it seemed only another confirmation of the perversity, the growing strangeness of the baffling world into which they had passed somewhere west of Fort Bridger, where the very face of the earth defied their expectations. With the water drawn at Twenty Wells they slaked their thirst, watered the parched animals, cooked an evening and a morning meal, but all avoided their own reflections in the mirrorlike circles that plunged so mysteriously toward the center of the earth, walked cautiously on the balls of their feet as they approached them. Some, indeed, felt so superstitious about the place that they neglected to fill their water kegs before pulling out.

———————

A TOWERING ROCK FORMATION, RISING VERTICALLY OUT OF THE plain, had been in sight since early morning, and as they drew near, it more and more resembled the ruin of a castle or redoubt, laid waste in a bloody siege centuries before. Despite its grim decay, they welcomed any relief from the monotony of the endless plain, and the rocky mass helped them measure their progress. It loomed to the right of the trail when they discovered the crystal-clear spring, the small hollow vivid with grass, and though it was only midafternoon, they immediately agreed to make camp for the night. Patrick Breen and his friend Pat Dolan raced ahead to the sparkling pool like rambunctious schoolboys, lowered themselves onto a stone ledge, and scooped double handfuls of the cool water into their mouths, spilling it over their faces and shoulders. Others had already dropped down beside them when the two men began to wretch, gagging and spewing and clawing at their throats. The spring ran with pure brine, so intense that it had scalded their lips and left them with rings of painful blisters around their mouths.

The party pushed on for another fifteen miles before finding a spring that ran with sweet water and a lush, sprawling meadow for the stock. A post had been hammered into the ground beside the spring with a board nailed to it, and the board still trailed a few shreds of paper. Here and there half-legible fragments of words could be distinguished, but there was no sense to be made of them. Many hesitated to drink from the water, despite their aching thirst, out of fear the Indians had poisoned it, a common trick to spare their arrows when they wanted to pilfer a wagon train.

Tamsen discovered a scrap of paper wedged between sprigs of damp grass, plucked it out and read the word "Two." She waved the tiny scrap overhead. "If we can just find enough, perhaps we can glue them back together." Then, imagining the intact message pasted to the board, she exclaimed, "That's it! The birds have pecked it apart to get to the glue. It must have been flour and water. But they wouldn't have wanted the paper. If we can just find enough . . ."

She hesitated, then asked everyone to move back, or their heavy shoes might trample what remained. "The children will be better. All the smaller ones. They're built closer to the ground," she added with a laugh, "and their eyes are sharper than ours. Children," she called, and clapped her hands overhead. It was the gesture with which she had announced the end of recess at the Sugar Creek schoolhouse.

Tamsen divided the children into teams, promised a prize to the victors, then sat with her drawing board on her knees, a glue pot balanced on the corner. Elitha raced across the grass with two scraps in her hand, and their edges met. Tamsen mated them in turn to a shred that still curled from the board, and they fitted perfectly. They were quickly glued into place, though they revealed nothing of the message once written there. Others followed, with the looping tails of "g's," and then the entire word "two" again.

Though she repeatedly urged them to keep back, many of the adults moved close enough to peer over her shoulders, watching her swift fingers dart across the board, arranging and rearranging, rejecting combinations, reconsidering, then fastening another wayward piece in place. The surface of the board resembled shredded lace, and few of the onlookers believed that a readable message would ever emerge. The illiterates—and there were several in the party, as well as some who recognized no word in English—were slack-jawed with admiration at fingers that could so easily shape the shattered alphabet, mould indecipherable letters into words, pushing those into the curious shapes of phrases. It seemed a kind of witchcraft, the mysterious casting of a ritual spell. For them, Tamsen might as well have been deciphering the scrawled lines in a man's palm, or reading messages in the spilled entrails of a sacrificial animal.

The last bits and pieces the children brought her so proudly, breathlessly, contained no markings, and Tamsen puzzled over what remained, composing them into possible combinations, her fingertips gently probing for the sense. She seemed to have thirteen words, though one consisted only of the letters "rivin," and of those she could make no sense whatever until she pushed them behind the clearly legible word "hard."

"Hard driving," she said—half to herself, in confirmation, half to satisfy her curious audience. "Yes," she nodded, "that must be it. Someone is telling us to expect hard driving. Warning us, I suppose." At that moment she recognized the careless scrawl with

251

which the words had been composed, remembered seeing it twice before—once on the far slopes of the continental divide, again at the head of Weber Canyon.

"It is another communiqué from Mr. Hastings," she announced in a clipped voice.

"Did you find his name?" Bill Eddy asked.

"No, but I recognize his hand. It's halfway between printing and cursive. Ask Mr. Reed."

Jim Reed stepped forward, tugging Hastings's last message from the pocket of his waistcoat, where it had been folded ever since he left the Weber to ride forward and locate their guide. He held the deeply creased page beside the board and nodded.

"It's from Hastings, all right."

"But what does it say, Tamsen," Betsy Donner wailed.

"It says . . . ," she began hesitantly. "At least, I think it says, 'Two days and two nights.' " She frowned and clamped the board as if she had suddenly grown dizzy. "It says," she pronounced carefully, " 'Two days and two nights . . . hard driving . . . cross desert . . . next grass and water.' "

"But that's impossible," Jacob Donner muttered, and looked to the others for confirmation. "It's not that far. Everybody knows it's not near that far."

"The lying, motherless bastard!" The sound that came from Bill McCutcheon was like an explosion. "The stinking, low-down son of a bitch!"

His profanity offended no one, for most were too dismayed by the news to spare the energy any final gesture of fastidiousness would have claimed. Hastings had explicitly and repeatedly told them the dry drive was no more than thirty or forty miles, that they could make it in, at most, a day and a night. Bridger and Vasquez had confirmed the estimate. Now Hastings informed them it would take two days and two nights on a drive without water or feed along the way. That meant the distance was at least seventy miles, if not eighty.

"How could any damned fool make that big a mistake?" Eddy wondered.

"Maybe he was bad at arithmetic," Tamsen suggested, but there was no humor in her brusque syllables.

"He's just a stinkin' polecat of a liar," McCutcheon fumed.

"Give him credit, at least," Reed suggested, hoping to cool tempers enough to work out a reasonable plan. "Hastings did what he could. He came all the way back to warn us."

"That's true," George Donner agreed.

Tamsen stared at the board, then struck it with a clenched fist that sent board, glue pot, and the loose fragments of paper flying from her lap. "It is *not* true," she insisted, lowering her voice to moderate the defection. Apologetically, she raised her eyes to her husband's troubled face and repeated, "It just isn't true, George. Hastings has never ridden back. Hastings has always moved on. He didn't wait for us at the head of the Sweetwater, and he didn't wait for us to catch up with him at Fort Bridger, and he didn't ride back to the Weber when Jim Reed nearly killed himself to go and fetch the man. He wouldn't have crossed the desert for two whole days and nights, then spent another two whole days and nights coming back to leave a note glued to a board, then crossed the desert again to join up with his train. Three times across the desert? I don't believe it, Mr. Donner. I think he posted this notice before he pulled out. I think he knew all along what the distance was. Mr. McCutcheon's a lot closer to the truth. Hastings is too busy saving his own hide to come back and leave us a billet doux. And now we'd better get busy and save ours!"

Without a word, George Donner slowly turned away to unyoke his teams and lead them to water. His feet seemed to drag as he moved, and his shoulders sloped forward as though he hauled some massive weight behind him. Tamsen's anger was diluted by shame as her eyes followed his shuffling, uncertain motions. He had not been alone in giving such blind faith to the geographical ramblings of a former temperance lecturer. James Reed had always made the most impassioned arguments for the Hastings route—even against the firm advice of authorities like Jim Clyman. George had never pressed the case, he had only taken the spark from Reed's self-assured, fast-talking enthusiasm. But George Donner was their captain, and he now bore sole responsibility for a decision all the men had reached, not just unanimously but with the stubborn determination of disciples following the footsteps of a messiah across the burning sand.

Feeling the dull ache in the hand with which she had violently struck the drawing board, watching her husband's clumsy movements, Tamsen felt too weary to rise and light yet another fire, haul pots and skillets from the wagon, to prepare another of the meals whose bland, unvarying flavors seemed as hateful as the constant sage and the endless choking dust of endless, laboring days. She remained rigidly seated while George led all the animals to water, then returned to set up the family tent. When he stood, after hammering in the pegs, she saw suddenly the whorl of hair at the base of his neck, and below it the crosshatched wrinkles in his skin, like the diamond pattern scored in the fatty covering of a baked ham. Something went dry in her throat, caught in it. Trying to stem the disruptive tide she felt moving within her, she forced her eyes away. John Denton and Milt Elliott were scrubbing themselves over a wooden bucket, their arms draped in the ecru lace of suds. Elitha was teasing Coalie with scraps of meat, and the dog danced rhythmically on his hind legs like a circus performer. The smaller children were playing hide-and-seek, and Frances's serious face appeared in fragments, peeking through a wagon wheel that segmented it into brief, sunburned wedges. George suddenly eclipsed her view of the children's game, and Tamsen saw again, as though magnified by crystal lenses, the single unruly tuft of hair she had once sought to tame with her fingers. It seemed to proclaim some terrible knowledge, an impalpable mass of human sorrow concentrated upon the nape of the man's frail neck as he went mutely about his task, fumbling with the frayed lengths of rope and silvered canvas that would thinly roof them from the sky. When the rawness scraping at the back of her throat mounted higher, she stood quickly and joined her husband, to help him arrange their temporary bed of quilts and buffalo robes.

THE CAMP WAS STRANGELY SILENT, WITH EVEN THE VOICES OF THE children stilled, during the two full days the men and women of the Donner Party spent preparing for the desert crossing. The chafed shoulders and sore feet of the oxen were treated with tallow and tar, buckets and kegs were soaked to make them watertight, and food was prepared to last the passage. The men scythed grass and packed it into every nook and cranny of the wagons, even lashing bundles to the sides and suspending them underneath. They planned to cross the desert without stopping for more than an hour or two at a time, and they were, according to Hastings, "Two days and two nights" from the next grass and water. Given Hastings's brand of arithmetic, that could mean as much as three, if they had any problems. Even the scowling Bill McCutcheon would not have guessed that it would take them closer to six desperate days to complete the next stage of their journey.

9

south of Utah Lake
Sunday, September 30th, 1846

This entry must be abbreviated, for the sun has long descended and we intend to depart this place before it again shows its fiery face, in order to avail ourselves of the cooler hours to begin our crossing of the desert. According to a bulletin from Mr. Lansford Hastings, which we found posted here beside a refreshing spring, the dry drive ahead will occupy two days and two nights. This greatly exceeds our initial expectations, and the communication provoked a great and general sinking of the heart. We have been at pains to load every available vessel with water, as well as laying in sufficient grass for the animals.

Our journey from the Wahsatch led us around the shore of

the briny Utah Lake, and from there through a barren terrain in which most of the springs were made undrinkable by the heavy infusions of alkali and salt. A delightful exception was the region christened "Twenty Wells" by Mr. Reed, and indeed the vertical shafts of these springs were so regular as to seem put down by the most exacting engineers, or the sharpest biscuit-cutter! Equally remarkable was the natural action which refilled them to the very brim (never a drop more or less) whenever water had been drawn out. Mr. Denton, who always makes precise notes and sketches of such natural oddities, attempted to plumb their depths, but resigned after paying out 70 feet of rope.

On the shore of the desolate Utah Lake we buried the invalid Mr. Halloran, whose pitiable struggle for life ended in the afternoon of August 24th. On the day following, fellow members of the Masonic brotherhood provided the ritual burial service, thus compensating somewhat for the absence of any relation to mourn his passing.

Young Edward Breen seems to be mending nicely, as though the arduous trail which drained Mr. Halloran's last feeble reserves has actually worked a curative effect on the boy. These mysterious regions, whose waters flow to the Pacific, frequently seem to reverse our expectations, as though holding up a mirror to our Atlantic souls.

10

THE TRAIL FROM THE SPRING WHERE THE DONNER PARTY HAD camped for three nights led due west, and the sudden rising of the sun flooded the sandy plain with carmine and gold. The light silhouetted an unexpected range of hills ahead, and the track seemed to aim for their heart, rather than bending to north or south. By noon the hills had swollen into mountains, steep and forbidding, and the trail pointed to the highest peak. Nothing had prepared them for such an obstacle in the desert road, for yet more hated mountains to be scaled, but they goaded the straining oxen up the steep slope, and those with heavier loads climbed down to help push the wagons the final hundred yards up the pass. To the west the land twisted upward again to a crumbling volcanic ridge, and beyond it there was only a blazing flash of white, like the eye of a furnace, to announce the real desert that still lay nearly a day's drive away.

The sun was setting as the last wagon rolled down from the mountain, and the party rested for an hour, giving grass and a little precious water to the teams without unhitching them. As the first stars appeared overhead, a bitterly cold wind poured from the thin sky with the whine of homesickness, knifing through the emigrants' thin clothing, and there was no fuel for a fire. Some dug beneath their loads for warmer outfits, but most stood flailing themselves with their arms while they chewed at mouthfuls of cold beans and brittle biscuits smeared with lard. The earth was now so thickly laced with salt that it sparkled in the moonlight like autumn frost, and they could almost imagine sleeping brown fields waiting for the awakening of spring. But despite the chill air, the earth itself seemed to pulsate with heat. It was a ghostly, godforsaken landscape, and no one complained when George Donner raised the call to pull out again.

The second dawn found them at the top of the snaking volcanic ridge that dropped to the floor of the desert itself. Many looked back at the desolate plain they had just crossed as though it now seemed a fertile garden, with its few forlorn clumps of withered sage, its lonely, weathered sentinels of greasewood. Ahead of them, and as far as the western horizon, there was nothing to relieve the bareness, the gray-white layer of leprous skin stretched tautly over the face of the earth. Only the vivid memory of the painful trials they had survived kept some from turning back, wheeling along the ridge and moving east again when George Donner's family wagon began its descent.

The trail looked deceptively firm, but it was increasingly hard work for the oxen, wading through light, ash-like sand and dragging wagons that often sank in it up to their hubs. Thickly lathered and soon too weak to bellow for water, some of them collapsed, dropped to their knees, and could not be raised again. They were left to feed the flocks of vultures that gyred overhead and began to pluck at the animals' bulging eyes even before the brief dying was over.

In sudden panic, one of George Donner's wheel oxen slipped its yoke, twisted in the harness, and rammed the wagon with such force a horn cracked off at the base. While it lunged for its mate with the remaining horn, John Denton put a single rifle shot through the maddened animal's brain, then helped hitch one of the spare oxen in its place, but the replacement was not broken to the wheel, and continually strained sideways to escape the pursuing wagon. The rebellion slowed the Donners even more, but by now all the heavier wagons had dropped behind, with the lighter rigs belonging to Eddy, McCutcheon, and the Breen family nearly two miles in advance. James Reed and the Donner brothers were now slowly bringing up the rear, burdened by the rich, heavy cargoes that had initially assured their status in the group. Keseberg hung back with them for a time, perhaps sparing his oxen, but panic finally gripped him, and he pushed them ahead, flailed the whip across their haunches until they sank groaning into the sand, blackened tongues sliding obscenely from their mouths. When further beating, as well as curses and prayers in three languages, failed to raise them, Keseberg ordered Dutch Charley Burger to help shift some of the goods from the supply wagon, which would have to be left behind. They were adding the reserve yoke to the animals unhitched from the second wagon when two bulls suddenly shouldered them aside and raced across the sands in a frenzied search for water. The men pursued, but were rapidly outdistanced.

Salt dust mixed with sweat to form a thick paste on the skins of the emigrants. When they tried to wipe it away, the salt crystals lacerated their flesh, and so they left it to whiten their sunburned arms and faces like theatrical paint, but they rubbed continuously at their eyes, which burned as though drenched with caustic soda. The albino Baylis Williams suffered so acutely that his sister bound his pale eyes with a strip of flannel, and he stumbled behind her with one hand hooked into the sash of her dress. Most of the party walked beside their wagons, heads down to moderate the painful glare, but there was no shelter from the roasting heat that cracked their lips, charred their skins, burned through the worn soles of boots and shoes. The universal torture denied the men and women even the luxury of complaint. Each was tightly wrapped in the cocoon of his private suffering. After the first night they did not halt again for rest, and each new dawn found them moving along the tracks of the Harlan-Young Party like beads drawn sluggishly along a string. If the tracks had not sliced with such mathematical precision through the sands, had the sun not so pitilessly duplicated their westward course, they would have imagined they moved in a circle, that the trail inscribed in the sand was their own, that they were doomed to follow it until it consumed them, like a serpent inch by inch swallowing its own tail.

If there was little water to spare for the animals, there was scarcely more for the adults in the party, and soon even the children were being given only a careful teaspoonful at a time. Tamsen felt she could not endure the rasping, whimpering cries Georgia and Eliza made, that rose even above the brittle rattling of the prairie schooners, but far worse was the bewildered silence that wrapped them after the third day, huddled beneath a tented quilt in the family wagon. Every few hours she gave the smaller children lumps of loaf sugar with a few drops of peppermint oil.

"Don't chew it," she told them. "Let it melt slowly in your mouth."

For a time, the remedy seemed to help. Then, at Noah James's suggestion, she gave each a flattened bullet to suck in the hope it would deceive their awful thirst. Only a few inches of water re-mained in one keg, and its constant sloshing tormented them all with dreams of splashing rivulets and springs, while mirages multi-plied cooling crystal lakes on the horizon. The treachery of those visions was almost as cruel as the relentless glare of the sun.

When they reached the salt flats, the entire party rapidly picked up speed, drew closer together again, but soon lunged into the sink, where the brittle surface would not bear the weight of even the lightest wagon. All sank several inches into the salty slush beneath, and it scalded the raw feet of the oxen. Each family now sought its own path, anxious not to plunge into the mire churned up by other struggling teams, and the Donner Party fanned out across the desert, more and more resembling a routed army in clumsy, undisciplined retreat.

When Reed's palace wagon broke through the crust of salt, George Donner thought of unhitching one of his own teams to help pull it out, but then he saw the top-heavy form shift, tilt, and settle above its axle, like a once proud clipper ship with the hull ripped open against a reef. It was soon so deeply wedged that Reed could not open the door, and had to splinter it apart, tear it with a raw, cracking noise from its hinges, to free his terrified wife and children. The Donners waited for Reed to shift teams and reload some of the lighter, more precious possessions from the stranded family wagon. When the job seemed finished, he hurried again to his palace car, struggling through the doorway with the great pier glass his wife had received as a farewell gift from her friends in Springfield. Its weight was so immense that he stumbled, and neither Tamsen nor George could believe he would attempt to add it to his overburdened supply wagons. After walking a few feet, Reed raised the mirror in the air and jammed it into the marshy ground, where it flared a challenge to the sun.

By the time the Springfield party was under way again, the others had all disappeared from sight, and soon there was another delay while George Donner unyoked a dying team, regrouped his staggering animals, and abandoned a supply wagon. It was their fourth day of travel through the merciless inferno, and there was no sign they were nearing the westward edge. As he had done before when the last threads of hope began to unravel, Reed proposed to ride ahead for relief. He would try to bring back water, and could tell the others if they stood a chance of completing the crossing or would have to abandon their wagons. Before mounting Glaucus, he instructed Milt Elliott to push the oxen forward every possible inch, but if they began to fail, he was to unyoke them and drive them to water, together with the loose stock. When the animals were refreshed, they could return to haul in their stranded goods and supplies.

THE COSTLY BOLTS OF FABRIC THEY HAD SALVAGED WERE PACKED
so tightly across the back of the family wagon that they formed an
impenetrable wall, and the air had become so dense that Tamsen felt
the children would surely suffocate. She pushed at the barrier with
her feet, but the tightly wrapped bundles were held rigidly in place.
Edging forward, she gripped the side of the wagon bed in her hands,
and using the new leverage, thrust again with her legs. Something
eased, and she imagined the air had become lighter. A bolt had
slipped, twisted, to reveal a chink of light, but it was still too tightly
wedged to drop away. Tamsen hammered her fists into the widening
gap with the frenzy of a prisoner hacking his way to freedom,
dislodging the stone whose mortar he had chipped away a stealthy
grain at a time with the handle of a tin spoon. Suddenly it dropped,
dislodging two others and opening a glaring window in the rear of
the wagon. Many of the wrappings had been torn, and Tamsen
propped herself on a sill of striped taffeta, felt her face caressed by
a fluttering edge of muslin, as her lungs strained against the boiling
air. She dislodged the sill, watching the bolt of taffeta, striped in rose
and green and the thinnest hint of cerulean, strike the salt crust,
bounce and tumble and unfold two neatly creased lengths against
the whiteness, like a precise bed of flowers set down by a fastidious
gardener. She ripped open the paper that concealed a rectangular
bundle of lavender silk and played it out slowly between her fingers,
felt it flow away from her as easily, swiftly, as the string of a kite
rapidly mounting the spring air. She smiled, then laughed aloud as
the draft from the moving wagon caught it, twisted the silk into a
ribbon, a royal pennant that fluttered bravely behind them until a
sudden whirlwind caught it, flung the stuff upward, churned it into
a vast rose. Tamsen let the final inches slide through her hands,
consigning them to the air. For a time, dense black damask embroidered in gold dragged a funeral pall behind them, then lace billowed,
fluttered into a bridal veil, only half visible against the glowing salt,
so that it seemed even more gossamer and fragile. Pink organdy
blossomed from the back of the Donner wagon, the crimson hem
of a bishop's velvet robe trailed the sand in stately, measured pace,
followed by the serviceable gray challis of a matron's second-best
dress. A diaphanous cloud of lawn, sprigged with ribboned bouquets,

floated beneath the startled eyes of the vultures, who would later descend to peck testingly at the dainty embroidery. Clutching the pinked ends of the cloth, Tamsen pushed four, five, six bolts onto the ground, watched them tumble playfully, bouncing and unfurling multicolored lengths that spread a brilliant rainbow in their wake.

JAMES REED PROCEEDED ALONG A TRAIL OF WASTE AND DESOLA-tion, littered with furniture, crates of household supplies and empty water kegs discarded to lighten the emigrants' loads. A brass bed-stead gleamed incongruously against the sand, complete with feather mattress, bolsters, and thick down coverlets, all new and probably stitched on long winter evenings, while heads nodded with talk of the bounties of California. With every mile there were more dead or dying cattle in sight, and stranded wagons whose distant hulks thrust out of the salt plain like vacant tombs. Glaucus skirted a trench where someone had started to dig a cache for his more valuable possessions, then abandoned the strenuous work and moved on, leaving a Saratoga trunk and a pine crate behind, perched at the edge of the shallow scar in the sand.

Reed passed Hardkoop's wagon without a greeting. His reti-cence had less to do with the old Belgian's fragmentary English than with the remote look in his eyes. They scarcely seemed to focus as they turned to stare at the horseman, and his hands were frozen into hooks that were insensible to the reins dangling there. The oxen were not being driven but simply lunged ahead in some feverish dream of water. A short distance beyond Hardkoop, the Wolfingers babbled without interruption, like siblings reunited after a half cen-tury of painful separation, each too eager to tell his own tale to catch the sense of the other's recitation. Reed observed that Mrs. Wolfinger had removed her heavy ruby necklace, which nestled in her lap and seemed to liquify in the intense sun. From time to time she attempted to pluck it up, but it scalded her fingers, and she sucked at them without interrupting her narrative.

After a two-hour ride, Reed saw the trail begin to curve slightly to the left and greeted the sprawling arc as a good omen, since the only reason for such a deviation would be the presence of water. He shaded his eyes, squinted against the glare, and could just make out a mountainous ridge ahead with faint spatterings of green. He had been saving Glaucus, but now he began to push the great mare, past a gateleg table that looked as though it had been rammed by a bull, past a parlor harmonium standing on its head, and then past William Eddy's wagon. The oxen had been unhitched and were obviously being driven on for water. A mile farther, the three wagons of the foolhardy Graves family lumbered along, their teams still apparently in good order, headed for the beckoning green of the ridge. When Reed arrived, there was nothing to welcome him but the treacherous greasewood and a view of the trail as it clutched the side of a steep promontory before plunging into yet another salt plain. He knew, now, that his own teams would never make the haul, that his family would perish if he could not get back to them, and though Glaucus began to stumble, Reed allowed her no rest. The mountainous slope had concealed the Murphy wagons, but when the trail had skirted it, Reed was nearly on top of them. The widow raised one hand in a kind of salute that smashed the brim of her felt against her sweating face. From the back of the wagon the thin, agonized voices of the children resembled the mewling of hungry kittens, and Glaucus shied at the sound.

It took nearly six hours for Reed to reach the spring that rose like a biblical miracle a few yards from the western boundary of the desert. Some of the luckier emigrants were already there, including William Eddy and the Breens. Eddy staggered from the spring under the weight of two buckets of water, then sat down clumsily between them. Having brought his family to safety, he now intended to set off into the desert again in the hope of reviving an ox that had lain down and refused to move. The Breens had already returned nearly ten miles to haul out their third wagon. They had come through without loss, as would the Graves family, though the wagons huddling beside the spring were so dried and split, the canvas so tattered, the spokes of the wheels so warped and sprung, they hardly looked worth saving.

While he rested beside Bill Eddy, Reed was aware of a grim tension between the young father and Patrick Breen, whose scowling glances repeatedly flashed in their direction. He could not be both-ered to ask their source, and he suspected his proud companion would have been reluctant to tell him.

At noon, when the sun flared so intensely overhead that earth and sky fused into a single mass, William Eddy realized that his wife and children would soon die without water. He had given them the last drops the night before, and now the three lay half-conscious in the wagon. When he saw the Breens halting, he raced forward with a tin cup in his hand, arriving just as Pat Breen was closing the cock on a water keg. The man pulled the final drop away on his finger and sucked it off.

"My wife and kids gotta have some water or they'll die," Eddy announced in a voice that suppressed every emotion.

"Well, there's no extra here," Peggy Breen bellowed from the wagon. Her husband hesitated, looking at the extended cup, but Peggy seemed to fly from the wagon, thrusting a rifle into his hands.

"We ain't got enough for our own!" she shouted. "Tell 'im, Pat."

"It's true," the man nodded slowly. "Ain't hardly got enough for my own. We're a mighty big family."

"Mine's a little family, but it's the only one I got," Eddy told him between clenched teeth. His eyes measured the dimensions of the keg, the time it would take him to reach it.

"No need to come beggin' 'round here," Peggy added emphatically.

Eddy stepped forward.

"Stand back there," Pat warned him. He tilted the rifle, dangled it warningly against his hip.

Tears stood in Eddy's eyes, but there was murder in the voice that whispered, "Out of my way, or I'll ram that goddamned rifle down your miserable throat." He looked neither to the man nor to the woman as he drew half a cup of water for himself, slowly downed it, then filled the cup to carry back to Eleanor and the children.

Now, as he stretched on the grass between the two brimming buckets, he saw Pat Breen unlash the barrel, tilt out what remained of the brackish water, and carry it to the spring to refill.

"Bastard," Eddy muttered, but Reed pretended to ignore him, and soon both men were distracted by the Widow Murphy's noisy arrival. She stood on the little platform that jutted over the rumps of the oxen, waving her hat in the air and bellowing "Hallelujah!"

After resting himself and his mount for an hour, James Reed began his return journey. Even those who had ignored him when he was riding west, perhaps resentful of the horseman overtaking them, hailed him vigorously, eager to know the distance that still separated them from water.

"You'll make it now," he encouraged Uncle Billy Graves. "It's less than five miles."

For Keseberg, whose oxen blundered so drunkenly against each other they could scarcely move in a straight line, Reed's information was less welcome.

"It's about ten miles," Reed told him.

"*Ach, du lieber Gott,*" the German swore. "*Scheiss Tiere!*" He reversed the whip to hammer at the wheel oxen with the handle.

"Mr. Keseberg, I'd advise you not to kill any more oxen. You'll need all you've got," Reed warned.

Keseberg stared resentfully at the fancy gentleman from Springfield on his prancing mare. "*Scheiss Tiere!*" he muttered again, but ceased to punish them.

Soon after his encounter with Keseberg, Reed passed the rolling wagons of Wolfinger and Hardkoop. "Fool's luck," he thought, as he paused again to scan the horizon for his own wagons. What he saw, soon after the full moon rose, was Milt Elliott and another hand driving his teams and loose stock. They were only following his own cautious instructions, but he felt a momentary flash of anger that they had abandoned his wife and children, left them defenseless and without a drop of water in the murderous salt plain. Then he remembered that one teamster would still be with them, and the clenched fist of his anger eased.

As the moon reached its zenith, he encountered the straggling rear guard of the train—the George Donners first, then the two wagons remaining to Jacob Donner—and knew that only his own stranded family was somewhere on the trail ahead. It was nearly daylight when he reached them, huddled against the cold with the teamster Walt Herron, Eliza and the half-blind Baylis Williams. Crowded together with the children in the center, they looked from the distance like an Indian burial mound, but they were wonderfully alive. Reed distributed the precious canteens of water, cautioning each to drink sparingly as they might have a long wait before Milt returned with the teams, then sent Walt Herron back with Glaucus.

Throughout the following day Reed watched for his teamsters, and when the dying sun revealed no figure moving against the distant horizon, he and his family set out on foot with the little remaining water and a few stale biscuits. Reed carried three-year-old Tommy, and Margaret Reed led Jimmy, who insisted he could walk for himself, but repeatedly stumbled when his feet caught in holes gouged by the oxen. They walked until all were so numbed by exhaustion and the cold desert wind that their legs refused to move, and then James Reed arranged the children in a tight circle, draped them in a pair of shawls, and ordered the five family dogs to curl beside them for warmth. The adults sat with their backs to the wind to provide a shelter, and soon the children slept deeply.

Their reprieve was brief, for suddenly all the dogs were on their feet, barking fiercely, and James Reed stood with his pistol cocked. A huge, panting animal loomed out of the darkness, and with a furious rush of hooves charged directly at the screaming children. The dogs turned it, and Reed fired a single shot in the air, fearful that a stray bullet would find a human target. As the mountain of flesh lumbered, wheeled, and swerved past him, Reed recognized one of his own steers, maddened by thirst. There was no hope of further rest for the terrified children, and the family pushed on again, reaching the wagons of Jacob Donner during the first hour of daylight.

Jacob and his family had slept for a few hours, hoping to gain strength for the last miles of their journey. The news they had for Reed brought fresh terror at the very moment when he thought the worst had been conquered. Soon after he had passed his teamsters, they had been distracted by a horse that lay down and refused to rise again. While the two were trying to heave and prod the animal to its feet, the oxen had stampeded, bolted in different directions, and vanished in the darkness as they sought the vague scent of water. The teamsters were out searching for the runaways, and Reed went to join them, leaving his little party to move ahead under the protec-

tion of the Donners. When he reached the spring for the second
time, he learned that his total stock now consisted of one horse, one
ox, and a half-lame milch cow.

11

Salvation Spring
Wednesday, September 9th, 1846
If our lonely campsite has any formal designation, it is unknown
to us, and so many have called it "Salvation" that the word seems
to have stuck. We have rested here since Tuesday morning and
will remain at least one further day to mend body, spirit and
wagons. The crossing of the great desert consumed not the advertised 2 days and 2 nights of hard driving, but six days and nights
of dreadful agony. The suffering and loss were so immense that
only now do I find the steady hand to set them down. Human life
was spared, but 36 head of working cattle either died in the
crossing or stampeded at the smell of water and have not been
found. Some of our party are still hunting, though there seems
little hope of finding the animals alive.

From our once-proud caravan there remain only 18 wagons,
many of those too battered and decrepit to see the eternal summer
of California. Drawn up near our "spring of salvation," they resemble nothing so much as the crumbling, decaying village of the
dead which we passed on leaving Fort Laramie, and round which
the mournful wolves had howled throughout the night. Even those
sly creatures could not survive in the wilderness of salt, but flocks
of ravenous vultures soared continuously over our heads, waiting
for another thirsty ox to perish. They had not long to wait. The
most terrible agonies were those of the dumb creatures and the
smaller children, who could not reason that even the unending
desert must have its end, and that if they are worth such tortures,

the valleys of California must be a veritable paradise. Only the nursing infants were spared the universal agonies of thirst. When our supply of water was nearly exhausted, I attempted to pacify the children with pieces of lump sugar flavored with peppermint drops. They seemed to find more relief in the flattened bullets they were given to suck, but these, too, were a pitiable substitute for the sustaining draught they craved. I exempt Elitha and Leanna from "the children," for they are too old for such motherly tricks, and have found adult duties and sufferings thrust rudely on them, but they are brave and sweet in their acceptance of necessity. Frances, too, has felt the abbreviation of childhood, and her dolls have long since disappeared.

We scarcely know whether thirst, heat, the blinding glare of the sun, the bitter cold of night or the corrosive burn of the salt-sand gave the most wretched discomfort, but without water, all would soon have perished. None were immune, and almost all suffered loss of property. Circumstances prevented our traveling as a unified company, and the fear of being stranded made most unwilling to pause and assist others in distress. It was, veritably, a case of "devil take the hindmost."

Luckily, none of our party have suffered so acutely as the Reeds, who have descended in one week from plenty to pauperage. The salt marshes claimed the noble palace wagon, and the 2 supply wagons were left behind by Mr. Reed's employees (at his instructions) in order to drive the teams ahead to water. While the men were seeking to raise a fallen horse, the oxen stampeded and spread to the four winds. No trace of them has been found, and Mr. Reed is reduced to his fine racing mare, an ox and a single footsore cow. Only through the promise of a generous share of the salvaged goods could he secure assistance in bringing in one of his wagons. What remains in the desert has been "cached," to use the term the French trappers gave to this artful process of conceal-ment. It consists in digging a deep hole into which the most valuable goods are lowered, then covered with a layer of earth or sand. Above this trove, less valuable baubles (but ones thought particularly appealing to Indian eyes) are strewn, and then covered with the remaining earth. It is hoped they will be too pleased with their gaudy find to seek further.

Mr. Reed has purchased one ox from the Graveses and one from the Breens—the sole families in our midst to have endured no material loss. In the single wagon there is little room for reserve supplies, and Mr. Reed today stacked bags of sugar and flour near the spring, announcing that any who wished might avail themselves without charge. Our own losses (1 wagon, 3 oxen, and a quantity of goods intended for the California trade) seem insignificant in comparison.

The men of our company vow that if they ever encounter Lansford Hastings, they will roast him alive. Mr. Eddy allows that such a fate would be much too good for the scoundrel, and is devising some more suitable treatment.

12

Sunday, September 13th, 1846

We have found a singularly pretty lake camp, and have only the wisdom of our Captain to thank that we arrived here so promptly. After leaving Salvation Spring we received another of the unhappy communications with which Mr. Hastings has "blazed" our trail. Milt Elliott and young Billy Graves were searching ahead for strayed cattle (without success) when they found the message, which announced another dry drive of approximately 40 miles. Rather than subject his party to further unknown hazards, our Captain sent scouts to examine the route. When they rejoined us, they reported that the Harlan-Young tracks proceeded north-northwest from the next spring and then veered back south again. By avoiding this detour and proceeding due southwest, we were able to shorten the dry drive by nearly 15 miles.

A snowstorm whistled about our ears as we left our refuge at Salvation Spring, though we were still in sight of the burning desert. The churning flakes confirmed our tardiness, and made all anxious about their shrinking provisions. Despite Mr. Reed's bounty, several families have been compelled to ration their food, and some are cautiously taking but two meals a day. A meeting was called yesterday to discuss the situation, and it was determined to send two men to Capt. Sutter's headquarters to purchase emergency supplies. Again the stalwart Mr. McCutcheon was among the volunteers, together with our remarkable Chicagoan, Mr. Stanton. Despite the latter's protests of loyalty, fears were expressed that an unattached bachelor might choose to dawdle in California rather than returning to his distressed companions of the trail. The skeptics seemed quickly to forget that the bachelor might as easily have remained with the Harlan-Young company while we were struggling through the Wahsatch. He chose, instead, to return at the peril of his life and assist us with our labors. It was finally agreed that our two former messengers would once more depart together, and they took their leave with the giant McCutcheon mounted on a spavined mare, the boy-like Stanton on an undersized, scrawny mule—the very model of Don Quixote and Sancho Panza embarking on new adventures.

A survey of our condition has confirmed that one of the Widow Murphy's supply wagons is beyond repair and must be abandoned, while Mr. Reed's makeshift teams have increasing difficulty to navigate the trail. As William Eddy has pitifully little to transport, the carriagemaker will shift his modest stores to Mr. Reed's wagon and add to it the strength of his own teams. Mrs. Murphy's son-in-law, William Pike, can then have use of the Eddy wagon. It is all a little like the nightly patching of a pair of shoddy work trousers! We are thus reduced to 17 rigs, and fear yet more will have to be abandoned.

13

Valley of Fifty Springs
Sunday, September 20th, 1846

For more than two days we have descended this fertile valley, which takes its name from the great quantity of its remarkable springs—some boiling hot, some tepid, and others delightfully chilled for the refreshment of the traveler. Game is plentiful, and the antelope and mountain goats seem so fatly content with their easy life that bringing them down is more like target-practice than hunting. We have had bountiful feasts, but also hundreds of Indians in the area come to seek the same. Despite their terrifying and unkempt appearance, these maintain a respectful distance, and our happiness would be complete if the trail did not move so vexingly to the south. It parallels a range of mountains higher than any we have yet encountered, and with no sign of a pass to bring us nearer to California.

The Breen boy is hobbling about on a makeshift crutch, but less and less dependent on it for support. He is, all in all, a miraculous tribute to motherly wisdom! His hardiness (or is it foolhardiness?) has assumed heroic proportions in Elitha's pretty eyes, and I fancy she hears wedding bells in her ears. She is not alone in her matrimonial daydreams, for a match is clearly brewing between Mary Graves and the dashing teamster, John Snyder. He is romantically handsome, like one of Scott's heroes, but his temper is pure blasting powder.

14

Mary's River

Sunday, September 27th, 1846

After three full days of a course that threatened to deposit us in
Mexico, we at last found a gap in the mountains and were able
to make a westward passage of 20 miles before descending into
another valley. Here we were frustratingly compelled to follow a
northbound creek, but this has brought us at last to the westward-flowing Mary's River. Our present location is familiar to all
California emigrants, and we rejoice to leave behind the windings of the Hastings route to rejoin the established trail. A troop
of shaggy-haired and otherwise stark-naked Indians came into
camp at early evening and let us know by signs that not only the
Harlan-Young Party passed this way but also a sizable group
approaching from the direction of the rising sun. These can only
be the fortunate souls who elected to travel via Fort Hall, and
who now have the jump on the short-cutters. The Indians also
communicated with some difficulty the fact that the peculiar
"sink" of the Mary's River still lies far beyond the horizon, and
this we must attain before beginning the final approach to California.

Mary's River is a most unprepossessing stream, hardly more
than a chain of stagnant, bitter pools, and the barren land all
about it offers such poor forage that we have concluded to divide
into two sections, despite the multiplied danger of Indian depredations. The Donner families will make up the forward unit, and
Mrs. McCutcheon accompanies us with the angelic Harriet. The
child pines for her brave, curly-headed father, who so dotes on her
that he frequently carries her about on one of his broad shoulders
—like a mite on the shoulder of a stallion! We daily expect her

father's return, together with Mr. Stanton and fresh rations from the California storehouse.

Eddie Breen has thrown away his crutch—or, rather, has chopped it up for firewood!

15

Mary's River
Sunday, October 4th, 1846

Nothing of any note has transpired in the last week, if week it was. For want of oiling, perhaps, our calendars have stuck, and none seem to agree on the day. By my reckoning, it is the first Sunday in October, and the nights have a chill much like that experienced at this season in Illinois.

We have traveled nearly 20 miles a day, following first the north fork and then the main stream of Mary's River. Heat and dust are our familiar daily companions. The two sections of our party camped together on Wednesday, though some called it Tuesday and others Thursday, but since then we have lost sight of the larger company that follows us.

The filthy, poverty-ridden Diggers grow pesky but show no real hostility. Nonetheless, the men have thought it proper to post a watch on the stock throughout the night. As Mr. Reed's teamsters now travel with us (except for Milt Elliott), we have guards aplenty, and the nightly duty imposes no unfair burdens.

There is still no sign of Messrs. Stanton and McCutcheon, but increasing need of their appearance.

One of our oxen has died. It had been failing ever since the desert crossing, and would not respond to all my clumsy doctoring. We now have no reserve, but are blessed to have lost no more of our stock.

The moon is once more at the full.

16

THE SECOND SECTION OF THE DONNER PARTY SOON LAGGED NEARLY three days behind the first, slowed by the sluggish pace of the teams belonging to Keseberg and Wolfinger. Even strengthened by Eddy's oxen, the Reed wagon could scarcely move any faster, and the Breens and Graveses were wrapped in the careless oblivion that protected them like the stony shell of a mollusk. Now that they had joined the main California trail, they only had to keep moving in a straight line, and there was no reason to push the weary animals, which they hoped to sell for a good price in New Helvetia. The party's progress was so snail-like that the Diggers, most of them on foot, had no difficulty keeping up. Their constant, skulking presence led Reed to propose that a watch should be set, but neither Uncle Billy Graves nor Patrick Breen was willing to have his well-earned sleep disturbed to sit with teeth chattering and stare for hours into the darkness. No longer a man of visible property, though the gold and bank notes he carried could have bought the entire train, Reed had little voice, and if the others thought at all about his misfortunes, it was only to conclude that he was being justly punished for his pride. Many blamed him still for the tortures they had endured in crossing the Wahsatch. It was his advice that had sent them clawing and scratching their way over the top.

The emigrants had turned away so many requests for food that the hungry Diggers rarely approached the train directly, and the few who did lacked the innocent, engaging smile of the young brave who caught up with the Reed-Eddy wagon as it crossed a low range of hills. The visitor spoke a few words of English, and amused the children with imitations of a driver yelling "Gee!" and "Whoa!" and "Huoy!" at his oxen. He also seemed, unlike the other Indians they had encountered, willing to make himself useful, and with thoughts of Robinson Crusoe, William Eddy named him Thursday. Peggy Breen scoffed that the day was really Tuesday, but Eddy stuck to Thursday; it was, in fact, a Friday when the young Indian attached himself to the rear section of the emigrant train.

"Do you think he's escaped from the cooking pot, like Crusoe's Friday?" James Reed asked.

"Wouldn't surprise me," Eddy answered. "A Digger will eat most anything. Gotta keep an eye on the dogs and the babies and your old boots when they're around. But what they like best is rotten harness leather boiled up with grasshoppers."

The two men laughed, and Margaret Reed smiled at their pleasure, for laughter had grown almost as rare as good grass for the stock, but she remembered with a chill the stories of Old Bill Williams and his peculiar dietary habits. She shuddered, a brief spasm that made her clutch the jolting wagon seat for balance, and seemed to hear Tamsen telling her not to be such a scaredy-cat. She missed her friend, the only woman in the train with whom she shared a real education, distant friends and acquaintances, and the little female intimacies that had thickened their relationship into a kind of sisterhood almost as secret, almost as elaborated, as the Masonic brotherhood to which her husband belonged.

Throughout the day, Thursday amused the company, acting as court jester and childishly pleased to be able to offer some simple service—fetching a bucket of water, getting a wagon over a rough spot in the road. Late in the afternoon, another Digger came in, perhaps inspired by Thursday's success, and the two got the dinner they asked for, amply paying for it by waking the sleeping camp when a grass fire broke out and threatened to ignite three of the tinder-dry wagons. In gratitude for their services, the emigrants gave them extra rations, and the two curled up at the edge of the camp to sleep, but they woke in time to disappear with Uncle Billy's best shirt and two of his oxen. When a horse was run off the following night, even Pat Breen saw the wisdom of setting a watch. Shortly before dawn, the animals seemed restless, but there was no sign of Indians, and only when hitching up the teams did the men discover that the Diggers had crawled up undetected to shoot their flimsy arrows into the haunches of several oxen. Most of the wounds were

275

so superficial that the animals scarcely bled, but one of the milch cows had suffered worse, and had to be abandoned beside the trail later in the morning.

The Indians' stealthy game continued throughout the coming nights, and William Eddy was attacked with a volley of arrows while searching for game, but escaped unhurt. It was less the direct losses they suffered than the constant watchfulness, the jittery anxiety, the sleepless nights, the children confined throughout the day in the roasting, prisonlike closeness of overloaded wagons, that caused tempers to fray in the straggling rear section of the train. Though their crooked, clumsily made arrows took no human toll, the Diggers were thus indirectly responsible for the death of John Snyder and the banishment of James Reed.

On Monday, October 5th, the wagons of the rear section rolled forward under a dense pall of yellow dust that stung the eyes and formed a thick, muddy scum on the water kegs. Except for Patrick Breen, who had assumed the trailbreaking position, the drivers could scarcely see beyond their own teams, but all felt the earth lifting, the oxen's feet churning, as they hauled up another sandhill. One of the Graveses' supply wagons, driven by John Snyder, stalled near the crest of the hill, and the dust was so heavy in the air that it was too late when Bill Pike saw the obstacle on the narrow track. He swerved, but wheels locked and the startled teams tangled together. Snyder was swearing and prodding at his own team when the Reed-Eddy wagon arrived, and William Eddy jumped down to help Pike prize the locked wheels apart.

Thinking it might be necessary to double-team the stalled wagon over the top, Reed had climbed down from the wagon box just as Snyder's temper exploded at the stupidity of the accident, and he began to flail his own oxen over the head. Knowing better than any man what it was to lose good working stock, Reed strode rapidly past Pike and Eddy and shouted up at the enraged teamster, "Don't be such a fool, man!"

"Fool?" Snyder bellowed. "Who you callin' a fool?"

"You," Reed snapped.

"Me?"

"Yes, you!" Then, consciously controlling his temper, he

added, "It isn't the first time some team's got stuck on a hill, and it won't be the last. We'll get you across."

"We?" Snyder laughed, throwing his head back to emphasize his contempt. "Look who's talkin'! A man without sense enough but to lose eighteen head in the desert. I'll get my own wagon across!"

Again the teamster brought his whip down hard across the bellowing oxen, trying to force them loose from the jumble of harness, and Reed shouted, "Stop that!"

"I may decide to take some hide off your fancy ass, too!" Snyder coiled the whip over his shoulder, but it was aimed in Reed's direction now.

"Just try it," Reed warned, and slid a hunting knife from his belt.

The sight of the polished blade so enraged Snyder that he suddenly jumped down from the wagon, reversing the whip and using the handle as a club. He brought it down viciously across Reed's head, opening a long gash that half-blinded him with his own blood.

It was at this point that Margaret Reed, alarmed by the angry voices, rushed forward and pushed her way between the two men— whether in the hope of acting as peacemaker or to ward off the blows aimed at her husband, even she could not have said, but the next blow landed on her shoulder with a loud cracking noise, another across her scalp. A crowd had gathered, but the dust was so thick that none could see clearly what was happening, and Reed saw only the blood that bathed his wife's face, speeding like a spring freshet through the yellow dust that coated her skin. Both men lunged again, Reed with the knife held level to his waist, Snyder with the whip handle raised like a flail, and their bodies locked, froze for an instant as hard and unyielding as a bronze tribute to gladitorial combat, and then Snyder slackened, slid to the ground with the handle of the hunting knife wedged high between his ribs.

The teamster's fingers seemed to caress it, examining the ridges and depressions of the bone handle, and then he announced, "I am dead." The words came slowly, and with each there was a fresh foaming of blood from his chest, the color of overripe raspberries.

W HILE THE OTHER MEN OF THE COMPANY DELIBERATED HIS fate, James Reed sat apart, holding his trembling wife in his arms and repeatedly reassuring her that in such a clear-cut case of self-defense, even Snyder's employer, Uncle Billy Graves, would have to see his side of things. If his own wounds were not evidence enough, those of his wife would convince even a rope-happy lynch mob. Virginia Reed had cleaned and dressed the long gashes in their scalps, trimmed matted hair away, wrapped them with strips of gauze that were now crusted with dried blood. Their forlorn appearance, however, seemed to win no sympathy from most of the council. Partly motivated by the fit of hysteria that convulsed his daughter Mary when she learned of Snyder's death, Uncle Billy Graves demanded an eye for an eye. Keseberg vigorously backed him; Pat Dolan was inclined to agree; Pat Breen wavered and finally muttered, "The law's the law." Only Milt Elliott and William Eddy argued Reed's case, but without property of his own Milt Elliott had no vote, and Eddy was so near destitution that he came near losing his.

Keseberg seemed to feel the matter was decided, for he left the circle of arguing men and began to unbolt his wagon tongue. When it was propped firmly upright, he attached a rope and stood back in clear admiration of his makeshift gallows. Ever since the episode of the buffalo robe, Reed had owed him a debt, and Keseberg had repeatedly scanned his fastidious ledger of debits and credits, accounts payable and accounts receivable, for more than a thousand miles. In the salt desert he had made another, minute adjustment when Reed interfered with the way he was handling his teams, and now he grunted with satisfaction at the tidiness of the settlement.

His reckonings, however, had not given proper weight to the persuasiveness with which Reed's two friends were repeatedly stressing his case, or the authority their arguments were lent by the weapons Milt Elliott and William Eddy now carried. If pushed too far, they would fight for Reed's life, but the threat required no words to make its effect on their listeners. The council agreed, finally, to substitute banishment for the death penalty, but insisted the offender take no water or food and no weapon with him. Those who desired Reed's death were thus spared the unpleasant business of actually putting a rope around his neck; hunger and thirst, Indians and wild animals, would be the executioners.

Reed at first refused to accept the sentence, refused even to consider it. It was unjust, it was barbaric, and worst of all it left his family defenseless. But Elliott and Eddy, who had heard the angry demands that the offender be hanged, made an oath to care for his wife and children.

"It's the only way," Eddy insisted. "We can't guard you all the time," he said, looking down at the double-barreled pistols he wore at his waist, the shotgun in his hands.

Milt Elliott was also a walking arsenal, and he shook his head sadly but agreed. "It's the only way, Mr. Reed."

In the end, only his wife's insistence persuaded Reed to accept the cruel verdict. It was for her, even more than the children, that he had wished to remain as protector and provider—the roles he had graciously played, then dramatically overplayed, throughout their marriage, treating her as delicately as a tissue-thin porcelain figurine that a single careless gesture might shatter. He had handled her reverently, admiringly, lifted her up in hands gallantly muffled by the softest doeskin gloves, placed her in a curio cabinet and gingerly turned the golden key. There, with her filigreed vinaigrettes and dainty stoppered vials of etched crystal, she had grown yet more precious and more fragile. He watched her now, the steady gaze and the unfamiliar tilt of her chin, the regal defiance with which she wore the bloodied cloth at her head, and he knew the rosewood cabinet had been smashed beyond repair—as surely as he had splintered the door of the Prairie Palace Wagon.

"Our supplies are low," she again reminded him, "and we have no idea when Stanton and McCutcheon will get through, if they get through at all. You will make it to the settlements," she told him, as though of all the uncertainties that surrounded them, this was the sole unquestionable fact. "And you can bring us relief if the others don't make it. If you stay, you won't be safe for a minute of the day or night, and I shall worry so that I'll lose my looks. Or what's left of them," she added, suddenly shy again.

They were gone already, her husband thought sadly, and they would never return. The suffering she had endured, almost always without complaint, had erased forever the fragile prettiness, the girlish freshness of her features, but it had left her with a handsomeness that surprised him when she turned and he saw, as through the eyes of an admiring stranger, the firm cameo of her matronly profile.

"We will manage," she assured him, and when he again started to protest, she blocked his words with her hand—not a finger tentatively pressed to his lips, but her palm firmly cupping his entire mouth. "It will be so much better for the children," she insisted, and her hand remained firm even when his tears descended to trickle warmly across her fingers.

James Reed remained in camp for the night and shortly after dawn stood by the shallow grave into which Snyder was lowered, wrapped in a dirty blanket, with a single board below him and another one above to discourage hungry coyotes. The condemned man then rode out while the others were hitching their teams, but on the pretext of searching the hills for game, William Eddy and Virginia Reed caught up with him a few hours later, leaving him with a quantity of biscuit, a blanket, a canteen for water, and a double-barreled shotgun and ammunition.

Two days after Reed's departure, Eddy and Pike were shot at repeatedly by Indians while hunting, and the increasing aggressiveness was underscored by a warning note from Reed the party found when making camp that night. One of the companies in advance of theirs had had a fierce battle with the Diggers, in which one man was killed and several wounded. In the alarm and confusion that followed the news, someone realized that Hardkoop was missing, and many of the emigrants imagined him lying beside the trail, his body studded with Digger arrows, the head savagely stripped of its silvery hair. The Belgian's wagon had been abandoned a week before, and he now traveled with Keseberg, but on rougher stretches of the trail everyone had to walk, and no one had noticed when the old man fell behind. It was Eddy who walked back along the trail and found him sitting in the center of the road, hugging his knees and weeping noisily. As Eddy helped him into camp, the old man babbled about Ohio, Antwerp, a son and daughter, but the rest was in a language his rescuer could not understand.

When the two men came within sight of the camp fires, Hardkoop suddenly stopped, clamping Eddy's arm in an iron grip, and whispered, "Keseberg make me walk. Say, 'walk or die, old man.' "

The following morning, Eddy watched carefully until Hardkoop had taken his seat in the Kesebergs' wagon, but for the rest of the day he was distracted by fresh problems of his own. Pat Breen and Uncle Billy Graves had demanded the return of the oxen they now claimed were only loaned to James Reed. Though Reed had promised generous bonuses when they reached California, the two men decided the murder of Snyder canceled any further obligation. With one yoke gone, Eddy was not sure he could even keep the wagon moving. Counting Eliza and Baylis Williams, he and Milt Elliott had three women, a half-blind youth and six children in their charge. He did not think again about Hardkoop until evening, when he anxiously searched all the camp fires without finding the man. Keseberg merely shrugged when Eddy confronted him, making it clear that the care of strays was not his responsibility.

It was Phillipine Keseberg who came to him later, darting frightened looks over her shoulder, to say they had passed Hardkoop shortly after noon, sitting beside the road and contemplating his bare feet. Somehow he had lost his boots.

The only remaining saddle horses belonged to the Graveses and the Breens, and nothing Eddy could say would persuade either family to risk a good horse for a worthless old man who was probably dead. Eddy gathered greasewood to build a beacon fire on a hillside, hoping it would guide the straggler to camp, and kept the fire high throughout the night, but the following morning the emigrants moved ahead without Hardkoop.

"It's the will o' the Almighty," Peggy Breen solemnly declared, and tossed an infant from one hip to the other, then made the blurred shape of a cross with her free hand.

"And it's too late to do anything now," her husband added.

William Eddy knew that Pat Breen was probably right, that if the old man hadn't died of fear and exhaustion, the Indians would have killed him, and that if the Indians had overlooked him, the coyotes would have done the job. But throughout the day he imagined Hardkoop crawling through the dust, dragging his bare, swollen feet behind him, and babbling of a son and a daughter while he struggled to catch up with the vanished wagon train.

17

Mary's River
Sunday, October 11th, 1846

We have not yet recovered from the grief and astonishment we experienced upon learning the tragic events that have befallen the rear section of our train. On Thursday, during the nooning, we were surprised to see a solitary horseman proceeding along the trail, and when we discerned the familiar figure of James Reed, our hearts sank, for we could only imagine that some general calamity had occurred, of which he was bringing us tidings. The Digger aggressions have greatly increased in recent days, and we have found ghastly signs of their bloody attack on a party in advance of ours.

It was, however, no general calamity which our Springfield friend had to communicate, but a specific one—namely, the accidental slaying of John Snyder, who was employed as teamster by the Graves family. He was a vain and boastful young man, but so full of mischief and merriment that his antics frequently enlivened our campfires, and he was generally well liked by all. The young ladies were particularly vulnerable to his handsome, manly features. If he had an enemy, it was in his own ugly temper, which at unexpected moments erupted like a volcano and seemed then entirely beyond his control. This apparently occurred again on Monday last when his teams became entangled with those of another wagon while attempting to pull a sandhill. When James

Reed approached to offer assistance, he found the teamster furiously beating his oxen, as though they were alone responsible for the accident, and the poor animals were bellowing with pain and fear. When he sought to restrain Snyder's wrath, Mr. Reed found it turned upon himself, receiving a deep gash in his scalp from the handle of a bullwhip which will certainly leave him scarred for the remainder of his life. Mr. Reed then drew a hunting knife—not with the intention of doing injury, but in hopes of cooling the young man's temper. The sight of the blade only enraged him further, and at the moment he struck again with his whip, Margaret Reed sought to intervene. She received a cruel blow to her shoulder and was also severely cut about the head. When Snyder lunged again, he fell upon the blade in Mr. Reed's hands and was dead of a chest wound within minutes. Even before the body was cold or Mr. and Mrs. Reed's wounds properly dressed, and while tempers in the party ran dangerously high, a council was called to determine the fate of the "murderer." All save Milford Elliott and William Eddy insisted on this cruel term, and most were for hanging the offender without delay. Mr. Keseberg felt so certain of the outcome that he had already raised a gallows and slung a noose from it. Cooler heads finally prevailed, but the compromise agreed upon seemed scarcely less cruel—namely, that Mr. Reed should be banished from the train without weapons, food or water. He rejected the sentence in the strongest manner, but his friends at last persuaded him that persistence in doing so would endanger not only his own person, but his wife and children. Margaret Reed pleaded most pitifully that he accept his fate, confident he would soon reach the settlements of California. As Mr. Snyder and Mr. McCutcheon have not yet returned, Mr. Reed may represent our sole hope of securing emergency rations from Capt. Sutter.

William Eddy and Mr. Reed's courageous stepdaughter had ridden after him with a rifle and a little food, so that he should not be entirely at the mercy of the wilderness, but he had found no game and was sorely weakened by hunger when he caught up to us. He remained but a single night and departed the following morning with Walter Herron, who formerly drove one of the Reeds' supply wagons and accompanied us when we were compelled to divide into two sections. The men are confident they can reach California in three or four days, and we pray they are right, for knowing our condition they refused to take more than a little bread with them, and will be reliant on the scanty game of the region. We are greatly distressed for Margaret Reed and her children, and will wait for them at the sink of Mary's River.

Misfortunes may truly be said to have multiplied upon the heads of this poor family, who once enjoyed the greatest luxuries and the most enviable position of our entire party. Their reverses make our own seem paltry, though they are a bitter dose to swallow. Diggers have repeatedly crawled near the camp at night and shot their clumsy arrows into the haunches of the animals. The bows are so weak and the arrows so small and poorly made, being intended principally for the hunting of rabbits, that the wounds are never mortal. However, some of the oxen receive so many of them that their haunches resemble giant pincushions, and the trickling loss of blood is sufficient to render them unfit for their labors. Several have had to be left behind, and some have been slaughtered out to provide fresh meat, but our salt is too scarce to cure it, and only the loin sections are removed, with the rest left behind for the perpetually hungry Indians. They hover in the hills like vultures, awaiting such windfalls.

In consequence of these losses, we were yesterday compelled to abandon the second of our supply wagons, caching the bulkier and more valuable goods in the lee of a sandhill. Into the giant desert grave went the books intended for my seminary in California, and which I had spent many months assembling. The loss of silver and years of Sunday dresses seemed, in comparison to the burial of these volumes, the most trivial inconvenience. That their knowledge and amusements lie now in the darkness of the blind earth is singularly hateful to me, but Mr. Donner promises to return in the Spring to retrieve them. It is certain they will not blossom in this wasted land. Mr. Denton begged to be permitted to rescue a slender volume by Keats from this premature burial, and I of course gave it to him gladly.

Near our present campsite is another grave, ravaged by the cowardly Indians, who dug up the corpse in order to steal the clothing, then left it for the coyotes. Coalie's barking called our attention to the gruesome scene, and the victim's bones were returned to their lonely resting place. Nearby was a rough wooden marker with the name "Sallee" carved on it, but nothing more.

18

Truckee River
Saturday, October 17th, 1846

It is my unhappy duty to record here a tragic episode which has only recently been made known to us. As it involves possible irregularities in the conduct of members of our party, Capt. George Donner has directed that this account be entered, to be presented to the appropriate authorities upon our arrival in California. The following statement is directly transcribed from his own words, and signed by his hand.

Not long after Independence we met up with a group of foreigners who had been living in Ohio and have traveled with them pretty much ever since. Two of the men were from Germany, and one was born in Belgium and couldn't speak much of anything but Belgian. These all seemed like good, prosperous people, and one of them named Keseberg could do the talking for the group. The others were Mr. and Mrs. Wolfinger (Germans) and Mr. Hardkoop (Belgian) and they being older folks, the trip was a lot harder on them.

Our party lost some working stock crossing the desert, and the Indians have killed some more, so that everybody has had to leave wagons and some of their goods behind. The wagons were all pretty bashed up, and a lot of them wouldn't have made it anyway. This was especially hard on Wolfinger and Hardkoop because they only had one wagon apiece.

Hardkoop couldn't keep up on foot and got lost in one of the bad desert stretches. Diggers killed some more steers near the sink of the Mary's River, and Wolfinger didn't have enough left to pull his wagon. This was last Tuesday morning, October 13th, 1846, and everybody was worried about getting across another long stretch of desert. Mr. Wolfinger wanted somebody to help him bury his property in a cache in the sand, and then maybe his wagon would be light enough to make it with reduced teams, but everybody was too busy with their own problems. The most we could do was let Mrs. Wolfinger ride in our wagon while he stayed to dig a trench. At the last minute, two of our teamsters named Joseph Reinhardt and Augustus Spitzer said they would stay and help, maybe hoping they would get a nice reward. My brother and I agreed we could spare them.

I hired these two men in Springfield, Illinois, when they saw an advertisement I published in the Sangamo Journal. They were partners who had come all the way from Hannover in Germany and were trying to figure out a way to get to Oregon or California. My brother and I divided their gear and some trade stuff between our supply wagons, but they were also promised regular wages for the trip. We don't know much about them, because they don't mix even with the other teamsters, and never did tell anything about what they did in Germany. They seemed honest, though, and were good workers who didn't complain about rough times. They mainly drove for my brother Jacob Donner, but sometimes for me.

I loaned the men a couple of shovels, and we left the Mary's Sink on Tuesday. Mr. Keseberg also stayed back a while, helping get things organized, but we don't know what was said because they all talked German. It took a whole day to get across the desert, but we made a stop at some hot springs in about the middle and thought the others would catch up to us there. When they didn't come, we were sure they'd find us on the Truckee River, which was our next stop, but it was two days after we hit it before the two Germans came up to us today, October 17th. According to their story, a whole pack of Indians came swooping down on them just after we left, and there was some hard fighting. Mr. Wolfinger was killed, and the wagon was burned, and they were lucky to get way with their skins. They were tired and dusty, but didn't show signs of any fight, and a lot of our people thought maybe they had robbed Mr. Wolfinger and maybe killed him. Mrs. Wolfinger, who can talk a little French with my wife, said her husband had plenty of gold and paper money in a special pouch underneath his shirt. When I questioned the two men separately, Reinhardt said they had searched the body in case there was money or a watch to take for his widow, but didn't find anything. Spitzer claimed they were so busy getting away from the Diggers that they didn't have time to look, and that if there was anything on him the Indians and buzzards have it now. Whichever way they tell it, the story is a little different, and looks like it ought to be investigated.

These are all the facts I know, but I have stated them as fair and thorough as I can.

Signed
Captain George Donner

19

Truckee River
Sunday, October 18th, 1846
The terrible deserts of these regions are all behind us! We traveled for a day and a night and part of a morning to cross the last desolate plain, and on Thursday the trail debouched into the narrow but fertile valley of the Truckee. In this cool, sweet ribbon of blue water we have bathed away the hated dust and slaked again and again our aching thirst. The cattle have fed day and

night from the wide green meadows bounding the river, and are so swollen from constant feasting they look for all the world as though about to freshen. We could use their increase, for the recent toll on our stock (and on men and goods and wagons) has been dreadful.

We were reunited with the second section of our party at the sink of the Mary's River, where the bitter and sluggish course suddenly sprawls across the earth like the fingers of some giant hand, and then vanishes without a trace. It was a mournful setting for mournful reunions. Our friends to the rear had suffered even more than ourselves from raids by the cowardly Diggers, and were compelled to abandon several of their wagons. They had also overstrained their remaining teams in two days of rapid travel to catch up with us. Inasmuch as a 40-mile dry drive still lay ahead, we determined to rest for a day, but the grass and water were so poor they did little to revive the animals. When some of the boys took them to better pasturage a short distance from camp, the Diggers attacked once more with their arrows, injuring 21 head. None were killed, but many were unfit for labor.

Hardest hit by this fresh catastrophe were the Wolfingers, the George Donners and the little Eddy family. The sad fate of Mr. Wolfinger has been told in the preceding pages. His wife sits opposite me as I write—a tall, well-mannered lady who is so stunned and grieved by the loss of her husband, which has left her alone and penniless on a foreign shore, that she scarcely seems in possession of her right senses. William Eddy's losses are nearly as extreme, but he is young and full of unquenchable manly resolve to overcome them. The Digger raids whittled down his makeshift teams until there remained but a single ox, and he was forced to cache his small store of worldly goods. He now proceeds on foot, carrying his older child, while his dainty wife Eleanor walks bravely at his side with the baby in her arms. Their sole provisions consist of a bag containing about 3 pounds of lump sugar. Similarly reduced, the aged Mr. Hardkoop repeatedly fell behind, and one night did not come into camp at all. Mr. Eddy begged for the loan of a horse in order to search for the straggler, but both the Breens and the Graveses refused to risk a valuable animal for a worthless old man. Mr. Eddy is not vengeful, but he has had his vengeance even without willing it. Today a mare belonging to Patrick Breen became bogged in a sinkhole. When the owner asked Eddy's aid in pulling her out, the young man reminded him in a soft voice of Mr. Hardkoop, and walked away from the scene. While Mr. Breen was seeking other help, the struggling animal was smothered in the mud.

Our fears for the welfare of Margaret Reed appeared at first to have been unfounded. She had nobly borne the family's recent reverses, and seemed determined to take upon herself the confident and controlling role her husband had vacated. With Milford Elliott's loyal assistance she bravely met the obstacles of the trail, and impressed even her husband's enemies with her fortitude and resourcefulness. She and her children had traveled together with the Eddys, however, and the loss of their wagon has literally stranded the poor woman. Only with the promise of princely rewards to be paid in California could she persuade the Breens to carry 2 scanty bundles of clothing and a few supplies in one of their wagons. We could offer no relief, for our single wagon is so overloaded that there remains but a tiny crevice for Georgia and Eliza to wriggle into. All the rest must walk, but the Reeds share our cooking fire.

It is a miracle that not a single footsore traveler fell victim to the last dry drive, for all suffered from hunger, thirst, heat, dust and exhaustion. We halted but once, in such a diabolical setting it could have been an outpost of hell itself, and might have blunted even the quill of Dante. There were more than a hundred holes gouged in the earth, and all bubbling and boiling and oozing bitter, sulfuric water. Save for brewing coffee, the water was useless, and the jets thrown up were a constant danger. One steaming spring was contained by a pyramid of red clay nearly eight feet high and six feet across at the base. Here the water rumbled like the threat of angry thunder and occasionally spurted long jets of steam from holes in the side. Only the most unmerciful weariness, and the desire to let those carrying small children come up, sufficed to make us linger more than a moment in this hideous inferno.

Thus can be imagined our breathless joy upon first sighting

the thin green line of the Truckee. Many rubbed their eyes and squinted as if testing for a mirage, but the beckoning line grew steadily, and as they made out the sturdy silhouettes of cottonwoods, several ran forward for the last mile and flung themselves into their cooling shade, laving themselves with the crystal water flowing beneath their arching boughs. For none was this relief so necessary as for the Eddys, who had sustained themselves for nearly two days on sugar, a few cups of water, and the little coffee we could persuade them to take from us. Mr. Eddy wasted no time in borrowing a gun and shooting 9 plump geese, 5 of which he distributed about the camp. He would have done better to keep them all for his famished wife and children, but even the Graveses and the Breens had their share.

We have found along the way several communications from Mr. Reed, and have often passed his campfires. Any signs of his safe passage are wonderfully consoling to the outcast's family, but lately there have been none, and we all anxiously scan the trail for them. Hopefully Mr. Reed and his companion are now safely in California, and we will soon be feasting with them there!

20

THE TRUCKEE NARROWED, TWISTED, CURLED BACK UPON ITSELF, and the emigrants had to cross, then recross it, at least once an hour. With fresh teams the descent into the shallow riverbed would have been at worst an inconvenience, but for ones that stumbled helplessly at the slightest obstacle, progress along the fertile valley was agonizingly slow. Even those families who had suffered no major losses, the Breens and the Graveses, now hoarded their remaining supplies with the sly cunning of squirrels sensing a sudden, early frost. Hunters had little luck in bringing back game, while the fat, speckled trout that flashed in the river were sated with their regular diet of tiny frogs, and ignored the baited hook. The emigrants had grown almost oblivious to physical obstacles, and were so numbed by their constant struggle with the trail that most concentrated solely on placing one foot before the other, on keeping their torn and ragged boots from slipping in loose gravel or catching on the exposed root of a tree. Several had discarded their boots when even emergency lashings of rawhide would no longer hold them together, and wore thin Indian moccasins. Eddy's were so lacerated that they gave him no protection, and at the end of the day, stiff with dried blood, had to be peeled from his feet. Yet all were so accustomed to such abuse that Keseberg scarcely winced and did not even pause to swear when a stob passed through his left foot. Only when the stob held him, and he looked down to see it protruding as cleanly as a well-honed knifeblade, did he begin to howl in a trio of languages.

Because few of the emigrants looked up from the trail, Charles Stanton was nearly upon them before they raised a shout of welcome, then spilled forward to surround him and his heavily laden mules with a noisy chorus of greetings and questions and complaints. Stanton rode the lead mule, one leg cocked loosely over the animal's back, a switch in his hand, and a mischievous smile on his face for those who had muttered that a bachelor could not be relied on to return to the train. Like the Indians who accompanied him, he was dressed in baggy homespun shirt and trousers and wore a polished leather sombrero nearly as wide as his shoulders. Anxious questions assaulted him like a hailstorm, and he ducked his head to ward them off. The barrage lifted and then began again, but he could only hear fragments that had to do with slaughtered oxen, with Indians and broken wagons, desert graves and knifings and hunger and thirst. It was as though by pouring out the tale of their disasters to this gentle, blue-eyed man, their memories and their dreams could be purged. He had been beyond the fabled mountains, had descended into the eternal summer of California and returned to nourish their starved, aching bodies.

Stanton was nearly as perplexed by the noisy onslaught as the two Indians, Salvador and Luis, who had accompanied him from Sutter's. The urgent, claw-like hands that plucked at his clothes, the mouths twisted in desperate recitations, bewildered him, and they bore no faint resemblance to the jubilant reception he had expected. He felt the mule grow restless, the muscles in his haunches twitching, and feared the nervous animal would launch his heels into the throng. As he slid to the ground he saw the frightened face of Amanda McCutcheon, ashen even beneath the coppery burn of the sun. Clutching her daughter tightly in her arms, holding the child before her chest like a living shield, she was a still point in the stormy congregation. She alone seemed too terrified even to phrase the question that now, and after so many lonely, terrified weeks, could at last be answered.

"Mac's fine," Stanton shouted to her.

As the woman moved forward, the crowd stepped aside, quieted, and she seemed to float toward him. The child in her arms might have been a sacrifice she was preparing to lay gratefully at his feet.

"He's just fine," Stanton repeated. "Had a bit of a fever, that's all. I told him he'd better rest up and take his medicine like a good boy." Stanton was clearly amused to report that the giant had toppled again and the city slicker had saved the day, but the joke he had rehearsed about Jack and the beanstalk was blunted now by the marks of suffering in the young mother's face. She seemed far older than he remembered; the whole company did—as though they had moved through some extraordinary time warp in his absence, as though the days had mysteriously bloated, swollen into years.

"I've got some good news for Mrs. Reed, too," Stanton announced, looking about the crowd for her, then realizing she had edged nervously forward and was already standing beside him.

"Good . . . news?" she whispered.

"Well, when I saw him your husband was skinny as a polecat, but Sutter should fatten him up quick enough."

"Where . . . ?" she began, but her breath jerked with the effort of controlling her tears. She would not give her husband's jurors the satisfaction of seeing her weep.

"It was in Bear Valley," Stanton explained. "We were on our way back up the mountains already, and stopped to visit with some of the Hastings people that were still camped there. That's when

Mr. Reed and Mr. Herron showed up, with a horse so skinny you could have played 'Yankee Doodle' on its ribs."

He would have left it at that, but Margaret Reed had to know more, wanted to hear every detail of her husband's perilous journey, and Stanton told her all he knew. The men had lived on geese along the Truckee, but had to make do with wild onions in the mountains, and even those were scarce. Once they had found five beans lying in the middle of the road, spilled from a passing wagon, and had stopped to build a fire and boil them up. Whenever they found an abandoned wagon, they practically took it apart with their bare hands, looking for a little sugar or flour, but all they ever found was a tar bucket. When Reed scraped away the tar with a stick, he saw that the bucket had once contained tallow, and rolled up two pieces the size of walnuts. Herron managed to swallow his, but after a single taste of the rank fat, Reed became so ill that his companion had feared for his life. But they had made it, the people from the Hastings party had stuffed them full of beans and biscuits, and they were heading down to Sutter's when Stanton led his mule train out of Bear Valley.

Even for those who had recently demanded Reed's life, the story of his salvation was a tonic. California was not far away, and the last chain of mountains thrusting across their path could be crossed and crossed again: Stanton had done it and Reed had done it and the Harlan-Young Party had done it, and it would soon be their turn. The voices that rose from the crowd now were full of the excitement and celebration Stanton had originally expected. Men slapped him on the back, asked him where he hid his muscles, and women wondered at the fineness of the homespun he wore. What kind of man was Sutter, they asked, and how many days to California, and what was the weather like, and was there game ahead, but most of all they eyed the heavy packs on the mules. There were seven of them, five loaded with dried beef and flour, and it seemed an incredible bounty. Only Stanton realized, at first, how pitifully inadequate they were for so many hungry travelers, and that they would have to be carefully apportioned according to the size of a family and the state of its reserves.

While the Indians unloaded the mules, Stanton tried to survey the general condition of the party.

"What have you got left?" he asked Peggy Breen.

"Nothin'," she said flatly.

"Nothing at all?" He looked at the plump baby slung against her broad hip.

When the woman remained silent, her stern features set like granite, Stanton addressed the entire group. "I'll need to know what stores each family has, so I can divide things fairly. But you'll all have to be honest with me. Nobody will get left out," he promised.

Each member of the party could have told, almost to the ounce, what remained in any family's flour barrel, whether they had coffee or salt left, if there was still a sack of dried beans that hadn't been opened.

"Now, Mrs. Breen, are you sure you don't have a little sugar or flour?"

"Maybe a little flour," Peggy Breen admitted. "But not much," she quickly added, and glared at the circle of hungry eyes that watched her.

It resembled a circle of vultures, Stanton thought, and one would have to treat them warily. "Mrs. Donner?" he called.

"Yes," Tamsen answered.

"Would you help me make a survey of the camp?"

"Of course."

"We'll have to make a list of each family's provisions, and how many mouths there are to feed."

"I'll just get some writing things," she told him, thinking that in some cases—the Eddys, for example, or the Reeds—there would hardly be any need of them.

When Tamsen rejoined him, Stanton was instructing the Indians to stand guard over the supplies.

"Not bad work for a botanist," Tamsen told him. "And one from Chicago, to boot!"

The strain of the last hour eased. Stanton tipped his sombrero and thanked her with the broad flash of his smile.

THE ELATION THE PARTY FELT OVER STANTON'S ARRIVAL faded quickly as the meagerness of individual portions was weighed and then weighed again in the hands. On the night of his arrival, the air was dizzily laced with aromas of biscuit and beef stew, but the following morning the threat of hunger again stalked the Donner Party. Throughout the day the Murphy family loudly debated their alternatives. As the largest single contingent, they had felt entitled to the largest share of emergency rations, but had hardly gotten more than the Eddys, as they still had coffee, beans, and a little flour remaining. If Stanton's relief had proved disappointing, it had nonetheless impressed them with the generosity of Captain Sutter, and by late afternoon they had determined to send out their own relief mission. While the women started the evening meal, Bill Foster and Bill Pike, Lavina Murphy's sons-in-law, began preparations for an early morning departure.

Pike was cleaning an old pepperbox pistol, which he intended to take along for defense, when one of the women called out that she needed more firewood.

"I'll get it," Pike answered, but remained seated for another minute, talking excitedly with his brother-in-law about the adventure that lay ahead of them, how much better it would be than poking along with the dilapidated wagons. He had begun to load the pistol, carefully easing the blunt bullets into the oiled chambers.

"My biscuits are gonna fall," a voice wailed.

"Comin' right up," Pike shouted, as he stood quickly and handed the pistol to Foster to hold. It instantly exploded with a roar that sent Foster tumbling from the log on which he sat, while the full charge of bullets slammed into Pike's face.

Their hands gloved with flour, the women rushed to the fallen men, and while Sarah Foster held her groaning husband in her arms, Harriet bent over Bill Pike and tried to wipe the blood from his face. She dabbed it cautiously, gently at first, with the wadded hem of her apron, then scrubbed at it more vigorously, until she realized the face was no longer there, and she began to vomit. Mrs. Murphy clamped her daughter's shoulders, pushed her firmly away from the twitching body and forced her head down between her knees. Some indistinguishable sound escaped the torn pulp that had been Bill Pike's face, a noise like water gurgling in a primed pump, and his elbows jabbed the ground as if he wanted to sit up. Lavina Murphy tried to cradle his head, but something slid between her fingers, slick and warm and rapid as the entrails of a chicken, and she let the head drop. In that instant the will that had sustained her, that had sustained the entire family for hundreds of miles, snapped suddenly and irreparably. She began to moan, then to howl, and to rip fistfuls of iron-gray hair from her own scalp.

THE DAMP SNOW THAT FELL DURING THE HASTY BURIAL CLUNG to the mourners' clothing, and the figures standing with bowed heads might have been clumsily hewn from alabaster. Bill Pike's body had been wrapped in a buffalo robe and placed in the shallow grave without a board above or below it, and when the first shovelful of earth had been spilled across the stiffened bundle, most of the men turned away to hitch up their teams.

Having distributed the emergency rations and gotten a good night's sleep, Charles Stanton should have returned at once to New Helvetia. Mules were worth their weight in gold in California, and Sutter had threatened to hang Salvador and Luis if they lost any. Stanton had no family of his own to tie him to the train, and his lingering meant three extra mouths to feed—his own and those of the strangely silent "vaqueros." But he had promised James Reed to do whatever he could for Mrs. Reed and the children. When he gave the troubled father his hand in seal of that promise, neither would have imagined that the woman and her four children were struggling westward on foot, entirely dependent on the fraying charity of others. It was less their obvious suffering than the uncomplaining spirit in which they accepted it that canceled Stanton's plans to deliver his supplies and return immediately to Sutter's. He took Mrs. Reed and the children under his protection, and he refused to permit them to walk. There was one mule for their clothing and supplies, another for Mrs. Reed and Tommy. Patty was mounted behind Salvador, Jimmie behind Luis, and Virginia locked her arms around Stanton's waist as their mule picked its way along the riverbed and into Truckee Meadows.

Hoping to strengthen their teams for the hard climb ahead, the emigrants rested for several days in the broad, lush meadows. Stanton warned that the trail went straight up over vast shattered domes of granite, and their weary animals could certainly not pull the grade unless they first put a little meat on their protruding bones. When pale silver clouds churned about the distant peaks, some worried about snow, but Sutter had assured Stanton the bad storms rarely came before the end of November, and that was still a full month away.

As the emigrants lingered, Brigadier General Stephen Watts Kearny began his own uneventful march to California. The trail to Santa Fe had been, in contrast, high drama. Counting the army and the traders who followed it, the general had headed a caravan that numbered over fifteen hundred wagons and twelve thousand oxen, beefs, horses, and mules. Rumor was nearly as thick as the omnipresent dust, and Kearny's dragoons repeatedly formed at cavalry point, galloped ahead with sabers flashing and guidons fluttering, to discover another empty pass or ravine. Only at Apache Canyon did the New Mexico governor make a token resistance, with his personal retinue and a militia consisting entirely of conscripted peasants and Indians. After having trees felled across the narrowest point and perching a few small, antique cannons on them, the governor announced the hopelessness of the cause and sent the army home.

Santa Fe, the Royal City of the Holy Faith of Saint Francis, did not even trouble with the charade of resistance. Kearny and his staff, with the army following in column, simply marched into the Plaza of the Constitution and raised their sabers to the ritual flourish of bugles as the flag went up. Then, after refreshing and amusing himself at a series of balls in his honor, establishing an English-language newspaper for the town, and attending theatricals in which the fierce Laclede Rangers appeared as chorus girls, he was ready for California. Taking the desert trail south of the Donners, he arrived at San Diego with only a single bloody skirmish to record in his logbook. After that, Kearny's principal opposition would come from the glory-hungry John Charles Frémont, who was canvassing the recent emigrants to compose his own California Battalion, which ultimately included Edwin Bryant, Owl Russell, Lansford Hastings, and James Frazier Reed.

THOUGH WILLIAM EDDY HAD NO AMMUNITION TO WASTE, HIS patience was nearly as short as his powder, and when he saw the Digger pointing an arrow at one of the few remaining saddle horses, he leveled the shotgun and sent a blast into the Indian's chest. The figure lifted, spun in midair, and slid down a ravine. Eddy scrambled after him, hoping to recover some of the shirts and spoons and strips of harness that had disappeared during the night. The hillside was steep, and using the shotgun to keep branches from raking his face, he lowered himself with one hand clutching at pliant saplings and bushes. The body had come to rest against an aspen, hunched as though in prayer, showing Eddy the ragged holes where the lead had slammed through the lungs and out the back. Turning his head aside, Eddy flipped the body with his foot, surprised by its lightness, and looked down to see the oval face of a boy of twelve or thirteen, the eyes still staring in disbelief at the twin barrels pointed toward him, frozen by the lead balls that exploded his lungs.

21

Truckee Meadows
Sunday, October 25th, 1846
We have reached our final waystation on the great road to California, and rest now in the broad meadows bounding the Truckee. Some of our party were so impatient to be off that they have preceded us. The Breens, whose oxen had suffered less than ours, commenced the ascent early on Friday, together with their bachelor companion Patrick Dolan, the Kesebergs and the Eddys. Mr. Keseberg seriously injured his left foot a number of days ago,

stepping on a sharp stob, and was mounted on a horse belonging to the Breen family. What duchies he pledged in exchange, I can scarcely dream. Yesterday the second section departed, consisting of the Graves and Murphy families, together with the Reeds and Mr. Stanton. We are not sorry to remain a while in the peaceful embrace of these meadows, for the last weeks have witnessed frequent disharmonies in our party. The alarming shortage of supplies and the continuing depredations of the Indians have set nerves a-jangle and put tempers on a short fuse.

It is not surprising that we have suffered numerous accidents —some slight and avoidable, others far more grave. The deep wound in Mr. Keseberg's foot could easily become poisoned before he has the benefit of proper doctoring. None of our misfortunes, however, have been so cruel as that which has befallen the Murphys. On Tuesday, the day following Mr. Stanton's return, the family concluded to dispatch their own messengers to Capt. Sutter to bring back emergency supplies. Mrs. Murphy's sons-in-law, William Pike and William Foster, had begun preparations for departure, and Mr. Pike was cleaning an old pepperbox pistol which he had bought at Fort Bridger. This is a clumsy-looking instrument, said to cause frequent unnecessary injuries, and to be of little use either for hunting or for defense, due to the uncertain aim. Just as the weapon was loaded, someone called for more firewood, and Mr. Pike rose to his feet to answer the request, handing the pistol to his brother-in-law. Before the latter had it fully in his grasp, there came a fearful explosion, and the shots passed directly through the head of Mr. Pike. He was dead almost instantly, and both his young widow and Mrs. Murphy are inconsolable. Indeed, we fear that Mrs. Murphy may never regain her peace of mind, and the entire burden of shepherding this numerous clan now falls on the shoulders of Mr. Foster, who is still so numbed by the accident that he is scarcely capable of speech. Mrs. Murphy's oldest son, John Landrum, is but 15, and so slow in his development that he can offer no real aid. Of all the grievous losses we have suffered, this is surely the most senseless and wasteful. Mrs. Pike now has two fatherless children, Naomi (3) and Catherine (1), to provide for.

I have already mentioned that Mr. Stanton returned to us. We met him several miles east of the Truckee Meadows, leading a train of seven mules that had been put at his disposal by the generous Capt. Sutter, together with supplies of flour and dried beef. Two Indians—"vaqueros," as they are called by the Spanish —had accompanied him. They are taller and duskier than the Diggers, and perform amazing tricks with a coiled rope. The rations they brought seemed pitifully meager for so many hungry mouths, but California now lies only a few days to the west, and we shall soon know plenty once more. Mr. Stanton brought us the joyful communication that Mr. Reed, with Walter Herron, had succeeded in reaching California, and immediately took Mrs. Reed and her children into his care. He is a gentle and great-hearted man, who risked his life to bring us succor, though he had no family of his own in our company. Mr. McCutcheon was detained at New Helvetia by another seizure of his chronic malaria. Our old friend Mr. Bryant, together with Hiram Miller, was also present at Sutter's, and this news brought obvious relief to Milt Elliott.

Mrs. Wolfinger still cannot accept her husband's death, and we have twice found her attempting to return to him along the trail—once late in the night, and barefoot. Her fine silk gowns have not done well in competition with the wilderness, and she makes a most dolorous appearance.

Our little rear guard, now rested and refreshed, will begin the mountainous ascent tomorrow morning.

22

THE DONNER BROTHERS ADVANCED THROUGH THE FOOTHILLS AT A stately pace, as though consciously rejecting the panic and angry confusion that had stamped their journey from the Wahsatch. On the first day they crossed the Truckee forty-nine times, but their movements showed neither haste nor annoyance. Between them they still had three wagons, a fortune in bank notes and coin, a dozen healthy children, devoted wives, loyal teamsters, and a freshened vision of new earth to be conquered. The worst trials were behind them, and they sat tall again, stroking their patriarchal beards, congratulating themselves on the wisdom of their venture.

The slight drop over a ledge of stone would certainly not have cracked an axletree if the desert heat had not dried it so badly, and George Donner's family wagon would not have capsized if it had not been so top-heavy with freight rescued from the abandoned wagons. It tumbled as suddenly as a horse whose foreleg plunges into a prairie dog hole, and the tiny cave in which Eliza and Georgia were curled collapsed around them, clamped the children in the smothering grip of tents and bedding. Georgia was soon freed, but Eliza seemed to have been spirited away, and only after the sheet iron stove, crates and trunks, barrels and harness and tools had been flung to the ground did her body emerge. The child's face was blue with suffocation, her arms and legs twitching convulsively. Tamsen vigorously chafed the child while George dribbled brandy between her parched lips until she gasped noisily and her breath jerked in whimpering sobs that told them she was alive. But it was hours before she had revived enough to force a few frightened words through her throat.

The teamsters cut a pine and hauled it to the makeshift camp where George and Jacob Donner worked it with hatchets, chisels, and mallets into a new front axle. They were giving it the final smoothing when Jacob's rusty chisel struck a knot in the wood, jumped from his grip, and gashed the back of George's hand. He clamped his wrist tightly to slow the gushing blood, and Tamsen washed it repeatedly with cold water. Blood still welled in the cut as she gently packed it with lint, tamping it down and adding fresh layers until the uppermost seemed dry. It was, she thought, like riprapping a swamp to make a firm passage, with the deadly waters continuously seeping through, to clutch at unsuspecting travelers. Here and there the lint discolored again as blood rose from the deep tear in George Donner's flesh, but most of it remained dry, and Tamsen bound the hand tightly with strips of linen, wound them into a thick mitt that would cushion it against accidental blows, and knotted it at her husband's wrist. Her own hands were so vivid with the blood he had spilled that she might have just returned from harvesting cherries.

V
PROSSER CREEK

1

Prosser Creek
Tuesday, November 3rd, 1846

While the snow falls so thick it blots out the horizon, we huddle like a family of Esquimaux around our cheery fire. A sudden storm obliged us to make camp here yesterday, and we must wait until it passes before seeking to catch up to the main party. They are three or four days in advance, and may already be dining with Capt. Sutter. The necessity of strengthening our team for the mountain passage compelled a delay in our departure from the Truckee, and an alarming accident cost us another precious day. We were proceeding through the rocky foothills when a sudden drop in the road splintered the forward axletree of our sole remaining wagon. Georgia and Eliza were buried by the shifting load, and we feared they would smother before we could free them from their prison. While a new axletree was being fashioned, Mr. Donner received a deep and painful gash in the back of his left hand, which is reluctant to close. In chopping saplings to reinforce our makeshift igloo, he scraped the wound against the back of a tree, and tonight the edges are badly inflamed.

So heavy was yesterday's sudden snowfall that it was thought advisable to erect some more substantial shelter than our threadbare tents could afford. Wood is plentiful and the men all set to felling pines. A crude breastwork had been formed before the fury of the driving snow so increased that the business of cabin-making had to be abandoned. I wrapped the girls in blankets and buffalo robes and they were stacked like giggling cordwood in the shelter of the logs. By morning three feet of snow covered logs and girls, who had to be shoveled out of their beds, but the downy covering had kept them warm, and even my frowning Frances found it all a miraculous adventure.

Out of fear the storm would renew itself, the men determined to erect simpler emergency shelters. Ours huddles to the south of a great split pine which serves us as hearth and chimney. The family tent forms the main salon, but this is enlarged by a semi-circular lean-to of pine and tamarack branches, which provides a handy storeroom. Over the whole is heaped everything that might discourage the icy wind—quilts, buffalo robes, antelope skins, India-rubber coats and sheets, with yet another layer of brush piled over that. The interior is cheerily lighted by a pair of blazing pine-cones. With poles driven into the ground and longer ones secured to them, we have rack-like beds elevated above the muddy floor, and I sit now à la Turk on one of them, warmed by the fire that dances from the pit scooped at the foot of our lofty pine chimney and lined with stones. The Jacob Donners lack this luxury, for their temporary quarters have a simple smoke hole in the center, and they are continuously enlarging it to release the smoke and shrinking it to deter the falling snow. Mr. Denton and the other teamsters are quartered across the creek in their version of a Sioux wigwam, which threatens to collapse with each faint gust of wind and makes dreadful sighing noises. There is abundant firewood, but our provisions are so low we shall have to move on with the greatest dispatch at the first sign of a thaw. It is said that such early snowfalls in the western mountains are always of short duration.

Mrs. Wolfinger resides with us, and we have succeeded in providing a guest chamber with a length of cord and a blanket. In that slender privacy she now weeps her way to sleep, as she does each and every night. Whether her tears are for her lost husband or herself or for the unlucky pair of them, we do not know, for she no longer seeks to communicate beyond the pale of her grief. Without the consolation of a husband or of children who look to her for nurture, the poor woman seems brittle and lifeless, like an uprooted plant left to wither in the sun.

According to the description provided by Mr. Stanton, the place at which we have settled is named Prosser Creek, though it divides into two distinct streams at this point. In a sheltered bend near our temporary quarters I was able to gather a large quantity of the tuberous cattail root which we sampled first in the Wahsatch, and which resembles the potato when roasted. The waters of Prosser Creek have their origin in Truckee Lake, whose shore we must traverse before ascending the pass to California. We cannot reach our destination soon enough.

2

Prosser Creek
Thursday, November 5th, 1846
The snow gives no sign of ceasing, and the thermometer continues to fall. We are not alone in this icy fastness, however, for the remainder of our party is encamped approximately six miles ahead, on the shore of Truckee Lake. The information was brought us by John Denton and Solomon Hook, who yesterday hiked westward to survey the condition of the trail, returning with unexpected news of those friends we thought already safe in the warm valleys of California. All efforts to cross the snow-clogged pass, by wagon or on foot, have been unsuccessful, and the others also wait for the promised thaw. The bouncing Breens are of course snug as bugs in a rug, having taken occupancy of an abandoned cabin conveniently found on the site. The unfortunate Margaret Reed and her children, together with the little Eddy family, occupy one of the wagons, for Mr. Stanton assures them the pass will soon be clear, and it is not worthwhile to erect any

better shelter. Mr. Eddy shot a coyote, but has seen no other game, and though fish are numerous in the lake, they refuse to be tempted by the baited hook.

Mr. Donner's injured hand gives him such discomfort that he has tossed and turned without sleeping for two nights, and his weariness is so acute that he can scarcely rise from bed in the mornings. Frequent soakings diminish the pressure of the swelling, but the relief is only temporary.

We have decided to slaughter some of the oxen, for there is nothing to feed them but dried rushes, and they bawl with hunger. If we delay any longer, the weaker will certainly die, and there will be even less meat on their pitiful bones.

3

JIM SMITH WORKED WITH JACOB DONNER AND HIS YOUNG STEPSONS, slaughtering three oxen and a cow that had ceased to give milk weeks before. Across the narrow creek, Antoine and the Germans were dressing two steers for the teamsters, piling stiffened haunches like cords of firewood beside their wigwam, then heaping snow over them to protect the stringy meat from the sun. George Donner was feverish, weakened by the pain that gnawed at his hand, and it was Tamsen who supervised the butchering of half their remaining stock, with Jean Baptiste and John Denton to assist her.

The little New Mexican raised the axe high over his head, straining on tiptoes, then heaved it forward, but the blade glanced off one of the ox's horns, jerked out of his hands, and plunged from sight in a drift of snow. The animal's startled cry was almost human, a piercing bellow of fear that seemed to continue without pause for breath, while the trembling legs churned feebly in the snow. Its bowels opened, and the air was suddenly thick with the stench of its panic. John Denton braced himself, straining at the length of rope around the steer's neck, but the animal was so dizzied by hunger it hardly resisted him.

Jean Baptiste dug the axe from the snow, stood again before the great curving horns, and bounced lightly up and down on his toes. "*Muerte!*" he shouted, and chopped the blade in a series of rapid strokes, slashed it again and again between the bulging eyes. The animal sank slowly forward onto its knees, flopped into the snow like a bundle of rags, but the bellowing continued, climbed in pitch until it was a shrill keening sound. Again Jean Baptiste flashed the axe in the air, brought it down so hard that the blow lifted him from his feet, sent the axe flying from his grip and spun him to the ground. His eyes were parallel with those of the bleating animal, and he stared into them as though pure contempt might split the great domed skull that deflected his blows. Then the New Mexican stood, flicked snow from his clothing with the backs of his fingers, and sauntered away, a matador contemptuous of an unworthy opponent. He sat on a log and announced, "Finished."

"But it's not finished," Tamsen said. "We can't let the poor thing suffer like this. It's got to be killed."

"He dead soon," Jean Baptiste assured her.

"But he is not dead now."

"Soon," he repeated, and began to whistle to himself.

Tamsen knew by now this peculiar blend of childishness and vanity and stubbornness, that it was useless to try to push him. Her fists balled, her nails dug into her palms as though punishing them for their weakness. It would all be so much simpler, cleaner, if she could match will with muscle, but she knew the weight of the axe was too great for her. Once more, as when it refused to follow Tully into death, she thought of her own body as a traitor, and the surge of contempt she felt canceled her irritation at Jean Baptiste's peevishness. Throughout their journey she had seen men exhaust themselves with bouts of arm wrestling and other loud, boastful contests at which they spent their strength as carelessly as drunken millionaires, while her own arms and shoulders had repeatedly rebelled, refusing to shift the burdens she commanded them to shift, and all her force straining against a picket line did nothing to break the plunge of an overloaded wagon. If Samuel Shoemaker had not been

309

off hunting, she would have taken the rifle and put a bullet through the agonized animal's brain, though it seemed a foolish waste of ammunition. If two grown men and a woman couldn't do the job, they might as well all give up, crawl into their beds, and never rise again.

"Mr. Denton," she called briskly, "I think we need your help."

"I don't know, Mrs. Donner." He stammered unintelligible syllables, let the slack rope droop to the ground.

Tamsen ignored the hesitation, picked up the freshly honed knife that rested on a stump beside her, and carried it to him, clapping the handle firmly into his palm.

"Here," she said, and leaned her weight against a horn to expose the artery throbbing at the side of the steer's throat. With the fingers of one hand she dragged the loose folds of skin away to show him the exact spot where he would have to sink the knife. "It's deeper than it looks," she cautioned, "so don't be timid."

Denton paled, and his jaw worked as though something unpleasant had lodged in his own throat.

"For goodness sake, don't be sick, Mr. Denton! I know it isn't very poetic, but it's got to be done."

The man started to reply, clamped a palm before his mouth.

"I've got enough sick people to worry about," she reprimanded him. "Now stop this nonsense!" She consciously used the tone she would have used with a wayward child, and it seemed to startle or shame him out of his seizure.

"I'm sorry," he muttered.

"Don't be," she reassured him. "Just help me get this over with." She bunched her skirts, twisting them into a knot at her waist and jamming the knot under the band of her apron, then straddled the steer. Gripping the horns, she angled her slight weight against them, forced them to the side until the neck was almost parallel with the ground. "Now," she said.

John Denton hesitated, staring at the length of razor-sharp steel protruding from his white-knuckled grip.

"Now!" she commanded, and he reached out to slash tentatively with the knife. A thin trickle of blood filigreed the animal's hide, and its bellowing became a raw scream. Tamsen clung to the broad sweep of the horns as the animal heaved beneath her. "Again, but deeper!" she shouted. "You've got to cut the artery," she insisted, and with such urgency that he plunged the blade to the hilt in the animal's flesh, drew it out and plunged it in again. Feeling the rhythmic tremor beneath her, as though the earth itself were heaving and splitting its crust, Tamsen slid from the back of the steer and raced to fetch the bread pan resting against the stump. When she returned with it, John Denton still stood beside the quivering animal, and she elbowed him aside to push the pan beneath the hot cascade of blood, wedging it in place with fistfuls of snow, so that the steer's convulsions would not dislodge it and spill the precious fluid.

"Would you bring me the kettle?" she asked without looking up. Then she added, "Please?" and heard him turn, his boots crunching in the icy crystals of fresh snow.

She emptied the brimming pan into the kettle, then filled it again, while the bellowing ceased and the animal's great eyes revolved backwards in its skull like those of a broken doll.

"The next will be easier," she assured John Denton when she stood again, "but first we'll have to dress this one out."

Jean Baptiste proved surprisingly adept at the skinning, and he and John Denton had soon peeled off the animal's hide, which Tamsen spread on the snow and scraped of its meager layer of fat, while the men carved away the steer's haunches, hacked off the legs with the axe, then severed the great tongue that sprawled in the snow. They split the carcass like a rotten log to expose heart and liver and kidneys and sweetbreads and tripe. Even the lungs were torn from their cage and carried to the pit dug on the north side of the lean-to, with fresh layers of snow packed tightly around them.

"The girls and I will do the rest," she told the men. "You get on with the slaughtering. But bury all the bones, too. We can use them for soup."

Elitha, Leanna and Frances helped her carry buckets filled with lengths of intestine to the creek, where they shattered ice thin as window glass to lower foot-long sections into the clear water. They used sticks to scrape them out, then hold them open so that the brisk, cleansing current flowed through. Had she been less weary,

Tamsen might have wondered at the ease with which her three young assistants performed the task. They knelt together at the edge of the creek, dipping the slick pink lengths in and out of the numbing water, as though washing skeins of finely spun wool.

4

Prosser Creek

Sunday, November 8th, 1846

We have slaughtered out half the remaining stock and packed the meat in a snowy larder. To prevent all our supplies from being spoiled by a sudden thaw, we have spared the stronger animals, but these too will have to be butchered if they grow any thinner. It is certain none are strong enough to pull even the lightest rig. Like good Indians, we found a use for almost every part of the oxen and cows. Their hides have been added to the roof of our quarters, where they provide us far more protection from the elements than they provided their original owners.

Mr. Donner's hand does not respond well to my poor doctoring. It is soaked regularly in a hot borax bath, but the festering continues, and our store of sulfate is exhausted. My patient receives a good dosing with tonic both morning and evening, and the largest portion of our nightly broth, but is often so weak he can scarcely quit his couch in the morning. I nag him, however, to take the clear air and sunshine whenever possible, for our makeshift home is very damp, and this can do his condition no good. The children are mercifully and miraculously well, though fretful when bad weather confines them indoors, and I would gladly trade a pound of salt for a few books with which to distract them. However, we scarcely have a pound remaining.

There is no fresh news from the lake camp.

5

Prosser Creek

Thursday, November 12th, 1846

The skies have finally cleared, and tomorrow a party will cross the pass on foot, with Capt. Sutter's mules breaking a trail for them. Milt Elliott arrived this morning with the happy news, and our teamsters all departed with him—Antoine, Samuel Shoemaker, Jim Smith, and the two Germans. Mr. Denton at first insisted on remaining behind to give what service he could, for both Mr. Donner and his brother are poorly, but we assured him Jean Baptiste could keep two fires burning, and that he should take this opportunity. In the end, he agreed to accompany the group only to spare us the rations he would otherwise consume. If we are further delayed, he will bring relief from the settlements, and I know that we can rely on his loyalty.

The Graveses quickly grew tired of their gypsy caravan, and have built a cabin. With the assistance of Mr. Stanton and Mr. Eddy, Margaret Reed secured a shelter for herself and the children built against one of the end walls. After much shameful bargaining and begging, she also persuaded Mr. Breen to give her one yoke of oxen, and Mr. Graves to supply her with another. For these scrawny creatures she has pledged double the number of prime young animals to be delivered in California. I have sent her a little coffee and some sugar, as well as mitts for the girls.

Though he is not at the moment fit to make the journey himself, Mr. Donner is greatly encouraged by the departure of the California travelers, and thinks it cannot be long before they send relief. He has been up and about most of the day, busy with a dozen chores and showing much of his former energy. With the heavy bandage he wears, he looks to be carrying a great snowball constantly about with him!

6

Saturday, November 14th, 1846

Our dispirited teamsters returned to their wigwam this morning. Jean Baptiste was chopping wood when he caught sight of them, and ran to the tent shouting the news that Mr. Reed was coming to our rescue. Would that it had been so! A party of 15, including Sarah Fosdick and Mary Graves, attempted to make the crossing, but the snow was so soft and resistant that they had scarcely proceeded beyond the head of the lake when night forced them back. The snow was 10 feet deep and the pass still more than 3 miles distant.

The men are cruelly disheartened by this failure, but say they will try again if the weather remains clear. None in the lake camp were able to give them food, and all they have had to eat since Tuesday morning is the small lump of frozen beef they took with them. I have made a pot of soup to help warm their stomachs, but their spirits admit no thaw. Their disappointment is certainly great, but with the exception of Mr. Denton they respond like spoiled children denied a promised bag of sweets.

7

Sunday, November 15th, 1846

The teamsters let their fire die out last night, and Mr. Denton came to us soon after dawn to ask Jean Baptiste's help in starting it again. His companions seemed indifferent about whether this was accomplished or not. Mr. Denton's eyes are strained and sore from the intense light of the sun reflected by the snow, and the others might have spared him this added responsibility.

I visited Jacob and Betsy at noon, and was surprised to find the entire family abed, including the children. Jacob complains still of "a touch of the gravel," but the others are all sturdy and well. Their quarters, however, are dusky and dank and vile-smelling, and I encouraged them to take advantage of the clear, dry air and the warming sunshine, which in sheltered corners feels quite summery. But they were not to be budged, saying they required less food and could remain warmer swaddled in their buffalo robes. Mary, however, played for a time with Georgia and Eliza, and her cheeks were quickly full of roses. My breadpan has become a sledge that spins wonderfully across the snow.

In other circumstances one might spend many contented hours in thoughtful admiration of the bold panorama of gleaming white mountains that ring the horizon, with the dark slashes of green that accent them. The hardy conifers never lose their needles, and bend with yielding grace to the weight of the snows. They seem to wait like fairy princesses, wreathed in icy sleep, for the touch of the wand of Spring.

Mr. Donner's wound is closing, but I do not like the puffiness that surrounds it, or the angry color.

8

SHE MIGHT HAVE BEEN UNWRAPPING AN ANTIQUE PORCELAIN CUP, A fragile family heirloom densely cocooned in strips of softest linen. Tamsen unlooped a single layer at a time and wrapped it neatly around the fingers of her left hand, then lifted the next careful strand, wound it, lifted another. The frayed strips tied them together, linked his bandaged hand to her slender fingers like the intricate web of a spider. Tamsen raised and lowered the shrinking coils, gathered them around her fingers, and as the thick bandage melted from her husband's hand, it gathered thickly on her own. Later she would boil the strips and hang them to dry before the fire, to wait in readiness for the next dressing. When she reached the final layer, she paused, for there was no way to remove it without causing him pain. He winced at her gentle tug and made an involuntary sound far back in his throat that resembled the whimpering of a hungry puppy. She jerked an inch of the dressing away, and he helped by pulling against her, making no sound now. Then the center of the wound was exposed, and though the remaining loops of linen were crusted tightly to his skin, it caused him less pain when they were peeled away.

Tamsen quickly twisted the last, stiffened length onto the coil, tugged it from her fingers and dropped it into her lap. She raised the hand to the light, measured the swelling with a cautious touch.

"It seems less feverish," she told him.

George Donner nodded. "It doesn't throb quite so bad as it did last night."

"The hot water seems to help. We'll have to bathe it more often. That's what brings the swelling down."

"Yes."

Her thumbs lightly massaged his forearm, ruffling the hair.

"That tickles," he protested, and tried to force a laugh at her game.

Tamsen's motions had revolved her husband's wrist so that she could see the discolorations that flowered just beneath the skin, but she made no comment, lowered the hand casually to her lap.

"It doesn't hurt near as much as it did," he told her. "And I can move it more."

"Don't," she warned, as she felt the gentle pressure on her thigh. "You could break open the scab again."

"You're the doctor."

"Oh, I wish it was true, Mr. Donner. Even such a one as Mr. Bryant."

"Why, that rascal would have me chewing pine bark."

"I would, too, if I thought it would help." She turned her head away suddenly, sharply, to ask Elitha if the water was hot enough.

"Not yet," came the reply.

"Don't scald me again!" George Donner warned. "You're not plucking a chicken, you know."

Until Elitha brought the steaming basin to his bedside, the husband and wife distracted themselves with the inexhaustible subject of a relief expedition. With wives and small children in the mountains, Reed and McCutcheon would certainly arrive soon with supplies. Even Walt Herron would do all he could for them, and Hiram Miller might at least be worried enough about his trade goods to want to see them all down from the mountains. But the next attempt to cross the pass might go better than the last one. The travelers would have the benefit of the path tramped along the lake shore, and the weather seemed a little warmer. The sun might already have begun to thaw the pass, as it had shrunken the drifts surrounding the camp. Their phrases had become ritual, and neither troubled to seek a variation.

"Reed's got letters to Sutter. That'll help get things organized," George Donner said.

"And he must be worried sick about Margaret and the children. It nearly killed him to have to abandon them the way he did, and he knew they hadn't much left to eat."

"Well, we know he made it to California."

317

"Yes," she agreed, and like carefully drilled actors who drop not a line of dialogue even when the stage set topples around them, who forge through their roles despite sticking doors, a bell that refuses to ring, the hem of a dress ripping loudly as it snares a table leg, they ignored the stench of decay that rose from the festering wound in George's hand. It resembled less the smell of spoiled meat than the sharp, penetrating stink of rotting fish.

9

MILT ELLIOTT APPEARED AGAIN ON NOVEMBER 20TH TO ANNOUNCE that another attempt to scale the pass would be made the following morning. Elliott also brought the incredible news that William Eddy had succeeded in killing an eight-hundred-pound grizzly. After planting two bullets in the animal's shoulder, he had somehow beaten it to death with a club, though one swipe from the bear's massive claws could have taken off his own head. He had been hunting with Bill Foster's gun, and Foster had claimed half the meat in payment, while Uncle Billy Graves got a generous portion for the loan of a team to haul in the carcass. The remainder would have to sustain Eleanor and the children until Eddy could return, or until Reed and McCutcheon came through with relief.

In preparation for the renewed effort to cross the mountains, Milt Elliott purchased from the Donners a blanket coat, pantaloons, socks, shoes, and tobacco, signing a pledge to pay for them at the current California rates. He left the camp at Prosser Creek in the late afternoon, accompanied once more by John Denton, Antoine, Samuel Shoemaker, Jim Smith, Joseph Reinhardt, and Augustus Spitzer. Each carried a six-day ration of lean meat and a few pieces of loaf sugar. Denton had tried to patch a pair of goggles to protect his eyes from the glare of the snow, but the lenses were splintered, and his breath frosted them so heavily they were soon useless. The two Germans lagged far behind the rest, and though there was now a smooth path linking the two camps, they lunged repeatedly into the loose snow, and their moccasins were rapidly encased in ice. The two seemed indifferent to their frostbitten feet, and stumbled forward only because others led the way. As long as their wigwam was in view, with a faint thread of gray smoke lifting from it, they would pause from time to time, revolve slowly in their tracks, and stare at it, as though regretting the snug beds they had left behind.

10

Monday, November 23rd, 1846
The men returned to us today, having crossed the pass and then reversed their steps to save the mangy hides of Capt. Sutter's mules! Mr. Denton is especially bitter, as the failed attempt nearly cost him his remaining eyesight, and he now adopts the colorful western jargon whenever describing Mr. Stanton and his "persnickety" ways. Even Mrs. Murphy, with 3 of her younger children, had gambled on the continuing fair weather, and there were 21 travelers in the party. The snows had nearly all melted near the lake, and higher up the crust was thick enough to hold a man's weight. The mules, though, kept breaking through the surface, and practically had to be carried over the pass, where the snow measured 25 feet in depth. Even with such a hindrance, all got across and made camp in a sheltered valley on the western slope, but melting snow kept putting out their fire, and none got any sleep that night. The next morning the mules were so spent they refused to move on, and without them Mr. Stanton likewise refused to budge, having pledged to return all the animals in good condition to Capt. Sutter. The two Indians also dug their heels in, and without the guides they had counted on, most of the party were afraid to proceed farther, for they could see nothing but

endless snow-covered mountains to the west. Only Mr. Eddy argued strongly that they should abandon the beasts or slaughter them and pack the meat along, and he offered to take full responsibility, but little Mr. Stanton remained stubborn as Sutter's mules. In other conditions his scruples would be admirable, but I cannot think Capt. Sutter would so value his skinny animals as to place a score of men and women in jeopardy in order to protect them. Mr. Eddy pleaded, threatened, and came near to giving Mr. Stanton an old-fashioned thrashing, but all to no effect. Only Milt Elliott and Mr. Denton seemed to share his determination, the rest being so discouraged and exhausted and cold they decided to turn back. Mr. Eddy, however, has lost none of his fierce resolve, and is planning to depart once more on Thursday, without the mules and with whatever souls are brave and strong enough to accompany him. He says if none are willing he will go alone.

Mr. Denton stays for a time with us, so that I can better tend to his injured eyes. One of our Germans, "Gus" Spitzer, has remained at the lake to try his luck with the Kesebergs, who have built a lean-to onto the sheltered side of the Breens' cabin. I should not like to be dependent on the charity of such a moody and close-fisted man, but perhaps the sense of common patrimony will overcome his meanness. The injury to Mr. Keseberg's foot has not healed, and Spitzer hopes to make himself useful to the family. In any case, there is one less mouth for us to feed, and the reduction is welcome. The animals we slaughtered out were so wasted by hunger there was scarcely any meat left on their bones. That is stringy and without a solitary grain of fat, and has to be taken without benefit of bread or salt. I fear the remaining animals will soon have to go into the soup pot.

The returning travelers were so weary that they tumbled into bed without a fire, and when they arrived I could not spare Jean Baptiste to make one for them. Indeed, I have been so occupied with keeping the children clean and dry, in bathing Mr. Donner's hand and Mr. Denton's eyes, in patching clothing and trying to keep the dogs from digging up our remaining supplies, that I have not had time to call on our neighbors "across the square." Jacob's gravel seems to get no better, and he hardly picks at the little ration of food Betsy gives him. Mr. Donner's hand likewise shows no improvement. His womenfolk are all well, however.

11

WHEN MILT ELLIOTT ARRIVED FROM THE LAKE CAMP WITH THE news that Eddy would depart the following morning, George Donner's spirits soared. Like his wife, he had developed a keen respect for the young father's resourcefulness, his refusal to be defeated by circumstances that would have sent other men toppling. It was hard to provoke Eddy's anger, but his laughter was quick and eager, like his almost profligate generosity. Above all he had resiliency, deep reserves of physical stamina from which he drew up fresh energy as he might have drawn clear, sparkling water from an artesian well. Where others bogged down in despair or self-pity, he lowered his broad head and plodded on, wasting little time in argument or bellyaching complaint. He knew what he wanted and he was ready to pay the price, even when it seemed cruelly, outrageously high. What he wanted now was the safety of his wife and children, and he wanted it with a fierceness that could cross mountains if not move them.

Perhaps Eddy stirred in George Donner some memory of his own younger self, of trails blazed and wilderness uprooted, of timbers freshly planed by his own hand, sweet with the perfume his labor had released, as they rose into the stout, pale cubes of smokehouse and barn. Eddy's body had not yet begun to proclaim restrictions and limitations, to whisper cautionary tales, and sometimes to rebel. It responded easily and unquestioningly to his commands, like a loyal hunting dog, its fidelity not simply beyond reproach but so automatic, so primal, as to resemble the unwilled beating of the heart. Now George Donner measured each day the steady progression of the poison in his body, turned to the tent wall so that his wife and daughters would not see him as he studied the inflamed traceries beneath his skin, like the mapping of a monstrous unexplored territory, a region of dark and fetid decay. Eddy's resoluteness might have caused other men to despair at their own weakness, might have provoked George Donner to anger or shame as he contemplated his failed captaincy. Not only did the elected leader of the party, the man charged with their safe passage, lag days and miles behind the rest, he now nursed a rotting arm and hugged the warmth of his bed while his wife performed both her own chores and most of the captain's. Had he been a jealous man, or less generous in spirit, he might have resented the girlish brightness with which Tamsen now spoke William Eddy's name and related his most recent adventures to the children. His slaughter of the grizzly had been decked in the language of fairy tales—the slaying of the giant, the ogre, the monstrous, panting beast. But like her he clung to the belief that if any man could get through the mountains, with or without a guide, it was Eddy. And in that determined young man from Illinois, himself a father though young enough to be George Donner's grandson, the crippled man caught the echo of his own questing youth. The thought of Eddy's mission invigorated him and redeemed his own failures, distanced the humiliation he had felt as the party's spirit crumbled.

When Milt Elliott brought him news of Eddy's intentions, he clapped his knee in jovial salute. "If there's any man can get through, it's Bill Eddy!"

"I reckon that's true, Mr. Donner."

"You're darned right, it's true. And if he gets hungry, he'll bite off a grizzly's head for breakfast."

"Pick his teeth with the claws."

"Skin it with his bare hands and make himself a nice bed."

"That's Eddy," Milt agreed. But his excitement was shaded with regret. "I still don't feel right about leaving Mrs. Reed."

"Well, I think it's a fine thing the way you've taken care of her and the little ones."

"It's a promise I made." Then, as though this sounded too halfhearted, he quickly added, "I don't mind. The kids are about the only family I've got, and maybe I ought not think about leaving them."

"Mrs. Reed has Eliza and Baylis to help her," Tamsen reminded him.

Milt shook his head. "Baylis is mighty weak, and Eliza can't do much more than nurse him. But I've cut enough wood to last six or eight weeks," he said. "We're sure to be back before then."

"Of course you are."

"Still, I can't help worry who's to cut and haul firewood if that runs out."

"If she had to, Margaret Reed would do it," Tamsen told him.

"Handle an axe?" It seemed to him a curious sort of joke.

"Yes, handle an axe."

"Well, ma'am, that just don't seem right." He blushed suddenly, realizing that Captain Donner might think he meant it wasn't right for Mrs. Donner to have to do so much man's work now. "I mean, I gave Mr. Reed my word of honor," he explained. "He was always square with me."

"We know what you mean, and we know how much you've helped Mrs. Reed," Tamsen assured him. "You can help her now by trying to bring back supplies."

"What I still don't understand," George Donner said, "is why Jim Reed hasn't showed his face yet."

"Oh, I reckon he'll be along any day now."

"You and Mr. Eddy may even meet up with him somewhere in the mountains," Tamsen added.

"That'd be a fine thing, wouldn't it? Then we could show him the way to the camp."

"And we'd have salt again!"

"And beans."

"And bacon."

"And biscuits."

"Me, I thought I couldn't ever look down the barrel of one of Eliza's biscuits again, but now I reckon they weren't so bad after all."

Tamsen stood and snugged her apron more firmly around her

waist. "If you two keep on, you'll talk yourselves right out of a bowl of my famous soup."

"What kind of soup would that be?" Milt wondered.

"I'll let you guess."

"Would it maybe have a little ox belly in it?"

"It might."

"And a little water?"

"Yes, and quite a lot of melted snow."

"And not too much salt."

"Just a pinch."

"Pepper?"

"Two corns to every pot."

"A feast!" Milt Elliott shouted.

"That's not all," Tamsen said, and gave the men a mysterious smile.

"Potatoes?"

She shook her head.

"Beans?"

"No. Cattail roots and laurel leaves and a pinch of sage."

"A dish fit for a king, Mrs. Donner. Does it have some french-ified name?"

"No, it's just my famous Prosser Creek chowder."

"Well, I sure came on the right day."

"If you'd come an hour later, we might have eaten it all." The simple remark jolted and unnerved them, and the three adults each avoided the others' eyes. She had veered too close to the truth that shadowed their waking hours and remorselessly infiltrated their uneasy sleep. Tamsen laughed nervously, turned to the simmering pot and said over her shoulder, "We'll just wait for Mr. Denton. He's taken a little chowder to the teamsters."

"They're too lazy to do for themselves," George Donner explained. "Without John to fetch wood, they don't even keep the fire up half the time."

"Hibernating, maybe," Milt suggested, and looked up as a blast of cold air announced the Englishman's return.

He stared for a moment, apparently surprised to see a visitor, though Milt Elliott moved regularly between the two camps. Denton seemed about to make some remark, but only nodded in rapid greeting as he vigorously slapped snow from the shoulders of his coat.

"Hello, friend," Milt said, and something in his tone, some unexpected tenderness in the way he pronounced the simple words, caused Tamsen to glance over her shoulder at the two men.

"Hello, Milt. Planning another hike?"

"Tomorrow. Want to come?"

"Might as well. I don't have anything else planned."

"And the others?"

Denton shrugged. "They'll want a personal invitation. Preferably an engraved one, with ribbons on it. They're awfully particular about the company they keep."

"I'll go over after I've had my chowder. What's the weather like?"

"So-so. A little snow, but not too bad."

Milt stood, leaned closer to the Englishman, and asked, "How's the peepers?" His arm raised as though he wished to test the inflamed skin around John Denton's eyes.

"Better," he answered, and slapped again at his shoulders, though the little remaining snow had quickly melted. "I've had the best nurse in all of Prosser Creek."

"Sure they're strong enough to take the sun?"

"I hope so."

"Maybe . . ."

"No maybes. I intend to go with you. I want to go with you," he stressed.

"That's mighty fine by me, friend."

Tamsen interrupted their hesitant dialogue. "Milt, would you take a bowl to Mrs. Wolfinger?"

"Indeed I would!" And he stood with it before the blanket that draped the entrance to the woman's quarters, repeating "Knock-knock-knock" until her voice made a faint, unintelligible reply and her trembling hand appeared at the edge of the blanket. Milt lowered his shaggy head over it, spilling a tangle of curls forward as he loudly planted a kiss there, then quickly pushed the bowl into Mrs. Wolfinger's grasp. Georgia and Eliza thought it a wonderful joke, and during dinner one would suddenly stare at the other, say "Knock-knock-knock," and receive a cascade of giggles in return.

NEITHER MILT ELLIOTT NOR ANY OF THE DONNER TEAMSTERS LEFT the camp on Prosser Creek the following morning, for the light snowfall that had begun the previous evening increased in strength, fell steadily throughout the night. By day it alternated with rain and sleet to blot out the sun, drown the horizon in dense twilight, and even the angular shelter of the teamsters was no longer visible from the opposite bank of the creek. It was Thanksgiving Day, but that knowledge only deepened the gloom within the tent, muting even the voices of the restless children. The driving wind seemed to seal the chimney, and smoke refused to rise. It billowed through the Donners' tent, stinging eyes and drifting gray ash, while the earth beneath the emigrants' feet became a muddy wallow. Jean Baptiste dug a narrow trench against the brush wall of the circular lean-to, and it was declared a temporary privy that mingled its stench with the smell of pine smoke, the molding ox hides overhead, mildewed clothing, and the rotting flesh of Captain George Donner's injured hand. Six adults, five children and three dogs huddled in the narrow, gloomy interior, occasionally rising to check the progress of the storm and to gulp in the clean, icy air that painfully stiffened their lungs. By midafternoon it was so dark that the woodpile could no longer be seen from the entrance.

To distract herself, Tamsen knitted, and while she did so, she attempted to distract the smaller children with stories of knights and dragons and enchanted princesses, of sturdy heroes who escaped from tortuous, impenetrable dungeons. John Denton taught Milt the chorus and a dozen verses of an English folk song, with Elitha and Leanna occasionally joining them in pale, tuneless sopranos. Rolled in a buffalo robe, George Donner faced the tent wall and seemed to be sleeping. The staccato of Tamsen's needles underlined all other sounds, like the ticking of a clock, and even when her arms grew numb she felt she must not stop, that time itself might cease if the rhythm were disturbed. When the others grew bored with their diversions, sank then into dull-eyed silence, she used the bright metallic needles as a weapon with which to keep the howling wind from the hearth. Feeling the tendons cramp along her forearms, she worked faster, not just carrying the clumsy burden of time but trying to speed it forward, accelerating its dull progress, and she drove the needles until the cramps extended into her wrists, then her palms, and her hands hooked into painful claws. The knitting dropped into her lap, and she clutched the knotted muscles in her arms, looked down to see that the shawl she had been working with soft, loose stitches had tightened and narrowed until the wool was drawn so taut the edges twisted together, curled back into a deformed flower. Her mouth set in a grim line, she jerked out the needles, tore a row of unruly stitches away, then another, not pausing to rewind the yarn but letting it spiral to the muddy ground. She tugged so fiercely at the woolen mass, ripping apart the work of the long, empty hours, that John Denton and Milt Elliott lifted their heads from their arms, blinking away a dazed sleep, and stared at her questioningly. When she had finally undone her work to the point where the original stitches flowed in slender, gently interlocking "Q's," like a model copybook exercise, she bit off the yarn, rolled the knitting together, and spiked it firmly in place with the needles.

She stood then, tightening the knot that secured her apron, smoothing her hair, and crisply announced, "It's high time I thought about Thanksgiving dinner!" Puzzled eyes turned toward her, followed her brisk motions as she crossed the shelter and unlocked the small horsehair trunk that did service as both fireside bench and table. She carefully lifted out a limp cotton sack containing a double handful of beans, and slowly added them to the soup. Tamsen let the firm, glossy ovals slide through her fingers, recalling the bulging sacks that once clicked cheerfully with the jolting of the wagon. Beyond that memory were others, so remote they were like a pleasant dream only half-remembered after a night's restful sleep: the intense green of plants winding thickly around slender poles silvered by rain and sun, the damp pods, fat and pungent, gouged open by her thumbs, spilling their shiny seeds, the sprightly rhythm of their dropping into the tin pan, the firm bulk of the torn shells gathered up in her apron, curved moistly against her stomach like a child waiting to be born. Singly, caressingly, she drifted them into the cauldron, watched them plunge from sight to drown in the watery broth. While the men and the children began to stretch, yawn, edge closer to the fire, she scraped the mold from a small strip of lean, smoked bacon, diced it finely and sprinkled it into the bubbling pot. Between the crackling logs she buried all the remaining cattail roots, and she sent Milt off to fill another kettle with snow. This she set directly on the fire, and when it began to simmer, dropped in a miracle of dried apples and a few raisins. The men and the children watched her performance without a word, but by now they formed a tight semicircle around the hearth, and an apple ring bobbing merrily to the top of the kettle was an inexhaustible source of fascination. Even Mrs. Wolfinger had gradually eased aside the partition separating her from the others, swung her feet to the floor and merely stared for a time from her gloomy alcove, then left the bed to shuffle forward, wearing a blanket tied about her shoulders, but with the brilliant ruby necklace gleaming against the coarse wool. Tamsen lowered the lid of the trunk, to use it as a serving board, but did not trouble to lock it again, for all its wonders were spent.

THE STORM NEVER ACHIEVED THE INTENSITY OF WHAT THE EMI-grants would have described as a blizzard in Illinois or Indiana, but it settled down to its work as though it intended never to stop again. On Thursday there was almost as much sleet and rain as there was snow, and on Friday much of the snow melted as it fell, but by Saturday it lay nearly a foot deep around the camp. The wind had gradually shifted to the east, roaring down on the shelters with an icy cold that lanced through the slightest crack or crevice, and soiled clothing was stuffed into the worst of them. Fearing that if he waited any longer he might be cut off for days or even weeks from the lake camp, Milt Elliott prepared to depart. Eddy would certainly want to leave as soon as the weather broke, and Milt intended to be there. The thought of such a journey once more stirred George Donner out of his lethargy, and while his wife recited a series of messages for Margaret Reed and Eleanor Eddy, he took a seat on the empty truck angled before the fire.

"Let's not be wasting any more of Milt's precious time," he said. "The man's got to be off, and there's still business to be done."

"Business?" Tamsen wondered.

"Milt can be my courier. I'd like to send a letter to Captain Sutter."

"A letter?"

"You sound like Echo Canyon," he laughed. "Yes, I'd like to send a letter. Would you get me some writing things, child?"

His merry, assured tone was like some pleasant melody she had heard once, years before, and then forgotten. It made the fire seem brighter, warmer, the air less dank. "At once," she assured him, wiping her hands on her apron, and quickly had her journal propped on her knees, with a loose sheet of paper, the ink pot and pen.

"No, no, I'll write it myself."

"But . . ."

"I only write with one hand anyhow, and I can use this one as a blotter!" He raised the bulky white mitt, waggled it over his head. "Besides, you've got to watch the chowder doesn't stick."

She surrendered her precious writing materials, and in the oversized, chunky scrawl of a schoolboy, he began with the notation "Donners Camp Nov 28 1846." He formed the words under his breath, syllable for syllable, as his hand sprawled the letters across the page. "This is to certify that I authorize . . ." George Donner squinted one eye at the paper, then raised it to his guest and said, "Milt doesn't sound like a real name. What is it, Milt?"

The man coughed, said "Milford," coughed again.

"Milford? Nice name, that."

"Well . . ."

"Nice, solid-sounding name. Better than Milton, I reckon." George Donner paused, grinned mischievously as he said, "Or Milk-weed."

"Kids used to call me Millstone and Millwheel," he admitted with a bashful shuffle of his feet.

"I'll stick with Milford. One 'l'?"

"Just one."

"Just one in your family name, too?"

"No, double 'l' and double 't'."

329

"Kinda wasteful, isn't it? You could do with one of each. Takes longer to write that way. More ink. Never mind." He continued then, sounding the syllables, pausing to consider weights and measures, and signed the letter with a satisfied flourish. It read:

Donners Camp Nov 28 1846
This is to certify that I authorize Milford Elliott and make him my agent to purchase and buy whatever property he may deem necessary for my distress in the mountains for which on my arrival in California I will pay cash or goods or both.—2 gallons Salt— 150 lbs Flour—3 Bus Beans—50 lbs Cake Tallow—5 pack mules and two horses. Purchase or hire.

Signed
George Donner

"That ought to 'bout do it," he concluded, and using his bandaged hand to anchor the paper, he folded it twice, ran his thumbnail along the creases and handed it to Milt. "I'll trust you to deliver it to Captain Sutter personally."

"Word of honor."

Pushing aside the canvas flaps that blocked the entrance to their shelter, George and Tamsen Donner watched Milt Elliott trudge along the creek, turn and wave once before he vanished suddenly behind a curtain of snow. George was stooped, balanced with his good arm angled across his wife's shoulders, and when their guest disappeared from sight, his weight sagged against her, and wordlessly she locked her arms around his waist to guide him back to his bed.

12

Sunday, November 29th, 1846

For five full days and nights, with only brief intermissions, a storm has swirled mournfully about our frail shelters. It came suddenly and with unexpected intensity, following a spell of clear, sunny weather which had emboldened several of the men to make another attempt at escaping this lonely place. Mr. Eddy was so fired with brave resolution that he would certainly have reached his goal, had not this new fickleness of the mountain climate confined us all to our damp and drafty hovels. Milt Elliott arrived on Wednesday to announce the departure of the expedition, and remained until yesterday, in hopes of the storm abating. There was nearly a foot of snow on the ground when he departed. Though we were fearfully crowded with an extra guest to house, his cheerful presence often lifted the gloom of these days. His is a stout and generous spirit, and Mr. Reed will be perpetually indebted for the services he has provided Mrs. Reed and the children.

On Thanksgiving Day (November 26th) our expanded company had a jolly if somewhat meager feast, followed by hearty rounds of song. Some of the verses were ill-suited to maidenly ears, but provided a welcome tonic for us all.

While we regretted Milt's departure, it was fortunate he did not linger for another day, as there were more than three feet of snow on the ground this morning, and it continues to fall. Our woodpile is nearly exhausted, and the fierceness of the storm makes it difficult to gather more. No living thing could possibly cross the mountains now without the aid of wings.

13

November 30th, 1846

The wind has eased, but on level ground the snow is higher than my head. We can keep but a small fire going, and I have packed the children into bed to keep them warm.

14

December 1st, 1846

The wind has risen again from the west, building drifts higher than our shelters. There is no sign the snow intends to let up before spring. Jean Baptiste and Mr. Denton have dug a tunnel in order to lay in a fresh supply of wood.

15

December 2nd, 1846

More snow. The remaining cattle have wandered off in search of shelter, and have certainly perished of the cold. We will look for them as soon as the storm abates. Their absolute loss to us would be an unimaginable calamity. The snow is a little less heavy than yesterday, and a weak sun filtered reluctantly through the clouds this noon.

16

Dec. 3rd, 1846

The snow mercifully ceased sometime in the night, but the sky is still obscured by threatening clouds that swirl along the slopes of the mountains. The temperature has risen a notch, and we hope for a thaw. *Evening.* No sooner had I completed the remarks above than the snow recommenced. It falls still. I can write little, for the fire is so low my ink freezes unless I keep it in the coals. Our supply of pine-cone lamps is exhausted, and we live in unbroken twilight.

17

Dec. 4th, 1846

The skies are clear at last, but the wind blows east by northeast and everything in the wilderness is cased in ice. We have begun searching for the strayed animals, and must find them soon, for our larder is nearly empty. Antoine has deserted us, preferring to try his luck with the company at the lake.

18

Dec. 5th, 1846

It is a fine, clear day, brilliant with sunshine, and even the children have been busy digging paths and ramps and tunnels to connect us to the teamsters, the Jacob Donners, a snowy "outhouse" and the blessed woodpile. Mr. Denton has returned to the wigwam, for its residents are too weak to keep a fire going, and he hopes to assist them. He also, I think, wishes to spare us the expense of his bed and board.

19

Dec. 6th, 1846

We all passed mid-day in the warming sunshine, which seems a miraculous gift after our dusky confinement. If the weather remains so fair and the crust on the snow holds firm, the men will certainly renew their efforts to escape.

Tonight we have a bountiful fire, and my ink is thawed, but there is unhappily little beyond our waxing distress to confide to these pages. Mr. Denton's eyes are somewhat strengthened, but Mr. Donner's wounded hand is dangerously infected. Jacob takes scarcely any nourishment, and Betsy spends much of the day in piteous tears. Most of my loaf sugar has been consumed, lump by lump, in attempting to still the children's constant hunger. I roast bones in the fire until sufficiently dry and brittle to crumble into the soup, as thickening. If we cannot find the strayed cattle soon, our hunting dogs will have to go into the pot. We have otherwise only one shriveled haunch remaining.

20

Dec. 9th, 1846

Milt Elliott has returned to us, in company with Noah James, to communicate the latest plan for escape. The resourceful Mr. Stanton and Uncle Billy Graves have devised a kind of webbed snowshoe, made from sections of ox-bows and laced with strips of rawhide. Our visitors had each borrowed a pair of these curious devices, which are so clumsy and heavy as to exhaust the wearer, but seem to serve their function of holding him firm on the crust of the snow. I tried a pair, but was unable to lift them, and remained as fixed as a war monument.

The unexpected guests arrived at the peak of a ferocious storm, which commenced this morning and continues now into the night. The customary route along the creek was thoroughly obscured, the trees that line it so deeply drifted as to resemble bushes, and the men several times lost their way, wandering in circles and requiring almost the entire day to reach us. Both have the cruel marks of frostbite on their noses and cheeks.

Mr. Stanton has sent me a letter, comically addressed to "Donnersville, Cal.," in which he requests a pound of our best tobacco and the loan of my pocket compass. Despite his assurances of the latter's safe and speedy return, I cannot let him have it, for the future safety of the children may well depend on its slender store of geographical wisdom. Mr. Stanton and his Indians have in any case the greater advantage of first-hand knowledge of the mountain trail. They will, however, get no further help from Capt. Sutter's mules, for these wandered away in the same storm that claimed our own animals, and have not been seen since. Indeed, all the remaining stock at the lake camp met with a similar fate, save for those belonging to the unquenchable Breens, who were provident enough to slaughter out all that remained alive only a few hours before the storm's commencement. It would not surprise me to learn that their guardian angel had also made a generous delivery of flour and salt!

Gus Spitzer has not fared well on the charity of the Kesebergs, and has been taken into the Breen cabin. According to Milt, the reluctant hosts had no choice, for the German stumbled through their doorway to beg for food and at once collapsed, his legs too weak to carry him farther. Baylis Williams is likewise too feeble to leave his bed, and Eliza is hysterical with worry, but the Reeds are reported to be well. They have eaten all the dogs save for Patty's beloved Cash.

Since yesterday evening there has been no smoke from the wigwam, and tomorrow Milt and I will pay a visit on John Denton and the remaining teamsters.

21

THE DRIFTING SNOW HAD SO DEEPLY BURIED THE HIDE-COVERED entrance to the teamsters' shelter that Milt dug for more than ten minutes to expose it, and then had to hack the frozen hide free with an axe before it could be drawn aside. The stench of decay and loose bowels sprang through the narrow opening like a wild beast freed from its cramped cage, slammed against them with the full fury of its long confinement. Tamsen gripped Milt's arm with a force that made him wince, and the pair swayed for a moment, their feet slipping on the icy ramp Milt had hammered out with the back of the shovel.

"Smells like a family of skunks moved in," he remarked, and

his feeble, boyish attempt at humor calmed her churning stomach. She was grateful suddenly for even this oblique acknowledgment of the awful misery within, infinitely preferring Milt's lack of subtlety to the calculated science of evasion. With George and the children she must plan every word and rehearse each careful inflection. The more desperate their condition became, the more they instinctively relied on her to wrap the grim truth in tinsel, and she was repeatedly startled by the extent of her newfound talent for deceit.

"Worse than that," she said, recognizing something more revolting than the mingled stench of urine, vomit, and excrement that billowed through the doorway. It was the smell of despair and hopeless surrender that provoked a deep sickness in her soul, a nausea far worse than what rose sourly from the pit of her stomach. That morning she had smelled it in Jacob's shelter, too, and had fled from it without turning, moving backward up the rough steps Betsy's sons had carved, slipping and stumbling and clutching at the mounded snow for support. Now, recognizing it again before she entered, she was prepared for it, and no mere horrors of the flesh could touch her where this far more savage horror crouched, waiting.

"You'd best bring some wood," she suggested. "They must be nearly frozen."

Milt lifted the entrance flap higher, ducked as though about to enter. "I'd better have a look first," he warned.

"No, I'll do that. You bring the wood."

"Are you sure, ma'am?"

"Yes, I'm sure."

He shrugged, stepped aside to let her move beneath his outstretched arm, then let the flap drop. The darkness inside was intense, with only the thin gray light leaking through the smoke hole to guide her to the reclining forms that might have been mounds of earth heaped around the pile of ashes and charred logs. As Tamsen moved forward her foot slid, and she looked down to see a pool of frozen urine with the shine of colored glass. She found a man's shoulder, shook him, and there was a sudden, sharp cry in guttural German, but it seemed to come less in response to her touch than from the dense thickets of nightmare.

"Mr. Denton," she called softly, but there was no answer, and she wondered if any of the others were still alive.

"Mr. Denton!" she shouted, then shouted the name again, even louder. When there was no reply, no movement, she stooped first over one figure, then another, shaking them, prodding them with stiffened arms, trying to roll them out of the blankets and hides that encased them as tightly as the cerements of a mummy. Suddenly one of the men sat upright, propped on his elbows, and as she distinguished the familiar profile in the gloom, she cried excitedly, "Mr. Denton!"

"Mrs. Donner?"

"Mr. Denton, the fire has gone out," she irrelevantly scolded, afraid to give words to the enormous relief she felt.

"I must have overslept," he mumbled, in a voice that rasped with long disuse.

"Only by a day or two!"

"That long?"

"That long," she emphasized. "It's two days since we saw any smoke from your fire. If you'd waited much longer, you couldn't have gotten out. It took Milt thirty minutes to shovel the entrance free."

"Milt?" he wondered.

"He came yesterday," she explained, "with Noah James. The people at the lake have been making snowshoes, and they're going to leave as soon as the weather clears."

Their voices gradually stirred the others awake, and all began to ask questions at once. Who was there? Was the storm over? Had Reed and McCutcheon come through? Had the missing animals been found? Could they have some meat? Could they have a fire? Someone, thinking he smelled coffee, begged for a cup, then angrily demanded one, then cursed loudly when no one responded. Another made the jerky, sobbing noises of a punished child. Milt returned, and the clatter of firewood stilled the teamsters, who raised up to watch the spark strike tinder, lick at a handful of pine needles, flow noisly up and over the logs. John Denton struggled to his feet, offering to help tend to his three companions, but his knees folded, and Milt caught him as he fell.

"What have you had to eat?"

"That," Denton said, gesturing to a kettle near the fire, but turning his head away from the glutinous brown mass congealed around fragments of bone and half-cooked strips of hide with the hair still on them.

"Mrs. Donner. . . .," Milt began, with a curious note of apology, but she was already scaling the slippery ramp, and soon returned with a small, compact lump of meat, scarcely bigger than her own clenched fist.

"That'll fix you all up good as new!" Milt said. "I'll get a bucket of snow, and we'll have some nice hot broth in no time flat."

"You've got to keep your strength up until the storm blows over," Tamsen insisted.

"And then we'll make tracks out of here," Milt boasted.

"Right you are," John Denton agreed, though scarcely able to sit upright by the fire. There seemed to Tamsen something courageous and tenderly patient in this eager acceptance of his friend's deceit. She recognized it easily, reflexively, for it was so like that she reluctantly practiced on her own loved ones.

THE GIRL CROUCHED ON HER KNEES BESIDE THE FIRE, HER HEAD bent, while Tamsen first brushed all the hair forward, then parted it with a big-toothed comb. Leanna made a protesting sound as the ivory comb snagged, and Tamsen put it aside to work the knot loose before continuing. Dividing the hair into fine, even rows, she examined every inch of scalp, and when she found a louse burrowing there she pincered it up between the nails of thumb and forefinger, dropped it onto the fire. Despite constant scrubbing, clothing boiled, bedding spread on the snow to air whenever there was adequate sunshine, vermin had invaded the shelter, flourished in the warm, damp interior, multiplied in cheerful defiance of all her caution. Wood mice had also sought the luxurious warmth, but those were more welcome. Coalie had caught the first, neatly biting off its head, but after that Tamsen and the girls snared them with a sieve, dropped them squeaking and convulsed with fright into an empty flour sack, leaving it to Jean Baptiste to butcher and prepare them for the cauldron. Each time he protested at the messy work, as he

339

had balked and pouted and protested when it came time to slaughter the hunting dogs, until Tamsen made it clear he would otherwise be obliged to share the teamsters' table.

Tamsen plucked another burrowing parasite from her step-daughter's scalp, and when it cracked between her fingers remembered an Indian mother feasting contentedly on just such delicacies. The sight had sickened her then, and she had fastidiously asked herself if life was worth sustaining in the midst of such filth and degradation, if she could possibly survive even a single night in the narrow spaces where men, women, children, dogs, and vermin nestled together. The Diggers, it was said, ate those same mangy dogs when game was scarce, as well as rattlesnakes and buzzards and the stinking flesh of coyotes. She could not understand why they would rely entirely on the vagaries of the hunt, or why they begged with such mournful persistence for a strip of bacon when nearby woods were full of berries and edible roots, but she understood now the constant, bottomless hunger that could so ill afford the luxury of discrimination. Had she thought they might help sustain her children's bodies, she would have dropped the hateful vermin into the caldron as well, instead of flicking them into the coals, where they crackled and shrank instantly to black pinpoints.

"Finished!" she announced, smoothing Leanna's hair away from her face, and the girl rose with a timid, embarrassed smile to give her place to Elitha.

Bundled tightly against the cold, Eliza and Georgia played in the entryway to the shelter. There, during the clear days following the first severe storm, the bowed wooden supports from the wagon had been firmly planted, the frayed canvas top stretched over them, to create a low, tunnellike entrance, with flaps of canvas and buffalo robes hung at both ends. It formed an antechamber that protected the main quarters from sudden blasts of cold air, and it offered space for an emergency supply of firewood. There Tamsen's youngest children had laid one log crosswise over another to form a seesaw, and they rocked forward and back in a constant, unbroken rhythm, chanting softly and solemnly in their secret language. For days both had refused all other speech. While they rocked, a single, intense ray of sunshine pierced the canvas overhead, danced on Eliza's plaid coat. Georgia pointed, and the two raised their voices to an excited warble as they stared at the clear yellow disc. Slowly, careful not to shatter it or frighten it away, Eliza slid her outstretched palm under the beam, felt its warmth tickle her skin, then clamped it firmly in her grip.

"Mama!" she shouted, pushing through the heavily draped entrance and racing to the fire with the clenched fist held rigidly before her.

"Mamamamamama, look!" She carefully raised her hand to Tamsen, slowly curled her fingers back, waited for the bright miraculous golden gift to be acknowledged.

"What is it, child? Did you hurt yourself? Show Mama where it hurts." Looking for some sign of a cut or a splinter, Tamsen also automatically felt the child's forehead for a hint of fever.

Eliza stared into her own empty hand and began to sob as she said, "Gone."

"What's gone?" Tamsen asked, and patiently repeated the question again and again, but was answered only by the agitated babble of a language she could not comprehend.

FOR A TIME EVEN JOHN DENTON TOOK PART IN THE RENEWED search for the missing cattle that had strayed off during the last storm, but he tired quickly and was persuaded to return to the comfort of the fire. Noah James, Milt Elliott, and Jean Baptiste continued the search, each equipped with a six-foot pole with nails driven through the end and bent upward into hooks. This was forced down through the drifts, twisted, then jerked out, in hopes that one of the nails would snag a scrap of hide. The three concentrated on the tamarack grove south of the Donners' shelter, reasoning that the weakened animals could not have wandered far in seeking protection from the wind. They moved systematically through the grove, stopping every yard or two and thrusting the poles into the snow between their feet, leaning their weight against the vertical lengths until they would descend no farther, twisting, drawing them out. A glance usually sufficed to confirm their lack of success, but at times a fragment of rotted leaf clutching the tip of a nail would briefly deceive them. They worked their way through the grove, turned, and made a parallel track as they searched in the opposite direction. Moving with the slow caution of the old, leaning on their staves as if for support, the three young men seemed ancient. When the snow began to fall again, driving with such vertical force it whirled through the grove to whiten their shaggy hair and beards, they resembled caricatures of Father Time, trudging toward an unavoidable rendevous.

THERE WERE STILL SMALL QUANTITIES OF COFFEE, FLOUR, AND sugar remaining, as well as a little meat, but the meat was cautiously hoarded now, a frozen lump precious as gold, in case one of the children should grow ill and require a strengthening broth. Discarded bones were boiled for soup, then boiled again until soft enough to crumble between the teeth. More thoroughly and more palatably than the hasty teamsters, Tamsen began to cook the stiffened hides that had been piled onto the roof of the shelter. In the beginning she avoided those that had molded after being repeatedly thawed by the heat of the fire or the reluctant sun, then frozen again. She and Jean Baptiste took down the best, scrubbed them with fistfuls of snow, and cut them into narrow strips. These she held singly over the fire, revolving each constantly so the precious hide itself was not charred, but only the unwanted hair singed away. When this was done, each piece was scraped on both sides, then dropped into a kettle to boil with a spoonful of crushed pepper. After several hours the strips began to dissolve, slowly losing their shape and blending together in a glutinous mass. Cooled, it produced a gluelike jelly that could be eaten with a spoon. The first attempts at swallowing a mouthful had made them all violently ill except for Mrs. Wolfinger, whose lips smacked in appreciation as if she were sampling a well-seasoned calf's-foot jelly. When the woman boldly helped herself to a second serving, the children seemed persuaded by her example, and George and Tamsen Donner were so relieved that they overcame their own revulsion. As she swallowed, Tamsen compelled herself to think of the classification of embroidery stitches, overcame the last spasm by whispering the word "bargello."

Preparing a single pot of the rank, sticky food consumed much of the day, and the air never entirely cleared of the musty, acrid odor of singed hair. Thus, Tamsen hardly noticed the smell when Georgia and Eliza tore away shreds of the muddy buffalo robe before the fire, singed them in the coals, then popped them hot and crisp into their mouths. Once she had paused to wonder that the rug seemed smaller, yet she had never connected that passing impression with the two girls who spent so much time playing beside the hearth. Only when she chanced to see a scrap of fur tucked furtively into the coals, then flipped aside with a twig, did she comprehend the earnestness of their play, and she had no heart to interfere. Even more than the inexpressible pity she felt for their gnawing hunger, she felt a sudden wave of pride at their resourcefulness.

22

December 13th, 1846

With brief pauses and drafty intermissions during which the sun occasionally winked through the clouds, it has stormed for five days. Today the snow has been heavier than any we have yet witnessed, and the entryway to our shelter requires to be shoveled free every hour, lest we be buried alive by the swelling drifts.

Messrs. Elliott and James are with us still. Had they not been compelled to lengthen their stay, I fear our teamsters (including Mr. Denton) would all have perished of hunger and cold. They had once more permitted their fire to die out, and had nothing whatever to eat except a vile-smelling pot of bones and hides, scarcely cooked at all, and which none could stomach. Milt has patiently tended to their needs, and Noah has made himself indispensible to Betsy, for Uncle Jake is nearly as helpless as the teamsters, though he and his family still have a quantity of meat. Certainly none of us have our hunger stilled, and all have got thin as rails, but none are starving. It is Jake's spirit that has surrendered, and his body only follows its cowardly lead. He has taken permanently to his bed, and manifests no interest in what occurs outside his nest.

Like Hansel and Gretel, we have begun to eat a house! Ours is made not of spicy gingerbread (whose very name is dizzying) but of hides. When singed and scraped and then boiled for an eternity, they create a kind of jelly whose unpleasant taste can be somewhat disguised by cracked pepper. Salt would help even more.

Whenever the weather permits, we continue our search for the missing animals, but the drifts are now so high I think we would have better luck searching for the much-sought needle buried in a haystack.

23

December 14th, 1846
The day dawned fair and clear, and if it holds, the snowshoers will certainly be making final preparations for departure. They have solemnly dubbed themselves "The Forlorn Hope." It is said about 20 people will make the attempt, including Sarah Foster, Mary Graves, Amanda McCutcheon, Harriet Pike and Sarah Fosdick. Three of the women leave nurslings behind, in the care of Mrs. Murphy. By that measure, conditions at the lake camp must be nearly as severe as our own. Milt, however, will not be joining the rest. He is reluctant to leave the teamsters, for he says they will not survive without his nursing.

24

Prosser Creek
Wednesday, December 16th, 1846

Jacob Donner died at noon this day, at the age of 65. At his wife's renewed urging he had left his bed and sat at a plank table laid in readiness for the midday meal. When Betsy Donner turned to tend the fire, he leaned his head onto his folded arms, and never lifted it again. Since our arrival at this place, he had seemed to drift deeper and deeper into sleep, until he finally dropped over the treacherous brink into that sleep from which there is no awakening. A brief service was read beside a grave chopped from the snow. In addition to his wife and her two sons by a prior marriage, Jacob Donner has taken cruel leave of five small children, the eldest 9 years of age and the youngest not quite 4. Noah James has moved in with the family to give them what assistance he can, but he cannot provide the guidance and authority of a father. George Donner not only grieves for the brother with whom he had shared so many of life's adventures and trials and delights, but continually berates himself for having planted visions of California in Jacob's mind.

25

December 17th, 1846

Late yesterday evening, John Denton summoned me to the teamsters' shelter, where Samuel Shoemaker had become hysterical. He was not violent, and his general bodily deterioration would have rendered any attempt at violence as harmless as that of a newborn kitten, but his wandering mind was indeed terrifying to behold. His voice was that of a child, repeatedly begging his parents for food, then for a feather comforter, and wondering why there was no fire in the grate. When his requests went unheeded, he wept most pitifully, but later became quite cheerful, and seemed to be playing Red Rover with his schoolmates, calling their names loudly and bidding them "come over." His last words, however, were "More porridge, please." Mr. Shoemaker was 25 years of age and in the peak of health until we were stranded here six weeks ago.

26

Prosser Creek

December 18th, 1846

I am dictating this report to my wife for the extra information it gives about the mysterious disappearance of Mr. Wolfinger, a former member of our party. A few hours ago Mrs. Donner and I answered an appeal from one of our teamsters, Joseph Reinhardt, to come to him without delay. He was about half dead and sinking fast when we got there but was holding on until he could talk to us both. At first he talked a lot of German and the only thing we could understand was "bad man." Then he screamed "Gott! Gott! Gott!" over and over again. Finally I got him calmed down some and he mentioned the name Wolfinger. "What about him?" I asked, and he answered, "Spitzer and me we kill old man." With Milford Elliott and Mr. John Denton and my wife as witnesses, I then asked him to repeat this confession and he did so very clear and not hesitating. Then he talked only German for a long time, getting weaker and weaker, but we could only understand him saying Mr. Keseberg's name several times and nothing else. At the end he screamed for a long time without ever taking a single breath and was dead. This episode made Mr. Elliott remember he had seen Wolfinger's rifle beside Keseberg's bed at the lake camp. Keseberg has a bad foot and was using the rifle like a crutch. Perhaps more facts will come from Augustus Spitzer, but he is at the other camp. We buried Joseph Reinhardt in the snow, fair and proper as we could, and have put his name on all his personal property. This did not reveal anything Mrs. Wolfinger, the widow, recognized as having ever belonged to her deceased husband.

Signed
Capt. George Donner

27

Dec. 19th, 1846

James Smith died this morning, drifting away like a sleepy child. Despite the gentleness of his surrender, this death seemed to alarm John Denton more than the others he had recently witnessed. Perhaps he reasoned that with his three comrades dead, his own life was now marked for extinction. With scarcely a word of explanation or farewell, and with his skin pale as the proverbial ghost, he departed for the lake camp early this afternoon. Milt will soon follow in Mr. Denton's tracks, for his patients have no further use of his doctoring, and he grows concerned about the Reeds. Noah remains with Betsy and her children.

28

WITH THE HELP OF JEAN BAPTISTE AND NOAH JAMES, TAMSEN spent most of the morning digging for buried treasure. The men cut a ramp into the snowbank where the remaining wagon had long since disappeared, then shoveled out the wagon bed itself to reveal the jumbled crates and trunks they had hastily ransacked, like startled thieves, when the first storm began. She remembered the search for bedding and warm clothing, her medicine chest, the alarmingly wrinkled, shrunken sacks of flour and salt. Now she sought presents for the girls for Christmas, and with a chisel Jean Baptiste broke open a box that she hoped might contain embroidered woolen shawls, but discovered only a quantity of cheap trinkets intended to charm the Indians. But perhaps, she thought, necklaces of bright glass beads, to glitter in the firelight, would after all please them more, even the little ones, and she pulled aside lengths of garish flannel and calico to grapple up an oblong parcel tightly packed in newspaper. Painfully stiffened with the cold, her fingers refused to release the simple knot that held the parcel, and she jerked at the string until it snapped, clattering its contents at her feet. The cruelty of the joke seemed too perfect to be the work of accident alone, and as she kicked the cheap mirrors angrily aside, scuffing snow over them, hearing one crack under the heel of a boot, she imagined the shock even the smaller children would receive at the unexpected sight of their own wasted faces. Each had grown day by day accustomed to the gradual withering of the others' cheeks, the hollows gouged around the huge, glistening eyes, but each would hold in memory's mirror an unblemished image of her own face. One of Tamsen's careful deceits, and one of the first, had been to conceal their sole mirror—not from her own eyes but from those of the girls, to spare them this unnecessary proof of their unending hunger. They were not starving, and they would not starve so long as a scrap remained to be boiled up in the big cast-iron kettle. If necessary, she would strip pine bark to make what the Indians called starvation food—hard, bitter balls of resin; she would also simmer harness leather, shoes, saddles, and George's Sunday braces. If the missing stock was not found in time, there was other meat frozen in the snow, its place of burial exactingly measured off, stride for stride, with the aid of her pocket compass, so that she could find it even in a storm, would know precisely where to dig even if the aspens marking their icy cemetery should be buried beneath the drifts. The children would live. Whatever her own fate, or George's, their five daughters would survive; if they hungered, and if their hunger often made her ache with helpless fury, fighting off a fit of wild hysteria that might have toppled their precariously balanced world, they did not and would not starve. Hunger itself became a measure of her careful rationing, and their thin faces measured it again, helped her adjust the portions that sufficed to keep them alive, healthy, strong, though their hunger never retreated far even after the rare meals fortified by a few ounces of meat, but crouched for a moment, gathering strength for a new attack. All this she accepted rationally; she had not made the terms or the conditions, but she would abide by them so long as she could bend them to her own unspoken purpose, fighting the ultimate hunger with smaller hungers as men burned a strip of pasturage to halt the fire racing across a nearby wood, and allowing the fat to melt from the children's bodies in order to toughen their leanness. She knew the mortal stakes of her elaborate bluff, and she accepted the risk, but she could not invite the children to hold up the hand-sized oval mirrors with their cheap, stamped-tin frames to confront the visible results of her strategy. It was enough that she must confront them every hour of the day, even behind tightly lidded eyes.

When the first mirror cracked under her heel, Tamsen thought, "Seven years bad luck," then wondered at the easy, careless luxury of superstition. The omen of the shattered mirror lightly presumed one would survive for another unimaginable span of seven years, the rich, eventful span of her marriage to George Donner, and not merely for seven fleeting days or seven weeks or seven months. The curse of spilled salt presumed the blessing of salt itself, and wood knocked to startle away evil spirits could not be the last length dropped onto the dying fire while wind screamed around the shelter like souls in torment. As she continued her search, she ignored the mirrors spilled at her feet, crackling like fresh ice on a pond, and finally drew from the crate the heavy packet of glass beads she had sought. Though the cold now ached in her joints and she had lost all feeling in the tips of her fingers, she selected her gifts carefully, holding them up singly and spinning them in the light, considering color and length, rejecting a pretty strand in pale pink that would have been perfect for Eliza, save that several beads had been crushed, and all this with the same patient care, the exacting eye that preferred genuine quality to a mere bargain, that she would have shown when shopping in the warm, snug interior of her favorite dry goods store in Springfield. Satisfied that she had chosen the best of those available, she slid them into the pocket of her cloak and quickly searched the other goods remaining in the wagon, thinking there might be some forgotten treat that would please George or Mrs. Wolfinger. She found nothing that would do for them, but she was rewarded with two unexpected treasures: a narrow tin containing watercolors and fine camel's hair brushes, and a ten-pound bag of rice overlooked in their original, hasty unloading. The rice, too, would be a Christmas surprise, and it would distract them all, perhaps, from the knowledge that it was Coalie that had gone to make the sauce, together with a spoonful of marrow, crumbled bones, and a handful of pine nuts. Constantly stirring, fearful that a single grain of the precious rice might stick and burn, she saw other women stirring rich stews thick with chunks of beef and bright garden vegetables. She saw them precariously raise steaming platters, mounded high with fried chicken, lift them dangerously over the heads of their guests, edging between crowded chair backs and wainscoting, while appreciative hungry murmurs urged them on. She saw herself on the first Christmas as George's bride, crouched before the unfamiliar oven ladling away the fat that streamed from the plump goose, pricking the skin to release fresh rivulets the color of antique gold, and later pouring on a cup of salty water to crisp the skin, worrying that the meat might be tough and dry or greasy and undercooked, that the dressing had fused to a pasty mass, that there wasn't enough gravy for so many, that there was too little of everything, that the mashed potatoes were lumpy, her pickles too sour, the beans too limp, that she had failed this first official test woefully and publicly before Jacob and Betsy, poor motherless Elitha and Leanna, William and William's wife, and George's grandchildren, and that worst of all the crusts on her pies (pumpkin, apple-raisin, molasses) would be tough and unchewable as shoeleather.

29

Prosser Creek
Christmas Eve, 1846

We have had a tasty stew with rice, and an evening of vigorous carolling. The girls all received beaded necklaces, and the fairest Indian maidens could not wear them more becomingly—not even those of Mr. Cooper. When we had exhausted our repertoire of Christmas melodies, Mrs. Wolfinger began to sing in a wonderfully rich soprano, treating us to both German and French verses, and making our little shelter ring like the stateliest cathedral. Jean Baptiste was powerfully smitten by the performance, and at this late hour is still flirting quite openly with the handsome widow woman. Mr. Donner says it is scandalous, but does not really mean it.

It has snowed off and on for four days, and tonight is particularly heavy.

30

New Year's Day, 1847

It is now two full months since we came to this place, and we have no more rations except for coffee, pepper, and a bit of sugar. If we are sparing, we have enough hides to last about a month, and by then we expect Mr. Reed will get through with relief. I try to visit Betsy and the children every other day, but the recent snows have made it difficult. Mr. Donner's hand shows a little improvement. Since Milt left, we have had no news of those encamped at the lake.

31

HER TWISTED FEATURES, THE HELPLESS AGONY AND GRIEF STAMPED so horribly across her face, would have sufficed to turn him away.

"I just can't do it. There's hardly enough for the children as it is. I just can't, Milt."

"It's all right, Mrs. Donner. I guessed maybe you couldn't."

The wind eliminated her reply as an angry hand might take a letter, tearing it across and scattering the pieces, only a single phrase falling face upward and in view: "One of you." She remembered his gentle motions as he nursed the teamsters and the refusal to think of his own safety, his dangerous journeys from the lake to the creek and back again, the games he devised for the children, his loyalty to the Reeds. Milt had arrived early that afternoon with Eliza Williams and the story of their failed attempt to cross the mountains. Milt, Margaret Reed, Virginia, and Eliza had departed together on the 4th of January, but on the second day Eliza was so exhausted she had to turn back, and after two more days of wandering in the mountains with a faulty compass, Virginia's feet were so badly frozen that the others had to retreat as well, with Milt carrying the girl most of the way. Margaret Reed had a pair of hides and a little meat remaining from the surprising inheritance Pat Dolan had left her when he set out with the Forlorn Hope, but it was a meager ration for four adults and three children. Somehow she had persuaded the Breens to shelter Patty, and Milt was determined to relieve her of the burden of feeding himself and Eliza.

"Eliza can't eat hides," Milt had explained to Tamsen. "She tries, but it won't stay down."

Before she could gather her wits for a pretense, she had admitted to him, "That's all we've got left. Hides and sometimes mice and a few bones. If it was just you . . ."

"No, I'll be O.K. Mr. Graves said maybe he could let me have a hide, and John's still got part of one he'll share. Guess we'd better be getting on back."

"Don't." She stayed him with a light touch of her hand and felt his arm tremble. He had wandered for four days in the mountains, for much of the way carrying Virginia Reed in his arms, had slept in the open, and then walked directly here with Eliza. "Stay the night," she insisted. "Stay until you get your strength back a little."

He had asked to talk to her outside, and they had left Eliza to warm herself by the fire while they stood in the inadequate shelter of the woodpile and Milt told the confused story of their attempted escape, of fires repeatedly drowned by snow, a compass that perversely contradicted itself. Trying to explain why Eliza surrendered earlier than the rest, he said, "She's been kinda funny ever since Baylis died."

"Baylis is dead?"

"Yes, ma'am, he was the first."

She had not known that death had visited the other camp as well. "Who else?" she wondered.

353

"Dutch Charley," he told her, "and Spitzer and Keseberg helped themselves to his money and his razor and two good-lookin' silver watches."

"And no one else?" Tamsen asked.

When he shook his head, "Nobody else," she released the breath caught in her throat as she waited to hear the death sentence for those who lingered still in her affection. But the Reeds were all alive, and Margaret Eddy and her daughter and old Mrs. Murphy, the Keseberg baby she had dragged into life with her own hands, and John Denton and Milt himself. Now, though she knew there was not so much as an extra spoonful of the day's ration of boiled hides, she was asking Milt to stay to dinner, agreeing to share her board with the Reeds' mournful servant girl as well. Whether Eliza Williams could stomach hides or not, she would somehow have her portion like the rest. It was a trick, Tamsen thought wryly, that she would far prefer to play with loaves and fishes.

"Don't," she insisted, when Milt told her it was time to return to the lake, and when the trembling that began in his arms extended to his whole body, shook him uncontrollably like a frenzied puppet, she held him tightly. All her reserve, her careful rationing, the miserly mathematics with which she measured off each strip of hide, were suddenly forgotten, and as he sobbed loudly against her shoulder, she tried to still him with the consoling melodies she would have whispered to a frightened child. It was not for himself but for all of them that he wept, and she knew that. When he did not respond to her comforting whispers, she raised his head between her hands and pressed his cracked, blistered lips firmly against her own. There was neither passion nor pity in the gesture. There was only the overwhelming need to say how much she cherished him, and the knowledge that if she sought to shape her feeling into words, it could only sound like a feeble apology for turning him away.

32

Jan. 9th, 1847

Milt arrived yesterday in the late afternoon with a pitiful account of his recent efforts to escape with Margaret Reed, her eldest child, and the servant girl Eliza Williams. They had departed around noon on Monday, leaving Tommy to the uncertain charity of the Breens, Patty with the Kesebergs, and Jim with the Graveses. The depth of Margaret Reed's distress is awesomely measured in that compromise, for she gambled the lives of her trusting children as well as her own in the hope of bringing back relief. Though Milt did his best to beat a firm path with his snowshoes, the surface was so soft that those who followed continually sank beneath it—often to their waists. On the second night their fire melted a deep well in the snow, and they were roused from an exhausted sleep to find themselves many feet below the surface, where the slightest movement might have buried them in an avalanche. Eliza Williams soon abandoned the struggle, but the others remained 4 days and cheerless nights in the threatening wilderness, until Virginia's frozen feet compelled them to turn back. According to Milt's description, the region to the west of the pass offers a mazy prospect no less perplexing than the Wahsatch, and his faulty compass was of no use in charting a course. It is to be hoped that the snowshoe party, which left 3 weeks ago, has fared better.

Milt and Eliza came to us in the hope of making themselves useful, but also to spare Margaret Reed the obligation of keeping them. Eliza cannot eat hides, but they are all the food we have, and scarcely enough of those for our own. The two spent the night with us, to recruit their strength, intending to return today to the lake, but a fresh storm has stranded them.

33

The storm continues, with the sky more gloomy and threatening than any we have heretofore witnessed. Milt and Eliza are still with us. Mr. Donner's hand has broken open again, and the wound is septic. The girls are well, and Frances is using her leisure to learn the multiplication tables.

34

Jan. 13th, 1847

It has snowed fast the entire day, and we estimate the new fall at about 3 feet. On the level the snow is nearly 15 feet in depth, and our shelter thus rests well below the horizon.

35

Jan. 14th, 1847

The storm surrendered yesterday evening, and the new day dawned bright and clear and sunny. We all spent the noontime out of doors, in the shelter of the woodpile, being nicely toasted by the sun. Milt and Eliza have returned to the lake.

36

OFTEN THE SNOW WAS SO TREACHEROUSLY YIELDING THAT TAMSEN was reluctant to let the smaller children move out of sight of the entrance to the shelter, fearful they would be swallowed by a snow-drift. But she prodded them out and into the fresh mountain air whenever the sky was clear. If she intended to sketch, Eliza and Georgia were usually propped upright beside her, wrapped in a single buffalo robe. With Jean Baptiste's help, the robe was stretched on the snow, covered with a quilt, and one of the girls placed at each end. Then the two were rolled toward the center, giggling when their bodies bumped together, their cold noses touched, and the bulky bundle, like a stout hollow log with eyes peeping from the top, was angled against a stump. From this snug position, they also watched Jean Baptiste as he split logs for the fire.

With only a few sheets of loose paper remaining, Tamsen used them sparingly, working on both sides, and repeatedly astonished by the variety of pastel tones that shimmered across the surface of the

357

snow, the deep mauves and blues bunching in the shadows. With each new sketch she shifted her position in a clockwise pattern, until she had completed the total panorama that surrounded their campsite: the peaks of distant mountains ornamented with plumes of silver clouds, nearer ones thrusting jagged, ice-glazed spars of rock toward the sun, and still nearer the faint, forked indentation that signaled the muffled creek beds, the twisted boughs of pines with their surprising, incongruous green, and sometimes only the tip of a branch that thrust from the snow like groping fingers. In the foreground of one sketch, the teamsters' conical shelter rises abruptly, its original structure long since erased by the drifts, as if detached and displaced from the range of mountains sprawling across the horizon. The low-ceilinged brush shelter in which Betsy Donner crouches with her six children is scarcely more recognizable as a habitation, for it has become an icy underground cave, with only a few inches of stovepipe protruding above the surface to hint at the twilight world below. The stovepipe is the work of Noah James, like the narrow, sloping tunnel connecting the shelter with the outside world. But in Tamsen's sketch stovepipe and tunnel entrance are no more than brief, transparent strokes of gray against the blue-white surface, with no further hint to the lives that still pulse deep beneath the snow, the lungs straining to draw breath from the rank air. Tamsen rarely goes there, for Betsy's whining monologue is such an incoherent jumble of dream and hope and memory that she can make no sense of it, and after a quarter of an hour begins to fear it is she herself who is mad, so hopelessly deranged as to be incapable of following her sister-in-law's brilliant and witty and informative repartee. She feels her mouth twitch open and shut but hears no sound issue from it, and knows that even if she could utter words of comfort or reproof they would sink unheeded beneath the ceaseless garbled stream of illusion and confession and tearful lament.

Tamsen sketches her own winter quarters on the heavy vellum endpapers of her journal. The front papers show the exterior view, with a profile more clearly defined than that of her neighbors. The curving trunk of the split pine, charred by the constant fire, forms a graceful vertical line, seeming to anchor the shapeless mound of the brush-covered tent sloping away to the south, the smaller projection of the former wagon top pointing along the well-packed trench, a band of purple, leading to the woodpile. A ribbon of smoke drifting from the larger mound, twining about the blackened tree trunk, lifts away to flutter across the deep azure sky, giving the scene a curiously cheerful and domestic look, the appearance of something snug, protective, nurturing. This is partly the effect of the tenderly radiant light flooding the picture, warming even the shadows. At a casual glance this luminous glow might almost have been the expression of something that loved and suffered for man. Under its alchemy, the dense, anonymous, snow-covered shapes seem to lift, to float lightly free of the urge of gravity.

In contrast, the drawing on the last pages of the journal has a heavy and melancholy effect, a feeling of airless claustrophobia. The hearth of piled stones offers the sole source of light, but the meager fire glowing there does not so much illuminate as weight everything it touches with a dense burden of shadow. Ochre, brown, black, and tones of dirty gray seem carelessly smeared, blotted, as though someone has sought to clean a brush of its muddy color by scrubbing it angrily against the paper. Only when held at arm's length do individual details become recognizable: the five girls huddled together on a single rack-like bed immediately to the left of the hearth, the figure of Jean Baptiste on his knees, shapeless beneath a dirty poncho, laying a fresh log on the fire. The bulky form only partially visible to the extreme left of the picture is George Donner, burrowed beneath the buffalo robe from which he rarely emerges. The looming shape to the right, that seems a rectangular shadow whose source is unaccounted for, is the blanket separating Mrs. Wolfinger's drafty alcove. Tamsen sits with her back to the entrance, and seeks to record the entire cramped scene, which compels her to distort perspective, to push back the walls to the right and left of her, angling them obliquely so that the narrow center of the shelter sprawls open, seems far wider than it really is, and exposes a yawning sea of mud that threatens to overflow the scene and drown the slender fire, whereas the actual space between the racks elevating sitter and sleeper above the mire is scarcely bigger than an average tabletop. The crowding of texture and form, the overlapping smears of somber color give to the sketch a gloomily abstract quality. It might be the rendering of a collapsing tunnel or even an abandoned mine shaft deep in the earth, with the flickering hearth no more than the struggling wick of a lamp. One might also take it for a hasty impression of dank, malodorous catacombs, the rack beds with their swaddled forms for niches hewn from porous rock, the distant light a cluster of spluttering votive candles.

37

Jan. 21st, 1847

We have scarcely more than a single hide remaining, and will soon be pressed to the direst extremes unless relief arrives. It is now more than a month since the snowshoers departed, and we daily expect some of them to return with emergency provisions. Mr. Reed is likewise long overdue.

I have sent Jean Baptiste to the lake camp for news and have given him a half-pound of tobacco to deliver to Mr. Denton.

38

Jan. 23rd, 1847

The renewal of the recent storm (the worst we have yet experienced) compelled Jean Baptiste to remain for two days at the lake camp. Our friends there have no encouraging news, and begin to fear the "Forlorn Hope" went astray in the mountains. Only Mr. Breen seems confident of their safety, and prays loudly to speed the arrival of beef and flour from Capt. Sutter. Mrs. Reed has moved her entire family into the Breens' cabin, which has a proper roof, whereas the hides that once roofed her own shanty have been eaten one by one. The infants in Mrs. Murphy's care are all sickly, having only a little sizing of snow and flour to take the place of the milk they crave. The Keseberg baby suffers similar distress. John Landrum, Mrs. Murphy's grandson, is not expected to live much longer, and the devoted widow is herself nearly blind.

Mr. Denton has paid me amply for his tobacco, twisting a note of thanks round a lump of purest gold extracted from his hearthstones. Having accidentally found a few bright flakes in the ashes, he obtained more by chipping away at rocks and burying the fragments in the hottest part of the fire. He seems very pleased by his discovery, though I wish he had sent us a like weight in salt.

The storm which delayed Jean Baptiste has renewed its onslaught, and its force waxes fiercely.

39

THERE WERE BRIEF INTERVALS OF SUNSHINE, AND THERE WERE hours when the wind dropped and a thaw seemed in the making. But after each tempting promise of reprieve, as cruelly empty as a desert mirage, the storm renewed its attack, hammering with snow and sleet and mountain wind, and trapping the emigrants for days at a time in the freezing shelters. For four nightmarish weeks all life seemed suspended, globed in eternal winter, and Tamsen ceased to record its declining rhythms in her journal, though each morning she noted the new date in columns that ran down a single page, and occasionally these were followed by cryptically brief notations: "thawing," "freezing," "wind W." But there were other measures of time, including the single hide that shrank in precisely measured strips, the melting snow that day and night dripped rhythmically through the roof of the tent, the deepening hunger that dizzied their motions, the long confinement stripping even more strength from weakened muscles, making the short journey to the woodpile a painful labor. Twice the fire died completely, and once the hearth remained cold for an entire day, the ashes finally buried beneath silting snow, for no one could remain upright against the thrust of the storm. Decades later, Eliza would remember two endless shivering weeks in which clothing and bedding were completely saturated with water, but it is doubtful if the discomfort lasted more than a few days. Quilts and clothing were rotated day and night before the fire in an effort to moderate the perpetual dampness, and India-rubber sheets were slung along the ridgepole to channel away the worst of the leaks. The system spared them, as well, the necessity of hauling heavy buckets of snow to melt for drinking water, and the boiled hides gave them all an unquenchable thirst. Their bodies rebelled against the diet in other ways, as well. Tamsen and Elitha both ceased to menstruate, though acute cramps told them their time was due, and the poison began to mount more rapidly from the wound in George's hand, soon extending well above his elbow. All suffered from alternating seizures of acute constipation, followed by uncontrollable, debilitating rushes of diarrhea, and all but the smallest children lost hair by the tangled fistful. Their eyes developed rheumy infections that sealed them shut in the night, and their teeth began to loosen, aching dully and sometimes bleeding from the gums. Only Jean Baptiste developed any acute pain, but was able to draw two throbbing teeth with his fingers, while Leanna lost one, and accidentally swallowed it in a startled gulp, when she bit into a fragment of bone that had not been sufficiently roasted. Tamsen's fingers were so shriveled that she feared losing her broad gold wedding bands in the snow. Beneath the dense layers of her clothing they nestled against her skin, twin orbits of gold suspended on a narrow velvet ribbon. For the time, she was powerless to treat these multiple symptoms of slow starvation, but she watched them as closely as she watched the steadily shrinking hide, and with as much well-camouflaged alarm as that with which she registered the relentless progression of the storm that annulled all hope of relief. So long as she could boil up yet another kettle of glue, so long as a single bone remained to roast in the fire, she could forestall the sole and awful alternative, but the compass was secure in its hiding place. A shovel meanwhile stood in readiness in the low antechamber, together with a hatchet and a sharpened hunting knife.

The heavy snows in the mountains appeared as drenching rains in the foothills, repeatedly halting the seven horsemen who departed Sutter's mill on January 31st to relieve the starving emigrants. With them was William Eddy. After battling the floodwaters of the American River, the men pushed on to Johnson's Ranch where other rescuers would join them, to slaughter and dry beef, pound wheat into coarse flour, and load the emergency rations onto pack animals. Fourteen men set out from the ranch on the morning of February 4th, and were soon deeply mired in the swampy trail. Drenched and half-frozen, they halted for two days to wait out a ferocious downpour, and lost another precious day in drying their packs so the food would not spoil. The following morning, after their first sleep in three days, the men moved out again, only to discover that the little stream that usually bubbled down Steep Hollow had swollen to fill the entire canyon. They felled pines to bridge the roaring waters, and working along the ridge leading to Bear Valley, encountered the first snow. The brittle crust collapsed beneath their weight, and the horses foundered helplessly in the drifts. Half of the burdensome supplies were cached at Mule Springs, and the useless animals sent back to Johnson's. Reluctantly, William Eddy also returned to the ranch; there had been too little time to recuperate from weeks of cold and starvation as leader of the Forlorn Hope, and he feared he would hold the others back. It took a week to climb from Mule Springs to Bear Valley on foot, and there half the party mutinied, refusing to carry fifty-pound packs across the frozen wilderness for three dollars a day. The promise of a bonus persuaded some, but three turned back, while others stumbled up the valley and across the divide to the Yuba River, taking turns breaking trail and caching even more lifesaving provisions along the way. Whenever a dead pine thrust up through the drifts they paused to fire the trunk, so that the charred sentinel could guide their descent. With each step they plunged knee-deep into the wet snow, often making less than five miles a day, and the exhausted rescuers once more lightened their packs.

On Thursday, the 18th of February, after two weeks on the

trail, the men of the first relief stood facing the treacherous pass. It was a mile away and five hundred feet above them; the snow, the thin air, their frostbitten feet made the climb an agony, but by midday they stood looking down at frozen Truckee Lake, and by dusk they had made their way across its snow-covered surface. The provisions they carried were now scarcely more than would be required for their own return journey. On the morning after their arrival, the three strongest members of the rescue party—Moultry, Tucker and Rhoads—departed for Prosser Creek, taking with them a small ration of jerked beef and a few biscuits for anyone who remained alive at the Donner encampment.

The men had been told the distance was no more than six or seven miles west, following the bed of the creek, but the creek wandered erratically, sometimes pointing due south, at times bending north, and often obscured completely by the drifts. After what they estimated to be more than seven miles, there was still no sign of habitation, though the exhausted trio repeatedly searched the horizon for a slender flag of smoke, repeatedly cupped hands to mouths to bellow "Halloos." His companions felt the mission was hopeless, but, as leader of the rescue operation, Dan Tucker doggedly refused to give up, sent his companions fanning out to search for footprints, smoke, or signs of felled trees. When they were nearly out of sight, he raised his rifle, butted it against his hip, and fired a shot that rumbled and echoed from the frozen landscape with a force that would have launched a whole series of avalanches in the mountains he had just crossed. Again he squinted to survey the glaring stretches of snow, saw nothing, and had broken open his rifle to reload it when a distant movement spun him around. The small, dark form was nearly a quarter of a mile away, but he had a hunter's instincts, and weeks in the mountains had finely sharpened his distance vision, so that he saw clearly the frantic, scrabbling motions. Even so, he thought at first that the figure crawling on all fours from a hole in the snow might have been a startled animal flushed from its lair, and only when it slowly, unsteadily rose to an upright position did he realize it was a child. As he advanced across the brittle white crust, he recognized it as a young girl, probably no more than fifteen, and dressed in clothing far too large for her size. She crooked both arms across her face to shield her eyes from the sudden, intense light, and seemed at first not to see him approaching. Then the arms slid away and she cupped her hands, staring around her as though through a pair of opera glasses. When she pointed them toward him, began to stumble rapidly forward, he tried to spring ahead but the treacherous crust shattered, dropping him to his waist in a snowy wallow. In the same instant, and as though the pair of them were connected by some invisible mechanism, the girl sprawled flat, skidded a short distance across the icy film like a bundle of rags. Her clothing seemed to drag her down, but she thrust herself clumsily to her feet as he climbed from the hole, the rifle held horizontally over his head for balance while he furiously kicked footholds in the snow. As the gap between them closed, he caught for an instant the absurd impression that she had begun to unravel like a knitted doll. Her hands spilled lengths of cloth onto the snow, and she paused to fling something at her feet. Hearing the crust crack another warning beneath his heavy boots, Tucker slowed, but she was now near enough for him to see that she had been unwrapping flannel coverings wound over her hands to keep them warm. He was also near enough to make a hasty revision in his estimate of her age, guessing by her awkward motions, her large eyes, the slight figure weighted by borrowed clothing, that she could hardly be more than eleven or twelve. He tried again to move more rapidly, to spare the child the painful effort each step plainly cost her, but again plunged into a drift and was still clambering out when she reached him, extended a bare hand tinted a vivid blue by the cold, and said with a hint of reprimand in her soft voice, "I'm Mrs. George Donner. We've been expecting you."

Tucker had little time to recover from his surprise, for Rhoads and Moultry had rapidly closed the triangle, and there were brisk introductions to be made, expressions of amazement, a jumble of questions and partially heard answers.

When the others paused to catch their breaths, Tamsen repeated the name "Moultry" several times, then asked, "Now why does that sound so familiar?"

The young man reddened, stammered that maybe she knew some other folks with the same name.

She shook her head, then suddenly asked, "Did you come out last summer?"

"Yes'm," he mumbled, wondering how this strange, tiny woman could know such a thing, or guess it.

"Septimus!" she said emphatically, making it sound like an entire sentence, a declaration.

"What?" he replied automatically.

"It was at Septimus Moultry's wedding that my friends Mr. Bryant and Mr. Thornton danced the night away. Is that you?"

"Yes'm," he admitted.

"Extraordinary," she pronounced, then stepped back to survey the trio of rescuers. She had sensed almost at once in their shy good manners that they were not mountain men but emigrants, farmers like her husband, and she now read something of their recent ordeal in the grayish patches of frostbite sprinkling their noses and cheeks. Only one of them carried a pack, and its limp outline seemed to shrink as she measured it with her eyes.

"Is that all you've brought for us?" she asked, blunt but not accusing, merely businesslike, wishing to dispense first with any unpleasant details.

" 'Fraid so," Rhoads admitted.

"Had to cache most of the rest," Tucker explained. "Half the men give out and turned back. But we'll take out anybody as can keep up."

"I see," she said, nodded thoughtfully.

"How many are you?"

"Well," and she spun the names off on her fingers, then summed them up, "Nine in our shelter and nine in the other. Eighteen in all."

Rhoads whistled. "We hadn't expected . . ."

"That so many of us would survive?" she wondered.

"Well . . ."

"The Donners are a tough breed," she announced proudly, then added, "all except Jacob, but he'd been sick for weeks."

Before the men fully realized her intention, they were being ushered to the hole from which she had recently emerged. Later, Rhoads would remember her as nipping at their heels like a sheep dog, but in fact she led the way, practically flying across the fragile crust, while they plodded cautiously behind her. For all the haste, she then requested them to wait.

"It's a mite cramped," she explained. "Let me just send the children out first." They soon emerged in the company of a scrawny, dark-skinned boy with absurd walrus mustaches, filing silently and obediently past without ever removing their eyes from the strangers, heads pivoting so far that the little one at the end of the stair-step line seemed to be walking backward. Then Mrs. Donner appeared again, smiled an apology for the delay, and announced, "Captain Donner will see you now."

The men had to bend nearly double to pass through the low entryway, and could hardly stand upright in the tent, where she stepped aside and nodded them to her husband, propped and cushioned on a rack of saplings like an oriental sultan holding audience from his divan. Confused by the ceremony, their eyes still adjusting to the faint light, the three visitors bumped and jostled together, scarcely knowing what was expected of them. They were confused, too, by the stench in the air, from which they instinctively shied. The other smells that had assaulted them in the crowded dwellings at the lake, that had taken almost as much determination to suffer as the mountain crossing itself, were absent, but there was another here, as sweetly fetid and rank as the breath of an ancient coonhound. It was Tucker who made out through the gloom the heavy bandage wrapping George Donner's hand and extending up his arm all the way to his shoulder, a plumply bulging form propped beside him on the bed like a swaddled child, and vaguely remembered something about the captain's wound, the infection.

Swallowing hard he stepped forward and said, "Tucker. Pleased to meet you, sir." Reassured by his example, the other men also presented themselves.

"Moultry."

"Rhoads. At your service, Cap'n."

Tamsen Donner provided seats, a trunk and a pair of stout sections of log, that sank threateningly into the muddy floor when the men took their places. She carefully put away the slender bundles Rhoads lifted from this pack, then sat at the end of her husband's bed, but leaned back so that the shadows wrapped her, and only the bright shine of her eyes was visible from time to time.

Like his wife, George Donner began his conversation with the remark, "We've been expecting you," but it was said with a weariness far more accusing than her own mild hint of rebuke.

"Well, we got here quick as we could," Tucker told him, and his partners nodded confirmation.

"Mr. Reed tried gettin' through a long time ago, but couldn't make it. Too much snow."

"Jim Reed? Is Jim with you?"

"No, sir, he's puttin' his own team together, I reckon. It was Mr. Eddy got us goin'."

The voices of husband and wife sounded in unison, "Mr. Eddy?"

"I knew he'd make it," George Donner sighed. "If there was ever one man could make it, that man was named Bill Eddy. Is he at the lake?"

"No, he had to turn back at Mule Springs. Halfway up," Tucker clarified. "Near 'bout as weak as a baby, he was, after all he'd been through."

"But Eddy made it to California!"

"Sure did, Cap'n."

"And the others."

"What others? You mean the ones got out with him? Well, it wasn't many. How many was it, Rhoads?"

"Five or six, I reckon," but he was clearly not certain.

"Two men as I know of," Moultry volunteered. "Mr. Eddy and some other man. But Eddy's the only one we seen."

"Mr. Stanton?" The anxious question came from the shadows at the foot of George Donner's bed.

"No, somethin' like Forster."

"Foster," George Donner said. "Bill Foster."

"That must be it," Tucker nodded.

"Are you sure?" Tamsen insisted. "Mr. Stanton was supposed to show the others the trail. He'd already been to New Helvetia and back again."

"That's right, ma'am. We all knowed him. He come four—

five months ago with Big Bill. With Mr. McCutcheon," he corrected.

"Hailed from Chicago," Rhoads added. "Real city feller."

"Charles Stanton." Tamsen pronounced the name as if she expected its owner to reply. Then, as though sharing some cherished family secret with her visitors, she told them proudly, "The snowshoes were his idea."

"Yes, ma'am."

"He and Mr. Graves spent weeks cutting down the oxbows so they wouldn't be too heavy."

"Yes'm. But Stanton he just couldn't keep up. Snow-blind, he was."

Tucker glanced quickly at Moultry, but the young man failed to see the reprimand in his eyes. Confidently he sketched the details as they had circulated among the emigrants camped now at Sutter's Fort, waiting out the spring rains. "Them snowshoes was mighty hard to manage, and Mr. Stanton couldn't keep up. Even the womenfolks was faster. Then he started goin' blind and was comin' into camp later and later every night. One mornin' he decided he'd had 'bout enough. Wrapped hisself up all cozy by the fire and sat there puffin' away at his pipe. One of the women asked was he comin' and he said he'd be comin' along soon. 'Y'all go on now,' he told her. 'Y'all go on.' "

"It isn't right!" Tamsen's voice had raised in pitch with the effort to control the anger that she knew was pointless, irrational. Twice Stanton had ridden ahead to bring them aid, and twice he had risked his life to return to them, though neither property nor family tied him to the train. Again and again he had tried to lead groups over the pass, and on the first attempt he and one of the Indians had pushed all the way to the windy summit, then returned to find the others so exhausted and so irritated by the delay that they refused to make the climb in darkness. Instead, they had fired a dead pine, huddled in its warming light, and fallen asleep. When they awoke, the drifts of fresh snow around them were ten feet deep, and the trail Stanton had plowed inch by painful inch was no longer visible. Later, when he refused to sacrifice Sutter's precious mules, he had brought down the wrath of the whole camp on his head, but

369

if they had followed his lead on the first night, there would have been no camp at Truckee Lake. "It isn't right," Tamsen repeated, but softly now, as she remembered other deaths without rhyme or reason —the deaths of sturdy young men primed for life, hungry for the future.

"So Eddy and Foster got through," George Donner remarked, trying to divert his wife's attention from Stanton's death, but himself silently enumerating the other men who would have died on the trek. There was Uncle Billy Graves, five years younger than himself, and the Donners' former teamster Antonio who had signed on in Independence. Pat Dolan and Jay Fosdick and two of Mrs. Murphy's boys had also accompanied Eddy.

As though sensing the man's troubled thoughts, and in a clumsy effort to comfort the captain's wife, Dan Tucker told them, "All the womenfolks made it." But the fact clearly puzzled him, for he repeated it, half to himself: "All of 'em."

"Are you sure?" Tamsen asked.

"That's what Eddy allows. Just two of the men and all the womenfolks."

"How long did they need? How long did it take them to get across?"

"Nearly 'bout five weeks," Moultry answered.

"Five whole weeks? But Stanton said they could make it in six or eight days, and he'd already been over the trail. So had Sutter's Indians."

"Didn't no Indians come back," Rhoads said. He hesitated, glancing at his companions, before he went on. "They was found by some of the local Indians, but weren't none come with 'em." The rescuers all knew why Luis and Salvador had not returned, for Eddy's guileless devotion to the truth compelled him to report the facts to Sutter, though his host repeatedly assured him such details were of no consequence. The Forlorn Hope had been too famished to wait for the tardy mechanisms of natural death to do the work for them, and when Luis and Salvador fell into the shallow-breathed stupor preceding death by starvation, a single bullet through the head provided fresh meat for the survivors. Eddy regarded the Indians as Sutter's personal property, and reported as candidly on their deaths as on the loss of the mules, omitting only the fact that it was Bill Foster who squeezed the trigger.

"I still don't see how it could have taken five weeks," George Donner objected, though westward from Fort Bridger time had stretched like an elastic band, and everything always took so much longer than the experts claimed.

"Well, they had a bad storm, got snowed up all over Christmas," Tucker volunteered. "Eddy said it took 'em more than a month."

"What did they eat?"

Tucker scuffed a toe into the muddy floor, then decided to suppress the answer in deference to Captain Donner's wife. It wasn't right for women to hear such talk. "At the end, Eddy killed him a deer," he explained, and the others accepted his evasion.

"So how long you think it'll be before Jim Reed gets here with supplies?"

"Can't rightly say, Captain. We was expectin' him to come along this trip, but he'd gone down to San Jose to try and organize some volunteers, and maybe the war caught him."

"What war?"

"The California war," Tucker said, surprised the news hadn't somehow penetrated the mountains. It seemed about all anybody could talk about these days. "War for independence," he added expansively, "and things has been hottin' up all 'round San Jose. But it goes right the way up and down the country." The theme clearly appealed to him.

"You don't mean to tell me Jim Reed's off playing soldier while his wife and children are near about starving?" George Donner remembered his friend's vigorous accounts of the Black Hawk War, the way he described it as the "finest chapter" in his life. "What a darned fool thing to be doing," he added.

Chastised, Tucker muttered, "Well, I guess he's not doin' much soldierin', but I think he got hisself a commission."

"How long has Mr. Reed been gone?" Tamsen asked.

"Well, he went south in December, and ain't been heard from since. Captain Sutter sent word out, but didn't get no answer back. Still, things has sure been hottin' up 'round San Jose."

"But you said he'd be coming in with his own expedition," Tamsen reminded him.

"I reckon he will, ma'am. He sure was all fired up."

Tamsen recalled the hours Jean Baptiste had spent aloft, scaling the tallest pine in the area to search the horizon for the first glimpse of Reed and McCutcheon. In the mind's eye they had all witnessed the arrival, the string of pack mules laden with supplies, the saddle horses dancing nervously across the snow, had rehearsed greetings and questions and complaints, had imagined the aromas of baking bread and thick, meaty stew billowing through the shelter. But Jim Reed was not riding toward them, he was cantering off with a spit-polish gloss on his oxblood boots, waving a saber overhead and chanting patriotic slogans and harvesting fresh medals for his lapels. He was not riding toward them but away from them, to the end of the continent, while their shrinking world disappeared beneath the snow. Only anger held their despair in check, and only despair blunted the anger both husband and wife felt at the news of this ultimate, mortal defection, this cowardly and vainglorious betrayal. If Reed had no regard for the ties of friendship, felt no duty to those who had embarked on this journey with him in a spirit of partnership, of mutual assistance and encouragement, surely he would be stirred by thoughts of a wife and children slowly starving to death in the mountains. But even if she had felt capable of controlling her rage while speaking of such things, Tamsen would not have broached them to Tucker and Rhoads and Moultry, to three strangers who had risked so much to come to their aid. Reed was suddenly as distant as the war itself, as distant as the ample barns on Sugar Creek; they were all distant, lost, banished, and she focused her remaining strength on the living. Mrs. Reed and her children numbered among them. This much Tucker could tell them—that they were alive and well, though they had no supplies remaining and must beg their daily rations of slop. They had no choice, then, but to try to escape with the men of the relief expedition.

"And Milt Elliott? Will he go, too?"

The name Tamsen spoke seemed to have no meaning to the trio of visitors, even when she repeated it. "Mrs. Reed's hired man, the teamster, Milt Elliott," she clarified.

"Him? He's dead," Moultry said.

"Milt is dead? Milt Elliott?"

"Well, I don't quite recollect his name, ma'am, but Mrs. Reed said she and her oldest girl had to bury their teamster all by theirselves. Froze his feet off cuttin' wood, then up and died."

"Milt," Tamsen whispered, but when she tried to summon an image of his face, she saw only the shaggy, tangled curls sweeping over Mrs. Wolfinger's outstretched hand.

"Any other folks died at the lake?" George asked, then added the explanation, "We haven't had any news in about a month now."

"Some of the littl'uns. Some of the babies," Tucker said, but did not know which, whose.

"None of the grown-ups?"

"Well. . . ," and Tucker seemed to hold back, his friendly, open face suddenly troubled and grieved, though he had neither friends nor relatives at the lake, could surely be touched by no death that might have occurred there before he arrived. But he had known William Eddy, had marveled at the man's lionlike determination, knew what he had survived and only survived with the most awful means in the struggle to bring help to his family, to the wife and children he talked about incessantly from sunup to sundown. And so he hesitated before he pronounced the words, then pronounced them softly, somberly: "Mrs. Eddy."

Tamsen suppressed a startled sob, suppressed as well the urge to ask about the children. Consciously she pushed the topic away, asking instead, "Did you meet a man named Denton? John Denton? He was Milt Elliott's best friend. An Englishman."

Relieved that the catalogue of death had ceased, Tucker said expansively, "Sure, there's an Englishman talks almost as funny as a Mex. He's one of the ones goin' with us."

Both husband and wife seemed to take heart from the news, to rouse a little from the gloom that had settled on them both, almost as tangible as the coarse ash from the fire, when they learned the reason for Reed's prolonged absence. They asked other questions then, described families and their relationships, but the three rescuers had only an oblique impression of the people they had seen, the wild-eyed ghosts, the walking skeletons that crept trembling from stinking dungeons, begging for food, and much of what they had witnessed they were already busy trying to forget. They could only say definitively that the healthiest and noisiest of the lot were a family called Breen, who had a proper cabin with a proper roof, a little meat still as well as a store of hides, and that they preferred to remain rather than risking the dangers of the trail. Otherwise, all the men at the other camp would probably be leaving with them, except for a German who was laid up with a lame foot.

It brought them, then, to the question of who would go from the Donner encampment and who would remain behind. Tamsen instantly named the five children, but Tucker shook his head, told her sadly that they could take only those big enough to walk for themselves. They would have to be big enough and strong enough to make it through the snow unassisted, and that automatically eliminated Frances, Georgia, and Eliza. It was also clear to them all, but carefully unspoken, that George Donner was no more fit for such a strenuous journey than his three-year-old daughter.

"Captain Donner and I will discuss it while you call on Betsy," Tamsen told them, "and I'll cook us all a little broth."

When the three men of the relief party departed that afternoon, they were accompanied by Mrs. Wolfinger, Elitha and Leanna Donner, Noah James, and two of Betsy's sons—William Hook and George Donner's nine-year-old namesake.

"Remember," Tamsen said to Elitha, "that you're a woman now." She tightened the bow holding the hood of the girl's cloak, then lightly touched a hand to her cheek. "You have your mother's earrings?"

Elitha nodded, fought back her tears, afraid they would childishly overflow if she attempted to speak, as they had done when she tried to say farewell to her father.

"You must take good care of Leanna. She's still just a girl, and she's not so strong as you." With those words Tamsen gently twisted her shoulders, turned Elitha around, and gave her a slight push. "Don't look back," she whispered.

Elitha joined the end of the column that snaked away from the camp with Rhoads and Moultry in the lead. Jean Baptiste had climbed the woodpile and watched their departure, sulking still over the men's repeated refusal to let him accompany them, their insistence that he remain to cut wood for the women, the eight children, and the crippled man who must remain at Prosser Creek.

Tucker lingered behind, clumsily seeking words to excuse the meager relief they had brought, but found none. Finally he said with a hearty confidence that rang false to both of them, "Well, I expect Mr. Reed'll be along 'most any day now."

"Yes, I guess so."

"Sorry we couldn't leave more rations," he blurted.

"We've got a piece of hide left, and we aren't so many now."

With genuine but guileless concern he wondered aloud, "And what'll you do when it runs out?"

"We're looking for some of the cattle buried in the storm," Tamsen answered. "Jean Baptiste has a prod with nails fastened to the end, and he pushes it into the snow in hopes of hooking something."

They both knew she had not answered his question, and he had no wish to press it. Besides, no one could guess where the cattle might have wandered in the panic of the first blizzard, and in places the snow had piled to a depth of more than thirty feet. The man and the woman understood that the search was hopeless, and the burden of that recognition weighted the icy air they breathed.

Then, with a little shake of the head, Tamsen seemed to say that the frozen peaks sealing the horizon left no room for evasion. "We shall have to begin on those who have died," she said, without pity or desperation or apology, but as calmly and casually as she might have noted the supply of firewood was growing low.

"We shall have to begin on those who have died," she repeated, as though her reply had perhaps escaped him, and with that she offered her hand in farewell. She might have been thanking him for the pleasure of a quadrille.

40

Prosser Creek

Friday, February 19th, 1847

The long-awaited relief has come at last! Seven men arrived at the lake yesterday, and three of them pressed on to our lonely encampment this morning. The names of our heroic visitors were Dan Tucker, Septimus Moultry, and Mr. Rhoads, whose Christian name we neglected to inquire. All had suffered greatly from exposure to mountain storms, but were still full of great-hearted resolution to guide to safety any who had the strength to accompany them. Elitha and Leanna have bravely joined the expedition, together with Noah James and Mrs. Wolfinger, who at the end seemed sustained by the faith that she was going to a rendevouz with her husband. We pray this is not so. Betsy's sons William Hook and sturdy little George have also gone along, and Jean Baptiste could only be restrained by the fiercest argument to remain behind. Mrs. Reed will go with all her children, and Mr. Denton, too. The loyal Milt Elliott, like Mrs. Eddy, could not wait for them, as both had already embarked on the dark journey into death.

The men brought us news from the lake and from the distant settlements. There is war in California, with numerous communities having risen up against Mexican rule, and Mr. Reed seems to have got himself involved in it while attempting to make arrangements for our relief. It is said he made the first effort months ago, but the weather compelled him to turn back.

Many of those who departed on snowshoes in December (including Mr. Stanton) perished of hunger and cold before reaching the promised haven. Of the 10 men who departed, only two are reported to have reached California alive, those being Mr.

Eddy and Mr. Foster. All the women, however, lived to complete the crossing, though there was disagreement at first about their leaving, for females were said to stand little chance of surviving the rigors that awaited them. Their greater endurance could have its source in the available food being divided equally among all members of the party, rather than being apportioned according to size and weight, and the men may have been obliged to do the heavier labor of breaking trail. Our experiences, however, have also frequently revealed a surprising stamina in the female constitution, once the time for mollycoddling is past. Most of the women who escaped with Mr. Eddy left behind small children, and maternal determination may also have inspired their efforts, whereas all but three of the men were bachelors.

Certainly we should be glad to know by what miracle the survivors sustained life during five weeks of fierce mountain storms, for they had taken with them dried meat sufficient to last but a few days. Those of us who remain behind have spoiled ourselves on broth and biscuit, which can last no more than a day, and our unaccustomed feast has meanwhile made a pot of boiled hides seem horribly repulsive to the eye, the nose and the stomach. Even of that, there is but little remaining, and we shall be obliged to choke it down somehow. When that, too, is exhausted, we must have the courage of other remedies. To do less would be equivalent to cancelling and annulling all our painful struggles to this date.

41

February 20th, 1847
This morning Betsy Donner paid us a rare visit, so wildly distracted and grieved we could at first make no sense whatever of her ramblings. She was also suffering from extreme frostbite but seemed unaware of her bodily distress, and came so near the fire she might

easily have lost a score of fingers and toes. Frances and I chafed her with snow and wrapped her afflicted hands and feet in warm flannel, by which time she had succeeded in communicating to us the source of her panic—namely, the disappearance of her eldest son, Solomon Hook. He was determined to accompany the relief expedition on their return journey, unable to comprehend that his younger brother should be elected to that company while he was declared unfit. But he has never been a strong child either in body or in wits, and long confinement had severely depleted both. It is feared that he slipped away in the night to follow his brother, and Betsy had searched for him since dawn, but herself became lost in the snow. To relieve her a little, I am caring for Sammie Donner, and Jean Baptiste has been sent out to hunt for the missing boy.

42

THE WASTED, HALF-STARVED OXEN THEY HAD BUTCHERED TAUGHT her that the vital organs suffered the least shrinkage, and the nourishment they contained was more concentrated than that of the stringy flesh. Left to himself, Jean Baptiste would have hacked off whatever part of the body appeared first through the snow he shoveled away, had she not remained to direct and assist him. Still pouting from Tucker's angry insistence that he remain behind, Jean Baptiste seemed distracted from the task he was now required to perform, not even registering the identity of the stiffened corpse from which he struggled to peel the frozen clothing, and the torn shirt soon covered the face of Samuel Shoemaker. It was easy enough to make the single incision from the breastbone downward, but opening the cavity was the work of four hands, and as she grappled with the unyielding carcass, Tamsen was grateful for the absence of blood, the anonymity of the snow, the invisible face, even for the moody silence of her collaborator.

Neither George nor the children asked how she had provided their evening meal, though even Eliza would have known there was but a single source remaining to them. Only Frances had overheard her mother's remarks to Tucker the day before, and it was Frances who wordlessly moved to the hearth, knelt there to watch the coals raked together, a fresh log angled across them, and began to fan the fire with her apron. With a brisk but unhurried rhythm she fanned until the coals glowed like lumps of molten gold, while Tamsen slowly revolved the liver she had skewered on a stripped pine branch. As the rich juices bubbled out and splattered, hissing, in the fire, mother and daughter were joined in wordless conspiracy before this bounty, like devout priestesses before a sacrificial altar. With their withered, clawlike hands, their immense, glittering eyes, their straggling hair, they seemed in that moment ancient, as if they had witnessed the beginnings of the earth and would witness its end, rocking back on their haunches in attitudes of timeless patience before the spluttering fire. The sweet smell of roasting meat dizzied them, filled the improvised shelter with its rare incense, while Frances encouraged the flames and her mother slowly revolved the scorched pine branch above them, their rhythms perfectly matched, forever entwined.

43

February 21st, 1847

Solomon Hook has been found, less than a mile from camp and walking in a circle. Thinly dressed, he had been exposed to the bitter weather for two days and nights, and the glare of the sun had almost totally blinded him. Jean Baptiste at first overlooked him, for the poor boy had trudged so long around the circle that he had carved a deep trench in the snow, and only the top of his bare head was visible. He has lost the power of speech, and communicates his simple needs with the gurgling noises of an infant. Betsy is nearly prostrate with the shock, but she and the two children are a little strengthened by the portions of stew I took them this evening.

44

NOW THAT THEIR EXTREME PLIGHT WAS KNOWN TO THE OUTSIDE world, the Donners felt confident that more substantial relief would soon be on its way. Captain Sutter had estimated the stranded families would have ample beef on the hoof to last them until March or April, but he had reckoned by Reed's statistics, which hadn't included the last heavy losses to Digger arrows, or the cattle that now lay deeply buried beneath the drifts. Eddy had corrected those errors, and if Sutter suspected the young father of exaggerating the distress of his wife and children, there were now others on their way who could bear more recent, more awful witness to their sufferings. The partial thaw that began in late February, slowly exposing the tangled brush skeletons of the shelters, offered further encouragement to the idea of speedy rescue. But there was no euphoria in either of the mountain camps, none of the hearty optimism with which Eddy's mission had once been discussed, for whenever the next relief appeared, it would be too late for Jacob Donner and Milt Elliott and Margaret Eddy. It would perhaps be too late for George Donner as well, and a whole herd of mules laden with flour and salt and beef and sugar and saleratus would not restore the grotesquely mangled corpses in their dooryard, or erase from memory the bright pink stains oozing into the snow as the thaw advanced.

Each day was devoted to the necessary, repetitious chores that sustained their lives. Because they were so plainly necessary, even Jean Baptiste did his share without grumbling. Because they were repetitious, even the worst of them soon lost their horror. Though they expected relief any day now, any hour, Tamsen was as scrimping and exacting and miserly in distributing their rations as though the supply of available meat must suffice for weeks. No ounce of nourishment was wasted: brains, hearts, lungs, intestines were even more strictly rationed than the rest, for they seemed more strengthening, and bones were boiled for soup, then either boiled again until they crumbled like chalk or crisped in the coals. An instinctive Yankee frugality had revived in Tamsen, complicated by the rigid distinction she silently drew between the honorable necessity of consuming the flesh that misfortune had provided them in their misfortune, and the disgrace of feasting and fattening from it.

Though they believed they had not long to wait for rescue, their estimates of time and of distance had so often been distorted, as if flung mockingly back at them from the bright convexities of a witch's ball, that they lived as though it would never come. They neither spoke of it nor tormentingly pictured it as they once had done, and Jean Baptiste no longer scaled the sentinel pine to squint for hours into the west, so that when the two strangers suddenly arrived on the morning of March 1st, the Donners' amazement was even greater than their elation.

Charles Cady and Nicholas Clark were an advance delegation from James Reed's own expedition, made up of seasoned, celebrated mountain men, French Indians and trappers and adventurers, some of whom had been recruited in Yerba Buena, where Reed's impassioned appeal for assistance had been answered by generous contributions of money, horses, and supplies. Unlike the men of the first relief, emigrant farmers themselves, including some who had recently traveled as part of the sprawling, amorphous overland caravan the Donners had accompanied, the majority of Reed's recruits felt no moral or sentimental ties to the stranded families. The recent war had disrupted trade, closed ports, and a drifter with no taste for soldiering could do worse than accept Reed's offer of three dollars a day for a hike in the mountains. Hiram Miller and Bill McCutcheon saw it all differently, of course, and so did old Caleb Greenwood, who claimed to be the first white man ever to lay eyes on Truckee Lake, but none of those rescuers advanced as far as Prosser Creek. That was the work of Clark and Cady, and the speed with which they moved suggests that tales of the Donners' fabulous riches had worked their charms. Certainly the Breens, as rank with peasant stinginess as with filth, the loudly contentious Keseberg, blind old Mrs. Murphy with the dying infants in her charge, would have had little allure to ambitious men with a chronic allergy to working for wages. Clark was a former sailor who had jumped ship to try his luck as a hunter, and who fell in easily with the carefree, daredevil Cady and Stone, partners who were always on a fresh scent of easy money. Reed called them collectively "the boys," envied them their prankish excess of energy, and was not surprised by the announcement that they could do without sleep, would even travel by moonlight, and intended to reach the lake camp ahead of the rest. They reached it, they made their rapid, unpromising tour of inspection, distributing a few stale biscuits to the survivors, and Cady and Clark at once set out for Prosser Creek, leaving Charles Stone behind at the lake cabins to wait for Reed and the rest to come up later in the day.

JAMES REED WAS AT FIRST PUZZLED BY THE RETICENCE, THE COOL formality, with which George and Tamsen Donner received him. Part of this he attributed to the terrible suffering the entire family had endured, part to the certain knowledge that George was dying —rotting away each and every day, and by slow, stinking, agonizing inches, as the poison which had etched his arm flowed into his body. He was too weak even to maintain the sitting position into which Tamsen had wedged him, and his speech was drunkenly slurred. Perhaps, Reed thought, the veiled distance into which both seemed to retreat was a screen thrown up to obscure their feelings of guilt, for he had seen ample evidence of the extremes to which starvation had driven them, but at least he had been braced for them, could control his revulsion. At the lake camp the scene had been far worse, the weakened butchers less skillful, the standards of housekeeping infinitely more primitive than here, but the thick curls of Milt Elliott's hair, frozen beneath a cap of ice, were still recognizable, though the skull had been sawed open. Cady and Clark had also told Reed that their arrival had surprised the Donners' handyman, the little New Mexican, at his work, startled him into flinging a severed

leg back into an open grave, where it rested now beside what remained of Jacob Donner. He felt a mortal revulsion, a baffled dis-
gust, and a vast relief that his wife and children had been spared this
horrible choice. Yet if it had been their only alternative, as it very
nearly was, he would have wanted them to seize it without hesitation
or guilt. Halfway up the mountains he had met Margaret, Virginia,
and Jimmy all stumbling like skeletons, like ghosts of the loved ones
he remembered, and they brought the awful news that Patty and
Tommy had not been able to keep up, had been sent back to the
camp of death. Days later, when he saw the crudely hacked and
mutilated body of Milt Elliott, dragged partly into the entrance to
the shelter housing Keseberg and Mrs. Murphy, he had vomited
until he feared he would cause himself some deep, internal damage,
but when he recovered he knew with certainty that Milt would freely
have given his body to sustain the children, to sustain Margaret
Reed, that not to take advantage of that means of survival would
have been a sinful waste. Even worse, it would have been suicide.

As though by a miracle, his wife and children had been spared
that fearful extreme, but he could measure its horrors in the figure
of Mrs. Murphy. There was no trace of the hearty, resolute widow
he had known on the trail, with her booming voice and bullying
devotion to her family. In her place was a withered hag whose hair
and clothing swarmed with vermin, and who had wandered so far
into the haunted grove of her mind that when Reed attempted to
question her, she first whined like a wounded dog, then tittered
girlishly and exposed her breasts. She had remained behind to nurture three children of her own and three grandchildren, while her
married daughters struggled to safety with the snowshoe party;
Amanda McCutcheon had also left her daughter in the old woman's
care, and when Margaret Eddy died, her two children found a home
in the dark, stinking cave deep beneath the snow. Four of her
charges were infants, and Lavina Murphy tended them as best she
could, dribbling into their mouths a thin gruel made of hoarded flour
and melted snow, while she watched them shrink to pale skeletons
with skulls grotesquely large for their bodies—too listless to cry out,
and in the end too weak to open their eyes.

In the Breen cabin, where he had found Patty and Tommy alive but too feeble to walk unassisted, some effort had been made to do battle with vermin and filth. Conditions were unimaginably worse in the hovel shared by Keseberg, Mrs. Murphy, and the three surviving children. The clumsily butchered corpse of Milt Elliott had given Reed his first clue, but even that had not prepared him for the unspeakable things within. Before they began the cleanup, he and McCutcheon stripped themselves and laid their clothes on the snow to avoid contagion. While Keseberg huddled in the corner, a blanket drawn over his head, and Mrs. Murphy stammered fragments of nursery rhymes, the rescuers built up the fire, heated water, and gently bathed the children, then oiled their bodies and wrapped them tightly in warmed blankets. When her turn came, Mrs. Murphy gave no more resistance than the infants, but Keseberg raged that he would not be touched. Perhaps he remembered the wagon tongue once raised for Reed's hanging, for his arms and legs churned as though they did battle with the angel of death. When McCutcheon pinned him roughly to the bed, the German whined that someone else, anyone but Reed, should do the job, but his protests were ignored. As McCutcheon moved about the hovel with a handkerchief tied across his face to filter the stench, he knew the bones of his daughter were among those littering the floor and tumbled in a heap beside the fire—most of them broken open, the marrow plucked out with twigs.

After what he had seen at the lake camp, Reed could not judge or blame the Donners. Tamsen's children were clean, healthy, warmly dressed, and her skillful hand had given the damp shelter a snug, homelike atmosphere. The fire burning so brightly on the hearth revealed no evidence of the horrors he had encountered on the previous day, and though he knew how his friends had survived, he could not condemn the extremes to which starvation had forced them. Admiring the dignity with which they accepted those consequences, he was even more wounded by the chilly note of accusation that slowly emerged from their elaborate but artificial show of good manners. They believed he had malingered, forgotten them all, been reaping glory while they gathered the slow, bitter harvest of death. He described then, in details he wished to forget, the agonizing struggle he and McCutcheon had made months before, when they had climbed as high as Bear Valley with twenty-one horses, many of them stampeded in the night by the Indian set to guard them. Those that remained sank leadenly through the surface of the snow with each laborious step they took, often disappearing up to their noses. The pack animals were the worst, had to be dug out every few yards, and what with plunging, digging, floundering through the deepening snow, they were making less than a mile a day, even with the day stretched to sixteen hours, when they turned back. Sutter had said a thaw still might come, that it was unusually early for such a storm, that if a thaw didn't come, if the snow got deeper and the train was really stranded somewhere in the high country, they could slaughter their cows and working cattle and hold out until March or even April. And when no thaw came, when the early winter clamped down as rigidly as the teeth of a steel trap, Reed and McCutcheon had set off to raise the alarm in San Jose, Yerba Buena, and Sonoma. The war had stripped the Sacramento Valley of almost every able-bodied man who might have helped mount a more extensive relief expedition, and Reed rode off on their trail. He had risked Mexican bullets and the flooded Sacramento and he was prepared now to carry his children to safety. George and Tamsen Donner questioned him only about his family, and they did so with genuine, affectionate concern, but James Reed told them as well an abbreviated version of his own trials since the day he had ridden away from them into banishment, himself nearly starving on the trail, and he told them not merely because his exaggerated aristocratic pride had been injured by their suspicions, but because he wished to lift the bitterness that added to the intolerable burdens his friends already had to bear. Slowly, patiently, persistently, he unfolded his own story, elaborating some episodes with more detail than he would later recall to his own wife and children, answering the questions they were too hurt to ask, seeking to reassure them of the constancy of his friendship. That much, at least, he could leave with them, in partial recompense for the fact that he brought so little in terms of literal, actual, immediate relief. They had heard the story before: pack animals were useless in the snow, while a man on foot could scarcely carry more than he needed for his own survival, and sometimes far less.

SHE HAD LEFT THE MEN TOGETHER AND JOINED THE CHILDREN, WHO watched Cady and Clark relocate Betsy Donner's tent, then shovel soft snow into the dark pit where it had once stood, littered with bones and bits of hair, charred logs, soured clothing, and human offal. Hugging the limp form of her youngest child, Betsy also watched the men's briskly efficient motions, but disinterestedly, as though a neighbor she scarcely knew, some itinerant stranger, were moving house again.

When James Reed finally emerged from saying his farewells to George Donner, he wordlessly guided Tamsen away from the others, walked a short distance with her along the frozen creek. "George says I am to persuade you to come with me," Reed told her.

"And leave him here alone?"

"He wouldn't be alone, Tamsen. Jean Baptiste is here. Cady and Clark are also going to stay and wait for the next relief. They'll do some hunting."

She shook her head emphatically.

"George warned me you'd be mule-stubborn," Reed said, trying to make it seem a joke, but she refused to acknowledge the gesture.

"No, Jim, I won't leave him. I can't. But please take the girls with you."

"Never. Not without you. I couldn't take the risk."

"Please," she insisted, with a rising catch in her voice.

"I've told you both we've already got too many children." He had also told them both that the first relief had been far too ambitious, that the lot nearly died because there were too many invalids, too many children, not enough snowshoes or supplies, and one bad storm would have finished them off. Counting his own son and daughter, both too small and weak to walk unassisted, there were already thirteen children to be shepherded across the mountains.

"But you're taking Betsy's children," she began, and instantly regretted the note of complaint in her voice. Yes, he was taking the demented Solomon Hook, as well as Isaac and Mary, but the little ones were so near death they might as well risk whatever dangers the trail had for them. Betsy could no longer tend to their needs, and Tamsen had already taken on an extra child.

"If you come along to help with the children, it might be possible. The Breens will have to take care of their own, and Mrs. Graves has to look after four. But she can't carry all four, Tamsen. The woman can hardly move herself."

"But it seems so unfair," she protested.

"Then come with us. I don't make you any promises, but I'll do all I can to help you. You know that. But I am not prepared to take responsibility for the girls . . . ," and here he paused, looked away from her pleading eyes before he added, "not after everything you've been through to keep them alive."

"But they're strong enough, Jim. They're skinny as rails but they're healthy. They're strong and they're healthy," she repeated, almost defiantly.

"Yes," he agreed, "they're the healthiest of the bunch, and the others would get all the attention, and your children would get almost none."

"But . . ."

And then he told her, interrupted her faint but persistent protest with the simple statement, "Mrs. Keseberg's daughter froze to death on the way out. Her mother carried her every step of the way, and the child froze in her arms. Several of the others will lose fingers and toes."

"I see," she pronounced softly, but he heard still the doubt in her voice, the refusal to accept the fact that other children should be spirited to safety while hers were left behind. It was for this moment that she had waited, that she had kept the children strong, walked for miles with them in the snow, insisted they leave their beds to play out of doors whenever the weather moderated.

Then James Reed reported what he had spared Betsy Donner —that her son had so gorged himself on supplies cached at Bear Valley that his stomach had bloated to the size of a watermelon, and he had died from his feast. If they weren't killed by hunger, they were killed by plenty, and if hunger and plenty spared them, they froze to death and were left behind, and not just the children but grown men like Denton, whose head, protruding from the snow, had provided a signpost just when they were convinced they had lost the trail. Even with someone to care for them, it was risky for children; without someone, it was sheer madness, and he would have his hands full with his own son and daughter. "Those are the facts," he said. "I'm sorry, but being sorry doesn't change them."

She had heard little of what he had said, other than his brief description of the death of Betsy's son. "The poor, dear boy," she whispered, and knew now that it would be wrong to send the girls off unprotected, especially while there was enough here to nourish them. It would be unfair to James Reed, and it would be far too dangerous for the children. Here they would all be safe together. She could keep them warm and dry, and with the supplies left by the second relief, paltry as they were, she could vary their diet a little from time to time.

James Reed sensed that he had won his point—not the one George wished him to make, for that was clearly hopeless, but the case urged by his own conscience. Now he reassured her again that Bill Eddy would soon be on his way, that a relief station was established and well stocked in Bear Valley, that the next rescuers would have an easier time of it, with a well-worn trail to guide them and with fewer people to bring out. "They may manage to get in with mules next time," he suggested, "and then they could even get George down."

"George is dying," she said, with a matter-of-factness that embarrassed him.

"Perhaps, but—"

"It pains him horribly even to turn his head now, and he faints whenever I try to change the dressing on his arm. He could never endure the jolting of a mule. The girls and I will . . . watch with him."

"He really does want you to go," Reed emphasized.

"Of course he does. It would ease his conscience," she answered, and again with a bluntness that made him feel awkward. Where others had sometimes described her as too "bristling" for their taste, James Reed had always been charmed by Tamsen's outspokenness, but now there was a hint of bitterness he did not recognize, though he knew it was a measure of her recent suffering, of the awful decisions she had been compelled to make for all of them. He had read their consequences in the hands she laid so lightly on his arm to stress her plea that the children be carried to safety beyond the mountains. The hands, like her face, were not so much wasted as distilled, refined, stripped of all excess. Hunger had not revealed the weakness of the flesh but the unyielding toughness of muscle, sinew and bone, exposing them like the intricate armature at the core of a clay sculpture. Her feelings, too, seemed laid bare by her ordeal, and his habitual gallantry worked no charms on them.

As though sensing his thoughts, Tamsen said, "I didn't intend any disrespect to Mr. Donner. He blames himself, though, for getting us so far behind schedule," she explained, "and even worse, he blames himself for getting us all into this in the first place."

"It was more my idea than his," Reed reminded her.

"I know. But it was also mine. I opposed it in the beginning, but in the end it sounded like a fine thing. We were putting winter and chills and fevers behind us forever, and there would be so many fine, brave, interesting things to do in a new country. Especially for the girls . . ."

When she faltered, James Reed could think of nothing to say but "It's almost over." He meant that their horrible ordeal was almost at an end, but Tamsen thought he was referring to her husband's dying.

"It could take weeks," she said. "He's the opposite of Jacob. George is a fighter!" she announced emphatically, and she was clearly proud of the fact, though his fight now brought him constant, unrelieved pain.

"So are you."

A hand impatiently waved away the compliment. "Just mule-stubborn," she responded, and this time managed a smile at the description. Then, suddenly weary with the topic, she said, "We're obliged to you for the supplies."

"It's not much."

"No, it isn't, but it will help."

"Cady and Clark ought to find game now."

She nodded. "We've seen bear tracks," she said. "Two sets— a mother and her cub, maybe."

"Splendid! There's nothing better than bear meat to build your strength. That's what Eddy got through on. You'll have to show Clark."

"Wouldn't he be enough? We've got Jean Baptiste, as well. Two extra men to feed is a lot."

"You won't have to worry. They've got their own rations—enough for at least a week, and by then Eddy ought to be here. And Clark will bring in game. He's the hunter. Cady can help you out around the camp, and Jean Baptiste can stay with Betsy. We're leaving another man at the lake to cut wood for Keseberg and Mrs. Murphy. He's a crony of these two. They're all young and tough, and they're prepared to stay behind to help out."

They had, indeed, seemed surprisingly eager to remain, and had he not been so relieved to be able to give his friends this solace and support, he might have wondered at the trio's cheerful acquiescence. Instead, James Reed left Prosser Creek not only with a lightened pack but with a lightened conscience, having provided generous protection for his friends, and never imagining that his decision was the equivalent of setting a pair of foxes to guard a henhouse.

45

March 2nd, 1847

We have just taken leave of a Springfield visitor, Mr. James Reed. Two men from the relief expedition he organized reached us at noon yesterday, and Mr. Reed himself arrived this morning—a veritable "sight for sore eyes" to all of us. He and Mr. McCutcheon had made a valiant effort to reach us at the end of October, and were deterred by the same early storm which stranded us here. Despite Captain Sutter's generosity, their subsequent efforts to organize relief were hindered by the current war for independence which has swept like an epidemic through California, making it difficult to recruit volunteers for such an expedition. The undue severity of the winter has also been an obstacle.

Of all the news Mr. Reed brought us of people and events beyond our frozen valley, none was more welcome or more wonderful than his report that our beloved daughters Leanna and Elitha Donner had reached safety, being but a short distance from a temporary camp established just below the snow line when he encountered them. Both were cruelly fatigued and famished, but had shown courage and independence of spirit during their ordeal, and Elitha had supported her weaker sister much of the way.

Also among those who had accompanied the second relief, Mr. Reed was amazed to see his stepdaughter Virginia staggering toward him across the snow, dazed and nearly frozen after six terrible days of journeying from the lake camp. The poor child was so exhausted and so overwhelmed by the reunion that she could speak not a single word, but when Mr. Reed persisted in asking to know where her mother was, Virginia pointed back along the trail, and there Mr. Reed found the wife he had so reluctantly left behind nearly five months before. On hearing his name spoken she had collapsed in the snow, and near her was their son Jimmy, who scarcely recognized his own father. Mr. Reed's overwhelming joy at this reunion was clouded by the news that Patty and Tommy had been unable to keep up with the others and were carried back to the lake to live or die on the charity of the Breens. Mr. Reed at once doubled his efforts, and mercifully found both children alive, though too weak even to stand without assistance. Mr. McCutcheon was less fortunate, as the golden-haired daughter who used to ride with such glee on his broad shoulder had been dead for more than a month.

Conditions at the lake camp are even more extreme than our own, and most of those remaining there (the populous Breens, as well as Mrs. Graves and her children) will accompany Mr. Reed when he departs tomorrow. Betsy's children Mary and Isaac, as well as Solomon Hook, will also be part of this group. Mrs. Murphy is unfit for travel, and still has the poor infants to tend, while Mr. Keseberg complains his foot is still much too tender for such an undertaking. Mr. Reed suspects he is fit enough but too lazy to make the effort. The girls and I will remain for the time with Mr. Donner. Nicholas Clark and Charles Cady, hardy and energetic young men who had accompanied Mr. Reed, will stay as well, hoping to offer us what service they can. Mr. Clark advertises himself as a skillful hunter, and we hope soon to see the proof.

We are assured that another relief, including Mr. Eddy and Mr. Foster, should reach us within the coming weeks. This fresh force is captained by a Mr. Woodworth, whose father was responsible for "The Old Oaken Bucket," which often rang from our prairie campfires. It will undoubtedly prove to our benefit if the son's mountaineering is superior to his father's melodies.

The recent thaw continues, and does much to improve the children's spirits. As they can spend part of the day in the open air, Captain Donner rests more easily, and he is relieved to spare them even a little the sight of his terrible agony. The fever and pain never quit him and will remain, I fear, until he takes leave of them, and of us.

46

THE DAY REED AND HIS MEN GOADED AND DRAGGED AND CARRIED THE refugees along the shore of Truckee Lake, Nicholas Clark located the tracks of the black bear and its cub, following them for nearly three miles and flushing them from a tamarack grove where they had been clawing among the roots. He shot the older bear in the shoulder, and as he fumbled to reload the wounded animal reared up as though about to charge, then spun around and began to lumber away, herding the frightened cub before her. Clark followed the bloody spore until dusk, then became fearful of losing his way or having to confront the powerful animal in the darkness. Early the next morning he resumed the search, tracking the wounded bear deep into the woods before giving up in exhaustion.

There was a peculiar stillness about the camp when he returned, and he was surprised to see Mrs. Donner standing alone near the creek, staring into the west. The temperature was dropping rapidly, and the wind pushed so hard against her that she clearly had trouble remaining upright. Perhaps, he thought, she was already hoping for the next relief, though Reed and his company had only left the lake the day before.

Clark ducked into the shelter to stow his rifle, then squatted before the fire warming his hands. He blew hard on his knuckles, rubbed the palms rapidly together to guard against damaging his numbed skin, and slowly spread his fingers, holding them at the edge of the light thrown by the fire. The warm currents of air washed pleasantly around his hands, and after a moment he rubbed them together, brought them closer to the glowing logs. It was then that the stillness struck him once more, like something tangible, menacing. He sprang to his feet, quickly surveyed the shelter, saw only the inert form of George Donner. "Cady!" he shouted, and when there was no reply, bolted from the shelter without pausing to button his coat, and cried the name again. He crossed to Betsy Donner's tent, lifted the flap, and had a glimpse of the New Mexican stirring a steaming pot, the demented woman sitting nearby and staring blankly at the child sprawled across her knees. "Cady!" he cried again, but no voice responded, and there was no one obscured by the bulk of the woodpile, and when he returned with the idea of waking George Donner, questioning him, he found the entrance barred by Mrs. Donner.

"My husband is sleeping," she said, in a tone that seemed oddly detached.

"Where's Cady?"

"Don't raise your voice," she warned. "My husband is sleeping."

"Your husband is always sleeping."

"Yes, it is better when he can sleep. Please don't be so loud."

"Where the hell is Cady?" he demanded.

"Gone," she told him, almost absentmindedly, and he realized that she was again staring past him along the creek, though darkness had now swallowed all but the distant silhouettes of the mountains.

"What do you mean he's gone? Where in hell would he go to?" His arms churned the air, demonstrating the foolishness of departure.

She focused on him now, stared so intently that he became restless, shuffled his feet like a naughty child awaiting a reprimand. In carefully clipped syllables, she told him once more that he was not to raise his voice.

"Yes, ma'am," he whined, "but—"

"Would you say, Mr. Clark, that your friends were honorable men?"

"What?"

"Are they men who can be trusted?"

"Who?" he wondered, genuinely puzzled by this cross-examination.

"Would you say that Mr. Cady and Mr. Stone are men of their word?" Her frown warned him that she expected a serious answer.

"Well. . . , well, sure," he finally brought out, trying to make the answer sound hearty and assured. Then, as he revolved the same question in his own mind, he knew they had skipped out on him, taken French leave. "The rats," he muttered.

"What did you say, Mr. Clark?"

"Never mind. They lit out after Reed, huh? And whose big idea was that?"

"Your friend Stone came this morning just after you'd gone off hunting. He didn't like his assignment at the lake. He said the others were all dying except Mr. Keseberg, and the two of them must have had a quarrel. In any case, Mr. Stone had decided to leave, and came over to see if anyone wanted to go with him."

"Double-crossing bastards!"

She pretended to ignore the remark, but could not ignore the deep chill of warning it struck in her heart. "They said they couldn't wait any longer. They were afraid of another storm coming and trapping them. They said Woodworth might not get through at all, that he'll just sit in the relief camp and get drunk until spring comes. Another storm would also wipe out the trail the others made." As she repeated their arguments, the panic struck Clark, as well. The weather was turning mean, he had missed the bear again, and when his own rations were gone, he would have to share with the Donners or do without.

"So they dumped me," he muttered when she had finished repeating the men's arguments.

"They waited until afternoon, but wanted to get at least as far as the lake before dark. They couldn't . . ." She hesitated, looking beyond him again into the thickening darkness, before she added, ". . . move very quickly with the children to carry."

"Jesus! They took the children?"

"Yes, I asked them to. If your friends were so frightened . . ."

"They weren't scared yesterday," he growled.

"Well, they had had more time to think things through."

"You bet they had, the snakes. What did they charge you?"

"Charge?" Her head jerked back as though someone had slapped her cheek with a glove.

"How much did they ask for?"

"Nothing. Nothing at all. I offered to pay, but they said they weren't doing it for the money. I had to insist. And then . . . well, they said maybe they wouldn't get their full wages from Mr. Reed if they didn't stay here as he told them to."

"So how much?"

"Five hundred dollars."

"Five hundred?"

"Yes, five hundred each."

He whistled, shook his head in disbelief. "You mean Cady and Stone both got five hundred in real money?"

"No, five hundred for each of the girls. We had an inheritance of fifteen hundred dollars in silver from someone who rode in our wagon for a while before he died. He was very fond of Frances."

"I just don't believe it," he said, stubbornly shaking his head.

"What don't you believe, Mr. Clark?" Her voice flicked him like a peeled switch.

"That they'd pull a deal on me like that. We was all partners," he complained.

"Then they cannot be trusted?"

"Now, I didn't say that, ma'am. But. . . ," and he began to

invent, partly to save his own pride, partly out of genuine compassion for the panic that now shook her voice. "But they ought not to have left you like that," he said. "They promised Mr. Reed. We was all to stay. That was the deal we had. And I guess I'll find that she-bear tomorrow, so we could ride out a storm O.K." His mind was measuring the weight of fifteen hundred dollars in silver, thinking how hard it would be to carry, knowing that with such a burden a man couldn't carry children very far. And though he spoke no word of this, Tamsen herself remembered Stone's scowl when she asked if he could take along some mementos for the children, then the way he brightened when he held the cloth-wrapped bundle in his hand and felt the curve of the silver spoons.

"It might have been the girls' last chance," she pleaded, as though trying to persuade him, to win his belated support for the scheme.

"I reckon you're right, ma'am. I reckon I'd have done the same thing if they was mine."

"Then you think the girls will be all right?"

"Sure they will. Cady and Stone wouldn't do 'em no harm." And that much he was sure of. Actively and deliberately, the men would do them no harm. They would also do them no good if doing good cost them a plugged penny or an ounce of work. Clark still had a vivid sailor's vocabulary for describing men who pulled such tricks, and he would have let it fly now had the tiny woman before him not recalled the kind of schoolteacher who could face down the biggest bully in the classroom. And he was not a bully. Nor did he have the careless, callous indifference of Cady and Stone. Otherwise, he wouldn't have frozen himself half to death on the track of a wounded bear that would like nothing so much as to bite his head off, whiskers and all.

She interrupted his thoughts with the question, "You will stay, won't you?"

"What?"

"I hope you will stay with us, Mr. Clark."

"Me? Sure, I'll stay." His first instinct, on learning that Cady and Stone had deserted, was to make tracks after them, to leave at once and travel at night if he had to, for there really did seem to

be a storm in the making, and Woodworth really was a drinker—
a rummy of a navy man who didn't know a damned thing about
mountaineering. On the other hand, if he left now, Clark figured,
he could probably forget about collecting any wages from Reed, and
if he stayed, he might have even more than wages. Besides, after
chasing bear tracks through the mountains all day, he was too cold
and too tired to pick up the trail of a pair of skunks.

"Sure, I wouldn't be leaving you. Guess you'll need some help."

"My husband and I are much obliged to you. We'll make it
worth your while."

She passed back into the shelter then, and he followed. Tamsen
let him know by a cautious finger to her lips that her husband and
the child cradled against him for warmth were both still sleeping.
He began to clean his rifle, calculating how far the wounded bear
might have gotten, wondering if there was a way to cut diagonally
through the woods to pick up the trail on the following morning.
Tamsen worked the small lump of dough she had made from the
flour James Reed had left them, and seemed to hear the girls' voices
repeating again and again, "We are the children of Mr. and Mrs.
George Donner. We are the children of Mr. and Mrs. George
Donner." She had made them recite the sentence like a litany while
she brushed their hair, then dressed them all in quilted petticoats,
linsey dresses, and heavy woolen stockings. Georgia and Eliza had
twill cloaks in garnet red with the matching hoods she had knitted
for them. Frances had only a wool shawl, but Tamsen had pinned
it firmly around her shoulders and topped it with a blue hood. "We
are the children of Mr. and Mrs. George Donner," they chorused,
and were still chanting the words when she led them from the shelter
to entrust them to Cady and Stone. Cady lifted Eliza, and only her
eyes showed over his shoulder, beneath the drooping peak of the
hood, as they moved away. Stone lifted Georgia and carried her
straddling his hip, while Frances followed them, jumping from one
deep footprint to the next, and turning only once to show her the
fiercely concentrated look on her face, like that of a determined and
somewhat crotchety old woman. Tamsen looked quickly away, and
when she raised her eyes again saw only flashes of garnet and indigo
through a stand of pines, and then only the green of the trees.

47

March 4th, 1847

Frances, Georgia and Eliza departed this day to join their sisters in California. The decision to send them from me was a grievous one, yet seemed the surest guarantee of their happiness and safety. A fresh storm appears to be gathering force, and the supplies brought by Mr. Reed were scarcely more ample than those we had from the first expedition. Nonetheless, I should not have considered sending the children had not Mr. Cady and Mr. Stone announced their last-minute decision to attempt to catch up to Mr. Reed's party. They are a full day in advance, but are very numerous, and with so many small children it is thought they cannot move rapidly. Charles Stone had been delegated to tend to those unhappy souls remaining at the lake, but found the job not at all to his liking. He also quarreled with Keseberg, who seems to have been made even more irascible by his long confinement, and repeatedly threatened violence. Mr. Stone came to our encampment at mid-morning to announce his intended departure and inquire if either of his friends wished to keep him company. Mr. Clark was absent hunting, but Charles Cady eagerly agreed, for both men were alarmed by the threat of a new storm, the scantiness of supplies, and Woodworth's unreliability. When it became clear they were determined to leave together, I begged them to carry the children to safety and paid them $1500 in silver for their charity to my daughters. Together with their older sisters, they will assuredly be better off awaiting me in California than remaining here not only in want but in daily witness of their father's terrible sufferings.

48

March 5th, 1847

The threatened storm descended upon us at noon today with a fury worse than we would have deemed possible at this season. Perhaps the winter is punishing us for having so prematurely rejoiced at its demise. The wind is the most violent we have known, and the sound of the splitting, crashing trees makes a constant thundering in our ears. I pray the children were safely across the pass when the blizzards commenced, and that the weather is kinder on the western slopes. But perhaps the men determined to wait out the storm in the lake cabins. None of us had thought it would come on so suddenly and so savagely. The girls were very warmly dressed, and so plump with all their layers of woolens and linsey as to resemble quilt-balls.

With the children gone, our temporary quarters suddenly seem much too large for us, and much too empty. Mr. Clark has remained to try his luck at hunting and to gather wood for our fire, so that Jean Baptiste can devote himself to the needs of Betsy and Lewis. We have seen none of them since the tempest commenced, but smoke rises from their shelter.

49

THE WIND, DRIVING ALMOST HORIZONTALLY, PUSHED A WAVE OF snow into the shelter when Betsy Donner thrust aside the canvas flaps. Tamsen looked up to see the woman enter with shawls and scarves flapping about her like the tattered canvas of a schooner running full sail into a typhoon. The woman rocked, swayed, then managed to right herself at just the moment Tamsen had decided she would surely capsize with Lewis balanced so clumsily in her arms. Betsy smiled with girlish brightness at her unexpected success, and Tamsen was relieved to see that her face no longer bore the marks of hysterical grief. Perhaps the children's departure with Mr. Reed had been, after all, the tonic she needed.

"Mind if I sit a spell?" Betsy asked.

"Of course. Do!" Tamsen was genuinely glad of the unaccustomed visit, the rare hint of cheerfulness, and quickly shifted bowls and spoons from the lid of the trunk to make a seat near the fire. Betsy settled herself comfortably, cradling the tightly wrapped child against her. She had swaddled him from head to foot in a blanket, and he resembled a Kansa papoose.

"Looks like we'll be snowed up again," Betsy remarked.

"Yes, it does," Tamsen agreed.

"I can't remember such a winter in all my born days. Never this bad." Her tongue made a clucking noise as she reassuringly patted the thickly bundled child.

"Nor can I."

"Can't even see the barn," Betsy sighed, and before Tamsen could think of a reply, Betsy asked, "How's George?" There was genuine concern in her voice, the same simple and vulnerable compassion that could send the woman into fits of helpless weeping over a toddler's skinned knee.

"Sleeping," Tamsen told her. "I changed the dressing this morning and put hot packs on his shoulder. He said it eased the swelling a little. There's no feeling left in his arm, but the shoulder pains him so much it hurts just to breathe."

"Oughtn't somebody fetch the doctor?"

"Well . . ."

"I don't want to go busy-bodyin' around, and you know a sight about medicine, but oughtn't George to have a real doctor?"

"Yes, Betsy," Tamsen said slowly, "I think he should have had a real doctor a long time ago. My medicine hasn't done him much good."

"You don't think I'm buttin' in where I ought to be buttin' out?"

"No, dear Betsy. I would never think that."

"Well, that's a relief. That's just fine, then," the woman sighed, and smiled again, pleased with the easy rapport, the sisterly sociability. She hummed softly to herself and rocked her youngest child on her knees.

"Did Lewis like his broth?" Tamsen asked.

"Oh, he just lapped it up like a little puppy," Betsy answered, bounced her knees teasingly and leaned over her son. "Just like a teeny tiny puppy," she said. "But I sure don't like the look of the weather. Never seen anything like it in all my born days."

"I don't like it either," Tamsen agreed, and used a broken axe handle to push the logs together, then added some brush to the fire to lighten the gloom of the shelter. Above the constant lament of the wind, there came the explosion of ice-heavy tree limbs ripped away, fracturing other brittle growth as they fell, and Tamsen shivered reflexively as she thought of Mr. Clark out gathering the fallen branches. The flames that now lighted Betsy's face gave it a soft maternal glow, and her eyes gleamed with the reflected merriment. Even the greasy hair that she had clumsily cut short to discourage the vermin seemed to fall softly about her face. Her jaw was heavy, her hooked nose too large, and the wasting of her flesh made them both seem even more exaggerated, but in that moment Tamsen found a strange beauty in her sister-in-law's unaccustomed repose. Perhaps, after all, she had found some hope and with it some

401

strength in the children's departure. Perhaps she could bear the coming grief of Sammie's death. The nephew that slept now beside George Donner was even weaker than the man. In the first days he had merely whined and fretted, throwing up the little food he was given, trembling constantly with chills, and scratching his face until it bled. Tamsen had made soft cotton mitts for his hands, had put him into bed with George to stay warm, and for two full days the child had made scarcely a sound. She had recently made balls of flour-and-water dough, boiled them for a few seconds before giving them to him, and he allowed them to melt in his mouth. Otherwise, he could eat nothing. Betsy never asked about the child, perhaps fearful of the answer she might receive, and concentrated all her frail energies on Lewis, the baby who was now hardly ever out of her arms.

"Lord, this weather sure does tire a body out," Betsy said, and suppressed a yawn.

"Why don't you go have a nice nap then? You could even have one here. We've plenty of extra beds now."

"I think maybe I'll do that," she said, but remained sitting before the hearth, faintly humming a lullaby, while Tamsen lowered tin bowls and spoons into the kettle that stood by the fire. She was grateful for the slight clatter of metal on metal, even glad for Betsy's off-key melody, for they helped distance the angry sounds of the storm.

Betsy Donner did, at one point, seem about to drift off to sleep, but her head snapped up and she said loudly, "Here I am just dozin' away when there's so many things to be done! I'll be leavin' you now."

"I'm glad you came," Tamsen said. In the four months of their icy imprisonment, Betsy had almost never visited. It was always Tamsen who must cross the snow, practically crawl on hands and knees to enter the neighboring shelter, until the decay of spirit there made even that a rare event.

"Tell George I said hello." With those words Betsy stood slowly, turned like a sleepwalker, and moved from the fireside. Tamsen glanced up to smile farewell and saw with horror the bundled child slide from Betsy's lap, as though she had forgotten he was

402

resting there. He bounced against the hearthstones, dislodging one and sending a blossoming of sparks into the air. As the blanketed form rolled forward, bumped the burning logs, Tamsen lunged after it, knocking the kettle and soaking her dress with the steaming water. She heard sparks snap in her hair, blinked away cinders, and seized an edge of the blanket to drag it to safety. Like a cornered animal, it seemed to jerk away from her, and she felt the frayed edges slide from her fingers, as her knee caught sharply against a stone. She lunged again, sank her whole hand into the cloth, made a fist, and jerked it away from the logs. They tumbled, spilling fiery embers, and she smelled the sharp, acid smell of her own singed hair. "Betsy!" she shouted, but realized the woman was gone.

Tamsen held the child tightly, patting at a smoldering patch on the blanket, and lifted the flap that covered Lewis Donner's face. The eyes had rolled so far back in the child's head that scarcely any color was visible, and the lips were drawn tightly away from the gums to show the tiny, even rows of teeth, like strings of seed pearls. In the first minutes, she thought the child had perhaps been killed by the fall, but when she felt the rigid arms and legs, looked again into the milkily vacant eyes, she knew he had been dead for hours.

50

March 9th, 1847
Elizabeth Blue Donner died this day at 46 years of age. She had failed almost constantly since the death of her husband in December. Her son Lewis died on March 7th, and the two were buried in a single grave. It was not possible to bury the child sooner because of the severity of the storm, which only began to abate yesterday afternoon.

Mr. Clark has killed a bear cub and hauled it back to camp. He thinks it is the same one whose mother he wounded before the storm.

403

51

March 10th, 1847

If the weather remains fair, Mr. Clark will journey to the lake camp tomorrow for news of the girls. The men may have remained there to wait out the storm, or have returned there after its force became clear to them. Mr. Clark has been promised a gold watch for the completion of this mission.

52

March 11th, 1847

Mr. Clark has his watch, and I have his report, which both gladdens and distresses me as it touches the welfare of my three daughters. Charles Cady and Charles Stone did indeed remain at Truckee Lake to wait out the recent storm, taking refuge in the abandoned Breen cabin, and leaving the girls in the care of Mrs. Murphy. As soon as the storm lifted, the men were on their way across the mountains, but neglected to take their charges with them. Their Judas portions of silver and the family mementos I had gathered together were, of course, snug in their packs. Mr. Clark was, I believe, genuinely distressed by the darkness and filth and absolute want in which he found the children. Mrs. Murphy is feeble in mind and body, and Mr. Keseberg has deteriorated to a state of savagery whose dimensions excel even those of nightmare. Mrs. Murphy accuses him of murdering her grandson Georgie Foster to satisfy his appetite for fresh meat. Such ravings cannot be taken in evidence, but Mr. Clark witnessed with his own eyes the way the German had hung the boy's corpse over his bed like a side of beef in a butcher's window—"to whet my appetite," he claimed. When I think that the children have lived for an entire week with such horrors, and all because of their mother's addle-headed haste, I cannot forgive myself. The perfidy of Cady and Stone makes the lies of Lansford Hastings seem fairly angelic.

Had it not been after sunset when Mr. Clark appeared, I would have departed at once for the lake, but must now force myself to wait for morning light. I have entreated Nicholas Clark and Jean Baptiste Trubode to remain here, and promised them a generous reward for their care of my husband and my nephew until such time as I can return.

53

THE CHILDREN WERE ALIVE, BUT THE DEEP STUPOR IN WHICH SHE found them terrified Tamsen more than any of the horrors she had witnessed in the mountains. Their faces, their clothing, the blanket covering them were smeared and matted with filth, as though they had lived not merely for a week but all their precious, fragile lives in this desolate cave, strewn with bones and strips of hide and scraps of human hair. Only by clamping her hands over her mouth did she suppress a scream, and she dammed hysterical tears with the knowl-edge that if she lost control now, they might all be doomed. This she told herself again and again as she began to shake them gently, then almost roughly, trying to rouse them from their deep, deathlike slumber. It was Georgia who responded first, without opening her eyes, "We are the children of Mr. and Mrs. George Donner. We are the children of Mr. and Mrs. George Donner." Frances and Eliza soon joined her, with voices weak and drunkenly slurred and uncoordinated, so that the trio came out as a meaningless babble. It did not cease when they recognized their mother, but raised in pitch as they flung themselves against her crouching form, their slight but eager weight easily toppling her to the ground, where hands sought her face, her hair, unintentionally clawing her cheeks, tearing a button from her dress, painfully gouging her breasts as they sought confirmation of the voice crooning their names, of the vision only partly glimpsed in the perpetual shadows of the shelter. Tamsen clutched them, returned each caress, measured their thin arms and legs with her fingers, stroked hair from their faces, made kissing motions with her lips whenever skin brushed against them, and constantly murmured their names. As they quieted, she tried to lock them all in a single embrace, to hold the three pulsing bodies packed tightly against her, flesh on flesh, but her arms were too weak, the journey to the lake had exhausted her, the fear and then the horror and then the release and then the joy flooding her had made her limp. She had not realized how tired she was, how greedily will had fed on flesh in these long months, the price exacted for the complex role of heroine, the toll of three nights without sleep. The children rooted against her body, their breath dampened her skin, and she reached again, sealing them for a moment in the tight circle of an embrace, locking her fingers to hold them forever safe and protected in this perfect orbit, and only when she herself became unconscious did the fingers slowly, reluctantly loosen their iron grip.

TAMSEN DONNER AND HER CHILDREN STILL SLEPT DEEPLY WHEN the third relief arrived, and woke only when William Eddy shouted at Keseberg, "I'll kill you! If I don't kill you now, you filthy bastard, I'll hunt you down later. You'll never get away from me. Never! You can go to hell and I'll follow you and cut your stinking heart out."

There were two men restraining Eddy, struggling to pin his arms to his sides as he lunged toward the corner where Keseberg crouched, his long, bony fingers shielding his face. One of the men Tamsen recognized at once as Bill Foster, but it took longer to make out the face of the Donners' former teamster Hiram Miller, with its unaccustomed growth of gingery beard. When they entered, the three men had overlooked the sleeping figures, went straight to old Mrs. Murphy, with Eddy and Foster breathlessly demanding to know what had become of their sons. The old woman angled a crooked finger at Keseberg, who crouched by the hearth preparing breakfast, conspicuously ignoring the visitors, and it was then that Eddy recognized what remained of his son.

"I'll kill you," Eddy whispered hoarsely, but was trembling too much to move, shaking from head to foot, all his muscles twitching and convulsing in a hideous, uncontrollable dance.

Keseberg said nothing for a moment, then pointed a long-handled spoon at Foster and croaked, "Eddy's boy is a lot more tender than yours was."

It was then that Eddy lunged, and Keseberg scrambled into a corner, yelping shrilly and covering his face with his hands.

His companions grabbed Eddy's arms, and Foster reasoned, "The bastard's crazy, Will. He's out of his mind. You can't kill him like that! He just did what we all did."

Eddy continued to struggle, but less violently, and spit noisily at the German. "I'll kill you!" he shouted. "If I don't kill you now, you filthy bastard, I'll hunt you down later. You'll never get away from me. Never! You can go to hell and I'll follow you and cut your stinking heart out." He sobbed, then spit again, sobbed raggedly as he shouted the words that woke Tamsen Donner.

When she recognized the former teamster, she called his name. Hiram Miller knew the voice was familiar, but couldn't place it at first. Instinctively, he spun around, dropping Eddy's arm, and saw a child move from the shadows beside the steep entrance to the lean-to. Eddy had turned as well, and the sight of her blunted his wrath. "Mrs. Donner," he said in surprise. "We didn't expect . . . We thought you were at the other camp."

"I . . . I came after the girls," she explained, then faltered, too weary and relieved and far too happy now to elaborate. "I'm just so glad you've come!" she said, and each of the men would remember for the rest of his life the triumphant smile she bestowed on them then, the welcome and the joy it contained. Eddy and Foster had hoped to rescue their infant sons, yet had half expected they would come too late. Hiram Miller felt a duty to his former employers, perhaps even guilt for having left them and his partner Milt Elliott to ride to safety with Edwin Bryant. Now the grief and frustration of the fathers, the guilt of the teamster, found release in the unexpected reunion with Tamsen Donner and the children who clutched at her skirts, staring with immense eyes at the newcomers. The men lifted them up and carried them out of the reeking pit into the sunshine, fed them on biscuits and jerked beef, and set coffee to boil.

When Tamsen had recovered a little from her surprise, braced herself with a steaming cup of sugar-thick coffee, she said to Bill Eddy, "I'll pay you well to take the girls out."

"You don't have that much money, Mrs. Donner." He saw the sudden pain flash across her gaunt features and hurried to correct himself, "Of course we'll take them out. We'll take you, too. Carry the lot of you pick-a-pack. I meant it's a thing . . . a thing money can't pay for. You can't buy it. Me and Foster know that. But don't you worry about a thing. You can depend on us."

Suddenly she felt so weak she feared she might faint, and braced herself against Eddy's arm. "I'm so . . . so . . . so . . . very sorry. Sorry about Eleanor. She was such a sweet, pretty thing. Sorry about the children. So very . . . very . . . sorry. And about Mr. Foster's boy, and about Milt and about the Keseberg baby. He . . . he fought so hard to come into the world. And about . . . all of it, and Mr. Donner. Please . . . so . . . sorry."

Hiram Miller twisted the top from a flask, insisted she drink from it, shoved it into her trembling hands and helped her raise it to her lips. She swallowed fire, and the burning cauterized her throat, scalded her stomach, snatched her breath away. When Hiram encouraged her to drink again, she shook her head. "No, I'm all right now," she assured the three men whose troubled faces leaned over her. "I'm just so relieved the girls can finally get out. It's what . . . what I've lived for."

"You, too, Mrs. Donner. You don't weight much more than one of the kids. Reckon I could carry you over one shoulder and Frances over the other."

Miller's thick-lashed brown eyes, almost too pretty for a man, seemed to beseech her to grant him this chance to show his loyalty, to make some recompense for leaving them, for leaving Milt. She meant to tell him simply that she could not go, not quite yet, but found herself saying instead, "You should keep the beard. It's very becoming, makes you even handsomer. But I'd trim it a little shorter."

Blushing, he measured the growth with his fingers, was about to reply when she raised her voice and informed the three of them, "I can't leave now."

"But we'll have to," Eddy insisted. "We can't afford to get caught in a storm the way Reed did. It was awful. The Breens were still stuck up there, half dead, and it took most of our own men to carry 'em back to Bear Valley. We'll have to get movin' pretty fast now."

"Then you'll have to go without me," she said almost casually. "But please take the girls with you."

"Don't you feel well, ma'am?"

"I do recollect feeling a mite better once upon a time, but I'll be fine now. Jean Baptiste and Mr. Clark promised to look after Mr. Donner and the baby, but they'll be expecting me back."

"Mr. Donner?" Eddy wondered. "Mr. Reed said . . . well, he thought . . ."

"Do you mean Mr. Donner's still alive?" Hiram Miller asked.

She nodded. "He was, at least, when I left him. And our nephew Sammie, too. But they . . . they can't last much longer."

"Mr. Reed said the captain wanted you to leave with the girls," Eddy protested. "You can't go back now, all that way. There may not be another relief come in for weeks. Most everybody's out already. Those two aren't goin' anywhere," he added, and jerked his head toward the entrance of the Keseberg shelter.

"Can't the two men take care of Mr. Donner and the baby?"

"They're both strangers," she said hollowly. "They're not friends and they're not family. I can't leave my husband and my nephew with strangers. Besides," she admitted, "all they can talk about is leaving. If I don't go back . . . I promised to go back as soon as I could do something about the girls."

"But Captain Donner wouldn't know. . . ," Eddy began.

"No, he would not. But I would know, Mr. Eddy, and that would be far, far worse." She stood, but somewhat shakily, and quickly sat down again. "You go first. I'd like to see the girls off."

"But . . ."

"Please?" she asked, forcing a smile to reassure them that this was really the better scheme. "I'd be so much obliged to you."

She had her way, and she waved farewells until the garnet-red cloaks and the indigo shawl shrank to dots against the snow, like flecks of color carelessly splashed on a pale watercolor sketch.

HER FIRST THOUGHT WAS THAT INDIANS HAD ATTACKED THE CAMP at Prosser Creek, and then that the black bear had sought savage revenge for the death of her cub. The brush shelters had been ripped apart, goods from the wagons had been tumbled to the ground, scattered over the snow. But when she saw the hammer and chisel with which crates had been splintered open, she knew the devastation was the work of Jean Baptiste and Mr. Clark, and later she would find the trail they had struck across country, to avoid anyone who might be approaching along the creek. Inside the tent cold ashes littered the muddy floor, the hearthstones had been ripped up and flung aside in the frantic search for treasure. They had taken her precious compass, but a glance told her the badly soiled California quilt was safe, and without dismantling the bed of the wagon, the men would not have found the gold concealed there. The family fortunes were secure, but Sammie Donner was dead, his body stiff and blue with cold, and Mr. Donner's breath was so faint and shallow that she did not trust her ears, but pressed her head against his chest and listened for long minutes before convincing herself that the muffled sound was the beating of his heart and not the pumping of her own blood. She was hardly able to stand, and lifting her arms was an agony. For a moment she wished only to lay beside her husband, the two sharing the last faint warmth of their bodies, and to give herself in oblivious surrender to sleep. "Soon," she thought, as she carried Betsy's child from the tent, scooped a shallow grave in the snow, and packed it hard over the emaciated corpse, canceled the hideous, unvarying grin on its face. "Soon," she whispered, as she rolled the hearthstones together and fumbled to kindle a fire. Sleep insisted, like an impatient lover taut with lust, and she promised she would come to him, would surrender utterly and without restraint to his frantic desire, as soon as she had brought in more wood, as soon as she had filled the kettle with snow and put it on to boil, dropping in a generous portion of bear meat to make a rich broth for Captain Donner in case he should awaken. In case he should ever again awaken. Yes, she agreed, she would come to him as soon as the fire had been built up high enough to burn through the night, so that the cold would not surprise them in their naked embrace.

54

FOR THE FIRST TIME SINCE THEY ENTERED THE MOUNTAINS, Tamsen's sleep was free of menacing dreams, and when she awoke she seemed to be emerging from a long hibernation, as though she might have slept for days, even weeks, and only the last smoldering fragments of wood on the hearth told her this was not so. Moving stiffly, she crossed to her husband's bed, quickly satisfied herself that he still breathed, and stooped to build up the fire. In its renewed light she saw the extent of the careless devastation she had been too weary to comprehend the night before—the wadding ripped from the linings of cloaks, her sketches trampled into the mud, balls of yarn clawed open, the feeble contents of the walnut medicine chest spilled, the trunk upended, and felt a bitter outrage at this violation of her home. Had anyone suggested she was in some way fond of this damp, reeking shelter with its awful history of privation and agony, she would have taken him for a fool. Yet now, when she saw trinkets and mementos bent, twisted, trampled, dirtied by the hands of greedy, ignorant men, it was an act of unspeakable desecration. Here, where the struggle for life had been fought so relentlessly, where the fraying wick of hope had been meticulously trimmed and husbanded, where taboo had been abrogated not as an act of viola-

411

tion but an act of faith, clumsy predators had entered, rudely flung aside the simple, necessary tools, the small comforts, the primitive and valueless treasures handled daily by herself and her daughters, once lifted up by Mr. Donner, by Milt and Mrs. Wolfinger and John Denton. If they had thrust filthy, grouping fingers beneath her skirts, thrust them insistently between her legs, she could have felt no greater outrage, no more loathsome breach of intimacy, no deeper wound to pride. They had left their dirt behind, and she moved with a fierce, angry resolve to purge it. What could not be ordered, cleaned or repaired, she threw on the swelling fire. It consumed fistfuls of wadding, the splintered walnut medicine chest, shreds of paper, a pipe with a cracked bowl, a canteen Jean Baptiste had left behind, a wooden doll that had once distracted Eliza. Even when this was done, when what remained had been shaken, brushed, straightened, organized, she felt still their cruel filth about her. With every vessel she could find, she hauled snow to melt on the hearth, and when it was hot began to strip away the intricate layers of clothing that insulated her body, threw them from her to be gathered later, bundled, buried in the snow. She made a paste from the ashes and scrubbed her body, scoured it punishingly, as though it had secretly collaborated in this unspeakable outrage, walking on tiptoe to ease the clumsy bolt, slowly draw back the massive door, only enough for the vandals to slither through, but enough for them to invade the sleeping, unsuspecting house. As she stood shivering, naked, she worked the slimy gray ash into her scalp, smeared a film across her face, rubbed it into her neck and across the curves of jutting collarbones that resembled bows so tightly drawn they must snap with the pressure, over sagging, wrinkled breasts like fruit eaten away from within by insatiable worms, across ribs as precisely etched against her skin as an engraving in an anatomy text. Her entire body trembled, but more with rage than with cold, as she smeared her gaunt hips, the fragile arabesque of her pelvis, thighs scarcely bigger than a man's arm. Then she rinsed the film away, scraping the residue with her fingernails until her entire body was covered with scarlet welts and furrows. She warmed strips of flannel and dried herself, and though she now became acutely aware of the cold, took her time in selecting pantalets and chemise, a challis dress and wool stockings and cashmere shawl from the small store of Sunday-best clothing she had rescued from the wagon, then jealously hoarded for her own rescue. When she was dressed to her satisfaction, she brushed her hair before the fire, feeling the heat tingle her scalp— brushed it forward across her face, then lifted it strand by strand, clamping each between her fingers, brushing it vigorously. The brushing continued long after the hair was dry, until her arm was too cramped to continue. Then she gathered the hair and knotted it swiftly at the nape of her neck, expertly easing her grip at the last moment, so that soft waves fell against her cheeks. She plucked the loose hair from the brush and consigned it, too, to the fire, where it crackled pungently in the flames. It was only then that she began to weep, not shedding polite, restrained tears of self-pity or helpless- ness or regret, but sobbing noisily, wailing a tremulous aria of purga- tion and release. Her weeping was without restraint and without specific reason; it was the overflow of suppressed anger and passion and grief that spilled forth eagerly after months of confinement behind the dense levees she had thrown up to channel it safely away. How long it continued, she could not have said; she only knew that before it ceased some awful, clenching pain had not only eased but given way to a curious joy, something endlessly rich, of which her tears became the demonstration and proof.

If her noisy indulgence woke George, he made no sign. It was nearly evening when he turned his head to stare in disbelief and then speak her name. "Tamsen," he said hoarsely. "Did you come back?"

She answered with a question of her own. "Did you think you could be rid of me so easily?"

THOUGH HIS BREATH GREW SO FAINT SHE HAD TAKEN THE MIRROR from hiding, kept it handy to measure the declining struggle, George Donner lived for nearly two weeks after Tamsen's return to Prosser Creek. Occasionally he roused enough to sip a little water or broth, with his head cradled against her arm, a cloth tucked beneath his chin to catch the dribbles his mouth would not hold. He seldom felt pain now, and did not protest when she shifted him slightly to remove soiled linen, sponge away his wastes.

She was too weak to cut firewood, but there were so many broken tree limbs littering the ground that she easily found enough. Once, dragging at a pile of brush, she exposed the haunch of one of their missing cattle, and in several trips managed to haul a generous supply of meat back to the shelter. She felt no hunger, yet forced herself to eat huge quantities, gorging herself to build the strength she would need for the coming journey, and perhaps with this excess to cancel the human flesh she had eaten in small, precise rations. Some of the meat was dried over the fire, Indian-style, in preparation for her departure, and snow was scooped over what remained of the steer, to protect it from spoiling in the sun. A new thaw had begun, and forms rose each day more and more distinctly from beneath the shrinking drifts. The teamsters' wigwam lifted into a tattered sentry on the opposite bank of the creek, the hubs of the wagons now peeped above the surface, and the stumps of trees Milt had felled towered over her head.

When her chores were done, Tamsen often sat beside her husband mending clothing—first, the things she would require in the days ahead, then things she knew would be left behind. So long as there was visible, measurable work to occupy her fingers, she took little thought of what it was, and surprised herself one day to discover she had not only mended a hole in one of George's socks, but sewn the top snugly shut as well. She chided herself for such foolishness, but she found other signs of absentmindedness, and though she tried to make a joke of it, she recognized an old acquaintance, caught a nod from that vacancy in which she had lived two long, uncaring, unfeeling years in Newburyport after Tully and the children had deserted her, and she feared she could not resist its allure. If madness claimed her now, the sea dragging her into its shadowy grottoes, opening huge wet jaws under the moon's cold wasted desolate face, she would not surface, would never gain the beach again to lie panting in a renewed embrace of earth as she had once done though landlocked and alien and mechanically performing unaccustomed tasks for William and for William's children. Tamsen abandoned her handiwork, spent hours outside the shelter, but when she returned again her old acquaintance nodded, tipped his hat, once even risked the impertinence of a wink. As her future narrowed, she began to dwell randomly on the past, to spend hours trying to recall the shape of an armoire, the color of a dress, the pattern of the bright, coppery hairs on Tully's arms, and then she became yet more absent-minded, and held even memory from her with stiffened arms. It was then that she began to wish for George's death, that she saw his continuing struggle as foolish, and at moments she hated him, hated this putrefying body that stood like an impassable mountain between herself and her children. Die, she whispered, and give this stupid agony an end. Give me, dear husband, my freedom. Release me from vows. And when he lingered still, each morning planting the pale, translucent blossom of his breath on her mirror, she discovered other reasons for so passionately wishing his death. Die, that I may see you pay with a last awful gasp for the agony you have inflicted for half a century and perhaps more on the women who always followed you so willingly, meekly, obediently, stupidly, wherever you piped your merry tune. Die, please, that I may be released from that spell, that commitment, that curse, freed forever from the whims of truant schoolboys. Die that I may join my orphaned and needy children. Die. Leave me. Go and prepare shady orchards and broad harrowed fields and with your two good strong manly arms raise a barn and a stout wooden house with wide, sloping eaves to make a silver curtain of the rain. Roof it tightly for me and for my daughters and for yours. Plane the floorboards until they are silken. Make a broad hearth, a generous mantel where a clock can stand, an oaken door frame for the kitchen where the growth of my children can be notched and initialed and dated. But do not linger. Sometimes she made her pleas aloud, as though reciting a prayer, sometimes to herself, but when George rallied briefly, said to her, "Go, Tamsen. Leave me, child," she knew that she would stay.

"Tamsen, go," he repeated, in a voice so hoarse and muffled that she had to hold an ear against his parched lips to distinguish words in the painful rasp of sound.

She placed the back of her hand against his cheek and told him, "No, Mr. Donner, it is you who must go before me."

55

Prosser Creek

March 26th, 1847

My husband Captain George Donner died this afternoon after a lengthy and painful illness. I have washed and prepared his body for burial, but cannot accomplish the latter without assistance. Hopefully the necessary rites can be performed before the wolves do their work. I shall depart within the hour to join my daughters in California.

56

THE DATE TAMSEN DONNER AFFIXED TO THE FINAL ENTRY IN HER journal was somewhat arbitrary. Since her return to Prosser Creek, she had kept no strict measure of time, but the moon was nearly full, and by this she made an approximate calculation that could be corrected later. The moon, luminous against the snow, would also serve as a guide for the first stage of her journey. It was not any superstitious fear of remaining for a night beside the corpse of her husband that prompted Tamsen's rapid departure. It was not even the danger signaled by the howling of the wolves, that had already dug up one of the oxen. She was no longer needed here, there was no reason to linger, especially not while five frightened, penniless children would be anxiously awaiting her. If she reached the cabins at Truckee Lake tonight, she could truly be on her way to California tomorrow. Only a few hasty preparations remained after she closed her journal, for most details had been checked and rechecked a dozen times, her small store of supplies kept in constant readiness. Two pouches were firmly sewn into the lining of her cloak, one for a supply of dried beef, the other for the precious journal composed for her daughters, and whose slender explanations they would now require more than she could have imagined when she so lightheartedly commenced it. In a drawstring bag she carried a hunting knife, nearly two hundred dollars in gold coin, and implements for kindling a fire. She folded the princely California quilt twice, placed the bag in the center, and made a tight roll to be secured with straps to her shoulders. In the spring they could send for what remained. There was money enough to pay men for the unpleasant job of salvage and burial, and she would not burden herself with the rest of the coin or the remaining family valuables. She did take the wagon spoke that was reassuringly smoothed to her grip, both for possible defense, and to support her unsteady progress through the snow.

She had crossed the trail only once, guided then by Clark's snowshoe tracks, and the little she remembered of the route had been so altered by the thaw that it found no echo in memory. Hillsides had shrunken or disappeared entirely, valleys deepened, and a whole forest barred her way where she had once moved lightly around clumps of slender bushes. A short distance beyond, the creek had swollen to shatter its roof of ice, overflowed to create a broad pond whose brittle surface sagged beneath her tread, then snapped to drop her into icy water that soaked her to the waist. Slowly, cautiously, she crawled the remaining distance, pushing the stave before her, hearing the ice crackle and chatter brightly, the water below mutter in response, terrified of being plunged again into the freezing bath. When she had at last reached firm ground, dragged herself upright, she proceeded a timid step at a time, testing her footing with the wagon spoke, but twice found herself suddenly wallowing in drifts that reached her shoulders, and even when the crust held her, she was hampered by the weight of her waterlogged clothing, which had begun to freeze into rigid armor. The moon brightly illuminated her treacherous path, but the iridescent blue light it struck from the snow flattened perspectives, distorted distances, made the landscape unreal, like a fancifully tinted plate in a book of fairy tales. The trees with their twisted and broken limbs were grotesque silhouettes, and their trailing, unseen fingers tore at the shawl with which she had covered her head, clutched at her feet and sent her sprawling. Once, in a clearing less than a mile from the encampment at Truckee Lake, where she realized that she had walked for an hour in a circle, she paused, leaning her full weight against the wagon spoke, reeling with the effort to keep her balance, and slowly tilted her head back to study the sky. Her neck was so stiff that only with a fierce concentration of energy did she force its obedience, and the effort so wearied her that she nearly toppled. Trembling, she raised her eyes to the moon, as though expecting to encounter the leering, malevolent face of a fiend, but saw only a harmless mother-of-pearl button, somewhat chipped and worn, stitched tightly to the sky.

EVER SINCE THE WOLVES HAD ROBBED HIM OF THE LAST PORTIONS of Mrs. Murphy's body, Keseberg had scarcely slept at night. There were other bodies remaining, and the carcasses of oxen and mules had begun to emerge from the snow, but much of the meat of both men and animals was spoiled, and the store he kept near the entrance to the lean-to was carefully preserved in snow, where wolves had more than once scratched noisily in the night, as though preferring his shrinking rations to those they might have had for the taking, without digging for them, only a few yards away. Though his foot hardly pained him now, Keseberg's leg was stiff, and hobbling about on a makeshift crutch to gather firewood quickly exhausted him. When the wolves made a feast of his freshest, choicest meat, he had made the effort of chopping the leg from a steer and dragging it into camp, but the unaccustomed labor dizzied him, and he found the taste of beef musty and rancid. He craved the flavors of heart, liver, kidney, brains, the faint saltiness and the strengthening richness they contained, but extracting them from half-frozen mules and oxen was too great a labor. So he waited night after night with Wolfinger's rifle beside him for the thieving animals to return, eager to protect the few choice delicacies remaining in his larder, the rifle oiled and loaded and ready to blast the slinking predators to hell. He would leave the first beast where it fell, as a warning to others, and he gloated as he rehearsed his triumph, saw the silvery body slammed by a bullet, buck and twist and leap once into the air before it sank into the spreading stain of its own blood. Often he dozed, embracing the rifle like a stiffly reluctant lover, but was instantly awake when the limb of a tree crackled or raked the ground, and listened intently for the rhythmic sound of curved nails slashing the snow, breath hotly panting just beyond the thin, unchinked wall. Satisfied that the noise was made by no unwanted visitor, he eased again into a light sleep. Then his patient watchfulness found its reward, for the shuffling that startled him into wakefulness paused only briefly, followed by a timid scrabbling, like that of some burrowing creature, perhaps only a rat, but perhaps some larger animal making its slinking approach. Suddenly the beast fell silent again, and Keseberg suppressed the sound of his own breathing, waited for the noise to resume, heard it then as it slyly approached the entrance, sniffing, scratching, once making a faint yelping noise. Perhaps, he thought, it was a wolf cub, even a young bear, and he drew his legs up, crouched with his back against the wall and the rifle steadied on his knees. Whatever was edging toward the entrance, it was almost certainly not one of the wolves for whom he had lain in wait so many sleepless nights, remembering the succulent delicacies they had pilfered from under his very nose. He had prepared himself to confront the most ravenous, ferocious wolf, had gloated over the rapid, uncomplicated cancellation of a debt, but because he did not know what kind of creature now prowled outside the lean-to, he felt an unexpected terror, drew his knees tighter against his chest, though the position made it more difficult to balance the clumsy rifle. For a moment, nearly paralyzed by fear, he had imagined some monster, some hideously deformed thing of evil, was crawling toward him, but he shook away the peasant superstition, told himself rationally and reasonably that only a wolf or a bear had the impertinence to venture so near a human habitation. Something heavy struck the well-packed ramp no more than a yard or two from the entrance—something solid, something made of flesh, and not some bodiless ghoul. Then the clawing came again, sharper and more rapid, and he thought it might be a wolf after all, suppressed a laugh at how readily his stupid victim had blundered into the trap, his nose leading him unerringly and fatally to the remains of Keseberg's evening meal. He grinned widely as he squinted along the barrel of the rifle, stilled its nervous bobbing, watched the bead at its tip dance erratically, then slowly come to rest suspended in the center of the faint rectangle of moonlight. With aching arms he held it poised there, framed by the rough logs, and when a shape appeared to eclipse the glow, he rapidly jerked the trigger. Trying to reload, he scattered most of the powder across the bed, and his shaking fingers refused to hold a bullet, but the stillness in the shelter calmed him, persuaded him he had killed the intruder with a single, well-placed shot. Thriftily, he saved the second bullet.

KESEBERG WOULD LATER RECITE MANY VERSIONS OF THAT NIGHT and of the days that followed, but most began with a tearful, melodramatic account of how Tamsen Donner, half-frozen and faint with fatigue, crawled into the lean-to hysterically babbling, "I must go to my children. I must go to my children." Her clothing was soaked from a plunge into the creek, and he did his best to make her warm and comfortable, but it was too late. When she lost consciousness, he labored for hours to revive her, chafing her frozen feet and hands, repeatedly calling her name, and she whispered one final time, "I must go to my children." When Dan Tucker, John Rhoads, and Bill Foster arrived at Truckee Lake on April 19th, they found the trail Keseberg had made going to and from the Donners' tents at Prosser Creek. He told them the pathetic tale of Tamsen Donner's final hours, and when the skeptical men demanded to know what he had done with the body, he boasted, "I ate it. It was the best I ever tasted! I took four pounds of fat from it!" Perhaps he was trying to distract them from the obvious signs of his search for treasure at Prosser Creek, the gold coins they had found concealed beneath his bed. They suspected him of murder as well as robbery, accused him, menaced him, and again he attempted to distract them by pointing to what remained of the blood he had drawn from the woman's body. Why, they demanded, would he have consumed her when there were other bodies readily available, ones he had already started on, when there were cattle and mules he could have eaten. Why? "Because the meat was so fresh. It was the best I ever tasted!" he assured them again, and licked his lips in demonstration, smacked appreciatively. The three men could almost believe his ravings, for at Prosser Creek they had found the skull of George Donner sawed open, the brains scooped out, though there was an ox haunch near the entrance to the shelter and a supply of jerked meat on the hearth. When the men of the last relief offered to share their rations with Keseberg, he flung them from him, said beef was too dry, and ate a farewell meal from the kettle he had been stirring when the three discovered him.

He had killed but not murdered her, and he despaired of persuading these tall, muscular, angry men of the difference, so he clung to his fable, wrung his hands, boasted of his appetite for human flesh. In doing so he punished himself, flagellated his own raw spirit, attacked a deeper guilt that never left him, but he also defied their righteousness. The outcast son of a pious, aristocratic family, he had developed natural gifts that should have assured his rise in society, his prosperity and contentment, but the very decisions that made other men heroes made him appear callous and villainous. His thrift was read as greed, shrewdness was reduced to animal cunning, resolution became stubbornness, and as the carefully laid schemes of his life collapsed, he lashed out in anger. He had not murdered Tamsen Donner, and he did not murder Georgie Foster, but took the dying boy into his bed one night to warm him, sentimentally thinking of his own dead son, the absent wife and daughter he might never see again. Accused of murder the following morning, he arrogantly strung the child's corpse on the wall, boasted of the tasty meal it would soon provide. Crazy or not, Mrs. Murphy would pay for the excesses of her slanderous tongue.

When Keseberg summoned the courage to leave his bed and discovered the body of Tamsen Donner slumped within the entrance to the shelter, he at once sought her pulse, sobbed forgotten prayers in the curiously formal, stilted German of his father's church, and then shrieked loudly, screamed in horror at this new outrage, this diabolical twisting of his intention. As though to plug the ebbing life, he thrust his fingers into the ragged holes at the front and back of her throat, where the bullet had torn its passage, but he could not help her. That she had not died instantly he knew only when he had dragged her to the fire and her arms sprawled on the earth, her palms crimson with her own brief effort to block the flow of her wounds.

He could not have known she would come crawling to him like an animal, scratching and moaning in the middle of the night, scaring him out of his wits. If she had only called his name, made some recognizable sound. While he searched her cloak and her bedroll, Keseberg repeated the argument to himself, elaborated it until he became incensed by her fiendish trickery, half believed she had sought to terrorize him. He remembered, too, the haughtiness with which the Donner brothers had joined with James Reed to banish him from the train, had persuaded even his closest friends to vote against him, when what he had done was a trivial thing, clearly no affair of theirs. He recalled Tamsen imperiously commanding him to leave when all he wished was to remain at his suffering wife's side, to comfort her, to ensure that she bore his son with the quiet dignity that became their station, their heritage, and not with the noisy squealing of a peasant or a pig. Keseberg opened Tamsen's bedroll, brightened at the familiar sound of gold coins chinking solidly together. The dirty patchwork quilt he flung into the corner, where filthy bedding and clothing formed a malodorous heap through which mice sometimes burrowed. Then he tore open the pouches in the heavy woolen cloak, lifted a fistful of meat to his nose and winced at the rancid smell. In the other pouch he found only a journal, though from the outlines he had expected a dense packet of bank notes, for the Donners were rumored to carry a great fortune with them. The journal he laid aside while he went about the familiar work of bleeding the corpse. He moved awkwardly, clumsily, for as more and more of his companions had died, he had donned their clothing over his own, as protection against the cold. Later, when he raided corpses, he sometimes found a waistcoat or shirt or tunic that took his fancy, and as he grew thinner it became easier to wedge new acquisitions over the old, until he resembled some grotesquely bloated scarecrow with bean-pole neck and wrists protruding awkwardly from the dense layers of tattered, trailing garments.

Before he could render the fat, Keseberg had to build up the fire, and by its renewed light he flicked through the pages of the journal, thinking at first it might reveal some clue to the location of the Donner fortunes. He found instead descriptions of geography and obscure plants, tiresome details about wagons and teams which could interest no one. How foolish it was to waste education on women, who had no need of such things, who could produce only prattlings like "I must extinguish wick and quill for another night of downy dreams." Irritated, he ripped the page out, crumpled it, and flung it on the fire, where the paper slowly unfolded into a vivid blossom. Further on there were recipes for tonics and talk of infusions and jellies and ridiculous comments on India-rubber overshoes. Keseberg looked at his own feet, clumsily wrapped in scraps of blanket, and snorted contempt as he tore out another page and balled it in his fist. Then he saw his own name, flashing from the center of the page as if emblazoned there, and read the passage aloud. "A German woman, Mrs. Keseberg, must soon be delivered of a child, and endures great discomfiture through the jolting of the wagons. The poor woman has already one small child to care for . . . ," he read, then paused to pronounce the name "Ada" before continuing. "I made some effort to distract the pretty little thing, but Mr. Keseberg let it be known that this was his wife's exclusive obligation. He is a proud man, and his squaw has much to bear from him." Yes, he was a proud man, and this much at least she had acknowledged, but to describe Phillipine as a squaw, an unwashed savage, was typical of these rich, smug Americans, who always thought themselves superior to foreigners, and he ripped the page away so angrily he ruptured the stitching that bound the sheets, and several others fluttered lazily to the ground. He read then of the death of the spoiled, overbearing old woman who had traveled with the Reeds, and whom they had all treated like royalty. They invented such airs for themselves, these crude men and women who understood so little of civilization. "Mr. Keseberg overturned and broke his wagon tongue . . ." Keseberg vividly remembered the panic, the awful noise, the mud that smeared everything, Reed's condescending remarks as he left him stranded in the wilderness with his poor bruised wife, his darling child, terrified and wailing with their pain and fear. The damp pages of the journal clung together, and he pawed them apart, licked his fingers and gouged the paper, smearing the ink, flung the paper aside until his eye found the name "Lewis Sutter Keseberg," and the phrase "his proud father," but the woman at his feet had paid more attention to the habits of the beaver than to the precious life of his newborn son. He stared at her ugly, twisted face, her shrunken cheeks and the thin, prim line drawn by her upper lip, and thought no woman so small-minded, so condescending, could comprehend what it meant to a man to produce from his loins a son, to give that son the glory of his own name. She who had had so many daughters, who had bred them like rabbits, could know nothing of that. Irritated as he was by what he found in the journal, Keseberg was oddly comforted by the fellowship of his own voice, and continued to read aloud passages that caught his attention, read Tamsen Donner's own biased account of Reed's cowardly murder of John Snyder, noting with satisfaction her remark that "Mr. Keseberg felt so certain of the outcome that he had already raised a gallows and strung a noose from it." Yes, someone had possessed the courage to act on his beliefs instead of spending all his time jabbering about each decision, playing the silly game they called democracy. In the entire company he had been the sole man brave enough to act on his convictions, and more would have followed his example had they not been so blinded by Reed's money and his fancy horse. Mrs. Donner, of course, felt sorry for them all, but the Donners and the Reeds were thick as thieves, smugly better than their traveling companions. Captain Donner even hinted that he had something to do with Wolfinger's death, and Mrs. Donner practically accused him of abandoning the stupid, whining Hardkoop, of feeding him to the coyotes. Fistfuls of paper flew into the fire, charred scraps tumbled on currents of air to be swept out the smoke hole, but then came a passage that paralyzed his hands, made him pant for breath: "Mrs. Murphy is feeble in mind and body, and Mr. Keseberg has deteriorated to a state of savagery whose dimensions excel even those of nightmare. Mrs. Murphy accuses him of murdering her grandson Georgie Foster to satisfy his appetite for fresh meat." Keseberg's eyes bulged with rage, the sound of the frantic hammering of his own heart seemed to fill the lean-to. Again he was the savage, the murderer—he who had sought to warm the poor shivering child. He had eaten it, yes, but what other use could the dead have? Was it better that they rot while others starve? Had he done worse than the rest? Had he committed some crime the others had not? *"Verdammte Scheisse!"* he screamed, and trampled the journal beneath his feet, stomped its lies and its stupidity, heard the boards crack, then plucked up the mangled pieces and jammed them between the burning logs. Slowly he calmed himself, felt oddly refreshed and restored by the overflow of his anger. It would not, in any case, be wise for others to read these vicious accusations, and as he warmed his hands he thought how simple it was to be rid of the frail evidence that might so unjustly argue his guilt. After the lies and insults he had read, he felt no further qualms in butchering this meat that providence had conveniently delivered to his fireside. The bones he would scatter in the other cabins, in the open graves, where they would never be identified, where any evidence of the bullet that had torn through her throat would be obscured by other evidence of what they all had done to survive. And the bones were no bigger than those of a child, indistinguishable from those of a young girl. Not a single bone or hank of hair would accuse him. A rib here, a rib there, Keseberg thought, and remembered an old German tale about a disobedient little girl boiled up for soup. The story had once terrified him, but it frightened him no longer, and he set almost cheerfully to work, thinking of the fine breakfast that would begin his day. The pair of heavy gold rings he found suspended from a narrow velvet ribbon were an unexpected bounty, for the woman's emaciated hands were bare of ornament.

VI
DEATH ROSTER

Brigadier General Stephen Watts Kearny concluded that the consolidation of America's latest territorial victory was now complete. Resigning his authority to a provisional government, he started east again from Sutter's Mill in May of 1847. With him rode the indefatigable diarist Edwin Bryant, to record the scene awaiting the company at Truckee Lake:

When the return party of General Kearny reached the scene of these horrible and tragical occurrences, on the 22nd of June, 1847, a halt was ordered, for the purpose of collecting and interring the remains. Near the principal cabins, I saw two bodies, entire with the exception that the abdomens had been cut open and the entrails extracted. Their flesh had been either wasted by famine or evaporated by exposure to the dry atmosphere, and they presented the appearance of mummies. Strewn around the cabins were dislocated and broken bones—skulls, (in some instances sawed asunder with care for the purpose of extracting the brains,) —human skeletons, in short, in every variety of mutilation. A more revolting and appalling spectacle I never witnessed. The remains were, by order of Gen. Kearny, collected and buried under the superintendence of Major Swords. They were interred in a pit which had been dug in the center of one of the cabins for a *cache*. These melancholy duties to the dead being performed, the cabins, by order of Major Swords, were fired, and with everything surrounding them connected with this horrid and melancholy tragedy, were consumed. The body of George Donner was found at his camp, about eight or ten miles distant, wrapped in a sheet. He was buried by a party of men detailed for this purpose.

Out of fastidiousness, perhaps, or respect for the gentle man who had given the ill-fated company its name, or concern for the orphaned girls he had seen begging at Sutter's, Edwin Bryant omitted any mention of the fact that George Donner's body, too, had been savagely mutilated.

The roster of death was now complete.

On the trail:

Sarah Keyes	Mr. Hardkoop
Luke Halloran	Mr. Wolfinger
John Snyder	William N. Pike

At the mountain camps (December, 1846):

Jacob Donner	Samuel Shoemaker
Baylis Williams	Joseph Rhinehardt
James Smith	Karl Burger

On the expedition of the Forlorn Hope (December, 1846):

Charles Stanton	Lemuel Murphy
Jay Fosdick	Antonio
Patrick Dolan	Luis
Franklin Graves, Sr.	Salvador

At the mountain camps (January and February, 1847):

Landrum Murphy	Augustus Spitzer
Lewis Keseberg Jr.	Milford Elliott
Eleanor Eddy	Harriet McCutcheon
Margaret Eddy	Catherine Pike

On the first relief expedition (February, 1847):

William Hook	Ada Keseberg
John Denton	

At the mountain camps (March, 1847):

George Foster	Lewis Donner
James P. Eddy	Samuel Donner

Elizabeth Donner   Lavina Murphy
George Donner   Tamsen Donner

On the second relief expedition (March, 1847):
Mrs. Elizabeth Graves   Franklin Ward Graves Jr.
Isaac Donner

At Sutter's Fort:
Elizabeth Graves

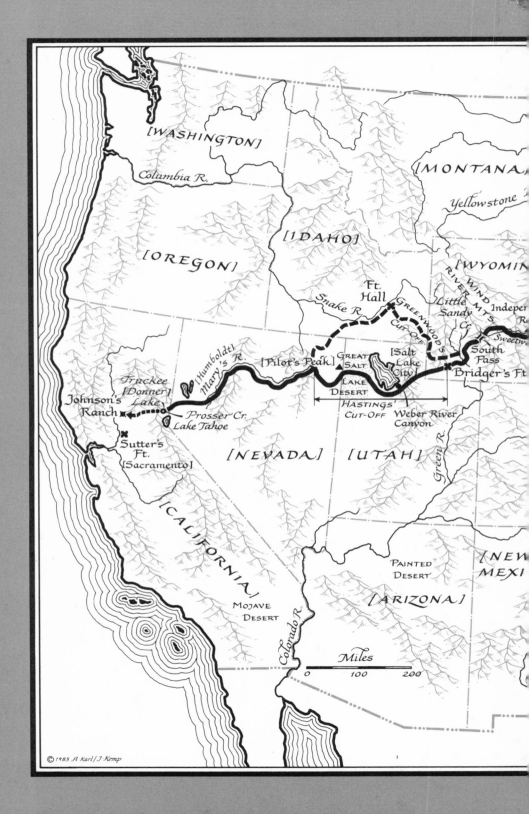

[WASHINGTON]

Columbia R.

[OREGON]

[IDAHO]

[MONTANA]

Yellowstone

[WYOMIN

WIND RIVER MTS

Ft. Hall

Snake R.

GREENWOOD'S Cut-Off

Little Sandy Cr.

Indepen R.

Sweetv

South Pass

Bridger's Ft

[Pilot's Peak]

GREAT SALT

[Salt Lake City]

[Humboldt] Mary's R.

LAKE DESERT

HASTINGS' CUT-OFF

Weber River Canyon

Truckee [Donner] Lake

Johnson's Ranch

Prosser Cr. Lake Tahoe

Sutter's Ft. [Sacramento]

[NEVADA]

[UTAH]

Green R.

[CALIFORNIA]

PAINTED DESERT

[NEW MEXI

[ARIZONA]

MOJAVE DESERT

Colorado R.

Miles

0   100   200

© 1983 A. Karl / J. Kemp